Girl A

Abigail Dean was born in Manchester, and grew up in the Peak District. She graduated from Cambridge with a Double First in English. Formerly a Waterstones bookseller, she spent five years as a lawyer in London, and took summer 2018 off to work on *Girl A* ahead of her thirtieth birthday. She now works as a lawyer for Google, and is writing her second novel. *Girl A* is now a *New York Times* and *Sunday Times* top ten bestseller and a Kindle number 1 bestseller. The rights have sold in 33 territories and a television series is being adapted with Sony.

@abigailsdean

Girl A

ABIGAIL DEAN

HarperCollins*Publishers*

HarperCollins*Publishers* Ltd
1 London Bridge Street,
London SE1 9GF

www.harpercollins.co.uk

HarperCollins*Publishers*
1st Floor, Watermarque Building, Ringsend Road
Dublin 4, Ireland

This paperback edition 2021
10

First published by HarperCollins*Publishers* 2021

Set in Adobe Caslon by Palimpsest Book Production Limited, Falkirk, Stirlingshire

Printed and Bound in the UK using 100% Renewable Electricity at CPI Group (UK) Ltd

MIX
Paper from
responsible sources
FSC™ C007454
www.fsc.org

This book is produced from independently certified FSC™ paper
to ensure responsible forest management.

For more information visit: www.harpercollins.co.uk/green

For Mum, Dad, and Rich.

1
Lex (Girl A)

You don't know me, but you'll have seen my face. In the earlier pictures, they bludgeoned our features with pixels, right down to our waists; even our hair was too distinctive to disclose. But the story and its protectors grew weary, and in the danker corners of the Internet we became easy to find. The favoured photograph was taken in front of the house on Moor Woods Road, late on a September evening. We filed out and lined up, six of us in height order and Noah in Ethan's arms, while Father arranged the composition. Little white wraiths squirming in the shock of sunshine. Behind us, the house rested in the last of the day's light, shadows spreading from the windows and the door. We were still and looking at the camera. It should have been perfect. But just before Father pressed the button, Evie squeezed my hand and turned her face up towards me; in the photograph, she is just about to speak, and my smile is starting to curl. I don't remember what she said, but I'm quite sure that we paid for it, later.

I arrived at the prison in the mid-afternoon. On the drive I had been listening to an old playlist made by JP, Have a Great Day, and without the music and the engine, the car was abruptly quiet. I opened the door. Traffic was building on the motorway, the noise of it like the ocean.

The prison had released a short statement confirming Mother's death. I read the articles online the evening before, which were perfunctory, and which all concluded with a variation of the same happy ending. The Gracie children, some of whom have waived their anonymity, are believed to be well. I sat in a towel on the hotel bed, surrounded by room service, laughing. At breakfast, there was a stack of local newspapers next to the coffee; Mother was on the front page, underneath an article about a stabbing at Wimpy Burger. A quiet day.

My room included a hot buffet, and I kept eating right up until the end, when the waitress told me that the kitchen had to begin preparing for lunch.

'People stop for lunch?' I asked.

'You'd be surprised,' she said. She looked apologetic. 'It isn't included with the room, though.'

'That's OK,' I said. 'Thanks. That was really good.'

When I started work, my mentor, Julia Devlin, told me that the time would come when I would tire of free food and free alcohol; when my fascination with platters of immaculate canapés would wane; when I would no longer set my alarm to get to a hotel breakfast. Devlin was right about a lot of things, but not about this.

I had never been to the prison before, but it wasn't so different from what I had imagined. Beyond the car park were white walls, crowned with barbed wire, like a challenge from a fairy tale. Behind that, four towers presided over a concrete moat, with a grey fort at its centre. Mother's little life. I had parked too far away, and had to walk across a sea of empty spaces, following the thick white lines where I could. There was only one other vehicle in the car park, and inside it there was an old woman, clutching the wheel. When she saw me she raised her hand, as if we might know each other, and I waved back.

Underfoot, the tarmac was starting to stick. By the time I reached the entrance I could feel sweat in my bra and in the hair at the back of my neck. My summer clothes were in a wardrobe in New York. I had remembered English summers as timid, and every time I stepped outside I was surprised by bold blue sky. I had spent some time that morning thinking about what to wear, stuck half-dressed in the wardrobe mirror; there really wasn't an outfit for every occasion, after all. I had settled on white shirt, loose jeans, shop-clean trainers, obnoxious sunglasses. *Is it too jovial?* I asked Olivia, sending a picture by text, but she was in Italy, at a wedding on the walls of Volterra, and she didn't reply.

There was a receptionist, just like in any other office. 'Do you have an appointment?' she asked.

'Yes,' I said. 'With the warden.'

'With the director?'

'Sure. With the director.'

'Are you Alexandra?'

'That's me.'

The warden had agreed to meet me in the entrance hall. 'There's a reduced staff on Saturday afternoons,' she had said. 'And no visitors after three p.m. It should be quiet for you.'

'I'd like that,' I said. 'Thanks.'

'I shouldn't say this,' she said, 'but it would be the time for the great escape.'

Now she came down the corridor, filling it. I had read about her online. She was the first female warden of a high-security facility in the country, and she had given a few interviews after her appointment. She had wanted to be a police officer at a time when height restrictions were still in force, and she was two inches under. She had discovered that she was still tall enough to be a prison officer, which was illogical, but OK with her. She wore an electric blue suit – I recognized it from the pictures accompanying the interviews – and strange, dainty shoes, as if somebody had told her they might soften her impression. She believed – absolutely – in the power of rehabilitation. She looked more tired than in her photographs.

'Alexandra,' she said, and shook my hand. 'I'm so sorry for your loss.'

'I'm not,' I said. 'So don't worry about it.'

She gestured back from where she had come. 'I'm just by the visitors' centre,' she said. 'Please.'

The corridor was a tepid yellow, scuffed at the baseboards and decorated with shrivelled posters about pregnancy and meditation. At the end there was a scanner, and a conveyor belt for your belongings. Steel lockers to the ceiling. 'Formalities,' she said. 'At least it's not busy.'

'Like an airport,' I said. I thought of the service in New York, two days before: my laptop and phones in a grey tray, and the neat, transparent bag of make-up which I set beside them. There were special lanes for frequent flyers, and I never had to queue.

'Just like that,' she said. 'Yes.'

She unloaded her pockets onto the conveyor belt and passed through the scanner. She carried a security pass, a pink fan, and a children's sunscreen. 'A whole family of redheads,' she said. 'We're not built for days like this.' In her pass photograph she looked like a teenager, eager to begin the first day of work. My pockets were empty; I followed her straight through.

Inside, too, there was no one around. We walked through the visitors' centre, where the plastic tables and secured chairs awaited the next session. At the end of the room was a metal door, without windows; somewhere behind that, I assumed, was Mother, and the confines of each of her small days. I touched a chair as we passed, and thought of my siblings, waiting in the stale room for Mother to be presented to them. Delilah would have reclined here, on many occasions, and Ethan had visited once, although only for the nobility of it. He had written a piece

4

for *The Sunday Times* afterwards, titled 'The Problems with Forgiveness', which were many and predictable.

The warden's office was through a different door. She touched her pass to the wall and patted herself down for a final key. It was in the pocket above her heart, and attached to a plastic photo frame, full of redheaded children. 'Well,' she said. 'Here we are.'

It was a simple office, with pockmarked walls and a view to the motorway. She seemed to have recognized this and decided that it wouldn't do; she had brought in a stern wooden desk and an office chair, and she had found a budget for two leather sofas, which she would need for delicate conversations. On the walls were her certificates, and a map of the United Kingdom.

'I know that we haven't met before,' the warden said, 'but there's something I want to say to you before the lawyer joins us.'

She gestured to the sofas. I despised formal meetings on comfortable furniture; it was impossible to know how to sit. On the table in front of us was a cardboard box, and a slim brown envelope bearing Mother's name.

'I hope that you don't think that this is unprofessional,' said the warden, 'but I remember you and your family on the news at the time. My children were just babies, then. I've thought about those headlines a lot since, even before this job came up. You see a great many things in this line of work. Both the things that make the papers, and the things that don't. And after all of this time, some of those things – a very small number – still surprise me. People say: How can you still be surprised, even now? Well, I refuse not to be surprised.'

She took her fan from the pocket of her suit. Closer, it looked like something handmade by a child, or a prisoner. 'Your parents surprised me,' she said.

I looked past her. The sun teetered at the edge of the window, about to fall into the room.

'It was a terrible thing that happened to you,' she said. 'From all of us here – we hope that you might find some peace.'

'Should we talk,' I said, 'about why you called me?'

The solicitor was poised outside the office, like an actor waiting for his cue. He was dressed in a grey suit and a cheerful tie, and sweating. The leather squeaked when he sat down. 'Bill,' he said, and stood again to shake my hand. The top of his collar had started to stain, and now that was grey, too. 'I understand,' he said, right away, 'that you're also a lawyer.' He was younger than I had expected, maybe younger than me; we would have studied at the same time.

'Just company stuff,' I said, and to make him feel better: 'I don't know the first thing about wills.'

'That,' Bill said, 'is what I'm here for.'

I smiled encouragingly.

'OK!' Bill said. He rapped the cardboard box. 'These are the personal possessions,' he said. 'And this is the document.'

He slid the envelope across the table and I tore it open. The will said, in Mother's trembling hand, that Deborah Gracie appointed her daughter, Alexandra Gracie, as executor of this will; that Deborah Gracie's remaining possessions consisted of, first, those possessions held at HM Prison Northwood; secondly, approximately twenty thousand pounds inherited from her husband, Charles Gracie, upon his death; and thirdly, the property found at 11 Moor Woods Road, in Hollowfield. Those possessions were to be divided equally between Deborah Gracie's surviving children.

'Executor,' I said.

'She seemed quite sure that you were the person for the job,' Bill said. I laughed.

See Mother in her cell, playing with her long, long blond hair, right down to her knees; so long that she could sit on it, as a party trick. She considers her will, presided over by Bill, who

6

feels sorry for her, who is happy to help out, and who is sweating then, too. There is so much that he wants to ask. Mother holds the pen in her hand, and trembles in studied desolation. Executor, Bill explains: it's something of an honour. But it's also an administrative burden, and there will need to be communications with the various beneficiaries. Mother, with the cancer bubbling in her stomach, and only a few months left to fuck us over, knows exactly whom to appoint.

'There is no obligation for you to take this up,' Bill said. 'If you don't want to.'

'I'm aware of that,' I said, and Bill's shoulders shifted.

'I can guide you through the basics,' he said. 'It's a very small portfolio of assets. It shouldn't take up too much of your time. The key thing – the thing that I'd bear in mind – is to keep the beneficiaries onside. However you decide to handle those assets, you get your siblings' go-ahead first.'

I was booked on a flight back to New York the next afternoon. I thought of the cold air on the plane, and the neat menus which were handed out just after take-off. I could see myself settling into the journey, the prior three days deadened by the drinks in the lounge, then waking up to the warm evening and a black car waiting to take me home.

'I need to consider it,' I said. 'It's not a convenient time.'

Bill handed me a slip of paper, with his name and number handwritten on pale grey lines. Business cards were not in the prison's budget. 'I'll wait to hear from you,' he said. 'If it's not you, then it would be helpful to have suggestions. One of the other beneficiaries, perhaps.'

I thought of making this proposal to Ethan, or Gabriel, or Delilah. 'Perhaps,' I said.

'For a start,' Bill said, holding the box on his palm, 'these are all of her possessions at Northwood. I can release them to you today.'

The box was light.

'They're of negligible value, I'm afraid,' he said. 'She had a number of goodwill credits – for exemplary behaviour, things like that – but they don't have much value outside.'

'That's a shame,' I said.

'The only other thing,' the warden said, 'is the body.'

She walked to her desk and pulled out a ring-bound file of plastic wallets, each of them containing a flyer or a catalogue. Like a waiter with a menu, she opened it before me, and I glimpsed sombre fonts and a few apologetic faces.

'Options,' she said, and turned the page. 'If you'd like them. Funeral homes. Some of these are a bit more detailed: services, caskets, things like that. And they're all local – all within a fifty-mile radius.'

'I'm afraid there's been a misunderstanding,' I said. The warden shut the file on a leaflet featuring a leopard print hearse.

'We won't be claiming the body,' I said.

'Oh,' said Bill. If the warden was perturbed, she hid it well.

'In that case,' she said, 'we would bury your mother in an unmarked grave, according to default prison policy. Do you have any objections to that?'

'No,' I said. 'I don't have any objections.'

My other meeting was with the chaplain, who had requested to see me. She had asked me to come to the visitors' chapel, which was in the car park. One of the warden's assistants accompanied me to a squat outbuilding. Somebody had erected a wooden cross above the door and hung coloured tissue paper across the windows. A child's stained glass. Six rows of benches faced a makeshift stage with a fan and a lectern, and a model of Jesus, mid-crucifixion.

The chaplain was waiting on the second bench back. She stood to meet me. Everything about her was round and damp: her face in the gloom, her white smock, the two little hands which clasped around mine.

'Alexandra,' she said.

'Hello.'

'You must be wondering,' she said, 'why I wished to see you.'

She had the kind of gentleness which you have to practise. I could see her in the conference room of a cheap hotel, wearing a name badge and watching a presentation on the importance of pauses – of giving people the space to talk.

I waited.

'I spent a lot of time with your mother in her final few years,' she said. 'I had worked with her for longer than that, you see, but in the final years I saw the changes in her. And I hoped that you, today, might take consolation in those changes.'

'The changes?' I said. I could feel myself starting to smile.

'She wrote to you many times in those years,' she said. 'To you and to Ethan and to Delilah. I heard about you all. Gabriel and Noah. Sometimes she wrote to Daniel and Evie. For a mother to lose her children, whatever sins she committed – she had lost so much. She would bring me all of the letters, to check her spelling and the addresses. She kept thinking that the addresses must be wrong, when you didn't reply.'

The tissue paper cast a fleshy light down the aisle. I had assumed that the windows had been an activity for the prisoners, but now I could imagine the chaplain, balanced on a chair after hours, dressing her kingdom.

'I wanted to see you,' she said, 'because of forgiveness. For if you forgive other people when they sin against you, your heavenly father will also forgive you.'

She rested her palm against my knee. The warmth of it seeped straight through my jeans, like something spilt. 'But if you do not forgive others their sins,' she said, 'your father will not forgive your sins.'

'Forgiveness,' I said. The shape of the word lodged in my throat. I was still smiling.

'Did you receive them?' the chaplain asked. 'The letters?'

I received them. I asked Dad – my real father, you understand, and not the rot in my bones – to destroy each one when it arrived. They were easy to identify; they came resealed, with a stamped warning of correspondence from an inmate at HM Prison Northwood. Soon after my twenty-first birthday, when I was home from university, Dad came to me with a confession and a box, and all of the fucking letters stuffed inside. 'I just thought,' he said, 'that in the future – you may be curious—' It must have been the winter holidays, because the barbeque was in the garden shed; he helped me to wheel it out, and we stood in our coats, him with his pipe and me with a cup of tea, and posted them into the fire.

'I think that you're in the wrong story,' I said to the chaplain. 'There's a narrative – you see it a lot – which builds up to a prison visit. Somebody inside, they're waiting for somebody else to visit. To be forgiven. The visitor's been mulling it over for years, and they can't decide whether to do it. Well. In the end they go. It's usually a parent and a child, or maybe a perpetrator and a victim – it depends. But they go. And they have a conversation. And even if the visitor doesn't *forgive* the person, exactly, they at least take something from the whole thing. But, you see – my mother's dead. And I never did visit.'

I had the mortifying sense that I was going to cry, and I pulled my sunglasses down to hide it. The chaplain became a lumpy white spectre in the darkness. 'I'm sorry that I can't help you,' I said, absurdly, and stumbled back down the aisle. The sun was finally starting to soften, and now it was time for a drink. I thought of a hotel bar and the weight of the first glass, settling heavy across my limbs. The warden's assistant was waiting for me.

'Are we all done?' she asked. Our shadows were long and black on the tarmac, and when I reached her they became one strange beast. Her shift was probably over.

'Yes,' I said. 'I should go.'

In the car, I checked my phone. *Is there such a thing*, Olivia had texted, *as too jovial?*

I held Mother's cardboard box in my lap and lifted the lid. A ragtag of possessions. There was a Bible, predictably. There was a hairbrush. There were two clippings, sticky with tape, which had been torn from magazines: one was an advertisement for beach holidays in Mexico, and one was for nappies, with a little row of clean, happy children laid out on a white blanket. There was a newspaper cutting about Ethan's charity work in Oxford. There were three chocolate bars, and a lipstick which was nearly finished. As usual, she gave nothing away.

The last time I saw Mother was the day that we escaped. That morning I woke up in the soiled bed and knew that my days had run out, and that if I didn't act then this was where I would die.

Sometimes, in my head, I visit our little room. There are two single beds, pressed into opposite corners, as far away from one another as they can be. My bed and Evie's bed. The bare bulb hangs between them, twitching at footsteps in the hallway outside. It is usually dull, but sometimes, if Father decides, left on for days. He has sealed a flattened cardboard box against the window, intending to control time, but a dim, brown light seeps through and grants us our days and our nights. Beyond the cardboard there was once a garden, and beyond that, the moor. It has become harder to believe that those places, with their wildness and their weather, could still exist. In the peaty glow, you can see the two-metre Territory between the beds, which Evie and I know better than any other. We have discussed the navigation from my bed to hers for many months: we know how to traverse the rolling hills of plastic bags, bulging with items which we can't remember; we know that you would use a plastic fork to cross the Bowl Swamps, which are blackened and congealed, and close to drying out; we have debated the best way to pass through the Polyester Peaks to avoid the worst of the filth: whether to take the high passes and risk the elements, or to pass through the tunnels of rotting materials beneath them and face whatever may be waiting there.

I had wet myself again in the night. I flexed my toes, twisted my ankles, and kicked my legs as if I was swimming, as I had done every morning for the last few months. Two. Maybe three. I said to the room what I would say to the first person I met when I was free: My name is Alexandra Gracie, and I am fifteen years old. I need you to ring the police. Then, as I did each morning, I turned to see Evie.

We had once been chained in the same direction, so that I could see her all of the time. Now she was tied away from me, and we both had to contort our bodies to meet eyes. Instead I could see her feet and the bones of her legs. The skin burrowed into each groove, as if searching for warmth there.

Evie spoke less and less. I cajoled her and shouted at her; I reassured her, and sung the songs which we had heard when we still went to school. 'Your part,' I said. 'Are you ready for your part?' None of it worked. Now, instead of teaching her numbers, I recited them to myself. I told her stories in the darkness and heard no laughter, or questions, or surprise; there was just the quiet space of the Territory and her shallow breathing, rushing across it.

'Evie,' I said. 'Eve. Today's the day.'

I drove back to the city through the early dusk. A thick golden light fell between the trees and across the open fields, but in the shadows of the villages and the farmhouses it was already dark. I contemplated driving through the night and hitting London before sunrise. Jet lag made the landscape bright and strange. I would probably end up asleep on a roadside in the Midlands; it didn't seem such a good idea. I stopped in a lay-by and booked a Manchester hotel with vacancies and air conditioning.

In the first bad year, we had talked only of escape. This was in the Binding Days, when we were only restrained at night, and gently, with soft, white materials. Evie and I slept in the same bed, each with one wrist attached to a bedpost, and our other hands holding. All day, Mother and Father were with us, but we went about our lessons (heavy in biblical studies, with some questionable world history), and exercise (laps of the yard, in vests and pants; on one occasion, some of the children from Hollowfield clambered through the nettles at the back of our property just to see us, and to guffaw), and mealtimes (bread and water, on a good day), without any restraints at all. Our famous family photograph was taken at the end of this period, before the Chaining commenced and we ceased to be portrait-ready, even by my parents' standards.

We talked of tearing the bindings with our teeth, or of slipping a knife from the kitchen table into a smock pocket. We could build up speed during a lap of the yard, then keep running, out through the garden gate and down Moor Woods Road. Father kept a mobile phone in his pocket; that would be easy to snatch. When I think about this time, I feel a terrible confusion, which Dr K – with all of her reasoning – never managed to resolve. It was on the faces of the police and the journalists and the nurses, although none of them could ever bring themselves to ask it. Why didn't you just leave when you had the chance?

The truth is, it wasn't so bad. We enjoyed each other's company. We were tired, and sometimes we were hungry, and on occasion, Father would hit us so hard that an eye was bloodshot for a week (Gabriel), or there was a guttural crack just below the heart (Daniel). But we had little knowledge of what would come. I have spent many nights combing through the memories, like a student in a library, wiping the dust from old volumes and examining each shelf, searching for the moment when I should have known: ah – there – it was time to act. This book eludes me. It was checked out many years ago, and never returned. Father taught us around the kitchen table, mistaking submission for devotion, and Mother visited us last thing at night to make sure the bindings were in place. In the early morning, I woke beside Evie, and the warmth of her body glowed against me. We still talked of our future.

It wasn't so bad.

I spoke to Devlin first, and asked to work from London for a week. Maybe more.

'Probate drama,' she said. 'How exciting.' It was early afternoon in New York, but she had answered right away, already half-cut. Around her, I could hear the hum of a civilized lunch, or a bar.

'I'm not sure if that's the word I would use,' I said.

'Well, take your time. We'll find you a desk in London. And some work, no doubt.'

Mum and Dad would be eating, and could wait. Ethan's fiancée answered the phone; he was attending the opening of a gallery and wouldn't be back until much later that night. She'd heard that I was in the country – I should come to visit them – they would love to have me. I left a voice message on Delilah's phone, although I doubted that she would call me back. Last, I spoke to Evie. I could hear that she was outside, and somebody near her was laughing.

'So,' I said. 'The witch is dead, it seems.'

'Did you see the body?'

'God, no. I didn't ask to.'

'Then – can we be sure?'

'I'm quietly confident.'

I told her about the house on Moor Woods Road. About our great inheritance.

'They had twenty thousand? That's news.'

'Really? After our resplendent childhood?'

'You can just see Father, can't you? Squirrelling it away. "For my God will meet all your needs" – whatever it was.'

'The house, though,' I said. 'I can't believe that it would still be standing.'

'Aren't there people who enjoy those things? There are some tours – in LA, I think – murder sites, celebrity deaths, stuff like that. It's pretty morbid.'

'Hollowfield's a little isolated for a tour, no? Besides, it's hardly the Black Dahlia.'

'We're a little more downmarket, I guess.'

'They'd be giving the tickets away.'

'Well,' Evie said. 'If there's a tour, we should certainly go on it. We'll be able to impart some real gems. There's a career there, if the law doesn't work out.'

'I think Ethan's already cornered the market,' I said. 'But really. What the hell are we meant to do with the house?'

Again, somebody laughed. Closer, now. 'Where are you?' I asked.

'At the beach. There's some kind of concert this afternoon.'

'You should go.'

'OK. I miss you. And the house—'

The wind was picking up where she was, whipping the sun across the ocean.

'Something happy,' Evie said. 'It should be something happy. Nothing would annoy Father more.'

'I like that idea.'

'OK. I'm going to go.'

'Enjoy the concert.'

'Well done, today.'

The plan was this:

Like undercover agents, we had been tracking Father's footsteps. In the Binding Days, we had kept a record, noted in our Bible with a stump of school pencil (Genesis, 19:17; back then, we still had a taste for melodrama). When we could no longer reach the book, I committed Father's day to memory, the way Miss Glade had taught me when I still went to school. 'Think of a house,' she said. 'And in each room of the house, there is the next thing that you want to recall. Franz Ferdinand is slumped in the hallway – he's just been shot. You walk into the living room, and you pass by Serbia on the way out, running. They're terrified: war's coming. You find Austria-Hungary in the kitchen, sat at the table with the rest of its allies. Who's with them?'

And Father occupied our house; that made decoding his days even easier. After so many months in a single room, I knew the sound of each floorboard, and the flick of each light switch. I could see the bulk of him moving through the rooms.

We had done several all-night stake-outs from our beds, so

we knew that he woke late. Even in the winter, it was already light when we heard his first, slow footsteps through the house. Our bedroom was right at the end of the hallway, and he was two doors down, so a night-time attempt would be no good; he slept lightly, and he could be on us in a few seconds. Sometimes I would wake to find him at our bedroom door, or crouching beside me, in contemplation. Whatever he was considering, he always resolved, and in time he turned away, into the darkness.

He spent each morning with Mother and with Noah, downstairs. The smell of their meals permeated the house, and we heard them at prayer, or laughing about something which we couldn't share. When Noah cried, Father took to the garden. The kitchen door slammed. He exercised: the grunts of it carried up to our window. Sometimes, just before lunch, he visited us, radiant, his skin sodden and red, a barbarian just done with the battle, wielding his towel like an enemy's head. No, the morning wouldn't do: the front door was locked at all times, and whether we went downstairs through the kitchen or right out of the window, Father would be waiting.

This was a point of contention between Evie and me. 'It has to be through the house,' she said. 'The window's too high. You've forgotten how high it is.'

'We'd have to break the lock on our door. We'd have to go through the whole house. Past Ethan's room. Past Mother and Father. Past Gabe and D. Down the stairs. Noah sleeps down there – sometimes Mother too. There's no way.'

'Why haven't Gabriel and Delilah left?' Evie asked. And whispered: 'It would be easier for them.'

'I don't know,' I said. There had been one night, many months before, when I had heard something quiet and terrible at the other end of the hallway. A thwarted attempt. Evie had been asleep, and I had never mentioned it. Now, with hope hanging precarious between us, I didn't think that I could.

After lunch, Father was in the living room, and silent. This, I believed, was our chance. With Father still, the whole house sighed and slacked. Delilah's whispers snuck down the hallway. Some days Ethan tapped on the wall, as he had done when we were very young and set on learning Morse code. Other days, Mother visited us. There had been a time when I pleaded with her to do something, but now I responded to her confessions in my head, and turned away.

'It's the only option,' I said to Evie. 'Once he wakes up, it's out of the question.'

'OK,' she said, but I knew that she saw this as make-believe, like the other stories I told to her to pass the day.

We had already discussed the window. With its cardboard cover, it was outside our scope of surveillance. 'It opens,' I said. 'Doesn't it?' I couldn't picture the latch, or whether the ground beneath it was concrete or grass. 'Maybe I am forgetting,' I said.

'I don't think it does,' Evie said. 'And it hasn't been opened for ages, now.'

We strained to look at one another across the Territory.

'So if we have to break the window,' Evie said, 'how long do we get?'

'It'll take him a good few seconds to know what's happening,' I said. 'And a few more to reach the stairs. Ten to get to our door, say. And then he'll have to do the lock.'

My neck ached. I lay back down. 'Twenty in all,' I said. The meagre number hung in the space between us. Evie said something else, too quiet for me to hear.

'What?'

'OK, then,' she said.

'OK.'

Our other obstacle was the chains, which had once been my greatest concern. But Father was clumsy. After the discovery of the Myths, and what happened after it, he didn't turn on the light when he left the room. I liked to think that he couldn't bear to look at me, but he was probably too drunk to find the switch; either way, it didn't matter now. I'd spread my fingers out as far as I could, so that he closed the cuffs around my thumbs and little fingers, rather than my wrists. So: it would have to be me, and it would have to be soon. 'He messed up,' I whispered to Evie, when I was sure that everybody else in the house was asleep. Her breath huffed across the bedroom, but she didn't respond. I had left it too late. She was asleep, too.

I contemplated the evening. It was dark, but it was still hot outside. I called room service, ordered two gin and tonics, and drank them naked on the bed. I had thought about going for a run, but the hotel was encircled by motorways, and I didn't want to pick my way around them. Instead I would drink, and find company. I changed into a black slip and leather boots, and asked reception for a taxi and another drink.

In the car, I thought that this was a good development: three drinks down, alone, Mother dead, and the strange city above and around me. I opened the car window as far as it would go. People queued outside dark doorways and sat on the pavements to drink. 'There's a storm forecast,' the driver said. He said something else, too, but we were at a crossing, and it was lost in a gale of chatter.

'I'm sorry?'

'An umbrella,' he said. 'Do you have an umbrella?'

'You know,' I said, 'I used to live around here.'

He caught my eye in the mirror, and laughed.

'That's a yes?'

'That's a yes.'

I had asked him to drop me somewhere local and busy. He stopped outside another hotel, a cheaper one, and nodded. The club was in its underbelly, down a narrow staircase, with a dance floor at the back and a vacant stage above it. It was busy enough. I took a seat at the bar and ordered a vodka tonic, and looked for somebody who would be glad to talk to me.

There had been times when Devlin and I had travelled so much that I would forget which continent we were on. I would wake up in a hotel room and walk the wrong way to the toilet, taking the route from my apartment in New York. I would come to in an airport lounge and need to read my boarding pass – really read it – to recall where we were flying next. There was always solace in sitting at a bar; they were the same the world over. There were lonely men with similar stories, and people who looked more tired than I did.

I sent gin to the man six seats down, who was wearing a shirt with a golden pin of wings, and searching for his wallet. He looked happy to receive the drink, and surprised; moments later he touched my shoulder, smiling. He was older than I had first thought. That was good.

'Hello. Thanks for the drink.'

'That's fine. Are you on the road?'

'I flew from Los Angeles today.'

'That's pretty dramatic.'

'Not really. It's a regular route. You're not from around here either?'

'No. Not any more. You're a pilot?'

'Yes.'

'Are you the main pilot or the second pilot?'

He laughed. 'I'm the main pilot,' he said.

He told me about his job. Listening to most people talk about their careers is tedious, but he was different. He spoke with sincerity. He talked about his training in Europe, and the first inevitable time that he flew alone. His hands reached for controls in the space between us, and when the disco lights hit them I could see small muscles shifting, just beneath the skin. It made you a drifter, he said, but a rich one. In those early years, he had lived in a state of anxiety, thinking always of the next landing, adrenaline pulsing through his body in the hotel beds. Now, he was arrogant enough to sleep well.

'The main pilot,' he said, still laughing. 'So. Where next?'

We danced for a short time, but we were older than the bodies around us, and neither of us was drunk enough. I was fascinated by a group of girls beside me, their limbs careening together. They wore a variation of the same, skin-slick dress, and laughed as one many-headed creature. Watching them, I touched the tired skin at my throat and at the corners of my eyes. The pilot was behind me, with his fingers slotted between my ribs.

'You can come to my hotel,' I said.

'I fly back tomorrow. I can't stay.'

'That's fine.'

'I didn't want you to be disappointed. Sometimes—'

'I won't be disappointed.'

It had been raining, as the driver promised. The streets were shining and quieter, and neon floated in the puddles. There were only taxis left on the roads, but none of them were stopping; we needed a busier junction. I watched the lights of the city slide over his face, and took his hand. 'There are things that I need,' I said. 'To make it worth my while.'

'Really,' he said. He had turned away from me, looking for a car, but I saw his jaw lift, and I knew that he was smiling.

In my room, I opened the minibar for drinks, but he stopped me, and sat down on the bed. I removed my dress and peeled my underwear to the floor, then knelt down before him. He surveyed me, nonchalant, just as I had hoped that he would.

'I want you to humiliate me,' I said.

He swallowed.

'You see,' I said, 'it needs to hurt.'

His fingers were twitching. I felt the familiar twinge in my cunt, like a new pulse. I arranged myself on the bed beside him, stomach down, with my head resting on my arms. He stood, came to me, with plans on his face. The turndown service had taken place, I saw, and there were chocolates on the pillow.

When he had left, I ordered room service, and I thought about JP. It was as though he had been waiting for my attention all day, patient and just out of view. One more drink, and I might have called him. I had his work number, which he always answered. I could have been distressed at Mother's death, alone in Manchester, and with no one else to turn to. 'And I'll be in London next week,' I would say, as an afterthought. 'Maybe even longer.'

I had heard that he lived in the suburbs now, with a new girlfriend and a small dog. 'Or a small girlfriend and a new dog,' Olivia had said. 'I don't recall.' I thought about the day that he left our flat. I had expected that he would rent a van or ask a friend for help, but he fit his belongings into two suitcases and a series of cardboard boxes, and waited on the street for his cab. It was raining, but he refused to come back in, as if the proximity would have made him change his mind. It wouldn't. There was nothing that either of us could have done to change things. I pulled my legs up to my chest and felt the scars on my knee, the skin smoother there. Then I touched the scars from the other surgeries. My fingers followed their familiar route. The scars were immaculate; in dim light, you couldn't see them. When I had pointed them out to JP, he was uninterested: 'I never even noticed them,' he said, and I liked him all the more for that. No, there was nothing that either of us could have done. To think of something else, I wondered if Evie's party was over. It was late, and later still where she was. I turned off my light and set an alarm for breakfast.

'Evie,' I said. 'Today's the day.'

The great expanse of the morning extended ahead of us, flat and barren. I had lived with the strange pain inside of me for many weeks by then, but today it felt worse; the blood smelt different. Then again: it was hard to distinguish that pain from the anticipation, which writhed in my gut like beasts breaking from eggs.

I tested the handcuffs, as I had done every day since Father's mistake. My left hand slipped through, but my right caught just beneath the knuckles. 'Is it warmer today?' I asked. I tried again, but it seemed harder still. My fingers were swelling with the effort. I had another idea: what Ethan, who had once loved to read about the Wild West, would have called a last chance saloon. But this idea was irreversible, and if Father visited us before lunch, I needed to be in chains. I would have to wait.

I listened to Father awaken. His footsteps lumbered slowly down the stairs, and I wondered if we had made a mistake. Perhaps it should be now. Then he was in the kitchen, and I heard the murmurs of early conversation, words interspersed with breakfast and contemplation, and probably some silent prayer. I had long abandoned Father's God, but still I closed my eyes, and prayed to older, wilder deities. I prayed for a while.

I woke again in the middle of the morning. I had been in a dense, dark place, just beneath the surface of consciousness. Cutlery clattered in the kitchen. The smell of Mother's baking padded up the stairs and curled on the floor of our room. There were a few scant strings of saliva in my mouth. 'Your first meal out,' I said to Evie; this was a discussion which usually escalated fast.

'Tea at the Ritz?' I asked. 'Or the Greek tavern?'

She tucked her legs closer to her chest and coughed, saying nothing, and I noticed the strange appearance of her feet, oversized at the end of each skeletal shin, like the shoes of a clown.

I had learnt not to imagine my parents eating, but this would be the last day, and so I allowed it. They sat hand in hand at the kitchen table. Noah surveyed them blankly from his chair. Mother had made an apple pie, and she stood to slice it. The top was golden, and brushed with sugar, and there were soft dimples in the crust where the fruit had tried to bubble through. The knife caught on the pastry top, and Mother pressed harder. When she broke through, steam and the smell of hot fruit rose around the table. She cut Father's slice, and served it on a warm plate, and before she helped herself she watched him eating. The crisp pastry and its viscous filling moving around his mouth. She feasted on his pleasure.

That day they had a long lunch, and Noah wouldn't settle. It was the middle of winter, I guessed, and by the time the living room door clicked closed, the light through the cardboard was dimming. The house was quiet.

'OK,' I said. 'OK.'

Before I could think any more about it, I pulled the chains taut.

My left hand contorted through the metal and came free. Still my right hand was too swollen to squeeze through, however hard I pressed my thumb into my palm.

Last chance saloon.

'Look away,' I said to Evie; even after all this time, there were some degradations which I didn't want to share.

When Delilah was nine or ten, she forced Mother's wedding ring onto her thumb, and it became stuck. Delilah was rarely in trouble, and I was delighted. I sat in the hallway, at the top of the stairs, and watched events unfold in the bathroom. Delilah was sitting on the edge of the bath, in tears, and Mother was kneeling before her, running a damp bar of soap between her fingers. With disappointing efficiency, the ring slid over Delilah's knuckle and landed with a tinny chime on the bathroom floor.

I pulled my hand through the metal, right to the sticking point, and started to twist it from side to side. There was already an indentation left from the morning's efforts; the skin there was bruised and close to breaking. I bit down on the sheet and moved faster. Unlike Delilah, I didn't intend to cry. When the skin split, my hand, black-red and wet, grinded through.

I laughed and cradled my arm to my chest. Evie's eyes were frightened, but she smiled, and gave me a thumb-up. I crouched on my bed and reached out into the Territory, searching with my good hand for something hard enough to break glass. My fingers passed through warm, damp patches, and things that seemed to move against them. I recoiled, and swallowed, and kept searching. Old food and small, rotting shoes, and mould on the pages of our childhood Bibles. Everything soft and useless.

Evie pointed, and I froze, expecting Father at the door. She shook her head and pointed again, and I followed her eyes beneath my bed. Underneath it – my whole arm shaking – my fingers closed around something hard. It was a wooden stake, grubby with old blood and its time in the Territory. I looked at it for a moment, remembering why it was there.

'Yes,' I said. 'Yes. Perfect.'

I stood up, unsteady, and shuffled to the window. Father had put little effort into securing the cardboard, and the tape which sealed it had started to decay. I eased the last few pieces away, bit by bit, until I was holding the board. 'Ready,' I said, and set it down onto the floor. Light howled into the room. Evie buried her face in her arms. I couldn't turn around and see the room lit by the day. It was time to go. I crossed the Territory; after all of our navigation, it was just three short footsteps to reach Evie's bed. I took her hand, as I had when we slept in the same bed in the years before, when things hadn't been so bad. She was still motionless: now I could see her spine and the exposed parts of her scalp, and how each breath was a little labour. I knew that once I broke the window, the seconds – our scant seconds, which we had spent so many months planning – would begin to pass.

'I will come back for you,' I said. 'Evie?'

Her hand fluttered in mine.

'I'll see you soon,' I said.

I lifted the wooden stake over my shoulder. 'Cover your face,' I whispered; then the time for quiet was up, and I swung the wood against the bottom corner of the window. It cracked, but it didn't break; I swung it again, harder, and the pane shattered. Downstairs, Noah screamed. Beneath that, I could hear footsteps underneath our room, and Mother's voice. Already, somebody was on the stairs. I tried to brush away the glass on the window ledge, but instead a shard lodged into my palm. There was too much of it, and there wasn't enough time. I hauled one leg onto the ledge, and pulled the other after it, and sat at the window, facing outside. Somebody was at the door; the lock was moving. I had told myself that I wouldn't look down. I pivoted around, and for a moment I was suspended, half inside the room and my legs in the winter air. 'We'll need to lower ourselves,' I had said to Evie, 'until we're hanging, so that we reduce the fall as much as we can.' The door opened, and I saw a flash of Father. The shape of him in the doorway. I let my body drop, but I was too weak to hang like we had planned it, and as soon as my arms locked, I fell.

The grass was wet, but the earth was frozen beneath it. As I landed, something in my right leg collapsed, the way that a building falls in on itself when the foundations are blown. The crunch ricocheted across the garden. I fell forward, and the impact shot the glass further into my hand. The air was too cold to inhale, and I was crying, I knew. 'God, get up,' I whispered. Slowly, I straightened, and pulled my T-shirt down towards my knees, and there, at the kitchen door, was Mother.

I waited for her to run at me, but she didn't. Her mouth was moving, but I could only hear the blood in my ears. We looked at one another for a long last second, then I turned and ran.

The garden gate was unlocked. I hobbled around the house, holding onto the walls, and then out into the road, following the white markers at its centre. The evening was a cold, dark blue. Here was the neighbourhood I remembered: Moor Woods Road and its quiet houses, each far apart from the next. Windows glowing like shrines in the gloaming. Father would be behind me. I couldn't expend energy approaching a doorway: he would catch me there, before the residents could answer. I could anticipate the precise weight of his hands on my shoulders. I screamed, trying to summon them from their living rooms, from their sofas, from the evening news. Festive lights hung from trees and over front doors, welcoming their inhabitants, and I thought, stupidly: Christmas.

The road curled downhill and my leg buckled, and I veered into the wall at the side of it, grasping at the wet stones. I steadied myself and kept going, in the shadows now, my feet slapping on frozen leaves and winter-long puddles. Pain was seconds away, like coming out of sleep; I was on the brink of it, and once it hit me I wouldn't be able to ignore it again.

I could see the end of Moor Woods Road. Beyond it, about to pass by, was a pair of headlights. I ran straight for them, my hands held up in appeasement, and the driver braked just before she hit me. The car bonnet was warm beneath my palms, and I left rusty handprints where I touched it. The driver was climbing out of her seat in silhouette; she moved tentatively towards me, and into the light. She was dressed in a suit and holding a mobile phone, and she seemed so bright, somehow, and clean, like a visitor from a bold new world.

'My God,' she said.

'My name,' I said, 'is Alexandra Gracie—'

I couldn't get the rest of it out. I looked back, up to Moor Woods Road: the street was silent and impassive. I sat down in the road and reached for her, and while she called the police, she let me hold her hand.

I woke once in the night, cold from the air conditioning, and folded the covers across my body. Already it was light outside, but I couldn't hear any traffic. It was nice to wake like this, with many more hours before morning. I would feel better then.

Just as I was falling asleep, my body started. I had been thinking of the fall from the window, fifteen years before. The impact, half dreamed and half remembered. A spectre of pain brushed my knee. Mother at the kitchen door. I rolled over. I stood in the garden in the dim winter dusk, in my sullied T-shirt and nothing else. My leg twisted behind me, like a ball and chain. It would have been so easy for her to stop me. This time, in the dream, I listened; I could hear her over my heart. 'Go,' she said. Further north they were preparing her grave, wielding shovels in the warm, pink dawn so that they could bury her before the sun rose. She said, 'Go.'

2

Ethan (Boy A)

ETHAN CALLED BACK BEFORE my alarm went off. He sounded like an advertisement for the morning: he had been for a run along the river; he was feeding the dog; he was cracking eggs for breakfast.

'Tell me everything,' he said.

I did so. He enjoyed my discovery of the article about his work in Mother's box of belongings; he asked me to recite it so he would know exactly which of his projects it referred to.

'Oh, that. That's a relatively old one.'

'It's a good job that she didn't have access to *The Times*,' I said. 'And "The Problems with Forgiveness".'

He ignored me. 'Will you be around for a while?' he asked. 'Being *executor*, and all.'

'I can work from London this week. I'll see how things go. We may need to visit the house, I guess.'

I could hear him contemplating it, recalling the windows, the garden, the front door and the doors after that. Each of the rooms. I was ruining his morning.

'We can find a time for that. Listen. Get a Friday-night train up to Oxford, stay with me and Ana. It's been ages since you've been in the country. And it would be nice to see you before the wedding.'

'It's work-dependent. I don't know how long I can stay.'

'Well, tell them your mother died. You'll get some leeway for that.'

The dog was barking. 'Fuck,' he said.

'I can go.'

'Friday. Call me when you're on a train.'

At the beginning – and at the end, too – it was just me and Ethan.

First born; last adopted.

It was a few months after we escaped before arrangements were made. I remember very little about that time, and each of the memories seems exaggerated, as if I've taken somebody else's story and imagined myself into the narrative. When they first woke me up, days after the escape and already a few surgeries down, they took me to a bath and washed me. My skin slowly came into view, whiter than I had remembered. It took hours, and each time they stopped I asked them to keep going: there was dirt in my ears, in the creases of my elbows, in the folds between my toes. When they finished, I held to the tub and refused to get out. 'There might be more,' I said, never wanting to leave the water and the warmth of it. It felt like the ocean would feel in Greece, where Evie and I planned to live.

Thin, downy hair had grown on my face and shoulders. 'Your body was keeping you warm,' one of the nurses said, when I asked her, and she kept her face turned away from me until she could leave the room. My bruises faded to a dull jaundice spread, and some of my bones began to retreat, back beneath fat and flesh.

I couldn't believe that people didn't enjoy being in hospital. That people could actually want to leave. I had my own room. I had three meals a day. I had patient doctors, who talked me through my body and why they had to open it. All of the nurses were tender, and sometimes, when they had left, I would cry in the clean, quiet room, the way that you cry when somebody is nice to you in the middle of a terrible day.

At night, and asleep, I called for Evie. I woke with people above me, consoling me, and her name still in my mouth. She was in a different hospital, they said, and I couldn't see her just yet.

A week after I first woke up, I opened my eyes and found a stranger in the room. She was sitting on the chair beside my bed, reading from a ring-bound file. In the moments before she knew that I was awake, I examined her. She wasn't wearing hospital uniform. Instead, she wore a sharp, pale dress and a blue jacket, and the highest shoes that I had ever seen. Her hair was short. Her eyes flicked through the words before her, and as she read, a line between them creased and softened, according to the sentence.

'Hello,' she said, without looking up. 'I'm Dr K.'

Many months later, I understood that it was spelt as a word – Kay – but by that time we knew each other well, and she liked my interpretation: 'It's far more concise,' she said.

She set down her folder and held out her hand to me, and I took it. 'I'm Alexandra,' I said. 'You probably already know that.'

'I do,' she said, 'yes. But it's better to hear it from you. Alexandra, I'm one of the psychologists who works with the hospital and with the police. Do you know what that entails?'

'The mind,' I said.

'Yes,' she said. 'That's right. So while all of the doctors and the nurses will be looking after your body, we can talk about your mind. How you're feeling and what you're thinking. Both what has happened, and what you would like to happen now. Sometimes the police might join us, and sometimes it will just be me and you. And when it's like that – when it's just the two of us – whatever you say to me is confidential. It's a secret.'

She stood up from the chair and knelt at the side of my bed. 'Here's the thing,' she said. 'A promise. I can understand minds, and I can work with them. I like to believe that I can make them better. But I can't read them. So we'll need to be honest. Even about the difficult things. Does that sound OK?'

Her voice was starting to distort. 'OK,' I said.

She said something more, but she was in motion, tipping away from me, and when I next woke it was night-time, and she was gone.

After that, she visited each day. She was sometimes accompanied by two detectives; they were there when she explained that Father had killed himself shortly after I left the house. The first team of respondents found him in the kitchen. Despite multiple attempts, it was not possible to resuscitate him.

Did they try? I wondered. Then: And how hard?

Instead, I asked how he had done it. The detectives looked at Dr K, who looked at me. 'He consumed a toxic substance,' said Dr K. 'A poison. There were many, many indications that this had been planned, and planned for some time.'

'There was a large supply in the household,' one of the detectives said. 'We speculate that this might have been the endgame.'

They looked at one another again. There was a relief to them, as if they had got something out of the way which had gone better than they expected.

'How do you feel about that?' Dr K said.

'I don't know,' I said. An hour later, when I was alone, I came up with my answer, which was: unsurprised.

Mother, they said, was in custody. She, too, had been in possession of a toxic substance, but had declined to take it; they had found her sitting on the kitchen floor with Father's head in her lap. She guarded the body like those dogs you read about, which refuse to leave their master's corpse.

'And the others?' I said.

'Rest, now,' Dr K said. 'Let's talk more tomorrow.'

I understand, now, that there were things that they were working to resolve. We had a whole team, a vast new family: the police; our psychologists; the doctors. They'd stand looking at old photographs of our faces on a whiteboard, headed with the names by which the world now knew us: Boys A to D; Girls A to C. There were lines drawn between us, and words written along those lines: 'Close proximity', and 'Potential violence', and 'Relationship to be determined'. New details would be noted, offered or ascertained from hospital beds. The map of our lives began to appear, like constellations at dusk.

Often, Dr K and I would sit in silence. 'Would you like to talk today?' she would ask, and I would be too tired, or in pain from one of the operations, or hating everything: hating her beautiful clothes and composure, and mortified, in contrast, by the way my body looked in the bed, the angles of it avian and strange, none of it working as it was meant to. At other times, when the detectives were with her, she would ask me about everything that I could remember: not just the Binding Days or the Chaining, but before that, when we were children. My audience recorded everything that I said, even the things that seemed irrelevant, and so I talked more: about the books that Evie and I liked, for example, or the holiday in Blackpool.

'How long has it been since you went to school?' Dr K asked. I was embarrassed: I couldn't remember.

'Did you start at senior school?' she asked.

'Yes. That was my last year. I don't remember the exact time I stopped, but I know where we were up to in all of the subjects – in almost everything.'

'How would you feel about going back?' she said, smiling.

After that, a hospital tutor came to visit me each afternoon. Dr K never mentioned it, but I recognized her quiet magic. She had procured a Bible for me to read, because I liked the familiar passages before bedtime. She sensed when I was becoming tired of the detectives' questions, and shut her notebook, closing the conversation. To say thank you, I tried to talk to her more, even when I did hate her.

Sometimes, too, we talked about the future. 'Have you ever thought,' she said, 'about what you would like to do?'

'Like a job?'

'Maybe a job, but other things, too. Where you would like to live, or places you'd like to visit, or activities you'd like to try.'

'I liked history,' I said, 'at school. And maths. I liked most of the subjects.'

'Well,' she looked up at me, over her glasses, 'that's helpful.'

'I had a book of Greek myths,' I said. 'So I'd like to go to Greece, maybe. Evie and I agreed that we would go together. We told each other the stories.'

'Which was your favourite?'

'The minotaur, obviously. But Evie got scared. She liked Orpheus and Eurydice better.'

Dr K set down her notebook and put her hand next to mine on the bed, as close as it could be without touching. 'You will go to Greece, Lex,' she said. 'You will study history and maths, and lots of other subjects. I'm quite sure of it.'

The team concluded that our best chance of living normal lives would be through adoption. Following careful consideration, each of us would be adopted by a different family. We had diverse, specific needs and problematic sibling dynamics; besides, there were so many of us. I have no basis for it, but I see Dr K lobbying for this approach, standing in front of the whiteboard and fighting for it. Above all things, she believed – with work, and with time – that it was possible to discard parts of the past, like an old season's coat that you never should have bought.

The frantic activity of that time was delivered to us in the months and years that followed, packaged in neat conclusions. The younger children went first: they would be malleable, and easier to save. Noah was given to a couple who wanted to remain anonymous, even to the rest of us; it was an approach approved by Dr K, and supported by secondary and tertiary psychologists. Noah would remember nothing of his time at Moor Woods Road. The first ten months of his life could be erased, neatly, as if they had never taken place. Gabriel went to a local family, who had followed the case closely, and who gave a series of emotional statements requesting that people respect their privacy. Delilah, who was the most photogenic of all of us, was adopted by a couple in London who hadn't been able to have children of their own. And Evie got luckiest: she went to a family on the south coast. Nobody told me much about it at the time, other than that she would have two new siblings, a boy and a girl, and that the family lived close to the beach.

I remember that Dr K was appointed to tell me this, and I remember asking her, absolutely sure that it couldn't be too much more effort, if they may have room for one more child.

'I don't think so, Lex,' she said.

'But did you ask them?'

'It's something I know,' she said, and then, unexpectedly: 'I'm sorry.'

That left Ethan and me. After many weeks of indecision, Mother's sister, Peggy Granger, agreed that she would see Ethan through senior school. She had two older sons, and she could handle another boy. The expectation was that he would leave her home after three years, when he had completed the school examinations that he had missed, although Ethan – being Ethan – was out in two. Peggy had visited us just before things became bad, and I had answered the door, so I was sure that she still thought of me. When she was asked, she denied ever having been to

Moor Woods Road. Besides, she said, and God forgive her, she wasn't used to teenage girls.

In the London office, people wanted to know two things: first, how was Devlin? And, once I had told them that: why was I back?

Let me tell you about Devlin.

Devlin always had an exciting project – a new project – which would ruin your life. She had endured sleepless weeks, and clients like Lucifer ('just as difficult,' she said, 'and just as charismatic'), and various uprisings from old, besuited men, all of which she had quashed. There would be moments, in the middle of a deal, when she would turn to me, and ask, quite nonchalantly, how I was. There was only ever one answer that Devlin wanted to hear: I'm fine. I am adapting to my third time zone in forty-eight hours; a typhoon has cut the Internet; I am tired enough to vomit with it. I'm fine. Devlin knew men who may (or may not) supply chemicals to Venezuelan drug barons; she knew the sultans of small Middle Eastern countries; she always knew precisely what to say. Her eyes and the hollows around them were the same shade of gun-metal grey. At forty-two, her heart – tired of two countries a week and five hours of sleep a night – rebelled against her, 35,000 feet above the Pacific and two hours out of Changi airport. 'I knew that something was wrong,' she said, 'when I didn't want the champagne before take-off.' A doctor rushed in from economy, and Devlin's heart settled. She woke back in Singapore, and asked for drinks for the whole plane – to make up for the inconvenience.

Afterwards, they performed some kind of operation on her heart, some deeply invasive surgery, and in meetings I noticed that she had developed a tic: she would touch her chest when she was angry or frustrated, as though she was reassuring a child.

I often imagined the scar beneath her shirt, the strange contrast of the rumpled flesh and the clean, pressed cotton.

Devlin had suggested that we fabricate a deal which required me to be in London, but as it turned out, a real one came along. One of Devlin's friends sat on the board of a technology company, which wanted to buy an exclusive genomics start-up, based out of Cambridge. 'My understanding,' Devlin said, 'is that you send them some DNA, and they predict your future.'

A slew of information had arrived on Tuesday evening. It was midnight in London; I opened the files as she spoke.

'Like a fortune teller?' I asked.

'A particularly sophisticated one, I hope. They call themselves ChromoClick.'

For the rest of the week, I slept under a thick cover of exhaustion, thrashing out of it every morning to the hotel alarm. I was in work in time for the start of London's day, and at night I joined Devlin on her New York calls. When I left the office, in the empty time before morning, the City was warm and dark, and I wound down the taxi windows to keep myself awake.

I ignored calls from Mum and Dad. I ignored the two hundred messages from Olivia and Christopher in our group chat. Throughout the day, Dr K rang at intervals designed to surprise me, and I ignored her, too. The only person I contacted was Evie. Our plan for Moor Woods Road was coming into place: a community centre, populated by things of which Mother and Father would have disapproved. We plotted a children's library; reading groups for the elderly; talks on contraception. Our suggestions became more ambitious.

'A roller disco,' Evie said.

'An all-you-can-eat buffet.'

'The country's premier gay wedding venue.'

Bill called me on Wednesday. Had I made a decision regarding my role as executor? There was a client on the other line, and a junior waiting outside my door. Bill was an anomaly: it was impossible to believe that the prison occupied the same world as the office. 'Give me until the weekend,' I said.

Friday evening, and still thirty degrees. I stood on the 18.31 from Paddington, emailing Devlin my thoughts on the genomics company's various misdemeanours, which had just been disclosed. A director had once left unencrypted hardware on a train, jammed with details of employees' sexual orientations, health conditions, and ethnicities. 'In short,' I concluded, 'there are issues.' Olivia had screenshotted photographs of the wedding and sent them to Christopher and me with eviscerating captions. 'Extremely strong canapés,' she wrote. 'Dress subpar. Gendered menu. What the fuck?' I reviewed my message to Devlin. 'For what it is worth,' I added, 'I am on a train. Will keep a lookout.'

I had asked for Ethan's address, and requested that he and Ana didn't meet me at the station. Their house was in Summertown, and I liked the walk: JP had studied here, and sometimes we had visited for a weekend. I wheeled my suitcase through Jericho and along Woodstock Road: there we were, at twenty-five, darting from the Ashmolean Museum, impersonating the death masks. Twenty-seven, and cutting away to Port Meadow with swimming costumes and champagne. Did she, I wondered – the small girlfriend – undress when he asked her to, and fill her mouth with it, carefully, before tasting him, barely concealed in the undergrowth? But she wasn't at fault; she had come long afterwards.

The colleges languished behind their gates, sleeping all summer.

Ana saw me coming along the street and waved from an upstairs window. I could see the flurry of her through the misted glass at the front door, just before she opened it.

If Ethan could have ordered a wife, it might have been Ana Islip. Her father had taught History of Art at the university for many years, and her mother was a minor member of a Greek shipping dynasty; distant enough to stay away from the business side of things, but sufficiently related to receive a monthly allowance. Ethan connected with Ana's father at Art Attack, which was an Oxford City Council initiative to rehabilitate victims of violent crime through art, and – having invited himself to a dinner at the Islip residence, which was out along the river, and made entirely of wood and glass – met Ana ten days later.

'Art Attack?' I said, when they narrated the story to me together. They each had assigned parts, and knew them well. 'Is that really what it's called?'

'Yes,' Ana said. Ethan, smiling, looked elsewhere.

On the day of the lunch, Ana had been swimming in the Isis. She was still drying off in her costume, on the bank, when Ethan arrived. It was a terrible day for him to be early.

'A fortuitous day,' Ethan said, and raised his glass.

Ana was an artist. She smelt, softly, of paint, and different colours scuffed her limbs. In each room of the house in Summertown, her canvases hung on the walls, or rested against them. She painted water, and the way that light fell on it: she painted the green-grey surface of the Isis, barely disturbed, and the ocean in the very last sunray before a storm. She painted the tremor of somebody setting down a mug of tea. There was an Ana Islip painting in my loft in New York, of the ocean twinkling under the afternoon sun. 'Greece,' she had written, on the accompanying card. 'My second home. Ethan said that you would like it.'

She flung open the door and embraced me. 'Your mother,' she said. 'God, I'm sorry.'

'Really. There's no need to be.'

'It must be complicated,' she said, and brightened, glad to have that part over with. 'Ethan's in the garden. Go, go. He opened the wine, even after I told him to wait. Oh, Lex. You look like you haven't slept in a week.'

I walked through the wood-panelled hallway, past Ana's studio and the living room, and out to the kitchen. Here, the house opened to the garden. The summer evening slanted down the skylights and drifted in through the great double doors. The conversion had been an engagement present from Ana's parents. Ethan's dog, Horace, lolloped inside to greet me. Ethan was sitting outside, with his back to the house. 'Hello, Lex,' he said. The sun was near-parallel with the earth, and for a moment all I could see was the white shock of his hair. He could have been any one of us.

I had last seen him in London, six months before, when he invited me to a panel discussion at the Royal Academy. The discussion was titled 'Education and Inspiration: Teaching the Young Artist', and Ethan was the chair. I arrived late, after drinks with Devlin – too late, conceivably, to enter the auditorium – and waited for him in the bar. Each table had a stack of cardboard flyers advertising the event, with a painting of two small children entering the ocean on the front, and descriptions of the speakers on the back.

Ethan Charles Gracie is Headmaster at Wesley School in Oxford. The school has a distinguished history and track record in the arts, and a number of acclaimed art initiatives at different age groups. At the time of his appointment, Ethan was one of the youngest headteachers in the country. Ethan is a trustee of several charities in Oxfordshire, has advised the government on education reforms, and gives lectures and seminars internationally, which address how education has helped him to overcome personal trauma.

I ordered another drink. The doors opened, and the crowd chattered in from the auditorium. Ethan was one of the last people to emerge, talking to two men in suits, and a woman wearing a lanyard. He caught my eye and a smile crossed his face, just so; none of the others even looked in my direction. He was holding a heavy jacket over one arm, and coming to a punchline. His palms turned up, to catch the laughter. He told a story just as Father did, with the same conviction, the telling of it travelling through his sinews and his muscles, through his whole body, but leaving his mouth and his eyes impassive, as if there was a faulty connection just beneath the face. People were waiting to speak to him, hovering at the periphery of his presence. I sat back. I would have to wait, too.

He found me thirty minutes later, and three drinks down. 'Hello,' he said, and kissed me on each cheek. 'Well. How did you find it?'

'It was very interesting,' I said.

'Did you like the suggestion,' he said, 'about the treehouses?'

'Oh, yes. That was one of my favourite parts.'

'You didn't even come in, did you.'

I looked at him and laughed. He laughed, too.

'I was at work,' I said. 'But I'm sure that you were wonderful. How are you? How's Ana?'

'She couldn't make it. Sorry – I was hoping she would be somebody for you to talk to. She's not well. I think it's – that nineteenth-century affliction – the artistic one. Very upper-class. What's the name of it?'

'Hysteria?'

'Less serious.'

'The vapours?'

'Yes. That's the one. She'll be fine.' His eyes were struggling to stay on mine; he could hear more important conversations all around us. 'Would you like me to introduce you to anyone? I'll have to circulate.'

'I still have some work to do,' I said, although I didn't. 'Circulate. It seems like a big deal.'

'There'll be bigger ones. Let me see you outside.'

Piccadilly was still crowded. There were blue and white lights above the road, and shoppers wizened with paper bags. It was cold enough to snow. Couples wore dinner jackets and gowns, and ducked into hotel lobbies. Each shop window presented some new, warm fairy-tale. December in London. I intended to buy something expensive, and to walk back to my hotel through Mayfair. I liked to see the doormen's outfits, and the glow of the apartments above the street. Ethan helped me into my jacket. I was still holding the flyer.

'That,' he said.

'Did you choose the picture, too?'

'Yes. Do you know it? *Children in the Sea?*'

'I don't.'

'Joaquín Sorolla y Bastida?'

'I still don't know it, Ethan.'

'It reminded me of you,' he said. 'You and Eve, perhaps.'

'It's an impressive biography,' I said. 'Even if you did write it yourself. I'm proud of you.'

He was already turning back for the Academy. Preparing a specific smile for his re-entrance. 'It's just storytelling,' he said. 'Isn't it?'

The story of Ethan's birth was part of our family folklore long before my own, and mine - ending with a girl born uneventfully in a hospital bed – was a disappointing sequel, which Father seldom told.

Mother was eight months' pregnant, and working at the reception desk of a nothing company an hour outside Manchester, where Father mended the electronics. At this stage, she struggled to reach the typewriter; the secretaries ridiculed the way that she walked; Father had to travel up from his basement office three times each day, bearing Tupperware and massages. There was little indication that the baby was coming, just an odd discomfort, the anticipation of a pain. Then the water was in her knickers and on the cheap office chair.

For the fourth time that day, Father ascended the stairs. One of the directors of the company, Mr Bedford – the villain of the story, in case there's any ambiguity – was already at Mother's side, holding her phone. Mother was holding it, too, and asking Mr Bedford to please *let go* of the receiver; she and her husband had agreed that the baby would be born at home, and they would go there now. Mr Bedford, it transpired, had dialled for a taxi to the hospital twice already, but Mother had hit the cradle before he could finish the order.

Mr Bedford was insistent. The baby was early, and Mother should be in hospital. If he couldn't call a taxi from the reception phone – which Father had now disconnected at the port, and whose cord he held aloft, well out of Mr Bedford's reach – then he would call an ambulance from his own office. My parents, trailing the desk phone and amniotic fluid, hit the road. They hobbled out of the office through the slow sliding doors and across the car park, and Mother keeled over in the back seat of the Ford Escort which they drove together to and from work each day. Father turned the keys in the ignition. Just as they pulled out, onto the A road, they heard the siren, and an ambulance swung past them, lights flashing.

'Mr Bedford,' Father would say, 'must have had a lot of explaining to do.'

At home, twenty minutes away, they laid out the soft, clean blankets which Father had bought with his Christmas bonus. They moved the cushions from the sofa onto the floor, and drew the curtains. Mother crouched in the makeshift bed. In the familiar gloom, her face glowed with tears and saliva.

Ethan was born forty hours later. At the end, Father said,

Mother kept falling asleep; he had to tap her head to wake her. (And did she think, now and then, of the blue and white lights and a hospital room?) They weighed the baby on the bathroom scales. He was seven pounds, and healthy. A son. He had torn his way into the world, had fought to get there early. They huddled on the floor, bloody and naked, like the survivors of some terrible atrocity. Like the last people in the world, or else the first.

The part of Ethan's birth that Father tended to omit was Mr Bedford's vengeance, a few weeks later. The Gracies had stolen company property and disobeyed direct managerial instructions. Besides, the other members of the facilities team disliked Father. There had been complaints about his fondness for public ridicule, and about the hours he spent at Mother's desk, kneading her body. Mr Bedford congratulated my parents on the birth of their son, and requested that they refrain from returning to the office. Their final pay cheques would be provided by post.

Mother didn't work again. For the next seventeen years, she was full of children, and she approached the role as a martyr. She was doing God's work, and she would do it well. We were never more precious than when we were inside of her; when she had us in the tight confines of her body, and we were quiet. In all of my early memories, Mother is pregnant. Outside, she wears thin dresses, with her belly button protruding like the start of a tumour, and at home, on the sofa, she reclines in knickers and a stained T-shirt, and feeds us. We clamour for her, sometimes two of us at a time, batting each other for the fuller breast. At my age, she had Ethan and me and Delilah, and Evie on the way. She smelt grisly, of insides. She leaked. The contents of her body were determined to reach the surface.

As a child, she had wanted to become a journalist. She lived with her parents and her little sister in a village surrounded by hills. Theirs was the last house on a terrace; there was a tilt to it, like the tower in Pisa. She committed to interviewing the whole village, and her father bought her a notepad from the newsagent to record her findings. On the first page, in her best handwriting, she wrote: *Dispatches from Deborah*. Each weekend, and sometimes after school, she trooped from house to house with her pad, investigating. She found that people were happy to tell her their quiet hopes – to win the lottery, perhaps, or to move closer to the ocean; to visit France or North America – and happy, too, to speculate about the relations of the new family in the next street along, who could be a couple, but could also, *quite* feasibly, be father and daughter. I've seen photographs of Mother at this time, and I don't question her early successes. She had her white-blond hair, and empathetic, adult eyes. You would tell her your secrets.

She hadn't counted on what she called The Parade. The first incident took place when she was ten years old, and about to take the exam for the grammar school in the next town along. It was the Harvest Festival in the village, and there really was a parade: each tenuous society decorated a float; mothers knitted scarecrows and slumped them throughout the streets; the children dressed up as miscellaneous crops and walked as one dawdling vegetable patch. That year, through a questionable democratic process, Mother had been elected Princess of the Harvest. She walked at the front of the procession, wearing a golden dress (a vast improvement, she concluded, on the potato outfit of the year before), and when the parade passed her house, the privates who were navigating the veteran float let off a round of celebratory gunfire.

From her position at the front of the crowd, Mother didn't see the accident take place. The rope attaching the Countryside Christian Church to their Morris Marina snapped, just on the crest of Hilly Fields Road. She heard the screams when the float hit her father, but she assumed that the crowd had simply become overexcited, and she waved more enthusiastically. When an organizer tried to bring her to a halt, she smiled politely and walked around him.

For a few days, there were national press in the village. Mother's father lost a leg in the accident, and a child – a pumpkin, home-stitched – had died. Mother was thrilled. She liked the slick, smart reporters, who had notebooks just like hers. She was royalty in the tragedy, both a victim and an unwilling participant. She offered a series of first-hand accounts, sitting solemnly in her living room beside her mother, with a tissue clutched in her fist. She concluded each interview by stating that – in light of the terrible events – she would very much like to become a journalist herself. She wanted to allow people to tell their own stories. In the back of her pad, she collected a series of names and phone numbers, with the title of each journalist's publication noted in parentheses. She allocated stars to the national publications, based on their professionalism and the amount of time they had been willing to let her talk; she would know whom to contact, when her time came.

Her other visitors were representatives from the Countryside Christian Church. Three women knocked at the door one evening, so softly that Mother discounted it, and they knocked again. They waited in the rain, a tentative distance from the door, with scarves tied over their hair and their faces shrouded in shadow. The oldest woman was bearing a basket of warm bread covered by a tea towel, and when she held it out, Mother started. She thought, for an inexplicable moment, that the basket concealed a baby.

'We pray for you every day,' one of the women said, and another added: 'And for your father.'

'Yes – for your father, too. May we see him?'

'He's still in the hospital,' Mother said. 'My mum's there now. And my sister.'

'If you are ever lonely,' said the oldest woman, 'you mustn't hesitate to join us.'

'It's important,' said the next, 'to welcome children with open arms.'

Her father returned home from the hospital a month later. The press were back in their cities, and the child's funeral had taken place, following the same route as the Harvest Festival. Her father was quiet and static, propped in front of the television. The left leg of his trousers dangled behind him, like the ghost of a limb. He could no longer clean windows. For the first time, Mother wished that the accident had never happened.

'And so The Parade began,' Mother said. The parade of Mother's misfortunes. 'Well,' she would say, when Father lost a job, or a teacher called, concerned, that one of us was not in school, or the first time that Father hit Ethan, 'what can you do about The Parade?'

When she was no longer known as the Princess of the Harvest, Mother started to care for her father, while her own mother took up extra shifts in the village shop. She had to ensure that he ate breakfast – her mother suspected that he was trying to starve himself – and check the stump for signs of infection. Her father sat in his chair, and Mother knelt on the floor before him. She was proud of her disposition. She touched the smooth, sealed skin, and the purple seam where the wound had been stitched. She thought: perhaps I should become a doctor. They were silent during the inspections. Her father no longer asked her about her latest interviews, and she had nothing to report.

Her other responsibility was her sister, Peggy. Peggy was eight, and a great inconvenience. 'She isn't as clever as you,' their mother said. 'She needs you, Deb.' When Mother finished her homework, she sat down to help Peggy with hers, and sighed at the juvenile nature of the tasks. She decided to get a number of questions wrong in order to avoid suspicion, but sometimes these were the simplest questions, and she hoped that Peggy would be called before the class, and asked to explain herself.

Mother failed the entrance examinations to the grammar school. Her family didn't comment on it, as if there had never been any real prospect of success. The Parade continued. She went to the local comprehensive, which was occupied by farming oafs and their future wives, all of them reeking of cow shit. She had a single friend, Karen, whose family had recently moved to the area; Karen was painfully thin and perpetually bored, and when she lit a cigarette you could see the bleeding stumps of her fingernails. The teachers said that Mother was distracted and didn't apply herself; but how could she, when she was so clearly meant to be elsewhere? She developed psoriasis on her elbows and underneath her eyes, and so became sensitive, which was how her mother explained it to the villagers who visited the shop, and asked what had become of her: Deborah is a very sensitive girl. To make matters worse, Peggy scraped into the grammar school, and began to speak to everyone in the family in a clipped, affected accent, which pierced each room of the tilting house – Peggy, for whom she had sacrificed everything.

Mother could sometimes be seen walking through the village to evening Mass at the Countryside Christian Church, still in her school uniform. She walked fast, with her arms tucked beneath her ribs and her stockings bunched at the ankles, and she was always alone. She liked to arrive just before the service began, and to depart before the rest of the congregation stood. She had heard that the village believed that she exemplified forgiveness, although for the most part she liked an evening away from her family, and the relieved smiles of the congregation, believing that she had pardoned them.

Mother left school at sixteen, with a few perfunctory

qualifications, and a place on a secretarial course in the city. When she could afford to do so, she moved out of the house in the village and across the moors to the suburbs; that saved her from having to witness any more of Peggy's ascent, or to care for her father, who was becoming confused. Over time, he had shrunk into the fabric of his chair, and when she kissed him goodbye, he flinched, as if she had hit him.

When Ethan and I were very young, and there was less competition, my parents would allow us to request bedtime stories. (Father saw books as inferior to his own tales; 'They didn't need paper in the days of Homer,' he said, neglecting to elaborate on the history of the paper-making industry.) Ethan's favourite story was that of his dramatic arrival into the world, which always culminated in Mother moving aside the living room rug to show the brown birthmark on the carpet. But my favourite story was that of the evening my parents met.

Karen had persuaded Mother to accompany her to the city on a Saturday night. 'You're getting boring,' Karen said. 'Even more boring than you used to be.' (At the time of the telling, Mother believed that Karen still lived at home, unmarried, and with mental health issues; 'Now who's boring,' Mother said.) They dressed in Mother's flat, Mother always in black, with the white shroud of hair down to her waist, and a sad Elvis song on the stereo, whatever the occasion. They boarded the local bus with a bottle of Riesling to share en route.

The evening was a disaster. They ended up at a pub beyond the city centre – rickety tables; slot machines; a sticky carpet – where one of Karen's old lovers was working behind the bar. They pretended to be surprised to see one another, although it was obvious to Mother that the whole evening had been contrived. She was the gooseberry, there to entertain Karen while the barman was serving. They drank free vodka and orange, and the barman winked at Mother when Karen visited the toilet. Just after eleven, somebody put on a vinyl – something heavy, which Mother had never heard before – and the barman and Karen started to dance. A toothless woman in sequins joined them, then one of the locals, barely able to stand, but gyrating his hips in Mother's direction. After a short time of moving her weight from foot to foot, she snatched her jacket from the bar stool, and left.

She didn't know where she was. She walked in the direction of the bus stop, tears in her eyes. In another life, she was already asleep, warm and oblivious underneath her blankets. In this part of the city, the buildings were far apart, and between their lights were wastelands of shadow, so dark that she couldn't see her shoes. She ran across the dead zones, stumbling at the puddles and potholes. She was quite sure that she had gone too far.

After half an hour, she came to the church.

It was set back from the road, at the end of a winding gravel path between graves. Its bricks were a warm, terracotta red, underlit through the night. It was after midnight, but the stained-glass windows were flickering: somebody had lit candles inside.

Thinking little, she parted the door. She could wait out the night inside, and leave long before the first Sunday service. At the threshold, she removed her shoes and tugged her dress down to her knees. She left damp footprints on the stone.

Five candles burned at the end of the aisle. She tiptoed towards them, glancing down each pew as she went. When she reached the pulpit, she turned back, as if addressing the congregation.

'Hello?' she called.

'Hello,' Father said.

Her heart jittered. He was standing on a balcony above her, his palms pressed against the railings.

'Hi,' Mother said.

'Hello,' he said again. 'I wasn't expecting anyone in.'

'I feel very stupid,' she said. 'But I'm lost.'

'That's not so stupid.'

'What are you doing here?'

'It's a side project. I'm testing some new lighting. Join me, if you'd like.'

He beckoned. Mother was still shaking. She didn't move, and Father laughed.

'Don't be frightened.'

'I'm not frightened. How do I get up?'

'Back by the entrance. Let me light the way.'

He disappeared, and bright light flooded the aisle. Relief rushed through her: foolish, to be afraid of the dark. She ascended the staircase as quickly as she could, hampered by her dress and holding onto the walls, navigating wires and banners and stacks of chairs. At the top, she looked for him, suspicious that it had been a prank, and that he would have hidden. Instead, he stood with his back to her, waiting.

'It sounds like you're having quite the evening,' he said. He held a fuse box in his hands. There were crevices of muscle along his forearms, and bright deltas of veins. The new, strange country of him.

'Yes. I shouldn't have agreed to it. I have this friend – an old friend, I suppose. It was her idea.'

He didn't yet deign to look at her.

'Where is she now?'

'With some guy, I think.'

'She doesn't sound like such a good friend.'

'I suppose not.'

He conjured a spotlight, which travelled down along the balcony, and rested on her face.

'Your hair,' he said. 'All of the lights land in it.'

(*All of the lights land in it*: an excellent line. While I try to deny it, there were times – when I was younger – when this would have impressed me, too.)

'Is this how you usually spend your Saturday nights?' Mother asked.

'No. Sometimes. I like the technology, you see. And I like to help out.'

Mother leaned against the railing alongside him. She let her hair fall against his arm.

'I've never had company before,' Father said, and smiled. 'This makes things much more interesting.'

'I'm not that interesting at all,' Mother said. 'I mean, I'm pretty boring. Actually.'

'I don't believe you. What's the best thing that's ever happened to you?'

'What?'

'Tell me the best thing that's ever happened to you. Nobody's boring when they tell you the best thing that's ever happened. Go.'

Mother thought of her princess dress, and the faces of the villagers watching the Harvest Festival. In her mind, they multiplied, so that she led the parade through a crowd of hundreds – thousands – of well-wishers. 'Fine,' she said. She knew exactly how she would tell it.

'See,' Father said, at the end. 'That wasn't boring. But it wasn't the best thing that ever happened to you, either.'

'It wasn't?'

'Of course not,' Father said. He concentrated on the fuse box, passing it from one great palm to the other. He was smiling, close to laughter. 'That's tonight.'

'This is a boring story,' Ethan said, whenever it was told. 'I don't know why you like it.'

'Do you think it ever happened?' Evie asked me, when she heard it for the first time. 'Or did they just meet at a Sunday service?' I was surprised by her cynicism, then surprised that I had never questioned the story myself. The fact was, I wanted it to be true. It cast my parents in a dark, glittering light: the lovers poised on their balcony at the very beginning of the tale. This was the version of them that I liked the best.

Ethan had his own plans for the house on Moor Woods Road. He kept them to himself through dinner on Friday night, and during Ana's artistic tour of Oxford on Saturday morning, but by lunchtime his opportunities were running out. Ana had made a Greek salad and found a garden umbrella, and we ate outside, talking about Ethan's work. 'Would you like to go for a walk after lunch?' he asked me, pointedly. I imagined him striding into the staffroom at Wesley to propose the same thing to a colleague, and how the connotations of that suggestion would linger when they had gone: a walk with Mr Gracie.

'Sure,' I said.

We walked out to University Parks, past the cricket pitches and the flower beds, and found a shaded path to the Cherwell. The open grass was a dull, desert yellow, but underneath the trees and by the river, it was still green. The sunshine snatched a little of Ethan's dignity. His skin was a shade thinner than white, and his more caustic lines – on the forehead, and between the eyes – no longer retreated when he smiled, but stayed, poised, on his face.

'Your hair's even darker,' Ethan said. 'I don't know why you do that.'

'Don't you?' I said. 'Really?'

'You look better blonde.'

I knew Ethan well enough to appreciate that this was a battle cry: a few notches out of the enemy's wall before he launched the main offensive.

'I have no desire to see Mother in the mirror,' I said. 'Besides, it's not in my direct financial interests.'

'Unlike mine, you mean?'

'It can't hurt,' I said, 'with lectures about your personal trauma.'

'Overcoming personal trauma. And I'm not trying to judge you, Lex, I'm really not, but you should come along. The feedback's been unbelievable. Everybody gets something out of it, I promise you. I'm in New York in the autumn. It could really help you out.'

My face was hot. I paused and swallowed, but Ethan didn't notice. A stride ahead of me, now.

'It's a great platform to talk about education,' he said.

'And about yourself.'

'Education *in the context of* ourselves. Do you even remember how happy we were to go back to school? I want all children to have that enthusiasm. To be able to rise above their circumstances. You should have seen the children I taught in my twenties, Lex. They were already shells. It's our kind of enthusiasm that I'm promoting. I don't know why you have a problem with that.'

'Please, Ethan,' I said. 'Everybody knows you start with a slide of the mugshots.'

'Sure. You have to get people's attention.'

We had reached the river. Punts trundled past between the trees. I sat down in the grass.

'With that in mind,' he said. 'I want to talk to you about the house. Eleven Moor Woods Road.'

I closed my eyes. 'Really,' I said.

'I think that this is a good opportunity for us. For all of us. A unique opportunity.'

'Well, it's certainly unique.'

'Listen. It's not so different from what you're suggesting. With a few changes. A place for the community, yes. But we need to put our name on it. The Gracie Community Centre, Hollowfield.

If you do that, you get the newspaper articles, the opening ceremony. You get access to more public funding. You help more people. Think about it. Shouldn't part of that place be dedicated to our family? Whether that's a speaker series, or some kind of memorial. We could – we could keep one room of the house as it was, so that people could understand what we went through. I don't know. I haven't finished thinking it through.'

'A museum.'

'That's not what I said.'

'Nobody in that community is going to want a shrine to yesterday's news.'

'They might do – if it brings other things with it. Attention. Investment.'

'We didn't exactly glorify Hollowfield the first time round,' I said. 'No, Ethan. It doesn't need our name on it. Just a community place, with a decent purpose. What's wrong with that?'

'It's a waste. I could do a lot with this, Lex. At least consider it.'

'There's no way.'

'You need me to consent to your plan, too, remember. It works both ways. Who else have you even spoken to? Delilah? Gabriel?'

'No. Just Evie.'

Ethan laughed. He waved his arm at me, as if dismissing a particularly frustrating schoolgirl, committed to failure whatever he might do. 'Of course,' he said. 'Of course.'

I told Ethan that I would walk back alone, and when he had gone I found a quiet patch of sunshine and called Bill. He didn't answer. I expected that he was at a zoo or a barbeque, with children attached to his limbs. Still sweating. Ethan had left me savage, and I called again.

He answered on the third try. 'I've given it some thought,' I said, 'and I accept.'

'Alexandra? Is that you?'

His voice was surrounded by music, and he was walking, as if searching for a quiet corner. I felt a worm of embarrassment in my gut. The Gracie girl, he would mouth, to his extended family. *Sorry.*

'I'm happy to hear from you,' he said, catching up on his minor triumph. 'And your mother – she'd have been happy, too.'

Mother's happiness: threadbare, like wearing rope. 'I wouldn't be so sure,' I said. 'Anyway. My sister and me – we have an idea—'

I walked him through the community centre, room by room. At the garden (daffodils, for the most part, and a patch of vegetables managed by children from the primary school), he laughed, and almost dropped the phone.

'It's perfect. Perfect, Lex. The other beneficiaries – do they agree?'

'It's a process,' I said. And, when he didn't respond: 'It's ongoing.'

'Ongoing' was a word from Devlin's Temporal Dictionary for Clients, alongside 'shortly', and 'as soon as possible'.

'We'll need to request funding, too,' I said. 'For the conversion. It's a lot more than you could have expected, Bill. You don't have to help with any of this.'

'I know. I know that, Lex. But I'd like to.'

I was to secure the beneficiaries' agreement. He would investigate the documentation. He mentioned planning applications, grants of probate, executor's deeds. A whole new language of death and houses. We would have to think about the best way to pitch the application to the council, he said, bearing in mind where the money had come from. Perhaps – if I fancied an adventure – we would travel to Hollowfield, to deliver it in person.

'The prodigal daughter returns,' said Bill, who, for all of his time with Mother, had clearly never read the Gospels.

After dinner, Ethan went out. He had a late appointment with some of the Wesley governors at a hotel in the city centre, and we shouldn't wait up for him. 'They loathed me, at first,' he said. 'Too young. Too high profile. Too – what was it, Ana? – too revolutionary. Now they want me to sup with them at the fucking weekend.' All dinner, he had been sullen, criticizing Ana's cooking and pouring wine with deliberate zeal, so that it slithered down the stems of the glasses and stained the wooden table.

'Thank God he's gone,' Ana said. 'Sorry, Lex.'

In silence, we cleared the table. Ana had painted the plates, so that olives and cypress trees emerged as you ate. 'Leave the glasses,' Ana said. 'I'll open another bottle.' I took a cloth from the sink and wiped the red rings from the table.

We sat outside, cross-legged and facing one another, like children about to clap hands. 'So,' I said. 'Tell me about the wedding.'

It was only three months away, now. They would marry on Paios, in Greece, which had its own airport, not much more than a shack and a concrete strip. Ana had holidayed there when she was a child, and had told her father, in no uncertain terms, that this was where she would get married. She liked the little white church in the main town, high on a hilltop, which she had believed, then, to be the top of the world. At nightfall, you could see every light on the island, be it a car or a house; she would contemplate a couple driving home from dinner, midway through an argument, or a widow, in bed, reaching to turn out her bedside light.

'Always such sad imaginings,' she said. 'I was such a melancholy child.'

She looked down from the sky, as if remembering that I was there. 'Of course,' she said, 'I had no reason to be.'

'I've booked my flights,' I said. 'I can't wait.'

'You're still welcome to bring somebody – if you would like.'

I laughed. 'I'll see if anything develops. I'm running out of time.'

'You'll be fine, anyway. Delilah will be there.'

'Well. That'll be an interesting encounter.'

Even in the dark garden, I could feel the flush of Ana's discomfort. She would have liked all of us to be there, matching in chiffon and joy, on Ethan's side of the church. Instead, Evie and Gabriel hadn't been invited, and Delilah and I didn't talk. Evie and I had spent some time speculating about the guest list, and the extent of Ethan's self-service. We concluded that her place had probably gone to an MP, or the chairperson of an international charity. 'Somebody useful,' she said, 'whom you would never want to sit next to.' She paused to shrug. 'It's not like we were ever close.'

'Lex—'

Ana combed the air with her fingers, as if she might find the words there.

'Sometimes,' she began, 'I just wonder—'

She stared hard at the kitchen, empty under elegant lights, at the other end of the garden. At last it was cool. The oak branches above us tipped and collided in the wind, drunker than we were. Ana set down her glass and caught the tears at the corners of her eyes. 'I'm sorry,' she said.

'That's OK.'

'Ethan has been difficult. Everything must be a success. The school, the presentations, the charities. The wedding. You know – don't you – that he sleeps badly. Right from the beginning, I would get up in the night, and see him reading, or at work. But now – I hear him, walking through the house. In the daytime, there is a barrier, when he's like this. Between us. I can't get behind it. I can't understand him. As long as we're happy, I'm happy. But he doesn't see things in this way.'

'Success at all costs,' I said.

'Yes. Quite. And behind this barrier, I worry that I don't know him at all. Sometimes he will look at me – let's say I ask a stupid question, or suggest that preparation for an assembly can wait until the next morning – and it's like I'm speaking to a new person, a different person, with his face. And' – she laughed – 'not one that I like all too much.'

'Does he ever talk to you,' I said, 'about our childhood?'

'He's told me some things,' she said. 'But not others. And, you know, I respect that. I've attended his presentations. I know how he's suffered. It's just – if there is anything that would make me understand. Whether I should try to make him talk. Any suggestions at all—'

Leave him, I thought. I could taste the words; I could hear precisely how they would sound when they left my mouth. Try to understand, I would explain, which of these two people – the person you met, and the person you perceive to be new – is my brother. I thought, too, of the aftermath: of Ethan walking into the rubble of all that he had built.

'Wait for him,' I said. 'When he's like that – I think he goes somewhere you wouldn't want to follow. He'll always come back to you.'

'You think so?'

'Of course.'

She tilted forward, onto her knees on the grass, and took my hands. 'Thank you,' she said. A tear dawdled on her face, but she was smiling. 'A new sister,' she said.

When I was old enough to understand where Ethan went each day, I would wait for him and Mother by the door, clutching a pillow in anticipation. He had been only an eight-minute walk up the road, at Jasper Street Primary School, but to me it seemed that he had traversed the world, and returned each evening triumphant and willing – if, at times, begrudgingly so – to impart all that he had learnt.

In Ethan's third year at school, when he was seven, his teacher was Mr Greggs, who implemented Fact of the Day, Word of the Day, and News of the Day. Each pupil in the class took turns to present their three items. These were the first things that Ethan taught to me when he returned home from school, while Mother fed Delilah. The presentations, Ethan said, were of mixed quality: Michelle, for example, had informed the class that she had come second in a gymnastics competition, as if that was *news*. Each time it was his own turn, Ethan left for school on the balls of his feet, fizzing with excitement, and I shouted the items after him as he went. I was quite sure that he was the cleverest person in the world.

I still recall some of Ethan's own facts; once, in a pub quiz and sitting beside JP, I took the pencil and paper and noted the capital of Tuvalu.

'Funafuti,' JP said. 'Well, you couldn't make that up.' We received a free tequila for the only correct answer, and as I set down the glass, JP shook his head. 'Funafuti,' he said. 'I'll be damned.'

Before joining Jasper Street Primary School, Mr Greggs had spent a year travelling the world, and Ethan described the contents of his classroom to me at teatime, with eyes like globes. He had a set of Russian dolls, which lived inside one another, and a little bronze model of the Golden Gate Bridge in San Francisco. He had a kimono from Japan, which you could try on – both boys and girls, because in Japan, anyone could wear them – and a cowboy hat from the actual Wild West.

Father had returned home from work and joined us in the kitchen. It was a dull Friday evening, February, and he was still wearing a coat, which smelt of the cold. He took four slices of bread from the freezer and slotted them into the toaster. 'That isn't a place,' he said.

'What?'

'The "Wild West". This Mr Greggs is having you on, Ethan. He can't have been there, because it isn't a real place.'

I looked at Ethan across the table, but he was fixated on his hands, which were pressed together, as if in prayer. Father smeared butter across his toast and shook his head.

'I didn't think that you would be so slow,' he said, 'as to fall for something like that.'

Father had rarely taught us facts, but he had taught us philosophies. One of these was that no person was any better than another, however educated or wealthy he or she might appear to be; specifically, no person in the world was any better than a Gracie.

'Who is this person?' Father called. 'Deborah?'

Mother came arduously from the living room, bearing Delilah in her arms and Evie in her belly. 'What?'

'Mr Greggs,' Father said. 'Ethan's teacher.'

'What about him?'

'Is he peculiar?' Father asked. He bent the final piece of toast in half and folded it into his smile.

'He was a bit delicate,' Mother said, 'at parents' evening.'

Father snorted. Pleased with that. He wore a blue boiler suit, which couldn't contain his laughter; his body bulged against the material, like magma at the crust of the earth. After his dismissal by Mr Bedford, Father worked as the electrician for a Victorian hotel in Blackpool, right on the seafront, and wore the same uniform required of the hotel cleaners.

'It's only temporary,' he said. 'Of course.'

When he first met Mother, Father had described himself as a businessman, which wasn't so far from the truth. In the evenings and at weekends, he still occupied an office space in town, with dirty white blinds and a sign which he had ordered from a printer: *CG Consultants: Ideas with a spark*. He dispensed advice on purchasing computers, fixed Walkmans, and hosted unpopular programming classes on Saturday afternoons. Children of all ages were welcome; on the better days, two or three glum boys would file into the room, accompanied by their mothers, who liked to tap on the keyboards and talk to Father. Father wanted to talk about computers; the mothers wanted Father to talk about himself.

Father spoke only when he was quite sure that his audience was listening to him, and so each phrase was weighed, prepared, and carefully proclaimed. The mothers at coding class leaned eagerly into the silences between his words: they liked his quiet temperament and his beard and his black hair, and the heavy hands which skimmed across the computer keyboard, and which were easy to imagine on your skin.

'Back to the breach,' Father said, and stood from the table. One of the coding club mothers had made an appointment to discuss whether she should purchase a Macintosh or an IBM. A busy evening at CG Consultants. Ethan waited for the front door to close; as soon as it had, he darted past me and Mother, and upstairs. He, too, went to work.

Sunday dinner: the fortnightly endurance of steak and kidney pudding. The burst of each slither of organ made me want to vomit.

Ethan had visited the town library on Saturday morning, and smuggled home a rucksack of books which he refused to share; he upended the swag onto his bed and bundled me out of the room. Now we awaited him at the kitchen table. Delilah was anxious, contorting in Mother's arms. Mother flopped a breast from her maternity dress and offered it to the child.

'That's it,' Father said, and stood up. 'I'll go and get him.'

There was no need. We heard the light footsteps on the stairs, and Ethan appeared at the kitchen door.

'Sorry,' he said.

He was quiet through the steak and kidney pudding, and quiet as we took the plates to the sink. He was quiet when Father asked him for liquor, which he took carefully from the Forbidden Cupboard and poured into Father's wedding glass, as he had been taught.

He, like Father, understood the importance of just when to speak.

When we were back at the table, and watching Father drink, Ethan cleared his throat. He was too nervous for introductions, and he came right to it.

'There is such a place,' Ethan said, 'as the Wild West.'

I looked up from the table. Father's lips were wet, and he licked them. He rolled the bottom of the glass around the table, and watched the amber surface shifting under the kitchen lights.

'What's this?' Mother asked.

'Where Mr Greggs went,' Ethan said. 'I've read about it. It's just a way of talking about the American Frontier, when people first got to that part of the country. There weren't any laws, just cowboys and pioneers, and saloon towns. It's different today, but you can still go. You can go to Texas or to Arizona or to Nevada, or to New Mexico, which is where Mr Greggs went.'

Father set down the glass and leaned back in his chair.

'So,' Father said. 'What you're saying is that you and Mr Greggs are much cleverer than me. Is that it?'

I swallowed, hard; I thought that a bite of the kidneys might have lodged between my throat and my stomach.

'No,' Ethan said. 'What I'm saying is that you were wrong about the Wild West. It *is* a real place, and Mr Greggs wasn't making a fool out of me.'

'What are you talking about, Ethan?' Mother said.

'Aren't you listening?' Father said. 'He's talking about how much better he is than the rest of us.' To Ethan: 'And what else would you like to teach the family? Please – do tell us more.'

'I can tell you about the cowboys,' Ethan said. 'And one thing

I read was about life as a pioneer. They received these letters, from other people on the frontier – from friends and family – telling them to go west—'

Father was laughing.

'Do you know the problem with thinking that you're so clever?' Father said. 'You become very boring, Ethan.'

Tears shook in Ethan's eyes.

'You just don't like it,' he said, 'because I was right, and you were wrong.'

The way that Father moved reminded me of crocodiles in the nature documentaries that I liked at the time, their bodies placid until prey touched the water. Father stood up, lunged across the table, and slapped Ethan with the back of his hand, hard enough to knock him from the chair and send a dash of blood across the table. Delilah, woken by the clatter, started to cry. 'I'm going to be sick,' I whispered to Mother, and made it only a few steps from my chair. Father stepped past me – crouched on the carpet, and faced, yet again, with the kidney pudding – and opened the front door. He didn't close it behind him, and the damp night air stole into the house and settled there.

Mother cleaned Ethan's face, and my vomit, and Delilah. Already, little disappointments had tugged at her jawline and her breasts. She was becoming sullen; the sharp eyes of her childhood photographs were hard and resigned. She finished the leftover liquor in Father's glass, then waited for him to return. She felt the tapping of the fresh child in her womb. The Parade marched on.

Some time deep in the night, Ethan returned. I could hear him downstairs, talking to Horace, and I fell asleep. When I woke up next, he was at the threshold, the hallway light behind him.

I remembered another doorway, at Moor Woods Road; how he had filled that, too. In silhouette, he hadn't changed.

'Can we talk?' he said.

The exposure of somebody awake while you're sleeping. I wore thin, cheap pyjamas, purchased at the station. They had bunched at the stomach and between my legs. I wrapped the sheets up to my neck, and squinted into the light. 'Now?' I said.

'You're my guest. Aren't you supposed to entertain me?'

'Actually,' I said, 'I think it's the other way around.'

He closed the door behind him. Into the room came the smell of tired wine. For a moment, before he found the light switch, we were in the dark together.

'How did it go?' I said.

He was leaning against the wall, smiling like he knew something I didn't.

'The best part of it,' he said, 'is watching them trying to decide if they want me to succeed or to fail.'

He paused, back in the hotel bar. I could see from his face that he was pleased. Had known exactly what to say. He had lobbed his slights, and they hadn't yet landed; they would hit the governors in bed, midway through the night.

'Anyway. How was your evening? You and Ana.'

'It was nice.'

'Nice. Nice *how*?'

'What do you want, Ethan?'

'I'd like to know what you talked about,' he said. 'For starters.'

'Nothing. The wedding. Her dress. The island. Nothing very exciting.'

'Moor Woods Road?'

'It's not really Saturday-night conversation. Is it?'

'I'd like you to know,' he said, 'that things are good for me, now. But I can't deal with interference, Lex. I can't deal with your stories, at a time like this.'

'My stories?' I said. I was starting to laugh.

'I've had to be selective,' he said, 'with what I've said to Ana. You understand that. I don't want to upset her. There are things – certain things – that she doesn't need to know.'

'Are there?' I said. Laughing harder, now. 'Certain things?'

'Stop laughing, Lex,' he said. 'Lex—'

He crossed the room and took me by the throat. Palm crushed against the cram of tubes and bone. Just for a second; just long enough to show me that he could. As soon as he let go, I clambered from the bed, coughing with the shock of it.

'Stop it,' he said. 'Lex. Lex, please.'

He held his arms up to me, his whole body in appeasement. As usual, the sentiment didn't reach his face. I leaned against the wall, as far away from him as I could get. Sweat shifted in my hair, down my back. The insect legs of it.

'Don't wake Ana,' he said. 'Please.'

'Certain things . . .' I said. I was waiting for my body to stop convulsing long enough to make the point. 'Like what? Like how you were next in line to the throne? Truly – Father's son?'

'That's unfair.'

'You know, I always used to think that it would be you who would save us,' I said. 'I waited. I would think – he isn't even restrained. Any day now. When he's eighteen. When he can leave of his own accord.'

'I tried, Lex. When we were little. Do you remember? When I still could. But by then – I was out of courage.'

We surveyed one another across the bed. He was smaller now. Ethan, with his deficit of courage, and a good face for sympathy.

'That isn't how I remember it,' I said. 'That isn't how I remember it at all.'

He sat down on the bed and brushed the creases from the sheet.

We listened for noise from Ana, but there were only the quiet floors of the house: the rugs and the bookshelves and the bay windows, undisturbed.

'For what it's worth,' I said, 'tonight – we talked about other things.'

He nodded.

'Go to bed, Ethan.'

'What I said before,' he said, 'about the governors—'

'What about it?'

'I won't fail,' he said. 'Will I?'

'I doubt it.'

Drunk, he smiled at me. Smiled all the way to the eyes. It was as if he was already forgetting.

'Thank you,' he said. He clambered to his feet and crossed from the bed to the doorway. I heard him retreating along the hallway to his bedroom, stumbling into a canvas halfway there, then the whispers of a mattress, of him and Ana. I sat with my back against the wall and my legs stuck out ahead of me, holding my throat where he had held it, tight then loose, confident in the control of my own fingers, the muscles obeying the motor cortex. I waited a while, until I started to enjoy it, and went back to bed.

When we were tired of the hospital room, Dr K helped me into a wheelchair, and we wound down the corridors. I liked the hospital courtyard, which was really just a balding garden between wards, populated by smokers and people making serious phone calls. The doctors demanded that I wear sunglasses whenever I went outside, but Dr K had recoiled at the frames provided by the hospital and promised to fetch me a pair of her own. I rolled out wearing pyjamas, blankets, Wayfarers.

This day, the detectives weren't with us. 'They've asked me to make a particular enquiry,' Dr K said. 'It's a sensitive matter, I think.'

We sat side by side, her on a bench and me in the chair. It could be easier to talk about the difficult things, she said, when you didn't have to look at one another.

'It concerns your brother,' she said. 'Ethan.'

I had suspected that this was coming. In the detectives' questions, Ethan was implicated by omission. It had been more than a month, I thought, since I had heard his name.

'You see,' Dr K said, 'he wasn't in the same condition as the rest of you. He was stronger. Nothing broken. He wasn't even in chains.'

Beneath the blankets, I wrapped my fingers around one another, and checked the surface. Making sure that she couldn't see them.

'There were sightings – reports – suggesting that he had been allowed outside the house.'

I saw the detectives hunched around a television, watching a year pass on the same dull street. Scanning for Ethan's gait.

'The police are questioning,' she said, 'whether he suffered at all. Or whether his role was altogether different.'

A month of detective work, for this moment. They would be waiting for Dr K to call, after our meeting, with tight jaws and the necessary documentation.

'Did he ever hurt you?' she asked.

I tried to make my face like hers: like a house from the outside.

'No,' I said.

'I shouldn't have to tell you,' she said, 'that the time for protecting people has passed.'

'There was nothing he could have done,' I said. 'Just like the rest of us.'

'You're sure?' she said. I allowed myself to look at her, then, over the top of my glasses, so that she could see that I meant it.

'Yes,' I said.

The house in Oxford was beautiful in the morning. A long rectangle of sunlight cut into my bedroom and rested on the duvet. The Islip canvas in the guestroom was a river in motion, and Ana had placed it behind the bed, facing the window, so that it was hard to tell what was the effect of the paint and what was the real light in the room. I kicked off the cover and stretched into the warm day. For a moment I imagined that the house was mine, and empty. I would take a book from the study and spend the morning in the garden. There would be no need to talk to anybody all day.

Downstairs, Ethan and Ana were in the kitchen, standing close together at the counter, their bodies touching. Reconciliation.

'How was the meeting?' I asked. Ethan turned to me, unperturbed.

'Excellent,' he said. He was wearing a polo shirt, and his hair was damp. 'They were after a general update, before the results days. It's impossible to predict, of course. But I'm positive.'

He served me a coffee. The whites of his eyes were sallow and cut with little red wires.

'You must have been back late,' I said. 'I didn't hear you come in.'

'Oh, not too late. There's sport at the school today, so I have to be on decent form. Ana and I are heading up. You're very welcome to join us.'

'Don't worry. I'm going to take the train back to London. I need to think about speaking to the others, like you said.'

'Well, we're making eggs. Stay for that, at least.'

We ate in quiet, looking out onto the garden. When Ethan

had finished, he pushed his plate away and took Ana's hand. 'Before I forget,' he said, though there could have been no chance of him forgetting, 'Ana and I discussed your proposal. About how to handle the house.'

My mouth was full. I nodded.

'It's a great idea,' he said. 'A community centre, in a town like that. No associations with us. It sounds good, Lex. Let me know what to sign.'

'I'm sure we can donate some supplies,' Ana said. 'Paints, paper. Anonymously, of course.'

'Right,' I said. 'OK.' I thought for a moment of Devlin in a negotiation, and how she might display a studied softness when her adversary least expected it; it was as if she had trusted you with her most precious secret, and you couldn't help but like her for it. 'We could talk about some limited publicity,' I said, 'if you think that it might attract more funding.'

'It's all very exciting,' Ana said. She clapped, stood from the table, and kissed Ethan on the head. 'Is it summer dresses?' she asked. 'Or more casual?'

'Wear a dress,' he said, and she nodded, and ran upstairs.

I turned to Ethan.

'What?' he said. 'I thought about it some more. I don't need it. Not really. Do what makes you happy. Besides, Ana loved the idea.'

'Are you sure?'

'Almost. There's a condition.'

'You've got to be joking, Ethan.'

'I'll sign off on all of this. But if we're doing it your way, you deal with it. Demolition, funding, whatever. I don't want to hear anything about it. I mean – look around. This is where I live now.'

I looked at the drowsy bees on the grass, and the eggy, hand-painted plates, and Horace dozing beneath the sunflowers which Ana had planted at the end of the garden. ('There's a local competition,' she had explained, seriously, 'between the old women of Summertown. But this year, I'm going to win it.')

'Even seeing you,' Ethan said. 'Sometimes it's too much.'

There were many responses to that, but each would lose me the deal. I nodded. 'OK,' I said. We shook hands, as if we were children placing a sombre bet on the capital of Tanzania. The memory made me smile, and the capital wouldn't come to me, so I asked Ethan. This, more than anything, was an offering of peace.

'It isn't Dar es Salaam,' he said.

'Well,' I said. 'Obviously.'

'Dodoma,' he said. He looked at me, triumphant and then wistful. 'Mr Greggs and his capitals.'

'I remember them.'

'Not Dodoma, though.'

'No. Not Dodoma.'

'Do you know,' Ethan said, 'I was giving a presentation last year, at a conference for headteachers. It's a big event. Headteachers from around the world. And at the end of my speech, when the applause started and I could actually relax, I looked up, and I was sure that I saw him in the crowd – Mr Greggs. He was near the back, but he was clapping, and I thought that I caught his eye. I tried to find him afterwards, at the drinks reception, but it was busy, and it was the last night of the thing, and I never did.

'Anyway. I decided that I would look him up. I requested the list of attendees from the conference, and he wasn't on that. I searched for headmasters across the country, thinking that the list might have missed him off, somehow. He didn't come up there, either. So then I search more widely. And it transpires that he couldn't have been at the conference, because he died. Five years earlier. He was still a teacher then, in some comprehensive in Manchester – dead in service.'

I thought of Ethan leaving for school on the days of his presentations, brimming with knowledge. 'I'm sorry,' I said.

'Well, what is it to me? But he was a good teacher.'

We could hear Ana on the stairs. The two of us stood, together, and watched her come through the kitchen. She was wearing a yellow dress, and when she walked into the sunshine she opened her arms, as if she would embrace us when she arrived. 'The strange thing is,' Ethan said, just before she reached us, 'each time that I speak, I think of him. I still like to think of him in the crowd.'

3

Delilah (Girl B)

Detective Superintendent Greg Jameson at sixty-five: fat and retired, like a show dog gone to ruin. Each morning his wife, Alice, makes the tea, butters the toast, props him up with the newspaper and an old hospital tray she took from work. 'To make up for the long, long nights,' she says. It is ten o'clock, and the bedroom curtains flutter in mid-morning sunlight, and in these moments, the night shifts are long forgotten.

His days are rich. He enjoys the garden, with cricket on the radio. He enjoys a weekly swim at Pells Pool, but only in the summer. Undressing on the grass, he is surprised by the great white mass of his stomach; by the grey hairs webbed against his chest. He is surprised not to sink. In the winters, he hibernates, with biscuits and sports biographies. He talks at local schools and at community centres in London, talking about his time on the beat, talking about his days as a detective, talking about how they could do the same. Some days they will ask interesting questions, and he'll know that they really listened, that the day was well spent; other times they will enquire: 'Did you wear a hat?'

Sometimes. He will think of it, then. Sometimes he had returned home in the early morning, his mind crawling with hatred for the human race, and he had contemplated packing a bag and driving to the loneliest place he could think of – Ben Armine, perhaps, or Snowdonia – and spending the rest of his days as a hermit. (Or, he reasoned, as the local eccentric; that way, he could maintain access to hot meals, and a pub.) There had been days when he couldn't speak to Alice because she was too incompatible with his shift: she believed that people were, fundamentally, good. She sang in the kitchen, and was upset when she received charity leaflets about cruelty to animals. What could he possibly say?

Yes. There had been a time when he had worn a hat.

Many of the cases were solved, and he doesn't think about them so much. Others hang open, like a door in the winter, and he can feel their draught.

For example: a twenty-year-old man, Freddie Kluziak, attended the party of a close friend in the function room of a pub. Second floor. The pub's surveillance camera was fixed on the stairs leading up to the party, and captured Freddie ascending with two acquaintances, carrying a birthday present. At the end of the evening, the lights came up, and Freddie's friends searched for him, to no avail. That was fine: he would have left early, drunk or tired. Two days later, his girlfriend raised the alarm. Nobody had seen him since the party. The surveillance footage arrived on Jameson's desk like a long-awaited invitation. The whole team gathered around, craning for the details. Jameson spent seventy-two hours accounting for each person who walked up the stairs that day, and each one of them walked back down, except Freddie Kluziak.

What perturbed Jameson the most was the present. That was gone from the scene, too. He felt absurd, telling Freddie's father that his son must have left via a window with a parcel in his arms, but at that stage they had excavated every wall of the function room, and the landlord was sick to death of them.

Or: a five-year-old child climbed up to a third-floor window ledge and jumped. George Casper was illiterate and near mute. He did not, his teacher explained, know how to turn the pages of a book: he would look at them like they were dead, flat things. He liked birds. This from the mother. Offered as an explanation. George had pushed a chair to the window, she said, to get closer to them. He rolled from the sill, a grubby Icarus, half-naked and with no vocabulary to shout. 'Which chair?' Jameson asked, and the mother couldn't remember; she had moved it to see the body below. Jameson lifted all three chairs in the flat and did not believe that a malnourished child could have moved any one of them. The rooms were a cacophony of DNA: the boy had stood on every seat; there were dregs of each resident in all of the beds; they tested some dog shit in error. Jameson did not know how the child had come to land on the concrete, but he looked at the parents and suspected that they were not just stupid, but cruel.

He was unprofessional, then. The only sordid months of his career. He walked past the door of the flat in jeans and a shirt, after work, listening to the family. He followed the stepfather to a pub and drank six whiskies – six – hoping to hear something before last orders. 'Where do you go,' Alice murmured, when he came in smelling of smoke, the folds of casual clothes sounding different from uniform as he undressed in the darkness.

One evening he passed the mother in the forecourt of the block. She was carrying shopping bags and her belly was engorged. It was too late to change direction, so he smiled at her, and she glanced away, then looked back.

'Aren't you the policeman?' she said, eyes roaming for uniform, or a badge.

'Yes. Yes. Just on a plain-clothes patrol. How are you?'

He carried her bags up the stairs. She was excited to be a mummy again, she said. They came out cute as puppies. 'Do you have children?' she asked, and he said no. He hoped to, some day. He wished her good luck.

That night he lay on the bed, fully-clothed, and Alice woke to him crying. The tremble of his body across the mattress. They had wanted a child for five years by then. He gathered her into his arms – maybe it was her gathering him – and his face dried against her hair. It was no good thinking about the unfairness of life, and they had resolved not to do so, but sometimes—

There were other things that they could do. There were children in the family. Alice's younger brother had three girls, and they looked after them often. Jameson and the eldest girl shared a birthday, and when she was ten he spent a whole day assembling a garden trampoline for the family party, with balloons tied to its legs. It was unexpectedly exhausting, and when he had finished, Jameson collapsed on the mat. Alice stood at the kitchen door, holding her tea, and laughing.

'Harder or easier,' she said, 'than flat-pack furniture?'

She set down her mug on the doorstep and clambered past him, up onto the trampoline. She bounced, threateningly, from foot to foot.

'Don't be ridiculous,' he said.

'Oh, come on!'

They held onto one another, shrieking, and knackered in seconds. The children were delighted with the trampoline, and for a short time it was a highlight of any visit to the Jameson household. Then the girls were teenagers and uninterested in adult company, and the trampoline became rusted, and buried beneath each new autumn's leaves.

The Gracie case came to him when he was fifty. January. He hadn't worn a hat for many years. He and Alice had just returned from work and had taken down the Christmas decorations. Something about the act embarrassed him, although he had enjoyed them in December. The undressing of the tree; the careful placement of the ornaments back into their boxes. Who had it all been for? They sat down for dinner in the kitchen – Alice was talking about hospital politics, and their niece's new boyfriend, and the grisliest trauma call of the day – and the phone started to ring.

He was summoned back to the office for the initial meeting.

The forensic team had sent over photographs from the house, and the Detective Chief Superintendent guided them through each room: this is the body of the father; Boy D was discovered here, in a crib; Girl B and Boy B were in the first room upstairs, restrained. The forensic archaeologists had started digging in the garden and at the foundations of the house, but it would be a long exercise. The children were in different hospitals, according to their specific needs; they were all malnourished, and, with the exception of two of the boys, they were each in a critical condition.

Seven children. Jameson watched the pictures on the screen, changing and yet the same. Same soiled carpets, same dank mattresses, same bags of rot. He thought of Alice, who would be curled on the sofa, wearing her glasses to watch the television. 'It sounds bad,' she had said, as he left. 'I'll wait up.'

'Don't, Alice.'

'I'd like to.'

There were two priorities, said the DCS. The first was the preservation of evidence; the second was the commencement of interviews. How did this happen? When were the children last seen; who were their friends; where were the other relatives? There would be medical reports tomorrow. They had the mother in custody. They had found an aunt, who seemed eager to talk.

'We can't speak to the children just yet,' he said, and Jameson understood that this had been a point of contention and that the DCS had lost.

Jameson was asked to interview Peggy Granger. 'After that,' the DCS said, 'you can work with Girl A. One of the child psychologists is already reading into her case. Dr Kay. Do you know her? Young. Very impressive – I've worked with her before. Groundbreaking, some people say.'

'Girl A,' Jameson said. 'Is she the one who escaped?'

He returned home in the middle of the night. Alice was lying on the sofa in lamplight, with two cups of tea on the carpet beside her.

'They always told me not to marry a policeman,' she said. 'And they were right.'

He knew that she would have been thinking of this all evening; calculating exactly what to say to make him smile. He lifted her legs up, then sat down and placed them onto his lap.

'I feel a hundred years old,' he said.

'You look at least two hundred and seven. How was it?'

'Terrible,' he said. She reached down and handed him a mug. 'And the villain's already dead.'

'I'm sorry,' she said.

'Do you remember,' he said, 'the evenings, very early on, when I would sometimes cry? I always thought that it was because of all of the terrible things that I had seen. All of the worst parts of the human race.'

'Sh,' she said. 'You don't—'

'But it wasn't,' he said. 'I think it was gratitude. I think that I was just so relieved. You see? For us, and this life.'

He came to know Dr Kay well over the months that followed. They spent many hours in the hospital, listening to the stories of the thin, wounded child. There were days when he found it difficult to look at her, and would focus instead on his notes, or the strange digital language of the hospital machines, which he didn't understand. All the time, the girl was becoming stronger, and if, on occasion, he questioned Dr Kay's methods, or what she chose to say and to withhold, she pointed to this. 'Each day,' she said, 'Girl A progresses. She's moving further and further away from that house – faster than any of the others. You see that, don't you?'

'Of course.'

'Well, then. Let me do my work.'

When the interviews were over and the evidence collected, he was assigned to other cases, although he asked about the children often, and he continued to supervise the Gracie case. One evening, Dr Kay visited him late, as he was finishing work. The last pale spring light was sliding from the blinds. He was packing his bag and thinking of his bed, the smell of it and the sheets worn just the way he liked. He thought, too, of the beds at Moor Woods Road.

Dr Kay was waiting on a cheap plastic chair, every part of her out of place: the softness of her sweater, the cat-eye glasses, her hands on her lap, with the nails painted by somebody else. 'Hello, Greg,' she said, and stood to embrace him.

'Coffee?' he asked, and she nodded, although they each knew that she wouldn't drink it. He took her backstage, to one of the interview rooms. The chairs had been abandoned at strange angles to the table, as though people had departed in a hurry. 'Make yourself comfortable,' he said. At the coffee machine, he found that he was frightened. He hadn't expected to see Kay until Deborah Gracie's trial. He took the coffee before the machine had finished, and it spat hot water at his hand.

'Are they all OK?' he said, when he was back. He placed the coffees on the table, and Dr Kay took one for the warmth of it.

'They are,' she said. 'You'll have seen the press releases, of course. "The current whereabouts of the children are unknown."'

'So – with families who'll care for them,' he said. 'People don't need to know any more than that.' He lifted his plastic cup, and toasted. 'May they all live long and happy lives.'

'There's an exception,' she said. She exhaled, covered her eyes with her hands. He reached for her.

'I only came to you,' she said, 'on the basis of what you've said to me before. About what particular people take for granted. About what you and your wife might want.'

She had covered her eyes so that she didn't have to look at him. Beneath her palms, her face was tired and hard. She knew exactly what she was doing.

Now, at sixty-five, the phone is ringing again.

Jameson is in the garden, working through the Sunday paper. Alice lies on the grass, reading the travel section. 'You're closer,' she says. He swears, and rises from his deckchair, gathering his body out of it. He counts the rings of the phone, aware that he is becoming slower; each year there seem to be more rings before he can reach it.

'Hello?'

'Hello, Dad,' I said.

'Lex. We've been worried.'

All week, Delilah had ignored my messages, until her voicemail greeting started to sound secretive, then spiteful. That left a long Sunday afternoon in London, with little to do. The streets were still quiet, although a few early drinkers clustered at the tables in the sunshine. Behind tinted windows, people wiped down tables and floors, reluctant to come outside. Here, the half-drunk pints and abandoned take-outs were starting to rot. Hot, dank smells sweated from the drain covers; the city couldn't hide its insides so well in the heat. I bought a coffee and sat in Soho Square to call home.

Dad wanted me to come to stay, for a few nights at least. 'All of this family contact,' he said. 'I don't know if it's good for you.' This was a tired debate, which was roused for special occasions: Dad had spent the last year arguing against my attendance at Ethan's wedding. When they adopted me, my parents moved as far away from Hollowfield as they could, and although Mum said that she had always wanted to live closer to the sea, I suspected that they also wanted to remove me from the region altogether. To them, the past was a sickness which my siblings still carried; you could catch it from a conversation.

'I'll come,' I said. In Sussex, they had boundless time and

intermittent Internet access, and they would want to hear all about New York, and my weekend with Ethan, and what, precisely, a genomics company was supposed to do. 'Just not yet.'

I told Dad about the prison and the chaplain's monologue. 'I should have referred her to you,' I said. 'My accomplice. Do you remember burning the letters?'

'Of course I remember. I remember that it was all your idea, too. You know, I could have come with you, to the prison.'

'I was fine.'

'I don't like the thought of you there alone.'

'Like I said. It was fine. And I have the others, too.'

'And will they be much use?'

'It's not looking particularly promising.'

'Have you been speaking to Eve again, Lex?'

Here it was: the old determination to preserve me from the rest of them. 'What if I have?' I said, knowing that he wouldn't answer. We were coming to the end of the conversation, and he always had to hang up on good terms.

'Look. If you can't come home just yet, at least see Dr K.'

'I don't think that's necessary.'

'Maybe not. But it might be a good idea.'

I thought of what Devlin said when faced with a suggestion she had no intention of entertaining: Thank you for your input. The polite disregard of it was crueller than disagreement or debate, which at least took a little effort. I saw Dad's damp handprints on the phone, and the little minutes of terror he had allowed himself over the last week, wondering why I hadn't called.

'I'll consider it,' I said. 'I promise.'

In my room at the Romilly Townhouse, I called Olivia. 'I'm at work,' she said. 'I'm in a terrible mood.'

'Oh.'

'They turn the AC off over the weekend. Who thought that was a good idea?'

'You can come to my hotel,' I said. 'I have a tab.'

'And air conditioning?'

'That, too.'

I met Olivia on the day that I arrived at university. We shared a bathroom. She was the kind of person whom you notice right away, even if they're on the other side of the bar and talking to somebody else. I arrived in the halls before her, and Dad helped me to lug my belongings to my room. He seemed older than any of the other fathers; 'I'll bring things from the car,' I suggested, 'and you take them down the hallway.' I had spent half a day searching for just the right duvet cover, dismissing Mum's suggestions as too juvenile; too middle-aged; too flowery; too feminine; just hideous. I settled on a dark blue cover embroidered with constellations, and the moon on the pillow, which, now that I looked at it, seemed deeply, irreparably embarrassing. Dad and I made the bed, and I smoothed down the cover. My hands were shaking. The bed was set in the corner of the room, and I would wake with my head beneath the window.

'Can we move the bed to the other wall?' I said. 'Do you mind?'

We rearranged the room. He sat down on my desk chair, holding his back, and pulled a list from his pocket.

'Your mother,' he said, and shook his head. 'Let's see. Knee-brace?'

'Yes.'

'You've got all of your food.'

'Yes.'

'You've got your fancy dress things.'

We had been informed of various events in the first few weeks of term, and accompanying costume requirements. 'I packed them,' I said.

'And you're going to go?'

'I'll see how it goes, Dad. You can leave now.'

'OK,' he said. He wrapped me into his arms and kissed my forehead. 'The welcome drinks,' he said. 'Promise me you'll go to those, Lex.'

'OK.'

The welcome drinks were tea and squash, which didn't seem especially welcoming. A student from an older year, appointed to put us at ease, asked me a series of polite questions. Where was I from, what subject would I study, how had I spent the summer. Over his shoulder, a girl in a denim jacket had just said something to make the surrounding group laugh.

I excused myself. I would shower and prepare for the first week of lectures. That was a whole five days away. In the still of the strange new room, with the sounds of the reception stretching out across the gardens, it seemed like a very long time.

I was at my desk, reading about old laws, when somebody rapped at the door. I tiptoed to the keyhole and watched the girl in the denim jacket lean against the wall and fold her arms. She waited for one beat – two – and, bemused, turned away.

I opened the door.

'Hello,' she said. 'This isn't the greatest introduction, but I think that we share a bathroom.' She stuck out a scrawny hand. She had vampiric dog teeth and crooked dimples, so each time you realized that she was good-looking, it surprised you.

'The whole welcome thing,' she said. 'It's a little awkward.'

Olivia was studying Economics. She had spent the last year as au pair to the children of an Australian oil executive, which had made her realize that money really, truly, genuinely doesn't buy you happiness. One of the daughters faced her down on her very first day and told her that she would be gone within the week. 'A year later,' Olivia said, 'she cried when I left. So that was a real triumph.' She had already met the guy living below us, who was called Christopher and was studying architecture.

His mother had sent him with brownies for the whole staircase, and he was stockpiling them under his bed, mortified. She looked past me to the little pile of belongings in the middle of my room, bunched together like there was safety in numbers.

'Hey,' she said. 'Great duvet.'

Olivia met me in the champagne bar at Romilly Townhouse, and hugged me carefully. She wore aviators and a suit and a fine silk scarf, embroidered with ants.

We talked about Italy and the wedding, and the torta al testo which the couple served at midnight. 'Truly,' said Olivia, 'the finest fucking thing that has ever been in my mouth.' We talked about genealogy and genomics, in a broad sense; Devlin's deal was confidential, and Olivia worked for a rabid investment outfit. 'My dad tried it,' Olivia said, 'in a sort of start-of-retirement crisis. I think he found out that we were from Wales – where my grandparents live.' We discussed the weather. We debated shopping in New York versus shopping in London. 'But,' Olivia said, 'don't you start to find the flattery *grating*?'

'Your mother,' Olivia said, as the fourth round of drinks was served. 'Oh, Lex. I'm not going to pretend like I know what to say. But she brought you into this world.' Olivia raised her glass. 'So. Cheers to that.'

At the beginning, I would try to tell Olivia and Christopher all of the time. We would be walking to the college bar, or drinking in the gardens in the rusty October afternoons, and the words would rush up to my throat, tasting of bile.

They knew that I was adopted and that I was older than I should be. I wonder now about all of the other strange aberrations which they left unquestioned: the photograph of me and

Evie on my bedside table, and my insistence on showering at inopportune moments, and my fortnightly journeys to London, where I walked through Fitzrovia, past the stern townhouses and the rainbow mews, to see Dr K. Did they consider whether they should ask me for an explanation? Did they debate exactly what the first question should be, in order to secure the highest returns?

If they ever did discuss my oddities, they concluded that they wouldn't raise them with me. Term was passing, and my history had become like an acquaintance's name: there was a point after which it became impossible to ask for it. I didn't mention Mother and Father until our final year, and then, it was only because I had to.

It was late October, and the week of Halloween parties and dinners. Each evening, mist seeped in from the Fens, like autumn's great party trick. Olivia and I recycled the previous year's outfits, which had been highly acclaimed: we were the dead twins from *The Shining*, with pale blue dresses and just the right knee-length socks, which we had found in a back-to-school sale. We walked into the college bar hand in hand, looking serious, and Christopher turned to see us. A plastic knife was protruding from his skull.

All of our favourite people were there, and 'Thriller' was playing on the jukebox. Olivia's new boyfriend had cycled over with a college friend whom I knew from the university running club and liked well enough. The early darkness still surprised us, as though the evening was going too fast. Soon we would be in spring term and close to examinations, and there would be no more nights like this one. We left the bar later and drunker than we had intended, still holding our plastic glasses, and started to walk along the courtyard towards the college gates. The fog lingered over the grass; through it, I could see the distorted lights of the buildings across the quad, but not if anybody was watching from the windows.

Halfway to the gate, I heard the sound of footsteps just before us – about to meet us – and from the mist came a collection of grotesques. There was Ian Brady, with his suit and his hair just so, and a drag Myra at his side. There was O.J. Simpson, his face a mask on a slight, white boy's body, and the black glove dangling – ill-fitting – from his hand. There was Shipman, with a fake beard and a real medic's coat. And then, towards the back, were Mother and Father.

They had captured Mother's white, white hair, the wig askew on the boy's head, and the odd, grey dress she was wearing when she was arrested. In the mugshot, it fell from her shoulder, and you could see the slash of shadow cast by her collarbone; they hadn't got that. Father was even less accurate. The tallest boy in the group has assumed his role, but he wasn't tall enough. The haircut was too good, and the eyes were too mild. That, I thought, wasn't really the imposter's fault.

'Tasteful, kids,' Olivia said, as they passed.

The plastic glass fell from my hand. The mist was thickening; now I couldn't see Olivia or Christopher, or my own hands. 'Liv,' I called, with the idea that I could do so quietly, before anybody else noticed, although I was already on my knees, and the grass was soft and wet between my fingers.

Ted Bundy, whom I recognized from the law society, helped Olivia to carry me to my room. She had dismissed her boyfriend. She ran two glasses of water and lay down beside me on top of the night sky.

'It was some kind of sporting dinner,' she said. '"Fuck-ups and Felons". Creepy as hell, though.'

She rolled over to face me, but I stayed on my back, following the cracks on the ceiling, trying to travel along them from one wall of the room to another.

'So,' she said. 'What happened?'

'I don't know,' I said. 'Maybe the drinks.'

She snorted. 'Come off it, Lex. You? It was the start of the night.'

'Then – I don't know.'

'Lex,' she said. 'I never asked – there were lots of things that I didn't want to ask. I guess I thought that you'd say them when you were ready. Maybe you never will – I don't know. And I don't really care. But you have to tell me if you're OK.'

I could feel the words sputtering up my throat, as they had done when we first met.

'If I tell you,' I said, 'can you promise me – that whatever questions you might have – and whatever you might think – we never have to talk about it again?'

'Oh, Lex,' Olivia said. 'Of course I can.'

'Do you remember,' I said, 'the House of Horrors – you would have been about thirteen . . .'

When we left the Romilly Townhouse, the evening escalated quickly. Olivia was a member of a whisky society with a bar nearby, and Christopher could meet us there. His new boyfriend was trying his hand at stand-up comedy, and Christopher couldn't bear to watch him; this was a good excuse to miss an evening show. 'It's not that he's bad,' Christopher said. 'It's that I'm on edge. I keep waiting for somebody to heckle. And if they do, I'll have to tackle them to the fucking floor.'

'Can you look into retorts?' I asked. 'That might be a safer bet.'

'We're working on it,' he said. He sighed. 'I preferred it when he was the funniest accountant I knew.'

'He wasn't that funny,' Olivia said.

'Olivia's in a dreadful mood,' I said. 'Ask her about the air conditioning.'

'My mood's improving. I just can't see him on stage.'

'You two are about forty drinks ahead of me,' Christopher said, and ordered another round. 'I had no idea that you liked whisky, Liv.'

'I'm not wild about it. But I like having somewhere to take people. You should always have somewhere to take people.'

'And somewhere with so much atmosphere,' I said. There was only one other person in the bar, an old man in a houndstooth suit: 'Is he dead?' Olivia had asked, when we arrived.

'Well, you should always have somewhere where you know that you'll get a seat.'

'Tell us about New York, Lex.'

'I moved house,' I said, 'to this loft. It's huge. Near the water, in Brooklyn. But it's shared.'

'I couldn't share,' Olivia said.

'It's me and this old woman. The old woman who owns the loft. There's a partition in between our spaces, but sometimes the partition falls down, and there she'll be, in bed, or watching a documentary. She's called Edna.'

'Edna's ripping you off,' Christopher said.

'Yes. Spend some more money, Lex.'

'I don't mind it,' I said. 'I've got used to it. She's very quiet. I'm never even there.'

'Leave Edna, and come back to London.'

'Well, I'm here now.'

'And you have to stay for my birthday,' Olivia said. 'It's the big one. Twenty-eight. I'm having the party two years early, before I'm too tired.'

'I'm exhausted,' I said.

'New York was a good excuse, but that isn't.'

The bartender collected the glasses. 'Which one did you like?' he asked. There had been tasting notes, but we hadn't read them.

'I liked them all,' Olivia said, 'and this one the best.'

'What about JP?' Christopher asked.

'What about him?'

Christopher looked at Olivia, a drink beyond subtlety.

'Will you see him?'

'I don't think there'll be time,' I said. 'I'm working for a psychopath.'

'He asks about you whenever I have to see him,' Olivia said.

'That's nice.'

'I say that you're doing great. I say that you're beautiful and rich.'

'Thanks, Liv. To be honest, I don't think about him too much. Just on and off. I'm OK.'

'If there's anything you'd like to know, I can find it out.'

'Well, I'd like very much not to talk about it.'

We tried to get into Ronnie Scott's for the later show, but there wasn't one on Sundays, and the club was about to close. 'Go home,' the doorman suggested. Christopher needed to meet his boyfriend; the stand-up hadn't gone well. I implored Olivia to join me for one final drink.

'Twelve fifteen,' she said, and recoiled from her watch. 'I'm out, Lex. I'm out.'

When her taxi arrived, she climbed in and lay down on the back seat, and looked at me upside down, through the open window.

'It's too hot for any of this,' she said, and then, laughing: 'Is it really Sunday?'

'It's the new Thursday.'

'So long. So long, my friend.'

The driver, bored with us, began to pull out. Olivia sat up and waved. 'London!' she shouted. 'Isn't it wonderful?' I nodded: yes, yes, it was good to be in the city. The taxi trundled into the night traffic. I stood on the kerb for a few minutes, considering a man I used to see in Marylebone, after JP. Only a short walk away. I had met him online according to his discretion, and I thought of him often, when I was listless in New York. It was a terrible idea. For all I knew, he could be married now.

I walked past the dark restaurants and the doorways, and back to the hotel. There was a freestanding bath in the middle of my room, which I hadn't bothered to run during the week. Now I sat on the chequered floor and watched it filling. When I was swaddled in the water, I reached for my phone. Ethan had messaged. Wesley won the cricket game. It was good to see you, as ever. A transmission from a whole different time. I squinted at the screen. Excellent news, I replied. Then, because I was soft and drunk: Honduras?

One last task for the day. I found the number I was looking for, and again there was the breathless voicemail, as though you had interrupted her in tears, or in bed. 'Delilah,' I said. 'Why don't you ring me the fuck back.'

Mother was finally examined more than a week after Ethan's birth. In the first few days, jubilant with the baby, the pain had felt like an accomplishment. On the seventh day, she was cowed by fever, and she prayed with her eyes on Father, imploring. He relented when Ethan was ten days old, and Mother was shaking too hard to hold him. She hadn't prayed hard enough.

After the infections were treated, and the tears stitched, the doctor informed my parents that if Mother decided to have more children, there was a significant risk of complications, and she should do so only in a hospital bed. The doctor must have been the kind of man whom Father tolerated: powerful; self-assured; difficult to argue with. I was too young to remember Delilah's birth, but I recall our visit to hospital to meet Evie, who was born late on New Year's Day.

Father had left us with Mother's sister, Peggy, who had married one of the boys from the grammar school. She was pregnant at the wedding, although she tied a great bow of chiffon low around her waist, and nobody was allowed to talk about it until the couple returned from honeymoon. By the time Evie was born, Peggy had two loud, gormless boys, one Ethan's age and the other a little older, and spent her days cleaning the new home her husband had purchased. Tony Granger was an estate agent in Manchester, and seldom seen. Ethan called him the Faceless Man: we only ever seemed to catch a glimpse of navy suit or polished shoes, disappearing into one of the rooms of the vast, white house.

Ethan liked to torture our cousins, the way that some children like to torture the household pet. He told them fanciful stories: if they could hold their breath underwater for one minute, then they might be recruited by the same secret society to which he belonged; there was a serial killer in town who was targeting small boys as they slept, and the only proven way to avert him was to stay awake for three nights on the trot. He would place a prized belonging from Benjamin's room beneath Michael's bed and await the ensuing tantrum, or knock one of the boy's glasses from the table, casually, when the adults were in another room. 'You're so clumsy, Benjamin,' he would say, continuing to eat, and Ethan – being slighter, and younger, and with my unwavering support – would usually be believed.

When Father came from the hospital to collect us, it was bedtime. Ethan and I had fought over who would read the bedtime story, and Peggy had deemed that we would take it in turns, in age order: first Michael, then Benjamin, then Ethan, and then me. Delilah, three and bored, ran from one room to the next, delighted to be awake. The book concerned pirates, and was significantly more dramatic than any of Father's bedtime tales, even if Michael read in a stilted monotone, and Ethan rolled his eyes (*'Alexandra* can read better than this') until it was his go.

I was nervous and excited about the opportunity to read in front of an audience, and as Ethan neared the end of his pages, my heart pattered faster. I really could read better than Benjamin – and maybe even better than Michael – and here was the chance to prove it. I cleared my throat, and had wrested the book from Ethan when Father knocked at the door.

'Another girl,' Father said to Peggy, then shouted for us.

'It's late,' Peggy said. 'Eight o'clock, Charles. They're in their pyjamas. They can just stay here.'

Ethan and Delilah had joined Father at the door, but I stayed on the sofa, holding the book. 'It's my turn,' I said. 'It's my turn to read.'

'Come here, Alexandra.'

'It's outside visiting hours anyway,' Peggy said. 'They can meet their sister tomorrow.'

'I'll decide when they can meet their sister. Let's go, Alexandra.'

'There are only a few pages left.'

Ethan looked up at Father. 'Come on, Alexandra,' he said.

'But it's *my turn*.'

Father held out his arm and brushed Peggy aside. He came into the living room without taking his shoes off and picked me up. I was still holding the book; he took it from my hand, easily, and threw it against the wall. Over his shoulder, I saw the faint footprints of dirt in the cream carpet, and Peggy and her children, standing in their light, bright hallway, becoming smaller in the night.

Mother had been opened up, Father said, once we were in the car. The baby couldn't get itself in the right position. They had cut her out. I looked to Ethan for an explanation, but he, too, was confused. Delilah started to cry.

At the hospital, I didn't want to leave the car. I thought of Mother on a cool, silver table, her torso splayed across the room. You could see each of her organs operating, as on the face of an expensive watch. The new baby crawled from the viscera, slippery with blood. In the car park, I reached for Ethan's hand, expecting him to ridicule me; he was eight, now, and above such gestures. But he held my hand and squeezed it.

Of course, it wasn't like that at all. We travelled along the vast, bright corridors, trying to pronounce the names of the wards. In maternity, a nurse spoke to us gingerly, the way that you might speak to a wounded and vicious animal, and took us to Mother. She lay on the bed, asleep, with her skin and flesh intact. At her side, in a small plastic cradle, was the baby.

Father didn't look at the child. He touched Mother's hair and face, waking her; when she saw him, she smiled. Ethan, Delilah and I crowded around the cot.

'I don't want her,' Delilah said.

'You're too small to even see her,' I said. The baby was still asleep. I took one of her immaculate little hands with my finger.

'She looks just like Alexandra did,' Mother said, and an odd, unwarranted pride spread across my chest. It had been worth missing my turn to read. Here was a new sister, who was just like me, and one day I would read to her.

'We'll call this one Eve,' Father said.

Delilah didn't change her mind about Evie. For nearly four years, she had been the youngest child, and she saw the baby as her usurper: a malicious courtier in her kingdom, smuggled in the guise of a child. The plan had been for Evie to sleep in Delilah's room, but that was no good; Delilah took the baby's blanket for herself, or left little ambushes for the child. Into the cot she snuck a fork, my pencils from school, the tweezers from Mother's dressing table. 'A present,' she insisted, 'for the baby.'

The house was reordered. I slept in the baby room with Evie, and Delilah moved in with Ethan.

Delilah didn't get away with things because she was cunning, like Ethan; she got away with things because she was beautiful, as Mother had been. It was an indisputable fact, like those required by Mr Greggs, and one to which I was becoming resigned. Each year at school, we would be summoned for photographs, including family shots. When Delilah first joined us, the photographer pretended to drop his camera. 'What a beautiful little girl,' he said. 'Here, here' – he handed her a fat teddy bear, which he had been using to cajole reluctant pupils – 'a few on your own, first.'

When the photographer had taken a set of pictures of Delilah from different angles, up close and further away, he beckoned for me and Ethan to join her in his frame. Delilah had discarded the bear; I picked it up from the dusty assembly hall floor, but the photographer shook his head. 'No,' he said. 'That's just for the prettiest little girls. And you're too old for that, anyway.'

My parents ordered the group photograph. Ethan was nonchalant, and Delilah was crowing, and I was looking up at the ceiling, with a red face, trying very hard not to cry.

Mother placed it in a cheap supermarket frame and hung it in the living room, where it was impossible not to look at it. Delilah, inspired, asked to see pictures of Mother as a child. 'We're the same!' she exclaimed, and, looking at me over the top of the photograph album: 'And so different from Alexandra.'

'We have the same hair,' I said.

'Yes, but a different face, and different eyes, and different arms and legs.'

When we were children, I considered Delilah to be foolish. Her school reports were damning: 'Delilah needs to apply herself,' the teacher would write, or 'Delilah doesn't have a great deal of natural ability in this subject, and will need to work harder.' I had heard two of the teachers talking about her one lunchtime: 'She's certainly no Ethan,' said one, and the other nodded: 'And no Alexandra, either.' When Delilah was assigned homework, she rested her head on her arms and reached across the table to Father. 'I don't understand,' she said, 'why I can't just have one of your stories instead.' Now, I think of the careful attentiveness on Delilah's face when Father was talking, and her adoration of Mother as a child, long before The Parade began, and I wonder if Delilah was, in fact, cleverer than me and Ethan – if Delilah was the cleverest of us all.

For some time, I complained about sleeping in the same room as Evie. I was disgruntled with Delilah, and disappointed that I would no longer have the opportunity to talk to Ethan last thing at night, which – ever since he had imparted his knowledge of the Wild West – was when we discussed our days at school. The baby room was crowded with Father's old projects: a computer slumped on the bedside table, exposing shiny guts; wires coiled beneath the cot. But Evie was a stern, quiet baby, and I began to like her. As Mother had said, she looked just like me. It was easy to allocate a baby's affiliations, and I badly needed somebody on my team.

Instead of talking to Ethan about my day, I whispered across the room to her. In one of Father's boxes, I found a torch; when the teacher allowed us to take books home from school, I waited for the house to settle into the night, then began to read aloud. 'She can't even understand you,' Delilah said. I ignored her. The reading wasn't just for Evie; it was also for me. Sometimes, if I caught her when she was whimpering and lifted her from the cot – just before she really started to cry – I found that I could console her myself. And I was usually the first to reach her; increasingly, Mother and Father were occupied with other things.

Some time between Sunday and Monday, my phone began to ring. When I woke like this, disorientated, from a dead sleep, I thought for a moment that I was in Moor Woods Road. Many years ago, Dr K had formulated a three-point plan to address these awakenings: stretch up to the ceiling; wait for the room to come into view; remember each detail of the day before, as specifically as you can. Soho cast an electric orange glow through the curtains, and the bath and the desk solidified from the darkness. Yesterday's dress lay on top of my shoes on the floor, as though their occupant had vanished. I thought of Olivia in the taxi, waving her scarf from the window as it went, so when I answered the phone, I was smiling. Just gone four. I waited for the caller to speak.

'Lex. It's been a very long time.'

'Delilah,' I said. Of course.

'I'm in London,' she said. 'I can come to see you. Where are you staying?'

'Romilly Street,' I said. 'It's the Romilly Townhouse. When do you want to meet?'

'I don't have very long. I'll be there in an hour. Maybe less.'

'What?'

'To see you. I'm coming to see you.'

'It's the middle of the night.'

'I'll see you soon.'

I tried to turn on a gentle light, but hit the overhead switch by mistake. Kicked off the bedcovers and lay in a stupor on the mattress. Cursed Delilah; hotel lighting; the novice percussion band rehearsing in my skull; the whisky society; the tilt of the earth; London in the heat; the distance from the bed to the shower. Under the cool, clean water, I made myself vomit, and rested my forehead against the tiles. Delilah.

When I had stopped shaking, I opened the window and sat down at the desk, and wrote a brief, broad letter of consent in respect of the house on Moor Woods Road and the accompanying cash, allowing for the establishment of the community centre as

Evie and I imagined it. I left the execution block empty. I didn't even know what Delilah's name was, now. The first grains of daylight scattered across the room. I ordered coffees from reception and drank them both. She would make me wait.

She arrived two hours after she phoned. She called again to check my room number, and a moment later her footsteps stopped outside my door. She waited a few seconds before she knocked, and I stood on the other side of the wood, thinking of her in the empty corridor, assembling her face.

Father kept the Bible on his bedside table, and whenever he couldn't divine an evening story, he asked one of us to fetch it. As with the tales of our parents' lives, we fought to hear our favourite book. I liked the Book of Jonah because of the whale. Ethan liked the Book of Samuel but hated the Book of Kings; it featured his namesake, but only to clarify that Solomon was much, much wiser. Delilah was happy to listen to whatever Father selected, which was usually something didactic. It was, I thought, her way of concealing that she couldn't remember which book was which.

On Sundays, we dressed in what I thought of as our uncomfortable clothes – high white collars and nipping waistlines – and walked through the town in Father's wake. We passed other, older churches, with congregations filing steadily inside – there, close to the centre, was the austere stone church at which we had been christened – and arrived at a square, beige box of a building, just before the industrial site. There was a white canopy above the door, where somebody had hand-painted: Welcome.

Attendance at the Gatehouse was poor. There was a group of indistinguishable men in overlong suits, all of whom played the guitar. There was a straggle of mothers, picking at the biscuits and the squash, who waved at Father as we arrived. Babies tumbled down the aisle. There were a few silent widows who sat towards the back and enjoyed the music. One of them, Mrs Hirst, was blind. Her eyes rested always on some distant past, which, at four foot five, was just over my right shoulder. We argued over which of us would have to lead her to the refreshments at the end of the service. We were frightened of her, we said, in the way that children say that they're frightened as an excuse for being cruel.

At the Gatehouse, my parents acquired the status of minor celebrities. Our family filled a whole pew, and the old women stroked our hair as we passed. One of the youngest mothers asked Ethan if we were albinos, which he didn't dignify with a response. Father delivered guest sermons on certain Sundays, which were just as popular as Pastor David's. When Pastor David contracted the flu, Father led his Tuesday-evening prayer group – and kept it.

CG Consultants had closed just after Evie's birth. The fact was that nobody in town – and very few people in the country – owned a computer. 'It's the pioneers,' Father said to us, 'who get slaughtered, while all of the settlers finish first.' Father had always been a religious man, but he had also been a businessman, and a teacher, and a man whom women liked to watch. We were learning about pie charts at school, and I saw Father's life allocated to a circle. As his other identities diminished, the slice of religion eclipsed the rest.

There were theatrics. The first time that somebody fell to their knees on the floor of the aisle – overcome, I assumed, with the Holy Spirit – Ethan caught my eye and looked away again, as fast as he could. I could feel his shoulders shuddering against the pew. It was less funny the next time, and the next; and less funny, still, when Father knelt at the front of the room, his heavy arms stretching to the cross, as if awaiting an embrace. Delilah knew just what to do. She danced in a circle, with her face thrown back to the sparse, wooden ceiling and her tiny fists clenched. At times, holy tears rolled down her face and into her hair.

It was at the Gatehouse that we first met Thomas Jolly. One Sunday, Mother seized Father's arm as we filed inside, and nodded towards a strange, bald man at the back of the church. During the service, I watched him. He didn't sing with the same zeal as Father or the men with the guitars, but he knew every word, and when Pastor David was speaking, he leant forward, his eyes closed, and smiled with small, craggy teeth. At the end of the sermon, he blinked and caught my eye, and although I looked away, I sensed his smile widen.

After the service, Father hurried us out of the pew. 'Jolly!' he said, greeting the stranger like an old, dear friend. He whispered something in Jolly's ear, and Jolly guffawed. Mother arranged us behind her, in a single, solemn line. 'Look at this family,' Jolly said, to Father. 'Look at these children! I've heard so much about them.' He shook my hand and placed his palm across my head. He was a slight man, but ropes of muscle wound around his arms, and his whole body trembled with a keen, contained strength.

'And another?' Jolly asked, and cupped Mother's stomach with both of his hands. She looked at Father, to secure his pride, and she, too, smiled.

On the walk home, Father was invigorated. 'Jolly's doing amazing things,' he said, 'all across the North West. And it's us he came to see.' He laughed, and lifted Delilah above his head. A thin rain was falling, and we didn't have an umbrella; the cold of it sat beneath my clothes. Autumn, trudging in across the moors. I walked faster, and Ethan ran to join me. Father was still holding Delilah, and now he took Mother's hand from the pram and swept her beneath his arm. 'My beautiful children,' he said. 'My family.'

Jolly was a pastor in Blackpool, just off Central Drive and close to the hotel where Father worked. Father had assisted Jolly in installing new technology throughout the church: there was an advanced projection screen, for videos and photographs, and state-of-the-art speakers, which Father had inherited from the hotel. 'The atmosphere there,' Father said, 'is like nothing else. It's electric. If you want to see the future of the church, that's where you go.'

The holiday was booked for late February, just before the new baby would arrive. Jolly was hosting a long weekend of sermons and events, and Father would provide technical and spiritual support. Ethan, Delilah and I were to miss school on Monday. 'This,' Father said, '*this* is learning.'

We would have two rooms at the hotel, he said. The best rooms, which overlooked the ocean.

We hadn't been on holiday before, but as soon as it was arranged, Father was rejuvenated, as if the promise of it was all that he required. He asked for his liquor every evening, and he described the town in great detail. There was a theme park, he said, and a huge Ferris wheel. We would be able to see all of the way home. Mother, watching him talk, smiled, and closed her eyes to join him in the promised land.

Her pregnancy had been difficult. There were complications with the caesarean scar, which hadn't been allowed enough time to heal before the skin was stretched again. (How long did they wait, I wonder – after Evie – before he wanted her, and did she protest in the few moments before he was inside her, silently, with her limbs, so as not to wake us?) She had shown us the fine, careful line through which Evie had come, sat low on her belly like the print of a waistband. Now, the scar tissue buckled under the new weight, and Mother spent a lot of time in her bedroom, with the door closed. 'She needs a break,' Father said. 'The sea air. She'll be fine.'

A few days before our departure, Father arrived home with a brown paper package. 'A family gift,' he said. Delilah tore open the parcel and held up a thin, red T-shirt, which was imprinted with a verse from Peter: *Grace and peace be yours in abundance.* A set of identical garments fell to the floor. There were six T-shirts in all, one for each of us and for Mother and Father. On the back, the T-shirts bore our names.

'Wow,' Delilah said. She distributed the rest with great care, holding each garment flat on her palms, like an offering.

We set off for Blackpool on a Friday evening, when it was already dark. Mother held Evie, who was grumbling; she would usually be asleep, or in my arms. 'Why didn't we go earlier?' I asked, but the car was quiet, and Father ignored me. It had rained all afternoon, and orange light glittered on the road. Delilah stroked the material of her new T-shirt, her fingers playing absentmindedly over the polyester. Ethan held a schoolbook up to the streetlights and squinted through the darkness. I wished that I had remembered to bring one, too.

'We'll need to be quiet,' Father said, 'when we arrive.'

I sat up taller. 'Are we here?' I asked.

We swung onto the promenade. The cold void of the sea extended from the sky. On the other side of the car was a cataclysm of lights: twinkling arcades, and men and women queuing outside the dance halls, and neon horses escaped from a carousel and suspended high in the night. Ethan rolled down the window. The slot machines chirped. A fat man in a ringmaster's suit beckoned us towards a doorway draped in red velvet. There was no queue there. 'Can you see the rollercoaster?' Ethan said, tugging me across the seat to look. 'I'm going on that.' Before we reached the hotel, Father pulled away from the seafront and parked along a side street, behind an ice-cream truck with shattered windows.

'Quiet,' he said. 'Remember?'

We took the bags and the pram, staggering beneath their weight, and followed Father into the dark. Wind skittered from the sea and down the lane. The streetlights here were broken, and I couldn't see my feet. I stood on something soft, which gave way beneath my shoe, and hurried on. Father led us to a little wooden gate and found the right key. Then we were through it, in the garden of the hotel.

My father worked at the Dorchester, Blackpool, which is still on the seafront today. When Olivia's parents took us to tea at the Dorchester on Park Lane, thirteen years later, I looked at my reflection in the vast courtroom mirror – champagne; velvet dress; the scones just replenished – and thought of the other Dorchester, which I had once considered to be the most exciting place in the world. There was a time when I thought that I would return with Evie. Here, I would say, the site of your very first holiday. I envisaged running through the Pleasure Beach from one ride to the next; winning an oversized stuffed animal; fish and chips on the beach, in the evening, when we were salt-battered and drunk. I found the Dorchester on the same sites I checked for business travel, and weekends with JP. But the reviews were terrible ('Avoid This Disgusting Place'; 'Vile'; and, at best, 'OK but needs serious updating'), and I knew, scrolling through the photographs, that the place I remembered no longer existed. If we returned, I would probably find out that it never had.

From the garden, we could see into the hotel's empty ballroom. Covered tables arranged around a wooden dance floor. Reflected in the wood was a glass dome onto the night sky. On a clearer night, you would be able to dance on top of the moon. Above the ballroom, I could make out the small, square lights of guests still awake in their rooms. Father was looking at them, too.

'It's important to be quiet,' he said. 'Do you understand?'

He opened a fire door, and let us into a narrow staircase.

The rooms were on the very top floor of the hotel, and reeked of paint. The radiators had been turned up high. 'See,' Father said. 'Brand new, and renovated.' Ethan, Delilah and I pressed our noses to the glass. Father had kept to his word. You could see out to the pier and to the big wheel, turning slowly through the night.

'I need to sleep,' Mother said. She lifted Evie from the pram and through the interconnecting door. She had developed a kind of forward lurch when she walked; it made you want to reach for her with every other step, although none of us did. Father followed her. We climbed beneath the covers in our new T-shirts, still whispering between the beds. Delilah, softer at night, asked me to stroke her hair. Leave the curtains open, I said to Ethan, last thing. I wanted to fall asleep to the lights of the promenade, rising up to our window.

If you've seen the photograph from Moor Woods Road, you'll have seen the picture taken on the pier at Blackpool. It was Saturday morning, and early. We had been too excited to sleep for long. Mother and Father took us to the beach before the first service began, begrudging but good-humoured, and we ran ahead of them, the cold, wet sand slapping beneath our feet, and seagulls spilling out across the sea. The sky was a thin blue, carved up with plane tracks and cloud. We teased the waves, running close enough for them to catch us and screaming when they came. Evie took tentative steps from me to Ethan, and back.

When we reached the pier, Delilah accosted a stranger to take the camera. 'T-shirts,' Father ordered. 'We should see the T-shirts!' It was just above freezing, and when we took off our coats and our sweatshirts, we shrieked at the wind on our skin. We were laughing, too; even beneath the pixels, you can see it. It's there in the way that we hold on to one another, and in my parents' faces. An artefact of the last good day, and much harder to look at for that.

Father had been right: in Jolly's church, there was an energy which the Gatehouse didn't possess. It wasn't the technology, or the crowded pews, or the thick red carpet where the worshippers writhed. It was Jolly, who was seized with a fervent charisma; who seemed to be at the pulpit and in the aisle and holding your hand, all at once; who cradled pallid, pot-bellied children as if they were his own. He hissed, and sweated, and spat. Everyone was welcome, and everyone had come: Jolly's comfortable benefactors, who had raided the wallets of reluctant parents; sunken-cheeked women, shivering in heels; bedraggled families, with innumerable children in tow. Here were the meek, ready to inherit the earth.

Between the services, Jolly had arranged breakout sessions. Mother and Father attended prayer groups and strategy meetings and Bible analyses, and Ethan, Delilah and I were sent to the children's workshops, which were held in a damp conservatory tacked onto the church, and occupied with toddlers, gunge-nosed and clapping at nothing. After the first day, Ethan protested. 'The other children are tiny,' he said. 'They can't even speak.'

We were walking back to the Dorchester. Father took two quick steps and tripped Ethan from behind. I recognized the technique from the older boys at Jasper Street, whom I tried to avoid.

'That's the problem with you and Alexandra, isn't it,' Father said. 'You always think that you're better than everybody else.'

Ethan righted himself and said nothing. From the walk, we could see the skeletal tracks at the Pleasure Beach protruding into the underbelly of the sky. I had seen the schedule for Sunday and had started to question whether there was going to be time to go on the rollercoasters, or on the Ferris wheel which Father had talked so much about. When we were back in our room, I asked Ethan if there was any way. On Monday morning, perhaps – if we behaved well tomorrow? He looked at me with the scorn which he usually reserved for his classmates, or Delilah, and I knew that all hope was lost.

'Don't be stupid,' he said. 'They were never going to take us to any of that. We only came here for Jolly and his boring church.'

I felt that I was about to cry, and turned away from him.

'And let me tell you something else,' he said. 'I don't even believe in it. Jolly, Father, God. Any of it. Nothing they say ever makes sense, if you listen to it.'

'Don't say that.'

'Well, it's true.'

'But not in front of Father, Ethan. Please.'

On Sunday evening, after the second service and once Jolly had embraced his followers, Father asked him to join us for dinner. 'We can try for a table at Dustin's,' Father said.

'What a way,' Jolly said, 'to spend the evening.' He clapped Father on the back, and his hand left a wet print on Father's shirt. He threaded his fingers into Delilah's, and, like a gentleman, held out his arm for her to lead the way. She blushed and covered her face.

'Off we go,' Father said.

Dustin's was Dustin's Bar & Grill, past the Dorchester and attached to another, grander hotel. The dining room was vast and lit by two dim chandeliers. Pink napkins had been stuffed into the wine glasses, and there were bread rolls already laid out at each setting, although few of them were occupied. Only one other family was at dinner, and when they saw us, in our identical clothing, the two teenage children whispered to one another, and smirked. Evie sat on the carpet and traced incomprehensible patterns with her fingers, and the rest of us took a seat. Mother looked at the menu, perturbed, but Father ignored her. He was ordering two bottles of wine, and recommending the steak. He was a regular.

'Can we get anything?' I asked, and Father snorted.

'Why not? This is a special night.'

We had only eaten in a restaurant once before, for Mother's

birthday, and I was still panicked by the range of options. I stared at the menu, hoping that it might reveal its secrets. Sausages and chips, or Dustin's Burger? The laminated card reflected back my face, in distress.

'Sometimes,' said Jolly, 'I look out at the congregation. You've got people nodding along, you've got people with tears in their eyes, you've got people possessed. But you know – you know in your heart – that most of them are cowards. They come for the music, maybe. For the comm*unity*. But they'll choose to be exactly what the world says they should be.'

Jolly bowed his head. Raised his glass.

'Not you, Charlie,' he said. 'I know it. I see it. You choose to be separated from this world. With a family like this – you can build your own kingdom.'

The waitress, clearing the other table, looked across at us, and away.

Father and Jolly talked with their eyes locked and their hands moving. Their teeth were grubby with wine. Mother sat eager for conversation, her head tilted to catch the scraps. I collected Evie from beneath another table and hauled her into my lap, and we played Peekaboo with a napkin until the food arrived. I watched Delilah's burger travel from the kitchen to her placemat, and stared, glumly, at the two wan sausages on my plate.

Father and Jolly drank into the evening, even when the food was gone and none of us were listening any more. When the waitress brought over the bill, Father took it from Jolly and counted out the cash. He was one note short, and Mother pulled out her purse. 'You would have let us off,' he said, to the waitress. 'Wouldn't you? Wouldn't you.'

She smiled politely, and took the money from Mother. 'I'll bring the change,' she said. With it, she brought a little pot of hard-boiled sweets, which she placed on the table between Delilah and me. 'You help yourselves,' she said. 'They're pretty good.'

'What if we want another drink?' Father said. 'You didn't ask us if we wanted another drink.'

'We're closing. There's a bar next door – that's open late.'

'OK. OK. We get the hint.'

We stood outside on the seafront. Father, still holding a wine glass, complained about the abrupt end to the evening. Tonight, the promenade was quiet and the Ferris wheel was dark and unmoving. It was just starting to rain. A couple hurried past us, hand in hand and trying to assemble an umbrella. I expected to say goodbye to Jolly, but he accompanied us back to the Dorchester, up the little staircase and to the two bedrooms on the top floor. Neither Mother nor Father made any attempt to discard him. It was as though the evening had long been rehearsed, and was proceeding just as they had planned it. 'Good night, little ones,' Jolly said.

'You go in there,' Father said, opening the door to our room. 'Go in there, and quiet, now.'

'Alexandra,' Mother said. 'Take Eve.'

'Why?' I asked.

'She's staying with you tonight. Leave her in the pram – she'll sleep into the morning. No disturbances tonight, please.'

'Why is he in your room?' Ethan said. Mother smiled, and cupped his cheek in her hand.

'Don't be rude, Ethan,' she said. 'Come on. It's time for bed.'

As soon as our door was closed, Delilah clambered onto one bed and jumped to the other. 'I'm not tired,' she said. 'Can we play with the baby?'

'No, Delilah,' I said.

'Hey,' Ethan said. 'Do you still want to go on a rollercoaster?'

We constructed the rollercoaster as follows: the desk formed a bridge between the two beds. For the dip, we lay the free-standing mirror face down and sloping from Ethan's bed to the wall, and slid down it on a hotel coffee tray. You had to abandon the tray just before hitting the wall, which only added to the excitement. After a few solo trips, the three of us sat on the coffee tray together and crashed straight through the mirror and onto the carpet, and lay groaning and giggling and shushing one another amongst the shards. Next door was quiet, and nobody came to us.

We became bolder. Ethan stood on his bed. 'I have a sermon,' he declared, 'which goes as follows. *I am the Lord.*'

'Shut up, Ethan,' I said.

'*I'm* the Lord,' Delilah shouted, and snatched for him. He ran across the desk and onto my and Delilah's bed, and bounced from one foot to the other.

'I'm sorry,' he said. 'You'll have to be my loyal servant, instead.'

Evie twisted in her pram and started to cry.

'Stop it, Ethan,' I said.

'Or you can be a leper,' Ethan said. 'That's your choice.'

Delilah pounced after him, shrieking between laughter and tears. As soon as she was on the same bed, Ethan tackled. The two of them collapsed onto the mattress, and the legs of the bed buckled. The frame hit the floor with an almighty crash.

There was a long, silent moment when it seemed that we had got away with it. Then the footsteps came, both up the stairs and from the room next door. Father emerged at one threshold, shirtless, and as he did, a stranger opened the door from the corridor. He wore a black suit, and the name of the hotel was embroidered onto his breast pocket. His name badge said: Nigel Connell. Welcome to Blackpool.

'Charlie?' Nigel said. 'What the fuck are you doing in here?'

He looked at Father, then at the rest of us. His eyes paused at the broken bed, and again at the shattered mirror.

'Fucking hell,' he said. 'Is this your whole family?'

'The rooms weren't being used,' Father said. 'I just thought—'

'But you can't just stay here. You can't just come here in secret and *stay*, without telling anyone. Without paying a penny.'

'Well, I can,' Father said. 'And I did.'

I crossed the room to Evie, who was still crying, and knelt next to the pram. 'It's OK,' I whispered.

'I'll have to escalate this,' Nigel said. 'After the speakers, too.'

'Do whatever you want,' Father said. 'You're a little jobsworth, Nigel. Aren't you. You're a sad sack of shit.'

He turned to us.

'Pack your things,' he said. 'Now.'

Outside, it was really raining. We hadn't had time to pull on our coats; Delilah had lost one of her shoes; Mother's lurch was the material of a cruel caricature. And Jolly – where was Jolly? The red T-shirts clung to our bodies, like cold hands between the bones. I reached the car just after Father and opened the door, but he pulled me back into the night. Ethan and Delilah were already waiting, there on the pavement. The firing line was complete.

'I'm going to hit one of you,' Father said. 'But I'll be fair. I'll be generous. You get to decide. Ethan. Who broke that bed?'

Ethan stared straight ahead. 'Delilah,' he said.

'Delilah. OK. Delilah?'

'It was Ethan,' she said. She was crying. 'I promise.'

'Well, then. Alexandra. It looks like you have the deciding vote.'

When I've thought of this moment, in jet-lagged hours of the night, or on a lonely winter Sunday, as it's going dark, the old squid twitches awake, and extends into my limbs, up to the throat and down through the womb. Shame.

'It was Delilah,' I said. 'Delilah broke it.'

As soon as the words were said, Father seized her arm.

'The rest of you,' Father said, 'into the car.'

He knelt amongst the crisp packets and the gravel, and bent Delilah over his knee. He pulled down her tiny purple trousers and her underpants, and smacked her five times, as hard as he could. By the time she could stand up, she was composed. She wiped the wet hair from her eyes and adjusted her clothes, and she gazed at me between the rivulets on the car window, to the warmer, lighter place where the rest of us were waiting. I remember the expression on her face, and I contemplate Delilah, wherever she may be – in another bed, or in the middle of her own Sunday afternoon – and I'm quite sure that she thinks of this moment, too.

'Come on in,' I said.

After our escape, Delilah came to me in stories. Here is my favourite. Delilah's psychologist was a young, supercilious man called Eccles, who positioned himself in the middle of every table, and enjoyed telling Dr K how satisfied he was with his patient's progress. In the victimhood charts, Delilah had surpassed Survivorhood, and reached Transcendence. 'Personally,' said Dr K, 'I have a limited tolerance for such categorizations.' Delilah gave the star victim impact statement at Mother's trial, and on this basis, Eccles was preparing the paper to end all papers, which he intended to see published in the *Annual Review of Psychology*, and, in all likelihood, reported worldwide. A week before its release, Delilah requested that all references to her be removed from the essay. She had rejuvenated her faith, and going forward, she would be working with God, rather than Eccles.

'Nice place,' Delilah said. 'I guess being smart still pays.'

She would still be the best-looking person in any room I could think of. She wore a white dress and a cut of lipstick, and a cross which you couldn't ignore. She slid from her jacket and threw it to the floor, and stretched out across the sofa at the end of the bed. Long, delicate limbs dangled down to the carpet.

'So,' she said. 'How are you?'

'I'm fine. I would have preferred a later meeting.'

'I was volunteering,' she said, 'when I received your call.'

She said *volunteering* in a way that implored me to ask for additional information. Instead, I said: 'Oh.'

'You sounded incoherent,' she said.

'I was catching up with friends. I wasn't expecting to hear from you.'

'Look,' she said, 'it was close by, and convenient. It isn't always so easy for me to get away. And you made it sound urgent.'

She gazed around the room – seeking out the calamity – and looked back to me, nonplussed.

'It's about Mother,' I said. 'I should give my condolences, I guess. I know that you were closer to her than I was.'

She laughed. When she did, I saw that there was a gap in her teeth. Halfway back, left-hand side. We had all required extensive dental work after the escape. I couldn't recall if it had been there then.

'How thoughtful,' she said. 'Thank you.'

'They're burying her on prison property. I thought that was best.'

'And after so much consultation.'

She closed her eyes. Exhaled.

'You didn't even visit her,' she said. 'Did you?'

'I had better things to do with my weekends.'

'Oh, I'm sure you did. I'm sure there was always a lecture to attend. Or – what? A dinner?'

She spoke to the ceiling, now, and I couldn't see her face.

'She would ask about you,' she said. 'She would come hobbling out, looking all around the room. Holding her stomach, like she's still pregnant. And every time she saw me, it was like she couldn't believe that I'd come. She liked to do these activities. Rather than talking, I guess. They'd put these special events on for Mothers' Day or Christmas or whatever, and she liked us to sit there, and – I don't know. We'd be surrounded by kids. Making wreaths, or greeting cards. You know. Crafts.'

'Crafts?'

'Crafts. We'd make one each, and sometimes, after that, she'd suggest we make one for Evie, or Daniel, or one of the others. But usually for you.'

'Delilah—'

'I know. They wouldn't have been to your taste. There were other days – she just wanted to know what you were up to. She wanted the link to your page on the firm website. Stuff like that. You weren't allowed to take phones in. I had to write down the whole fucking URL.'

'Why are you telling me this?' I said.

With a long sigh, she sat up. 'Don't you ever get tired,' she said, 'of hating them?'

'Not really,' I said. 'No.'

Delilah's victim impact statement: the great twist to Mother's trial. Ethan's statement was terse and condemning. He did not look Mother in the eye. My statement was read by Dad, while I was at school. Gabriel's statement was delivered by his adopted mother, and a well-used handkerchief. But Delilah: Delilah gave the people what they wanted. She was flanked by two police officers, who made her look smaller. Somebody had laminated her script, and the noise of it wobbled across the courtroom. She loved her parents, she said. They had wanted to protect their children – to do God's work. While they had made terrible mistakes, she recognized their intentions, and she had forgiven them. In the dock, Mother slumped amidst hair and tears. The newspapers described Delilah as sorrowful and conciliatory, which made me smile, even then.

She observed me, faint disdain in the lines between her eyebrows. 'It isn't good for you,' she said. 'It isn't healthy.'

A slight shake of her head.

'Hey,' she said, 'do you have any coffee?'

On the phone, the overnight receptionist was bemused. 'Didn't they arrive?' he asked.

'They arrived,' I said. 'Two more.'

'You must be having a difficult night, Miss Gracie.'

'Yes. That's true. Thank you.'

Delilah was appraising the room. She opened the wardrobe and ran her index finger along the dresses and suits. She took the complimentary body lotion from the side of the bath and squeezed it into her palm. At the desk, she read the note of consent and waited for me to hang up the phone.

'A community centre,' she said.

'There are two assets,' I said. 'The house at Moor Woods Road, and twenty thousand pounds—'

'Alexandra Gracie,' she said. 'Philanthropist.'

'Are you happy with it or not?'

'It was our home,' she said, 'and I'll be glad to see it used for such a good cause.'

She had retained her small, self-satisfied smile.

'The money's more interesting,' she said. 'Not least – where did it come from?'

This development, I enjoyed. Bill had emailed over the documentation when I was on the train back to London, and had phoned me right away. The money was attributed to the sale of a handful of shares in a technology corporation, he said, which Father had purchased decades before. 'If he had bought a couple of hundred,' Bill said, 'you'd be millionaires by now.'

A success, after all of this time. He would probably have declared himself the last major prophet. 'It's the pioneers who get slaughtered,' I said to Bill.

'I'm sorry?'

'No. Nothing.'

'The money,' Delilah said, 'should be divided between us.'

'The way I see it,' I said, 'is that the house is pretty worthless without some money to transform it. The council will want to see that we're committed – that we're willing to make a personal investment.'

'It's not for me,' she said. 'Although I know that's what you expect. I'm married now, Lex. He's a good man – an important man. But he's specific about his causes. And this – it's for a cause which is close to both of our hearts. But not to his.'

Ethan had found the wedding announcement on the *Telegraph* website. Delilah's husband was the heir to Pizza Serata, a chain of pizzerias marching north from Maidenhead. The marriage had taken place quietly, on a Friday afternoon. All I knew about Pizza Serata was that they had been exposed as donating to anti-abortion charities across the Atlantic, and that the pizzas were mediocre.

Delilah lay down on the bed and rested an arm over her eyes.

'How to explain,' she said. 'We were a family. Weren't we? At Moor Woods Road. Mother and Father – they tried to protect us. And there are consequences – aren't there? – to tearing a family apart? Removing that protection. Some people learn to live with it. But others don't.'

The coffees arrived. They were delivered by a new waiter in a clean, crisp uniform. A visitor from the land of the living. Delilah threw him a smile. 'You've saved my life!' she said.

The coffee was too hot to drink. We sat for a moment, cradling the cups and saucers. Delilah's hair fell around her face.

'Even me,' Delilah said. 'I struggled, at first. Alone for the first time, somewhere unfamiliar, and without our family. Mother out of bounds, and what happened to Father. There were things which I questioned, too. But God waited for me.'

She was convincing, Delilah. If you spent long enough listening to her, you could appreciate how she had convinced herself.

'OK,' I said. 'What do you need it for – the money?'

'It's Gabriel,' she said. 'He isn't well.'

'Where is he?'

'Not so fast. You don't get to start caring now.'

She held her coffee to her chest, like something she wasn't willing to share.

'He's in a hospital,' she said. 'A private hospital. He came to me out of desperation, I think. He knew that I would help him. And he's doing OK. I had enough money for the first month or so. You know that I won't beg you, Lex. But you need to understand that I care for him. And you have to accept responsibility – for what you changed.'

My brain was heavy, laden with last night's rust, but it was starting to grind.

'You didn't even know about the inheritance until today,' I said. 'So what was going to happen then?'

Delilah combed back her hair. Behind it, she wore her little smile. 'God loves a cheerful giver,' she said.

'You had already decided to ask me for money,' I said. 'Hadn't you?'

'Why else would I be here? It's an added convenience, I suppose, that now there's something you actually owe me.'

And Ethan wouldn't have helped Gabriel. A few weeks after he became the headteacher at Wesley, after the articles and the interviews, somebody broke into the house in Oxford in the middle of the day, when he and Ana were at a fundraising lunch. A witness had seen a man carrying a record player and television out of the front door; 'I didn't report it,' the witness said, 'because it was the man who lives there.'

'It could have been anybody,' I said.

'Come on, Lex,' Ethan said. 'You know exactly who it was.'

I nodded to Delilah.

'I've got the money,' I said. 'We don't need to use what Mother's left. And I can pay, for a recommended time frame, if you sign that form. But I want the name of the hospital. I need to speak to him myself.'

Delilah downturned her lips and wrinkled her forehead, in a freakish parody of my concern. She had made that face before, I thought, when we were children. We looked just similar enough for the impression to be accurate; that was why it hurt. 'You're so serious, Lex. You were always so serious. Whatever. Show me where to sign.'

She printed out her name at the bottom of the document, carefully, like a child in the term's first exercise book, and I took the paper to check it.

'I never did change my name,' she said, 'but I was always surprised that you didn't change yours.'

'The hospital, Delilah.'

I handed her the hotel notepad, and she wrote down the name of a well-known psychiatric hospital, an hour or so from London. Well, I thought. This will be expensive.

'I'd get to him quickly,' she said, 'if I was you.'

'And why's that?'

'The company Gabriel keeps – I don't think you'll be the only person after his cut.'

She looked around the room, retrieved her jacket, and crossed to the threshold.

'But you wouldn't know that,' she said. 'Would you?'

She had always walked with inverted feet. When she was little, it gave her a kind of bashful charm, but over time, Father became frustrated, and admonished her whenever he saw her toes beginning to turn. Now, I could only just make it out; she must have worked to correct it.

'I suppose I'll see you at Ethan's wedding,' she said. 'So we have that to look forward to.'

'Before you go—'

She had been standing in the darkness of the hallway, but now she stepped back towards me, into the early light.

'You don't really believe it,' I said. 'Do you? That they loved us? That they were trying to protect us? After everything that happened? You tried to escape, Delilah. I heard it. You and Gabriel. I heard what happened to him, that night in the hallway. The things that were done to us—'

Her face was changing.

'We each believe what we want to believe,' she said. 'Don't we? You more than anyone.'

A kind of resolution set across her features, then. It was the face that a child makes on the highest board at the swimming pool, when they decide to jump.

'Yes,' Delilah said. 'You like to pretend that you know best. But let me tell you what I think. I think you're the saddest one of all of us. When we were children, and we had all of those . . . *supervised visits*. Who were they protecting us from? Girl A. The craziest of the lot.'

'I'll sort out the money,' I said. 'And I'll let you know how long we can afford.'

'Do you remember what you said to me the last time we spoke?' she asked. 'How things became this way? I bet that you can't even remember that.'

'Goodbye, Delilah.'

'I'll pray for you, Lex. I always pray for you.'

'Well. Thanks.'

When I was sure that Delilah would have left the hotel, I walked through the lobby and up to Harley Street. Dr K's office was set back from the street, behind the branches of a spindly pear tree. I knew it from the blue plaque, and an old stone shell above the door. Karl Ghattas had lived there: Philosopher, Surgeon, Painter & Poet, said the plaque. 'I think that you should take it down,' I had said to Dr K when I first visited.

'That's enough to make anyone feel inadequate.' The street was still entombed in shadow, and I rested on the steps of the building and caught my breath. I found the windows of Dr K's office, with the curtains drawn. It would be hours before she arrived, and she could be travelling, or on holiday. Besides, it was Monday. It was time to go to work.

Here is another story. Mother was sentenced to twenty-five years in prison, before a full courtroom. When the judge announced his decision, he clarified that one of Mother's victims had made a specific request to approach her before she was taken from the dock. There was Delilah, with her arms outstretched. Ethan called me from the court steps, to castigate the whole hysterical process, and the next day, despite Mum and Dad's protests, I bought every newspaper and read the reports. A court artist had captured the embrace. The judge is grave. Mother's features are smudged with distress, and a fast pencil. But all you can see of Delilah is the back of her head. She could be weeping for the parents whom she had forgiven. She could be smiling into her noble, Motherless future.

We spent many sessions at the window above the plaque, with the court drawing on the table between us. Dr K seemed bored by this exercise. 'There's no answer to it,' she said, 'other than the one it would help you to believe.' But I was obsessed with it, for a while. I kept turning the paper, as if I might find Delilah's face on the other side of the page.

4

Gabriel (Boy B)

WE HAD COME TO the season of the wasps. In the taxi, one of the insects veered between the windows, until Devlin leaned across me, and crushed it between her phone and the glass.

'The question,' she said, 'is whether you're going to do it.'

On the seat between us was a pair of genomics testing kits, handed to us at the end of the day's meetings.

'Imagine,' Devlin said, 'if somebody had told me about the weakness in my heart. Would I have worked differently? Maybe I would be a yoga instructor. Or a gardener.'

'I don't think you'd have changed a thing. A nice gimmick, though.'

'They were full of them.'

Jake, the CEO and founder of ChromoClick, had led the presentation. He had already done the backstory: six years before, he had been working as a PhD student at MIT, mid-lab, when he was called from the room by one of the senior doctors in the Biology Faculty. At that moment, he was two hours into a day-long observation of a yeast strain, awaiting a potential mutation, and he was reluctant to leave the room. He knew that something was wrong when the doctor placed a hand upon his shoulder, and said, 'Spoiler alert, kid: the mutation never comes. Leave the yeast be.'

The news, which Jake had been half expecting, was that his brother had shot himself in the face, and Jake was half expecting this news because his father had shot himself before that, and his father's father before him. Jake was the exception: the mutation which, against all odds, had finally arrived. He returned to the lab.

ChromoClick was now the fastest growing genetic service company in Europe. Its reporting service provided an extensive analysis of health and ancestry to individual customers, and funded a research arm which was asking what Jake characterized as the big questions: how to extinguish fundamental flaws from family lines, and how fundamental those flaws needed to be to justify extinction.

'People have a natural curiosity about themselves,' Jake said, 'and we have a natural curiosity about helping people.'

'They told a good story,' I said.

'They want a good price.'

The motorway passed behind dim windows. It was the kind of hot, flat day when everything looks uglier than it is. Devlin held one of the kits to the light and surveyed the packaging as if it might reflect her.

'Dementia,' she said. 'A few coronary bypasses.'

I thought of my own list.

'I think my time for spitting in a pot must have passed,' she said. 'If anything of importance happens to be lurking in my DNA, it'll make itself known soon enough.'

The sky ahead was cluttered with buildings and cranes. 'We should talk about the drafting,' I said, 'before we hit London.'

Devlin wasn't listening. Still squinting at the test pack.

'Not you, though,' she said. 'There's still time for you to take up gardening.'

As it turned out, JP called me. The night receptionist, who treated each call with the same whiskery indignation, rang through to my desk and informed me that there was a gentleman on the line.

'Who?' I said. I was scrolling through the second page of

indistinguishable sushi platters, about to order dinner. 'I'm not expecting anyone.'

'He didn't have a real name,' she said. 'Just initials.'

'Ah. OK. Yes, you can put him through.'

The line clicked, and JP cleared his throat.

'Lex?' he said, after a moment.

'Hello,' I said.

'Hello. At last. You need a friendlier receptionist.'

'We don't do friendly. We do stamina and winning.'

'That sounds about right. Well. Olivia said that you were in town. I just wanted to say hello. I heard about your mother.'

'I'm fine,' I said, although he hadn't asked.

'Good. When do you go back?'

'It depends. There's a deal here, and some family things to sort out. Maybe a few more weeks.'

'Do you want to go for a drink or something, Lex? It would be good to catch up.'

'I don't know. This weekend – I'm going to see my brother. Early next week?'

'Monday?'

'Yes, Monday night. I'm in Soho.'

'OK. I'll find somewhere good.'

I could feel the old softening in my tone. I still wanted to amuse him. 'My expectations are higher these days,' I said.

'I guess New York does that to you. I'll do my best.'

'OK.'

'OK.'

So: the saga would continue. I sent a message to Olivia, expressing my displeasure, and ordered Health and Happiness.

It wasn't that we had ever been rich, or even comfortable, but we hadn't been poor. The poverty crept into our lives like ivy on a window, slow enough that you don't notice it moving, and then, in no time, so dense that we couldn't see outside.

Father developed strange fixations. They came like fevers, although some of them never left him. He decided that we were wasting water; it was a necessity, he said, and not a plaything, and he drew up a careful schedule of our weekly showers. When dinner was ready, he liked to serve it, and he did so with great deliberation. Our plates would be exactly equal, provided that one of us hadn't misbehaved or challenged him that day, in which case the guilty party would have a little less. He reread Corinthians and decided that we should better glorify God with our bodies, and we spent our evenings marching up and down the stairs, trying not to laugh. He was bored. He presided over the living room, planning his illustrious future: he would establish a website to present the truth of the Bible to children across the globe; he would become a pastor himself, and usurp David at the Gatehouse; he and Jolly would travel to America, to speak to the vast congregations there.

He spent a lot of time with Jolly in the kitchen of our house, with the liquor between them on the table, and meats sweating on their plates. He drove to Blackpool for Jolly's Sunday sermons, and in the evenings he required us to sit in the lounge, attentive, while he repeated the lessons. Mother nodded to his inflections and held out her cracked palms in supplication. At her side, Delilah smiled. On the longer nights, I would try to catch Ethan's eye, but he watched Father, his jaw clenched and harder than it had been a year before, and he didn't notice me.

Ethan had left the primary school. There were no more travel artefacts, or Facts of the Day. He attended the high school in between our town and the next, where there were eight classes to a year, crunched across five concrete blocks. There had been some problem in buying his school uniform, so that he and Mother arrived home separately, not speaking. I watched him leave on his first day, while Delilah, Evie and I were still eating breakfast. 'Why doesn't Ethan's blazer have a crest?' Delilah asked, as he left the kitchen. The front door slammed behind him.

He would lose things: his English Literature texts; his gym shorts; and, in late November, the blazer. 'You'll have to do without, then,' Father said, enthroned on the sofa with a tangle of wires and an amber glass.

'That's not really an option, though, is it,' Ethan said. 'You have to have one. You have to have one to go.'

'You're the one who lost it. Don't come crying to us.'

'Is there a second-hand bin?' Mother said. 'That kind of thing?'

That night, before bed, I thought of the teenagers who had watched us sit down to dinner at Dustin's, and the expression they had shared. The image returned to me often, and whenever it did, it made my stomach ache. I wondered if there had been other looks, that I might have missed. 'Was school good?' I asked Evie, to think about something else.

'Yep,' she said. Gabriel occupied her old cot, now, his limbs long enough to bump against the bars, and she was in my bed. It was a good sleeping arrangement for winter, when I couldn't feel much past my knees. 'We're doing animals from different countries.'

'Which was your favourite animal?' I asked. She was falling asleep, but I didn't want to return to Dustin's. I wanted to stay here, with her.

'The walruses,' she said. 'From the North Pole.'

'Why the walruses?'

She was quiet. I nudged her in the ribs, and she huffed.

'*Lex.*'

She was the first person to call me that. She had needed to ask for me before four syllables fit in her mouth. The name stuck. It was easier on the school register, and lighter for my parents to throw up the stairs. Besides, even my family wasn't entirely without sentimentality.

'Can't we talk about the walruses tomorrow?'

'Tomorrow? Well. OK.'

My stomach panged, again. I rolled away from Evie and tiptoed down the hallway. The bathroom door was locked, and through it I could hear the intermittent gasps of somebody trying not to cry.

'Ethan?' I whispered.

I cradled my stomach, knocked.

'Ethan? Ethan, I need to go.'

He opened the door and pushed past me, one hand across his face. 'Fuck off, Lex,' he said.

I sat on the toilet in the cold little room, examining the strips of mould along the bathtub, the clotted soap bars, the bathmat askew and still printed with the dirt of barefooted summer days. The teenagers in Dustin's had been right. We were odd and unclean. We were a spectacle. It made you uncomfortable just to look at us.

I tried to mitigate the dirt. I left for school a few minutes before Delilah and Evie, and went straight to the disabled toilet, which was set apart from the other bathrooms, just past the staffroom. I locked the door and removed my school jumper and my polo shirt. I leaned over the sink. I splashed cold water under my armpits and around my neck, and luminous pink hand wash after that. I unravelled a handful of toilet roll and dried myself, carefully, to stop any crumbs of paper from sticking to my skin. There was a pocked mirror above the basin, and I tried to avoid catching my own eye. There were a few mornings when the Year 5 teacher, Miss Glade, saw me opening the toilet door. She was always the last to leave the staffroom, lumbered with exercise books and a coffee and a leopard-print handbag. 'Are you feeling particularly disabled this morning, Miss Gracie?' she asked, or: 'Do you have your disabled parking card to hand?' But she never reported me, and when I provided my excuse – that the other girls' toilets were occupied, or that I had felt unwell – she always smiled, and waved me away.

My period posed a more significant problem. It came when I was ten; I had expected another few years to prepare myself. We had been informed, by a video in school, of the practicalities: the blood; the cramping; the sanitary products. It had seemed sterile and simple. Now I stood in the bath, half-naked and baffled. Nobody had mentioned the smell, or the clots, or what you were meant to do with one shower a week. I tried to reassure myself, in the same stern tone taken by the actress in the school video. It was a problem, and like any other, it would have a solution. For now, I lined my knickers with toilet paper and prayed. I was unconvinced about God's credentials in this particular sector. I would need a better plan.

My social currency had never been particularly high, but there was a handful of things that I could exchange for friendship. I was fast enough to be picked in the upper quartile in PE. I was intelligent, but quietly so. I didn't raise my hand in class, or share my marks. It had already occurred to me that, if I was going to be clever, I needed to be smarter about it than Ethan. I hovered at the periphery of a studious group of girls, who were preparing for entrance examinations to better schools, and I suffered their occasional ridicule, like a dog content with a kicking. You can endure an awful lot when you know that you'll be fed at the end of it.

'Why don't you ever have a sleepover, Lex?' Amy or Jessica or Caroline asked (to which I responded that my parents were too strict, so that it would be boring anyway). Or: 'My sister's in your older brother's class, and he's really weird.' (Yes, I would say, he really is; and then, feeling bad: He's really smart, though.) Or – worst of all, because I had given something away – 'When did you last wash your hair?'

The slights made it much easier to carry out my plan. Amy

was holding a party on a Saturday afternoon for her tenth birthday, and I walked across town to attend it. A heavy summer day, strung with flies. I carried my school bag, and wore a church skirt and one of Mother's old blouses; I had outgrown my jeans and T-shirts, and now they hung off Delilah. We sat in the family garden, sipping squash, and I watched the girls paint one another's nails. There was an odd number of attendees, said Amy's mother, and I would have to wait. I thought of Father's face in the event that I returned home with red nails – with glitter – and I smiled. 'Thank you,' I said, 'but I'm afraid that I'm allergic.'

When Amy's mother carried out the cake and the other girls started to sing, I slipped inside and upstairs, and locked the bathroom door behind me. I surveyed the clean porcelain and the concoctions around the tub. I considered climbing in and running it full, so full that it flooded under the door and down the stairs, and submerged the whole stupid house. No. That wasn't what I was here for. I opened the cupboards behind the mirror and under the sink. Plasters, pills, cleaning products. Outside, they were cutting the cake, and I heard my name. In the corner of the room, there was a prim hemp basket, sealed with ribbons. I untied the bows, lifted the lid, and opened a treasure trove of tampons and sanitary towels, stored in their cardboard packets, row after row in soft lilac, baby blue, hot pink. I imagined Amy and her mother in Boots, selecting the right boxes, and the resentment made me braver. I took an instruction leaflet and half of the products from each box and tucked them into my satchel, then I flushed the toilet, and rejoined the party.

On Saturday morning I took the Underground as far north as I could go, out of the tunnels and away from the city. By the end of the line, I was the only person left in the carriage, still blinking in the shock of light. The coffee kiosk at the station was closed.

See you Monday! said a sign, printed in Comic Sans and propped in the window.

I had spoken to Bill the evening before. He always seemed to call at a time when Devlin wanted something, so that whenever we talked, I sounded less grateful than I was. He had spoken to the council, he said, about our initial thoughts. I stopped scrolling through the ChromoClick report, and turned away from my screens.

'OK. How did it go?'

'They were unconvinced.'

'Unconvinced?'

'If you ask me,' Bill said, 'they'd like to see it demolished. You mention Hollowfield, and what do people think of? They think of the seven of you, standing in that garden. As soon as your mother died there were people sniffing around for scraps. Photographing the house for some feature or other. They mentioned something written by your brother, just the other day. I think they're tired of the whole thing.'

That, I understood. Ethan had sent me the essay. This one was titled 'Memento Mori: What Death Makes You Remember', and had just appeared in *T*. In the accompanying photograph, Ethan sat in monochrome in the house in Summertown, gazing out across the garden, with Horace in his lap. I didn't read the essay, but I did respond to the message: *Your kitchen looks fantastic.*

'We pitch it in person,' Bill said. 'That's what I think. You'll come across well, Lex. You know what you're doing. They'll see that this isn't some – some exercise in vanity. They'll see what you're trying to do.'

I pressed my forehead against the window glass. From here, with the buildings dimming to lights, I could be back in New York, with an empty weekend awaiting.

'In the meantime,' Bill said. 'How's the family?'

I picked up a hire car and drove towards the Chilterns. All summer, the sun had worn the fields, and now they were dull and patched, like cheap metal. The hospital had been built between two market towns, and I ended up visiting them both; there was a discreet turn-off, which I missed from each direction. Back in the first town, I found a cafe on the roadside and pulled over, already bored with the day. 'You've come too far,' the waitress said, warily. She was the kind of person who would inflate this encounter for the next customer and for girls' drinks tonight. By eight p.m., I would be psychotic, and seeking readmission. 'It's a green sign. You can't miss it.'

The drive of the hospital passed through forest shadows before opening out to an empty lawn. The white, white palace waited at the end of it, like the final destination in a fairy tale. The building had been the country villa of a Romantic writer, Robert Wyndham, and I had spent Friday night in bed and online, reading his accounts of evenings in the garden. There were visits from royals and ambassadors, and from Byron. There were statues of nymphs on the edge of the woods, designed to move in the dusk light. There were reports of pagan ceremonies and a great abundance of food and wine. These ironies were unacknowledged on the hospital website, and the statues had been removed.

There was a clump of smokers by the entrance, craning into the shade like flowers in reverse. A framed note explained that the interior had been refurbished last year, and had been painted in colours which promoted wellness. Wellness, it transpired, was white with a shot of pastel, and pink shirts at the reception desk. 'Hello,' I said. 'I'm here to visit my brother, Gabriel.'

'Surname?'

'Gabriel Gracie.'

'I'm afraid that Gabriel's occupied,' the receptionist said.

'Occupied?'

'He has another guest.'

'Who?'

'That isn't information which I'm able to disclose.'

The receptionist smiled pleasantly.

'Can I join them?' I said. 'I've come a long way.'

'Our policy is to allow one group of visitors at a time.'

'Really?' I said, and still the receptionist smiled.

'You're welcome to wait.'

I waited. The smokers traipsed past, lugging the smell of it. I turned the pages of a stale magazine, which seemed to be about houses and plastic surgery. An old fan turned behind the desk, moving the receptionist's hair.

Half an hour in, a man passed by, walking like he was heading somewhere more important. In the light of the reception, his skin was pallid, with the sheen of raw meat. Clothes stained at the collar and cuffs. When he was above me, he smiled, as if he knew me well. As if he had been expecting me. He had immaculate teeth: a last pocket of health, preserved from the general decay. 'Thank you,' he said, to the receptionist. 'As ever.'

Then he was outside, shielding his eyes against the afternoon.

'You're up,' said the receptionist. 'He'll meet you here.'

Gabriel came inconsequentially down the corridor. His face was clean and pale and preserved, like an undertaker's interpretation of my brother. He wore cotton trousers and mismatched socks, and a long, long shirt, buttoned to the neck. He gripped the sleeves, like they would roll away from him. Next to me, he removed his glasses, and smiled at a space close to my eyes, his pupils roving for the right spot.

'You found me,' he said.

'With a little help from Delilah,' I said. 'Yes. How are you feeling?'

'That's a dangerous question, around here. Can we go outside?'

'I don't know. Can we?'

'I'm not asking you to help me escape, if that's what you're worried about.'

We stood together, and I offered him my arm. I was surprised when he took it, and leaned against me. We moved as one cumbersome creature down the corridor and towards the sunshine. 'No further than the end of the lawn, please,' said the receptionist, and Gabriel chuckled.

'Do people actually escape?' I asked.

'Apparently. There are rumours that the whole forest's full of bodies – all of the sad, lost souls, you see – but I think they usually call for a taxi.'

'Do you want to sit down?'

'No. Let's walk.'

'One lap?'

'Let's try for that.'

He had lost most of his hair. The last clumps were shaved to the scalp. He pulled thick sunglasses from one pocket and a stick of gum from the other. 'Don't look at me too much, Lex,' he said. 'It's the medications. I'm a fucking mess.'

I wondered if he felt the same way about sunglasses as I did: the childish notion that you become invisible when you put them on. I had left mine in the car; I would have to allow him to see me, for now.

'Are you here for Ethan's wedding?' he asked.

'No. Because of Mother. The wedding's not for a few months.'

'It's nice, isn't it,' Gabriel said, 'that he's so happy.'

He laughed, but without much savagery to it. There was self-deprecation in all of Gabriel's laughter, which made you reluctant to laugh with him.

'You had another visitor,' I said.

'Yes. A friend. He comes every so often. Delilah, too.'

'I'm glad that you've kept in touch.'

'It's been on and off, over the years. She tried to keep me on the straight and narrow. And these last few weeks – she's been good to me, Lex. Once you get over the Jesus shit – she's been good to me. In the hospital – the real hospital, I mean – she was the only person I could think to call. I was hacked to bits, and she didn't bat an eyelid.'

'Well. It's hard to surprise Delilah.'

'Her husband's come with her a few times,' Gabriel said. 'But he always waits in the car. Anyway. Do you know what he calls her? "The Roach" – the last thing standing on earth.' Gabriel laughed. 'She told me it,' he said, 'like it was the greatest compliment she could have received.'

'The Roach,' I said.

'Yes. And he's right. She'll outlive us all.'

We stopped at a bench, the first one on the lawn, and he sat as old men do, checking that the chair was still there on the way down. The last time that I saw him, he had been a teenager, installed in front of the London skyline, on the television.

The truth is, Gabriel was the early triumph. He was inaugurated in a modest family home, with proper parents and a new sister. His happy ending is still available on YouTube, for public consumption. Here he is, starting secondary school on BBC News; talking to the camera on an episode of *I Survived*; receiving a birthday present from a middling footballer on *Children in Need*. Gabriel, with his crooked smile, strolling into breakfast television studios, both for an extensive, anonymity-waiving interview, and as an artefact dusted off for a feature called *The Big Debate*, which, that particular morning, was 'Child Abuse: Can we talk about race?'

'Are you going to tell me how you're feeling?' I asked.

He sighed, pantomime-wide.

'The thing about this place,' he said, 'is that I'm so bored of talking about myself.'

Gabriel's new parents, Mr and Mrs Coulson-Browne, had made it quite clear that he was a special child, so school, when it finally came – after nearly two years of one-to-one tuition, and at least three appearances on the actual television – was a disappointment. His psychologist, Mandy, had advised his adoptive parents that he might have additional requirements, or difficulties settling into the routine of school life; Mandy had a whole arsenal of carefully curated distraction techniques which the teachers wouldn't have the time to deploy. 'He'll be fine, I think,' said Gabriel's new mother. 'If you've done your job.'

'The important thing,' Mandy said, in their final session before school began, 'is to remember what we've learnt about communication. If you feel one of the Rages coming, you get up and out of that room. You tell a teacher, or you call me.'

The Rages had started at Moor Woods Road, although they only became the Rages afterwards, when Gabriel started working with Mandy. He might be chained to the bed, or exercising in the garden, and a minor occurrence – a fly in the room, or Evie straying clumsily into his path – would set off a mounting pressure in his head. It wasn't something that he could subdue or ignore; the pressure would continue to build until he released it. He would writhe in the chains so much that they left raw, weeping imprints around his wrists. He would throw his whole body to the ground and batter his head against it. Once, he bit Father's hand, as hard as he could and hoping that his teeth would meet. Although he was punished, terribly, he knew that he would do it again.

He had thought that the Rages would stop when he left Moor Woods Road, but that wasn't the case. Sometimes they happened in the Coulson-Browne household, where there was an unfortunate number of precarious items. Mrs Coulson-Browne kept a collection of crystal animals, and there was a set of wedding china displayed atop an antique cabinet (fake, Gabriel later ascertained, when he researched whether it would be of any value). Once, unforgivably, a Rage came in the dressing room of *Britain*

This Morning, when one of the runners insisted on taking Gabriel's relics from the House of Horrors from his hands, in order that they could be cleaned before they appeared in the studio.

But he and Mandy had worked on it. There was a tepee in the corner of his new bedroom, and he retreated there when a Rage was on the way. Inside, he kept a projector night light and the bear the Coulson-Brownes had given him when he first entered their home, which wore a T-shirt imprinted with *Survivor*. If he wasn't at home, he was to find somewhere quiet when the pressure began to build. He was to imagine the tepee and the slow movement of ocean mammals across the canvas.

'It's not going to be easy, Gabe,' Mandy said. 'A few steps forward, a few steps back. If you're heading in the right direction, then there's no shame in the stumbles.'

But school wasn't just a few stumbles. On the first day, you had to introduce yourself to the rest of the class with a funny or interesting anecdote, and he got off to a good start: he had been on television. He started by listing the specific programmes on which he had appeared, and then provided some key background information about his family – he had the attention of the whole room, now – but the teacher cut him off. 'Thank you for your contribution, Gabriel,' she said, but he knew from her face that he had somehow misspoken, and he returned to his chair in a fuzz of embarrassment.

The Rages became more frequent. There were times, at school, when he decided not to think of the tepee and the childish little lamp inside of it, and instead thought of what Father had done to him, or the fact that Mandy was marrying somebody from Scotland and would have to discontinue their sessions, or Mrs Coulson-Browne's failure to read the first page of his memoir. When he returned to himself, he would look around to see a ring of children's faces, and delight in their horror.

Delight: there was something to be made of that. Through the Rages, he acquired a kind of notoriety, which meant that a select group in his year – the parentless; the awkward; the rebels, and the frail girls who clung to them – accepted his company. They called themselves The Clan. The leader of The Clan was Jimmy Delaney, who had three tattoos and was rumoured to have fucked a student teacher on last year's geography field trip (although nobody, and least of all Gabriel, knew if that was true). At weekends, they gathered in parks, or in the bedroom of whoever's family was absent that night, and smoked sparse joints, or took it in turns to touch the girls who had turned up. Gabriel wasn't cool or useful enough to be at the centre of things, but he liked having people to sit with at lunch, and that they were interested in his story. When he was drunk, he would tell them everything that he could muster, but whatever he said, Jimmy pressed for more. 'Why didn't you just kill him?' he asked, about Father, and, 'Is it true that your old man was a pervert?' They were the kind of kids whom the Coulson-Brownes detested, and Gabriel liked that, too.

At home, his career was floundering. Mrs Coulson-Browne lobbied publishers and television studios, and contacted local celebrities, asking if they might be interested in meeting her son. There had been a small spike in interest upon the anniversary of the escape, and again during Mother's trial, but the story appeared to have reached its conclusion. It didn't help that Gabriel no longer looked like the angular child carried from Moor Woods Road, captured in a policeman's arms in a picture that was long-listed for the World Press Photo of the Year (Breaking News). Now, he was a scrawny teenage boy with glasses and Mother's dry skin and hair which got darker by the day.

He could sense that the Coulson-Brownes were losing interest in him. There was no cruelty in it, but a gradual detachment, as somebody might set aside a toy from their childhood. When he had first been adopted, the Coulson-Brownes had liked him present at their parties, which weren't really parties at all, but gatherings of neighbours, taking it in turns to see the insides of one another's houses. He would be sent into the lounge, armed with toothpick cheese and a bowl of crisps, and instructed to Work the Room. But ever since the Lawsons had come for dinner, it had been suggested that he stay in his room.

The Lawsons lived in the only five-bedroom house on the street and had a car with a 2.5-litre engine. Gabriel, precarious on the spare chair, and eating twice as much as everybody else, had sat through ninety minutes of side returns; prawn cocktails; the influx of traffic to the new estate; beef Wellington; other people's children. Finally, over caramel flan, the conversation became interesting. The Lawsons were narrating the story of their son, ever a risk-taker, who was encumbered in a Genevan hospital with a twenty-five-centimetre plate screwed to his left tibia.

'What's the one thing we told him?' Mr Lawson said. '"Stay on piste." And now where are we? Spending Christmas in ortho-paedics, in bloody Switzerland.'

'The price of those hotels,' Mrs Lawson said, 'at such short notice—'

'I have a metal plate,' said Gabriel, and the conversation crashed to a halt. He touched his jaw. Turned his head to show them. 'Here,' he said.

He had arrived at the hospital with severe malocclusion, he explained. He liked that he knew a word which they didn't. The growth centre in his left jaw was damaged, so one side of his face had turned out different from the other. Gabriel and Mandy had been invited to the X-ray viewer to survey the damage, and they sat together at a desk while a maxillofacial surgeon – that was the mouth – talked them through Gabriel's skull. It was funny, to see yourself in skeleton. The teeth were so much longer than you thought. At the end, Gabriel asked if he could come back post-operation, to see how the metal looked in his jaw. 'We've got a medic, here,' the surgeon said, and within a week, everyone on the ward was calling him Dr Gracie.

'Holidays in hospital were actually OK,' Gabriel said. 'They had this big chocolate egg hunt, at Easter. Christmas is probably pretty cool.'

Nobody was eating, now. The Lawsons lowered their eyes. Mr Coulson-Browne gave a tight, humourless laugh, and picked up his spoon. 'These hotels,' he said. 'How much are we talking?'

In her desperation, Mrs Coulson-Browne suggested finding Gabriel an agent, although she didn't know of anyone in particular. 'Besides,' she said, 'you have to think about which avenue you want to pursue, Gabriel. Whether that's television, or autobiography, or something like Matilda.'

Matilda was the Coulson-Brownes' real daughter, who had once been destined to become a ballet dancer; then, when she was overly developed, a West End lead; and, when she couldn't sing the requisite range, a backing dancer on a stadium tour. Finally, she worked as a choreographer on cruise ships, as far away from home as possible. Whenever she stayed with the Coulson-Brownes, she viewed Gabriel with a combination of trepidation and pity, and she tried to avoid being alone with him in a room. At the time, he had thought that she was frightened, although now, at the age that she had been then, he understood. She had been ashamed.

'What do you suggest that he do?' Mr Coulson-Browne asked, when Matilda was back from the Caribbean for Christmas, and they were sitting for dinner. Matilda looked at Gabriel, then at the table, and shrugged.

'I don't think I'm the expert,' she said.

'You must have *some* advice – from your experiences.'

'In that case, I think that he should try to be happy.'

'But his story!' Mrs Coulson-Browne said. 'That's a story that needs to be told.'

'There's somebody that I know,' Matilda said, 'in London. He's an agent for a few celebrities. They're not big ones, though. And he's not the most savoury of characters, from everything that I've heard.'

'See,' Mrs Coulson-Browne said. 'I think that would be very useful.'

'I'll give you his number,' Matilda said, to Gabriel. 'If you really want it.'

She wrote the name and number on a CocoCruises pad, and he repeated it, in his head: Oliver Alvin. 'You look after yourself, Gabe,' she said, and squeezed his shoulder. When she left for St Lucia in the New Year, he thought for a strange, stupid moment of asking if she would take him with her.

The first time The Clan asked him to feign a Rage was in a mock examination, in January. 'What we need,' Jimmy said, as they waited at the assembly hall doors, 'is extenuating circumstances.' He surveyed his cronies, smiling. 'Something traumatic,' he said.

'Has anyone got a weapon?' Gabriel asked. Nobody laughed, but they all looked at him and then at each other, and he realized that there had been a conversation – an in-joke – that he had missed.

'How are you feeling, Gabe?' Jimmy asked. 'Are you feeling angry?' He laughed, and slapped Gabriel on the shoulder. 'I could really do without this shit,' he said.

The hallway doors were opened; the students shuffled inside, clutching clear plastic pencil cases. The clock loomed at the front of the room.

Gabriel's seat was at the back. He rested his chin on his arms and surveyed the rows of heads. The clean, functioning brains within them, awaiting further instructions. Closer to the front, Jimmy turned to find him, and winked. The scripts were already on the desks. The invigilator directed the students to begin. When would be the right time, Gabriel thought, and could he really do it, here, on purpose – this strange, private thing, which he and Mandy had spent so many months trying to subdue?

It was a two-hour examination. He waited until half an hour had passed. He guessed at a few token questions, reluctant to commit to more. With every shift of the clock, his opportunity diminished; if too much time went by then the scripts might be counted anyway. At forty minutes, he stood up so quickly that his chair toppled to the floor. Then, with every head turning through the silence towards him, he began.

He threw himself onto the desk behind him and its occupant shrieked and darted from his path. With his tongue lolling, he slumped to the floor and began to hammer upon it, as though the ground might split and – at last – swallow him up. He hissed and howled every terrible word he knew, and, seeing the teachers advance, he flipped away from them, a fish on the deck, gasping and gnawing and seizing anything in his reach: the legs of desks and chairs and pupils retreating, and, at some point, a Hello Kitty pencil case, which he hurled at the advancing charge, scattering a whole rainbow of BIC Magic Felt Pens across the hall.

It took four of them to capture him, and, swaying mazy and half mad, march him to the headmaster. The students lined the corridor to watch him pass, and a few blinks of applause fluttered in the crowd. 'Amazing,' mouthed Jimmy, and Gabriel smiled.

After the examination, he did it on request. He performed at the leisure centre and at the cinema; at the supermarket, while The Clan carried out a few six-packs; at the entrance to an expensive restaurant, which the Coulson-Brownes booked for special occasions. There were moments, in the midst of it, when he couldn't tell if he was suffering from a Rage or feigning it; when he couldn't tell where his sickness ended and Jimmy's bidding began. The Coulson-Brownes balked at the school's suggestion that Gabriel succumbed to the Rages at particularly opportune times, and threatened what Mr Coulson-Browne's solicitor called a two-pronged reprisal: litigation, and the press. The school, conscious that Gabriel would be leaving at the end of the year, agreed to tolerate him for a few more months.

He took his real exams in isolation. He didn't know many of the answers. When school was done with, The Clan gathered at a table outside one of the town's more lenient pubs, and he drank until all he could see was Jimmy's face, floating in plural at the more important end of the table.

He had promised the Coulson-Brownes that he would look for a job, but for some months he left the house each morning and wandered the streets, applying for nothing. He dropped in on members of The Clan, most of whom had started college or apprenticeships, and who rarely asked him in. Jimmy, who had crammed for his exams, decided that he might want to go to university, after all. He was studying serious subjects, which took up all his time, and whenever Gabriel called by, he wasn't at home. Gabriel took night shifts at the bigger supermarket in town, which meant that he could sleep for much of the day; that prevented him from having to think about how to fill the hours.

He turned nineteen at the Coulson-Browne dinner table, two years later, over salmon en croûte and a shop-bought Victoria sponge. 'I hate to bring this up tonight,' said Mrs Coulson-Browne. 'But we need to know your plans, Gabriel.' She turned to her husband, encouragingly, and he nodded.

'As you know,' said Mr Coulson-Browne, 'we've been very generous.'

That was reasonable, Gabriel thought. He had first come to

this house half his life ago, on an introduction weekend. He had sat on the plump leather sofas and listened to how welcome he would be. He had mistaken the neat, beige rooms for things that he could fill. He looked at the wooden placemats, with scenes of the English countryside, and at the crystal animals, and at the piano which nobody could play. He would miss none of it. That night, he found Matilda's notepad, sat in his tepee, and called Oliver Alvin.

Oliver Alvin's office wasn't what Gabriel had expected. It was in East London, above a wholesale fabric store, and in the waiting room there was a woman wearing square black sunglasses, threading a tissue between the plastic and the skin to dry her eyes. Oliver's secretary, who was seventeen and still using Tipp-Ex on her nails, asked Gabriel to wait. There was nothing to read, so Gabriel surveyed the room. Framed photographs of Oliver and his clients looked back at him. He didn't recognize anybody.

Forty minutes after his scheduled appointment, the secretary asked him to go through: Oliver was ready to see him. Nobody appeared to have left the office. He stood, straightened his tie (which was Mr Coulson-Browne's tie, and which he had spent half an hour tying and untying that morning), and collected the portfolio which he had assembled over the last week, and which commenced with his photograph, beneath the words: 'Hello. I'm Gabriel Gracie, a survivor.'

Oliver was forgettably good-looking, like that actor in a soap, or a person in a stock image. His office smelt of expensive cologne. 'There are some things that you can do cheaply,' Oliver would tell Gabriel, in bed, a few years later. 'But not suits, and not aftershave.' Gabriel never did find out what the cheap things were, because everything about Oliver was expensive. He wore a vintage Rolex, which he had purchased from his watch dealer;

his shoes and his wallet had been made in Milan; he would order the oldest wine he could find on the menu. When Gabriel came into the room, he was sitting at his desk in a plum suit, typing on a MacBook. He didn't look up.

'I think that we have an appointment,' Gabriel said, and Oliver blinked.

'Gabriel,' Gabriel said. 'Gabriel Gracie.'

'Of course,' Oliver said. 'OK! Gabriel. So. Tell me about yourself.'

With both hands, Gabriel held out his portfolio. Oliver took it, turned a few pages, and slapped it onto the desk.

'Like I said. Tell me about yourself.'

What was there to lose? He started with Moor Woods Road. He found that Oliver was listening to him – nodding here, taken aback there – and, emboldened, he sat down at the desk and continued. He recalled all of the details that Jimmy had asked to hear, the meat off the story's bones, and he gave that up, too. When he stopped speaking he felt exhilarated, then exposed. He looked down to his lap and waited for Oliver's verdict.

'You're certainly more interesting than the Coulson-Browne girl,' Oliver said. 'I'll give you that. And it's in my remit. I've represented a number of victims – terrorism, near-misses, some really traumatic stuff – and they've done OK.'

Oliver frowned, calculating something crucial on his fingers.

'I'll be honest with you,' he said. 'It would be better if you were the one who had got the others out. The one who escaped. But there isn't much we can do about that. And there's still a few opportunities I can think of. Let me see what I can do.'

They talked business. Here he was: Gabriel Gracie, nineteen, speaking with his agent in the Big Smoke. They talked about what events Gabriel would and wouldn't be willing to attend ('How do you feel about gunge?' Oliver asked), if there was any way of contacting Girl A (there wasn't), and the cut to which

Oliver would be entitled (which seemed to Gabriel – even then – more like a fucking haemorrhage).

He celebrated with the Coulson-Brownes, with quiche Lorraine and champagne from France.

Most of the work involved true crime conventions. In his first year on the circuit, he would take to the stage to speak, but later on he tended to be assigned to a table in the lobby of a three-star hotel, sitting behind his name card and signing miscellaneous items. He was both impressed and disturbed by the extent of knowledge attendees had about his family. One evening, a woman presented to him a small, filthy T-shirt which she claimed had belonged to Eve. He recoiled from it and quickly recovered. Oliver would be unimpressed by his squeamishness, and he had no way of knowing if it was a genuine article. He considered the cardboard box of his own childhood belongings, which were stored and sealed in the Coulson-Brownes' attic, and wondered, fleetingly, what they might be worth.

There was increased demand for him in the autumn, when people started thinking about Halloween. These events were more challenging. At the true crime gatherings, he felt that people were waiting for him: when he started to speak, a hush descended across the room. The Halloween gigs were louder, and few people knew who he was. He appeared at universities, and at the night-clubs of small, sullen towns. He looked at the crowds, ragged in fancy dress, and understood that the majority of the attendees were the same age as him. They, like him, would have been nine years old when the police entered the house on Moor Woods Road, and were unlikely to remember much of the story. He was usually appointed to speak for five minutes and to introduce the next band, but he rarely filled the allocated time. 'You need to make it scarier,' a student representative instructed him. 'A little less depressing.'

He had expected that there might be more glamour to this

life. For the most part, the hotel rooms were tired and the beer was warm, and it was usually raining. He had anticipated spending his time in London, or perhaps abroad, speaking to journalists or to crowded halls. He had believed that his story could be an inspiration. In the end, he did make it to London, but not to inspire the masses. He moved to London because he was in love with Oliver.

It started in December, when Gabriel's work was drying up. An empty email from Oliver. Subject line: WE NEED TO TALK. They met for dinner in London, at the restaurant of a celebrity chef whom Gabriel had never heard of. Oliver looked unwell. The hair at his temples was damp, and behind the cologne there was another smell, something like old food, which Gabriel didn't recognize. Right at the start of the meal, as soon as drinks were served, Oliver came to it. 'You need to diversify,' he said.

'Sorry?'

'You need to add another string to your bow,' Oliver said, and when Gabriel continued to look at him, blank and anxious, he set down his glass and sighed. 'Let's put it this way,' he said. 'It's December. Nobody wants a survivor of child abuse for their Christmas party.'

Oliver proposed that Gabriel should accept what he described as more 'standard' work. Many of his clients, he said, needed to be flexible in order to get through the year. Oliver would accept an additional down payment to make this happen.

'I had thought that I could be, like – motivational,' Gabriel said, and Oliver snorted.

'You're a great kid, Gabe,' he said, 'but you're not motivating anybody.'

There seemed to be an infinite number of courses, served with stern deliberation. When they were finally outside the restaurant, Gabriel explained that he would need to leave. The last train home would depart in half an hour, and he wasn't sure how to get back to Euston. He had spent most of the meal trying not to cry, and was longing for the moment – the humiliating, private moment which must, finally, be near – when he could do so.

'You don't need to do that,' Oliver said. Cautiously, as if he was asking for permission, Oliver took Gabriel's index finger, then his middle finger and his thumb, and finally his whole hand, their fingers entwined. Oliver stumbled to face him – he was two bottles of wine down – and tipped his head upwards, until he was too close for Gabriel to see.

Gabriel had only ever kissed uninterested schoolgirls in the bedrooms of his friends, and Oliver's force amazed him. There was a dogged determination in his hands, on Gabriel's cheeks, and in his tongue, parting Gabriel's lips, and – later, in Oliver's bedroom, which looked south onto Tower Bridge, and which was precisely as Gabriel would have imagined it, right down to the black bedsheets and the touchpad lighting – in the rhythm of his mouth against Gabriel's penis. When Oliver was asleep, Gabriel stood at the window – he couldn't work the automated blinds, and had to prise them apart to see out – and surveyed the city, and thought pityingly of Jimmy Delaney, asleep in his university hall, with essays to write.

Gabriel returned to the Coulson-Brownes only once after that. There, he collected the belongings which he had salvaged from Moor Woods Road and took what he liked from his room. He left the tepee behind. The Coulson-Brownes provided him with a few months of rent on a flat in Camden, in exchange, he suspected, for never having him live with them again. 'This is it,' said Mr Coulson-Browne, 'this really is *it*, Gabriel', and Gabriel thought, triumphantly: Yes, it is.

Now he was tired, slack on the bench, without the energy to get back to the hospital. I jogged to the reception desk, collected a wheelchair, and helped him into it. The shadows of the forest fell closer across the lawn.

He didn't speak again until we were in his room. He manoeuvred from the chair, and I wheeled it out to the corridor, so that he wouldn't have to look at it in the night. 'Will you come again?' he asked.

'I can stay nearby,' I said. 'I can come tomorrow.'

I didn't know how to talk about the house on Moor Woods Road. It seemed impossible to ask anything of him when he was sitting on the bed, trying to take off his shoes.

'Has Delilah told you about the inheritance?' I asked.

'She mentioned it. She said that there's the house, and a little money.'

He lay down, and groped for his blankets.

'She told me about your idea,' he said. 'About the community centre.'

'And what do you think?'

'I need some time,' he said. 'Some time to consider my options.'

I paused, caught between the bed and the door. Gabriel, who had always been compliant.

'The visitor,' I said, 'earlier today. Is this something to do with him?'

At the bed, I took his hand. I wanted to comfort him, I decided, but I also wanted him to stay awake.

'Was that Oliver?' I said. And: 'Gabe – what did he do to you?'

He lay on his back, with his hands twitching on the blankets. Asleep, or ignoring me.

I sat on the lawn and rearranged the weekend. There were bed and breakfasts across the county: all of them were named after vegetation, and occupied. I found a spare room in a hamlet with nothing but a church and a pub, and drove there across the hot afternoon. Mum and Dad had intended to visit London on Sunday; they would have to wait. *Harder than I expected*, I said, by text. Another day at the asylum.

My host led me to a room attached to her family house, and presented a plate of biscuits and a handwritten Wi-Fi code. I was to use it responsibly. 'Thank you,' I said. 'This is perfect.' I thought of the Romilly Townhouse. The comfort that was to be found in its clean, vast spaces, and doormen appointed for discretion. 'I'll be outside with the little ones,' she said, 'and you're welcome to join us.' We each smiled, politely, quite sure that I wouldn't.

I opened my laptop. The desk looked onto a bright, brilliant garden. Sunlight darted through oak trees and flitted across the grass. I ate the biscuits and worked, and watched my host playing with her children. She was an actress: a dinosaur and then a princess, and now a bridge, under which they scrambled. The garden was strewn with discarded props. Delilah had been right, in one respect. I was such a serious child. Even my games had required absolute commitment. I tried to imagine joining the children around the flower beds, accepting the roles I was assigned. It seemed inconceivable. They would see through me and cut me from the cast.

Some things were for the best.

I watched for a little longer, then I closed my laptop, and walked to the pub.

That night, muddled from an afternoon of wine and in the strange, warm room, I dreamt of one of Robert Wyndham's parties. Long white tables adorned the lawn. Everybody was there: Delilah, Gabriel, Evie, Ethan and Ana. Everybody was well. I sat next to JP, who was telling some great anecdote, and I leaned into him.

The party was raucous; I was struggling to follow his narrative. Glasses chinked, and the table behind us shrieked with laughter. I hushed them, wanting to hear the story, but it was impossible to concentrate on it, and after a time I stopped trying. Opposite me, Evie was grinning and bored. She slipped from the table and across the garden, to where the lawn met the forest. I stood, too. By the time I had left the table, she was already turning to the woods. I called to her, but she didn't hear me, and in time she dimmed between the trees.

We moved to Hollowfield and to Moor Woods Road when I was ten, and in Miss Glade's class. Gabriel needed a bed; Ethan had started to lobby for his own room; Father had lost interest in the Gatehouse and had found a site to establish his own congregation. He would call it the Lifehouse. Whenever he talked about it, he built the pulpit with his fists, and etched the aisle with his fingers.

Delilah and I were the only ones to protest. 'I have friends,' Delilah said. 'Don't make me leave my friends, Papa.'

'Can't we at least wait until summer?' I asked. 'When school's over?'

Of all of the teachers at Jasper Street, I liked Miss Glade the most. She didn't encourage me to read in class, and she didn't praise me in public. Early on in the year, in October, she asked me to pop to the staffroom at lunch, and said that she had been impressed with my weekly book reports. Would I like to be assigned some extra reading – under the radar, no pressure, et cetera – just in case I was getting bored? On Friday lunchtimes, we sat in the windowless meeting room next to the school office and discussed whatever she had recommended. Miss Glade usually produced some kind of snack and asked that I helped her to eat it as we talked: a whole platter of fruit, for example, or a tray of flapjacks which she had baked. It always looked like far too much for one person, and I wondered how she had ever expected to finish it on her own.

The trouble came when Miss Glade spoke to Mother. Mother was collecting Delilah and Evie, standing in the playground with Gabriel and book bags and her jaundiced white dress, and Miss Glade asked if she could spare a moment. The others came in, too, and Gabriel roamed between the chairs and tables. He lifted crayons from their pots and took books from the shelves, giggling. He had a sharp, puckish face and a gappy smile. He would take items from strangers' supermarket trolleys and they would laugh, and forgive him.

'Isn't he lovely,' Miss Glade said. Mother nodded, shifting from foot to foot.

'It really does need to be a minute,' she said. 'We have to get back.'

'It's good news,' Miss Glade said, 'so it won't take long. I just wanted to comment on how well Alexandra's doing this year. Really top work, across the board. English, maths, science – the first tasters of some of the other subjects, too. It's been an excellent year, so far.'

Delilah rolled her eyes. Evie shot me a smile. Mother nodded away the praise, expectant, waiting for the great reveal.

'My recommendation,' Miss Glade said, 'is that you and Mr Gracie explore the idea of scholarships to some of the better secondary schools in the area. It's still a year and a half off, I know, but it never hurts to start thinking. A lot of these scholarships are dependent on family finances – and obviously I can't comment on that – but I can put together a prospective list, or talk you and your husband through some of the options. Whatever works.'

'Right,' Mother said. She looked at me, as though there was something I knew and was refusing to disclose. 'You're talking about Alexandra?' she said, to Miss Glade.

'That's right.'

'OK. Well. Thank you.'

'Should we put in an appointment,' Miss Glade asked, 'at a more convenient time?'

'I don't know if that's going to be possible,' Mother said. 'We're relocating in the next few months. Up to Hollowfield.'

'Oh,' Miss Glade said. 'I wasn't aware of that.'

She, too, looked at me.

'If it helps,' she said, 'some of the options would still be—'

Gabriel had spun the globe on Miss Glade's desk so fast that the Earth crashed onto the classroom floor. He froze, a cartoon culprit, and when the adults approached him, he cowered.

'It's no bother,' Miss Glade said, but Mother had already crossed the room. She rapped Gabriel on the hand and gathered him in her arms.

'See,' she said. 'It really isn't a good time.'

We walked home together. It was early December, but some of the houses had decorations up. Delilah and Evie ran ahead, pointing out their favourite Christmas trees. My breath muddled with Mother's in the air. 'As you know,' she said, 'I didn't go to the grammar school. And things worked out fine in the end.' I looked at the brown tape on the pram, and Mother's hair beneath the streetlamps, a brittle white and wrenched back from her face. Less of the light landing in it, now.

'I wouldn't mention this to your father, if I were you,' Mother said. 'He has other plans. Much grander plans, Alexandra.'

'But it wouldn't cost anything,' I said. 'To try.'

Delilah and Evie had stopped outside the biggest home on the street. In the window, there was an ornate doll's house, and in that house it was Christmas Day. Miniature children raced to the presents beneath the tree. The father reclined in his armchair. I looked for the mother in the bedrooms and in the kitchen, but that miniature was missing.

'It's beautiful,' Evie said. 'Isn't it?'

'Come on,' Mother said. She was beyond us, drumming her fist on the handle of the pram. I caught up with her before she could move on, so that she had no choice but to look at me.

'At least let me try,' I said.

She glanced away, as if she was embarrassed for me. She was smiling, just a little, and I suspected then that this had nothing to do with Father.

'I said no,' she said. 'Didn't I.'

Miss Glade didn't give up, although she abandoned the idea of enlisting Mother for support. Our Friday meetings became more fervent. You have to consider how other people may interpret this, she said. Don't just say that you like it – that isn't enough – tell me why. Her recommendations became more diverse: she brought in books about history; religions; the Romans and the ancient Greeks. In an hour we could unravel the string through the Labyrinth; slide through the hippocampus; scour coral for a male seahorse with eggs in its pouch. 'How long do we have?' she would ask me, when we came back to the little cupboard room. I narrated the time from the clock above her head, although she never seemed particularly interested in my response. I don't think that's what she was asking me at all.

'Alexandra,' Father said. 'You have a guest.'

He was standing at the bottom of the stairs. I had crossed the landing to clean my teeth, with *Fantastic Mr Fox* in my hand. My ritual was to stick the brush in my mouth and read three pages, whatever the book.

'What?' I said. 'Who?'

'Why don't you come and see?'

He swept an arm towards the living room, like a showman presenting a new, exotic act. I left my book on the side of the sink and padded down to him, into the downstairs lights and the smell of just-eaten casserole.

Miss Glade stood in the centre of the room, wearing a bobble hat and a duffle coat, impossibly clean. It was the first time I realized that she must exist outside of school. She had evenings, and a bed, and things that she thought about when she got into it. She was shorter than she was in the classroom, but Father did that: he shrank people. I folded my arms over my pyjama top, which was threadbare, thin enough that you could see my nipples through the material.

'Lex doesn't need to be here,' Miss Glade said. 'I came to talk with you.'

'Oh, we're a very open family.'

She was trying to look between us, but her eyes drifted to the corners of the room and the garbage bags there, the spill of old clothes and shoes and a few exhausted soft toys. Mother's blankets were piled on the sofa, stiff with dirt.

'Hello, Lex,' she said.

'Hi,' I said. And then, not trusting this version of her, the night-time version which didn't want to talk to me: 'What are you doing here?'

She looked at Father, who was already smiling.

'You remember the scholarship,' Miss Glade said.

'Yes.'

'I wanted to talk to your dad about that – and a few other bits and pieces. Nothing very important. Certainly nothing for you to worry about.'

Father spread down on the sofa, and gestured to the spare cushion. Miss Glade sat right at the edge of it, as if she didn't want our house against her skin. When she was there, she wrung her hands, still purple-white from the cold.

'If you don't want her to hear,' Father said, 'that's fine with me.'

Miss Glade looked at me with something sad and resigned in

her face. Something like a message, with the knowledge that I wouldn't be able to read it. 'I'm sorry, Lex,' she said. 'But I need to talk to your father in private.'

'OK, then.'

'OK. I'll see you tomorrow, Lex.'

Evie was already asleep. I lay on top of the covers with the light on, keeping guard, trying not to fall asleep. Miss Glade was one of the cleverest people I knew, I thought, but also one of the stupidest. She looked at me as if she was frightened for me, while she sat down there with Father, and wasn't even frightened for herself.

I never did find out what Miss Glade and Father discussed, but we left for Hollowfield a week later. I arrived home from school to find the family in the kitchen, Father standing with his palms flat on the table and Mother at his side. 'We've got a house,' he said. 'A house of our own.'

A little earthquake passed across Delilah's face. It started with tremors at her lips and at the corners of her eyes. 'I hate you,' she said, and her features crumpled.

'Already?' I said.

'It's become necessary,' Father said. 'All hands on deck.'

There were times when the exercise of packing seemed to be an autopsy of the house and the childhood we had spent there. Here, beneath my parents' bed, were the blankets on which Mother had given birth to Ethan. Here was a book about the American Frontier, never returned to the library. Here were unwashed liquor bottles, housing families of thin black flies. When we lifted the furniture from its cavities, we uncovered the house's worst ailments. The carpet beneath my bed was soft and matted, and tumours of mould had grown up to the mattress. There were putrid sleepsuits underneath the cot, each worn by any one of us, and never washed. The walls in Mother and Father's room were punctured, and when we held our fingers to the wounds we could feel the air outside, leaking into the house.

At the bottom of Mother's wardrobe, I found a notebook, sun-crinkled and close to disintegrating. I opened it in the middle. The handwriting was cumbersome – the writing of a child – but I didn't recognize it. *Dispatch 17*, it said. *I visit Mrs Brompton's cottage on a Saturday afternoon. She is in her garden, and in the mood for talking.* I smiled. Dispatches from Deborah. Mother's contacts from the world of journalism were recorded on the back page. They would be retired by now, I thought. Some of them would probably be dead. Had she ever called them? It seemed unlikely. The book had been forgotten, rather than hidden. I added it to the rubbish pile.

On my final day at Jasper Street, I embraced Amy and Jessica and Caroline. 'We'll miss you *so much*,' they said, and scrubbed at dry eyes. (I provided them with an excellent anecdote for future therapy – a tale of guilt, naivety, and horror – and when each new source close to the family stepped forward, years later, I would wonder if it was one of them.) Miss Glade produced a cake for the class to share – iced with an open book and *Good Luck, Lex!* – and when I cut into it, each of the layers was a different colour. I thought of Miss Glade in the kitchen of a small, warm house, wearing oven gloves and pyjamas, and I allowed myself a moment to reside there, with the smell of baking and a lifetime of Friday lunches. I hadn't quite forgiven her for the surprise visit to my house, but after the cake, I decided that I should try.

At the end of the day, she helped me to empty my desk into a plastic bag. I took all of the exercise books that I could carry, and slung my satchel over my shoulder. 'One more thing,' she said, at the classroom door, and handed me a present wrapped in newspaper.

'Should I open it now?' I asked, and she laughed.

'Lex, you open it whenever you want.'

I picked at the Sellotape and folded back the paper. Inside, there was a new, hardback book of illustrated Greek myths.

'Those are your favourites,' she said. 'Aren't they?'

I didn't know what to say. I nodded, and opened the book in the middle. There was a picture of the Underworld, and Charon ferrying Persephone down the Styx. She gazed back at the reader from the dark watercolours.

'Thank you,' I said. I made as much space in the bag as I could, and eased the book inside.

Miss Glade nodded, then reached down and hugged me, quickly and hard. When she let go, she looked surprised, as though she hadn't intended to do that.

'You look after yourself,' she said. 'OK?'

'OK.'

'Off you go. Your mother will be waiting.'

I set off down the school corridor, past the bright displays and the class photographs; past handwritten narratives of field trips and families and What I Did On My Summer Holidays. At the end, just before the door to the playground, I turned around. Miss Glade was still standing by the classroom door, her arms embracing her own body, watching me. I waved, and she waved back.

Hollowfield was stuck at the base of three tors, and hardly a town. The plughole of the moors. The welcome sign provided that it had a twin town, Lienz, in Austria, which I wondered about each time we drove past. How had the arrangement come about? Had anybody from Lienz actually visited us, to understand what they were welcoming to the family?

We moved house on a Saturday, in a van owned by one of Jolly's acquaintances. Mother was unwell, so Father, Ethan and I carried our belongings to the car. 'Do a last check,' Father said, before he would allow us inside, and Ethan and I walked from one vacant room to another, talking little. We had left only our rubbish, and dirt. The landlord recouped the cleaning fees five years later, when he sold photographs of the end of our tenancy to the press. The sad, stained spaces. As with most empty rooms at low resolution, it was easy to imagine that something terrible had happened in them.

We drove to Hollowfield through the gloaming. Clouds sagged over the hills. We passed the old factories, with their spindly chimneys and every other window kicked in. There was a functional high street with a second-hand bookshop, and a cafe just closing. Grey men stood at the door of the pub, their collars turned up.

'Is our house close?' Evie asked.

'Five minutes,' Father said. 'Maybe ten.'

He pointed out the site where he would build the new church. It was a dilapidated clothes shop with mannequins still sprawled in the window, but the footfall would be good, and he could always resurrect the dolls as statues – as part of his performance. We were driving out of the town, now, and we turned over the river, past a rotted water mill and a garage, and onto Moor Woods Road. The first few properties were cottages, neatly kept and gathered together, but as the road climbed, the houses dispersed and mutated. There was a dark barn, and a bungalow with a guard of rusted machinery. Evie opened the window of the van, counting down the numbers. 'The next one!' she shouted.

Number 11 was set back from the road. It had a grubby beige

front and a garage, and a garden at the back. It was – as they would later say – a very ordinary house.

Father had purchased the house on Moor Woods Road from an old member of Jolly's congregation. She could no longer manage the garden, or make it up the stairs without a break in the middle. Jolly had led negotiations. It was a house for a family, he said, and she had been happy for us to have it.

Her furniture still occupied the house. Under covers, chairs and tables and beds took strange, monstrous shapes. We tailed Father from room to room, guessing before he unveiled them. A boat, a body. A walrus. Before our first dinner at Moor Woods Road, Father arranged one of the furniture sheets over his head, and staggered into the kitchen, wailing. He said grace with a broad smile and his hand on Mother's thigh, and the sheet still hanging from his shoulders.

After dinner, Evie and I unpacked. In the moving boxes, our belongings had melded with everybody else's. There was a series of stern, ill-fitting outfits which we had both suffered, and we took it in turns to model them for one another. We traded T-shirts with Gabriel and Delilah, hurling them across the hallway. I had wrapped the book of Greek myths inside a jumper, partly to keep it away from Father – there were stories of the pagan gods, which was basically blasphemy – and partly to keep it away from Delilah, who would find some way to destroy it, or to make it hers. Once the house was quiet, I slipped the bundle to Ethan's room.

Ethan had his own space, but not enough belongings to fill it. Tired items had been given odd prominence. There was a crowd of plastic disciples on the windowsill. He had hung a poster of the human skeleton, dispensed in Year 6 science, on his wall. Father had already requisitioned a corner of the floor for his sermon notes. 'I think he hopes that I'll read them,' Ethan said, and nudged them away with his toe.

'Let me show you something really cool,' I said, and unwrapped the book. 'Miss Glade got it for me,' I said, 'but we can read it together.'

Ethan touched the cover, but didn't turn it.

'It's a children's book,' he said. 'Why would I want to read that?'

I peered at him, waiting for his face to crack. He looked blankly back at me.

'You like those stories,' I said. 'I only know them because of you.'

'And what good have they ever done for me? I'd throw it out, Lex, if I was you.'

Evie was more impressed. We would need to wait for another month before an additional bed arrived, and so that night, the first in our room together, we lay side by side on a stranger's mattress and held the book between us. I started at the rhythms of the house: water hammering through the walls; the creaking trees at the back of the garden. The floorboards seesawed beneath new, buoyant weight. 'In the beginning,' I read, 'there was nothing.'

I expected that things might be different in Hollowfield. I had mistaken the fact that nobody yet knew us for the hope that we could be whomever we wanted to be.

Jolly was often in the house, unannounced, wielding a tool, or eating with Father at the kitchen table. The conversations started clandestine; they exchanged glances when we wandered into the room. But in the evenings, voices rose to our bedroom. They used words like opportunity and beginning. Mother played the hostess, bearing delicate plates and topping up the men's glasses, and picking pastry from beneath her nails. There were some nights when I heard a third voice at the table: softer, less certain. Ethan had started to greet Jolly with a firm handshake, and call him 'Sir'.

Ethan joined in the tricks which Father and Jolly played on Gabriel, too. They enlisted him to assist them with fictional tasks or secret missions, each of which ended in his confusion. 'Hold this nail,' Jolly said, halfway up the stairs. 'Don't drop it – that's keeping your house standing.' And an hour later Gabriel was still there, clutching the nail determinedly in his fist. In the winter, Ethan sent him into the garden, to search for treasure buried by the last proprietor. He, Father and Jolly gathered in a coven at the kitchen window. 'Look, Lex,' Ethan said, and beckoned to me. I ignored him. At dusk, Gabriel returned bone-white and dejected, mud in the cracks on his palms. When they laughed, he laughed too. He laughed like he had been in on it, all along.

When I could avoid Jolly and Father, I did so. I still left for school early, in time to wash, and I took my time packing up my desk at the end of the day. I collected Delilah and Evie and Gabriel, and we ambled home together, stopping at the bookshop and at the watermill, and at the two mangy horses at the bottom of Moor Woods Road, who surveyed us with great suspicion. Mother didn't come down to the new school; she and Father had been talking of a new child, and she was conserving her energy.

And the days at school weren't so bad. The most surprising consequence of our move to Hollowfield was that I made a friend – a real one – who had arrived in Hollowfield a few months before, with braces and a southern accent, and who was almost as awkward as I was. Cara liked books and talking about them, and played the violin in assembly, standing timid and nervy at the front of the room right until she picked up the instrument. She played with a sway, which the other children mocked, and when she finished she had the expression of somebody who had just woken up. Cara never tittered when I was speaking, and there was nobody with whom she could share a side-glance. She didn't seem to mind that I was quiet in the classroom, only responding to the teacher's direct questions. All the same, I was careful about what I said to her. My parents worked away, I said, and when I described our house on Moor Woods Road, I was vague.

'I know it!' she said. 'The one near the bottom, with the horses?'

I nodded noncommittally. Cara sighed. 'I'm terrified of horses,' she said, and I smiled.

I was faring better in Hollowfield than Delilah, who didn't comprehend why she was no longer one of the most popular girls in her class, and better still than Gabriel. News had reached me from the younger classes that Gabriel was stupid, and easy to fool. The early years learned to read by narrating tins of words, and the majority of Gabriel's class was on Tin 6, which included DOLPHIN and PENGUIN. Gabriel was stuck with CAT and DOG, in the dull domesticity of Tin 2. When it was time for him to read, he held the paper a few inches from his eyes: there were opportunities to be gleaned from that. You could poke him from a distance, like a bull in the ring, and he might not be able to identify you. You could write something about him on a worksheet, and he wouldn't be able to read it, even if you waved it in his face.

'I don't get it,' Cara said, surveying him across the playground. He hovered beside one of the dinner ladies, as if he was anticipating an attack. 'You're pretty much the smartest girl in the school.'

That, I concluded, was why I couldn't interfere. In Hollowfield Primary School, I had crafted a precarious rung on the social ladder, tempered with a companion, and the begrudging respect of my classmates. In the evenings, I read to Evie or listened to Ethan, and at the weekends, we assembled in the Lifehouse, to sand the pews, or paint the walls, or pray for success. There was only ever enough time to make myself normal. This reassured me when I saw Gabriel alone at lunchtime, or sitting in the kitchen with that same tin of words, tracing the letters with his finger. Alone in the night, in a stranger's bedroom, it didn't reassure me at all.

Late in spring term, Evie and I waited on the school grass for Delilah and Gabriel. Going-home time had long passed; the last few parents were dispersing, holding school rucksacks and tiny hands.

'Maybe they've gone,' I said.

'Why?' Evie said. 'They always wait.'

'So – do we go and look for them?'

She was spreadeagled in the grass, squinting into the sunshine. 'You're closer.'

'You're younger.'

She threw a handful of grass in my direction. 'You're grumpier.'

She glanced away from me, then, over my shoulder, and straightened her face. 'Lexy,' she said.

The headmistress was coming across the playground. She stopped at the edge of the grass, stranded by her heels, and beckoned us.

'There's been a serious incident,' she said.

The incident was this: the night before, Delilah had packed Father's Authorised Hardback Holy Bible with Cross-References and Notes in her school rucksack. During afternoon playtime, she had retrieved the tome from her peg in the cloakroom and approached the cruellest of Gabriel's tormentors. 'Read this,' she said, and brought the book down across the boy's face. A corner had ruptured the globe of his eye. Teeth were loose. Father was on his way.

We waited for him on the chairs outside the headmistress's office, which were usually populated by the very worst children in school. Gabriel's hands were clutched in prayer, a gunge-nosed supplicant. Delilah sat with her chin up and shoulders back, the way Father liked us. 'What did you *do*?' I said, as soon as the headmistress had closed the door, and she snapped to face me.

'Drive out the mocker, and out goes strife,' she said. I wondered if she had shared this with the headmistress, too.

You heard Father before you saw him. His footsteps were heavy and unhurried, and each brought him closer than you expected from the last. When he arrived at the threshold, Delilah stood to meet him, offering herself for whatever punishment he might have derived on the drive. He would take his time with that, too. He stepped around her and handed me the keys, and rapped on the office door.

'Get out,' he said.

We walked in quiet procession to the van, and sat inside in silence. A few minutes later, the school door opened. Father picked his way across the playground, past the climbing frame and the little children's benches. He closed the door behind him and took the wheel, but he didn't start the engine.

'Next time,' he said. 'Leave the vengeance for God.'

With that, he started to laugh. He roared with it. He slapped the wheel, and the whole car quivered. Delilah smiled, first tentative and then wider. She had been suspended for a week, and she was to write a formal letter of apology, but at home she paraded around the house like a small, triumphant angel of justice. Raguel in miniature. In her days off, she was allowed to varnish the cross for the Lifehouse, while Father stood over her, telling Jolly the story.

The children woke me, bursting into the garden, and I was at the hospital early. Gabriel was at breakfast, no visitors permitted, so I waited in the chair at his window. His room looked out to the car park and was entirely absent of decoration. Little acts of preservation dulled the place. Every corner was rounded, and the furniture was bolted to the floor. A little band of children passed under the window, escorted by nurses. One of the girls was holding a bear in one hand and pushing an IV trolley with the other.

'There's a children's ward,' Gabriel said. He left the door open and settled himself on the bed. 'This was the place for us,' he said, 'right from the beginning. That way, we might have stood a chance.'

'We weren't crazy,' I said.

'Oh, come on, Lex. How could we have been anything else?'

'Is Oliver coming today?' I said.

'I don't know. Why?'

'Does he come every day?'

'He needs me. You don't understand, Lex.'

'So, OK. I don't. Explain it to me.'

So began the happiest years of Gabriel's life. Even now – even knowing how they would end – he was grateful for them. Oliver introduced Gabriel to his friends, a ragtag troupe of outcasts, who lived across the city in dark flats and industrial communes. Blake owned a photo studio in Soho. Kris was the girl who had been crying in Oliver's waiting room when Gabriel first travelled to London. 'God,' she said, when they were reintroduced, 'that was a terrible day.' Pippa had been on *Big Brother*, 'Season six,' she said, which meant little to Gabriel. Many of them had worked with Oliver in the past, Gabriel noted, but none of them did so now.

They collided on nights which fast became their own folklore. There was the time when they ended up in Blake's studio in the early morning, prancing for his camera in outfits prepared for a leather magazine shoot later that day. There was the time when Gabriel careened into Delilah as the clubs were throwing them out, stone-cold sober and handing out water bottles, of all things. He had faint memories of trying to discuss with her what had happened to them – all of his memories from this time were faint – but each time he did she would hold a finger to his lips and shush him: 'Let's not talk about that right now,' she said, and left her number in his phone. There was the time when, still awake at Sunday lunchtime, they drove up the M40 in Oliver's Audi and raided Ethan's house. Sighting Gabriel outside – Ethan's television in his arms and his hair Gracie-white in the summer sunshine – a neighbour waved, and Gabriel nodded back. Each of them offered their unique perspective on this moment on the way home, bawling with laughter.

('Is it still stealing,' asked Gabriel, 'if you steal from a psychopath?' 'Yes,' I said.)

The diversification was not what he had expected. Oliver had explained it to him the first time that he had visited Gabriel's flat. At that time, he had only a mattress, a toaster, a television and an armchair, and they made love on the floor by the doorway; he hadn't been able to wait. 'I've been working on it,' Oliver said, 'and some of it won't be easy.' One of his hands was in Gabriel's hair, and the other traced the lines from his hips to his groin, down and up and back down. 'Some of it may be undignified,' he said.

Gabriel, wanting to please him, smiled. 'Dignity's overrated,' he said.

It would only be temporary, Oliver promised. 'And then,' he said, 'your career really can take off.'

No. The work was not what he had expected.

Most of it involved waiting. He drove small, silent girls to hotel addresses, then waited for them to re-emerge. He was abandoned in houses devoid of furniture to wait for a courier to drop something off. In a haggard flat in Croydon he delivered a rucksack to a man with the look of a shaved cat, who invited him in and locked the door. 'I'd like you to dance for me,' the man said.

'Excuse me?'

'Just a little dance. And then you can go.'

A second man appeared, then, smiling at the first. Gabriel understood from the smile that they knew one another well. There was something about the second man that frightened Gabriel more than the first, an authority in the way he moved through the room. He checked the rucksack, took a beer from the fridge, and lay down on the sofa.

'Is this the errand boy?' he said. 'Oliver's?'

'Yes. He's going to dance for us.'

The second man started to laugh. 'Our friend Oliver,' he said. 'You tell him that we're looking forward to catching up.'

Gabriel fled from the room and flipped the lock, the laughter at his back. He crashed down a dim hallway and out into the evening. When he finally phoned Oliver, back in his flat with his hands still shaking, Oliver apologized, and said that those guys could be difficult. No, he shouldn't have to see them again. On the phone, Oliver was rasping and vague, as if he was just waking up, and Gabriel sensed then that something was waking in him, too, something which he had supposed was gone, but had only ever been sleeping.

And so it couldn't last.

Gabriel had heard rumours of Oliver's financial predicaments. Oliver often asked Gabriel if the Coulson-Brownes were good for a few thousand more: 'Make them guilty as hell,' he said, although Gabriel had known better than to try. Once, when lamenting the state of his Camden flat to Pippa and Kris – the creep of mould behind his bed frame, and the traffic noises outside, and the lonely stream of water which constituted the shower, which meant that you could only ever wash one limb at a time – he expressed his envy for Oliver's flat on the Thames, and the women glanced at each other, eyebrows raised.

'For all I know,' Pippa said, 'Oliver is flat-out broke. It's all on finance.'

'Count your wages with care,' Kris said. 'Seriously, Gabe.'

All the same, Gabriel was surprised when Oliver arrived at his doorstep at seven o'clock one morning, rolling two TUMI suitcases and smiling broadly.

'Would it be too much,' Oliver said, 'for me to crash here, just for a little while?'

'Of course not,' Gabriel said, and hopped from the threshold and into Oliver's arms.

'Fucking landlords,' Oliver said, crushing Gabriel more tightly than he had expected. They retreated back to bed, and a month later, with Oliver's suits in the wardrobe and his toiletries expanding across the windowsill, Gabriel came to the happy conclusion that Oliver didn't intend for the little while to end any time soon.

It was a difficult spell for Oliver's business. 'It's social media,' Oliver said. 'People think that they can do it all themselves.' He had relinquished his office in Aldgate, and worked on a laptop in the corner of Gabriel's flat. Whenever Gabriel walked past, Oliver appeared to be on YouPorn or Mr Porter, which could, Gabriel appreciated, constitute research. Besides, Oliver's difficulties bestowed Gabriel's role in their relationship with a new importance. He was no longer the tag-along, indebted to Oliver for his contacts and charisma. He could support Oliver as Oliver had once supported him.

And Gabriel could admit it: Oliver needed a lot of support.

Oliver, it transpired, was addicted to alcohol and cocaine, and Gabriel was addicted primarily to Oliver; then, as an inevitable accompaniment, to Oliver's own addictions, at first for Oliver's approval, and later – as tended to be the case – because he couldn't stop doing them.

The days were so long. He woke at eleven a.m., nauseous, and before he opened his eyes he sensed the impending dread of nothing to do until eight. On bad mornings, once he was upright, a plume of blood fell from his nostrils and onto his lap. He and Oliver would greet the day with a few Screwdrivers – 'Like they do in New York,' Oliver said – and amble to the pubs on the canal for lunchtime, or else walk down to Regent's Park and collect a few bottles of wine on their way. Oliver bought cocaine from an old acquaintance in Barnsbury, and when they felt that it was necessary – that it was the only thing that would do the trick – they would meander along the water and up to the estate, shielding their eyes from the glass towers and the wide, bright spaces at King's Cross. They would wake back in the flat, or in their favourite spot beside the allotment garden, and evening would be upon them. Gabriel didn't mind this in the summertime, when it was still light outside, but in the winter he was startled by the darkness and his own obliviousness to the time. He missed a number of jobs this way, and he knew that those clients would never work with him and Oliver again.

In the flat, there was always noise, bearing down on the walls. At any time, there was shouting in the street, sirens, the noise of heels on the pavement. Buses heaved towards the City. Gabriel could see the faces of the passengers on the top deck when they passed, features mutated by graffiti or steam. When he was hungover he sat on the arm of the sofa and watched them, calculating the hours left in the dwindling day. Waiting for it to end.

The worst thing was that the Rages returned. The first time was in the flat: the doorbell rang while they were sleeping, and a courier greeted Gabriel on the doorstep. 'Mr Alvin?' he asked. He was carrying a great selection of parcels – Gabriel had to make two trips up the stairs – which Gabriel and Oliver opened together. They were full of beautiful clothes, printed scarves and soft white shirts and a selection of silk ties, and as Oliver unwrapped a leather jacket, he began to laugh. 'I remember, I think,' he said, 'ordering these when I was fucked.'

Gabriel couldn't breathe.

'I thought – what else might my sober self need – but presents?'

The Rage seized Gabriel so quickly that he had no time to remember how to subdue it. All he could recall was that he was on the floor, his skull bucking against the carpet, watching Oliver's face above him. Humour had contorted into panic, and Gabriel felt a strange satisfaction spread beneath his fury, which lasted long after the Rage had passed. The parcels were returned.

Gabriel couldn't afford to pay the rent and to pay for his and Oliver's habits, and so he defaulted. There came a point when Oliver had sold his watch; his suits; half-bottles of cologne. Even the white goods from the flat had gone, which hadn't belonged to them in the first place. The only items of value left were the artefacts from Moor Woods Road.

Gabriel liked to think that he had resisted Oliver's suggestion to sell them for many weeks, but it was unlikely to be the case: alcohol made him pliant, easy to twist into this shape or that, and he was drunk all of the fucking time. Oliver had already created an account on a website which specialised in true crime memorabilia. They used a computer in the local library to offer out the items – Oliver's laptop had been sold, too – and worked on the wording together.

UNIQUE items from the REAL House of Horrors:
Your own piece of memorabilia from the Gracie House of Horrors.
Choose from:

- *Blanket owned by Gabriel Gracie (as seen in <u>this</u> photograph by Isaac Brachmann, nominated for several major awards)*
- *Diary of Gabriel Gracie (recordings from age 7–8) – approx. 20 pages*
- *Letter from Delilah Gracie to Gabriel Gracie WHEN CAPTIVE, 2 pages*
- *Never-seen-before family photographs x5*
- *Family Bible owned by Charles and Deborah Gracie*

Verification of goods available if required. Discounts negotiable for full set.

They slept together, their ankles entwined, and in the morning, when Oliver could move, they walked back to the library to check on the bids.

'Jesus Christ,' Oliver said, and flung his arms around Gabriel's shoulders.

There were some substantial bids for the individual items – a few hundred pounds for the diary, for example – but an anonymous bidder had offered two and a half thousand pounds for the full set. 'I've followed your story with great interest,' Oliver read, from the accompanying note, 'and think of you often.' He snorted, still gleeful. 'It sounds like you still have your fans.'

By the time bidding closed, six days later, the items had sold to the same bidder for just over three thousand pounds. Oliver went from the library to his dealer, and Gabriel returned to the flat with a range of envelopes, and unlocked the drawer of his bedside table. This was where he stored the little collection of items, close to where he slept and away from Oliver's sight. Now they would be preserved in a different house, one that he wasn't able to picture. He read his own laboured account of the days at Moor Woods Road, letters tumbling from their lines and landing, one on top of the other, at the bottom of the page. *Not a happy day*, he had written, and *Delilah is very pretty*, and *Lots of running today*. He had never been particularly eloquent, then or now; nobody had taught him, the way that his siblings had taught one another. He found that he was crying, and he tucked the diary into an envelope. Water damage might knock a few hundred off. It was time for the celebration.

That night he was as drunk as he had ever been. He bought a half-litre of vodka on the way to meet Oliver, and by the time he reached the pub he was smiling and soft. He couldn't see Oliver at the bar, or at any of the tables, and he walked through to the garden. There was a moment – he had just walked down the steps, and below the line of the afternoon sun – when the whole night came into view before him. Here was Oliver, his arm around a woman Gabriel didn't know. Here were his eyes, already wild. Here was his smile. Gabriel knew that he would consume whatever fell onto the surfaces before him, and that thoughts of the envelopes on his bed – of anything, very much – would stop here.

He woke up many hours later, in a bedroom which he didn't recognize.

He fumbled for his glasses. The world before his right eye was cracked in three.

There was a fur blanket on the bed, matted with his sweat, and a cat sitting at the threshold. 'Hello,' he said, and the animal turned, and padded away.

His clothes were on the floor: that was something. It was daytime: that was something else. He followed the cat into an empty hallway. Three doors were closed, but one was parted, and led to a dirty little kitchen. There was a half-eaten birthday cake on the side, and a few dying flies at the window. He drank water from his hands and tried to recall the evening. His mind usually teased him with disembodied memories, which would come into view days – sometimes weeks – later. An impromptu disclosure to a stranger, perhaps, about what his father had done to him, or a demonstration of generosity by Oliver at the bar which ended with his card declined, and Gabriel, feeling sorry for him, stepping in to pay. Today, though – nothing. He heard a shuffle behind one of the closed doors, and felt an urgent, nauseous terror. He hurried to the only door with a latch, and staggered down a dark stairwell and into the street.

He had a long shadow. It was probably the afternoon. There were Victorian houses – net curtains and chipped white fronts – and nobody around. The street signs said SW2. He didn't have his wallet or his phone, but his keys were still jammed into his pocket, and he held them like a charm and began the long walk home.

He walked for nearly three hours, staving off tears and with his tongue dry and swelling in his throat. When he reached the flat in the hot summer dusk he started to cry and then to choke. He crouched against the door, his face turned away from the revellers making their way down to Camden, and tried to think of something to say to Oliver, who might be in any number of moods: furious, because Gabriel had been an embarrassment for the evening; nonchalant, because he was still in his dressing gown, coming to; or, as Gabriel had been picturing it over Lambeth Bridge and all the way up through Westminster, frightened, and quickly relieved: he took Gabriel into his arms and they napped together until it was time to go out again.

But the flat was quiet.

There were only three rooms – the bedroom, the bathroom, and the living area with its two rusted hobs – so it wasn't difficult to see that Oliver wasn't there. Gone were his clothes from the bedroom rail, and the toiletries which the two of them had started to share, and the last few rations from the kitchen cupboards. Gone, too, were the envelopes which Gabriel had prepared the day before, packed with the items from Moor Woods Road. He felt the first pulse of panic and tried to subdue it. They would be here, somewhere. He looked for them beneath the bed; he opened the oven; he even pulled back the shower curtain and stared haplessly at the blackening bathtub. He was talking to himself, making the sounds that a mother might make to a sick child. On the sofa, he found a note, written on the back of a receipt from Tesco Express: *I'm sorry. I love you.*

When the Rage came, he didn't think about Mandy or the ocean mammals, or about his fucking tepee. He welcomed it like an old friend, the last one remaining, and he set about the absolute destruction of everything that he could reach. He tore up carpet and hammered his fists through plaster. He upended the bed, which they had slept in together. He smashed the solitary window to the street. When the flat was ruined, he took what Oliver had left in the kitchen – there were only scissors and a paring knife; the final insult, perhaps – and started on himself.

'And now,' I said, 'he's back.'

'He came to apologize, Lex. He was in a bad place, then.'

'But it's a strange coincidence.' I said. 'Isn't it? That he would turn up now – weeks after you were admitted – once he heard about Mother?'

He rolled his head away from me, across the pillow. 'You don't know him,' he said. 'You don't know anything.'

'It's been in the papers,' I said. 'Online. He could have seen it anywhere.'

'We could get better together. That's what he said. He's ready to try. And when we are – that money. That money could help us, Lex. We could get a place to stay. Somewhere quiet. Somewhere in the countryside, he said. Just the two of us.'

'This one, Gabe – I think you may have to do this one alone.'

I took the documents from my bag and left them on his bedside table, so he could see them when he woke up.

'I'll leave these here,' I said.

I waited.

I said: 'Think about it.'

Oliver: waiting against a car, wearing yesterday's clothes and the smile of somebody who was winning. He walked past me, making for the doors, and I thought of the train journey home; of the postponed burden of doing nothing. There was Delilah, thumping the Bible across the playground.

'Hey,' I said. 'Hey—'

He paused, and walked back to me. This close, his body was scrawny, diminished inside his clothes. There was sweat on his forehead and at the ends of his hair. He looked like a nocturnal thing, which could only stand the sunlight for so long.

'I'm Lex. Gabriel's sister.'

'I know who you are,' he said.

He gave a long, theatrical sigh.

'You all have that same look to you,' he said. 'Like some part of you's still starving.'

'How can you do this?' I said.

'Do what, now? Visit a troubled friend?'

He took a few steps away, back towards the hospital. 'You used him,' I said. 'But I can be more specific. Specifically: you defrauded him. You're defrauding him still.'

'Look,' Oliver said. 'If it hadn't been me – it would just have been somebody else. Gabriel – he always needs somebody.' He remembered something – the scene of some precise degradation – and chuckled. 'He's special like that.'

'He is special. He survived it. He very nearly escaped himself.'

There was a tremble to my voice. Fury, erupting as tears. Not here. On the train, maybe, in a swaying bathroom, with nobody to see it.

'Prison won't be so different,' I said. 'Do you think that you'll be special – when the time comes?'

I took his wrist. That's how it feels, I thought. Tighter to the flesh than you'd like it. And you – with your clean hands, and your nice teeth, and a propensity for smugness – wouldn't survive it.

'There's another interesting thing,' I said, 'about court proceedings. Even the small claims are on the public record. Even the ones that aren't successful. It's a good way to find people.'

He gave me a long grin, with a kind of pride to it.

'I can see how you got out,' he said. He nodded, agreeing with himself. 'You and me – we could have made some real money together.'

He rummaged in his inside pocket and conjured a scrap of paper. The card was warm, with worn corners, but I could make out his name, and the word Agent, in raised print. Then he was past me, and into the hospital. I waited on the tarmac, watching him walk away, and when I looked up to Gabriel's window, I saw the tired moon of his face, hanging there, watching too.

On the drive to the station, I wondered what would become of Gabriel, and then, as I often did, how his life would have turned out if Dr K had been assigned to take care of him – or any one of the others – rather than me. Her approach was different. She had acknowledged that from the beginning. She had become famous in her field over the years after our escape: she contributed to Supreme Court cases, and her TED Talk had nearly two million views. She mentioned me, of course, although only ever as Girl A. The lecture was titled 'The Truth, and How to Tell It'.

She had discharged me six years ago. July. I graduated from university the week before, with a First. My job at Devlin's firm was secure. The month had been dappled with sunlight and farewells, and now the rest of the summer sprawled out ahead of me. I would return home, to be with Mum and Dad, and to read in their garden, lying on the trampoline. I travelled to London in the late afternoon, begrudging the heat and the hassle of it; it felt like a final obstacle before weeks of freedom. Mine was the last appointment of the day.

Dr K's waiting room was at the bottom of a grand carpeted staircase, and she collected each patient in person. She still wore excellent shoes, and she always made an entrance. This time, she came down the stairs with a bottle of champagne in one hand and glasses in the other, and her arms open. I stood to meet her.

'Congratulations,' she said, holding me. 'Oh, Lex! Congratulations.'

Instead of ascending to her office, as we usually did, she led me through a fire door, and down the escape to a little paved garden in the shade of the building. We sat on discarded milk crates, and she popped the cork. 'I like to think,' she said, 'that this is where Karl worked at his painting.'

'Neutral territory,' I said. 'This is new.'

She asked about the graduation ceremony; about Christopher and Olivia; about my plans for the summer. Then, with her face turned away from me, up to the jumbled townhouses and the strips of sky between them, she smiled.

'I don't think that I need to see you any more, Lex,' she said.

'I'm sorry?'

'It's been nine years,' she said. 'More than nine years, actually, since that first day in the hospital. Do you remember it? I'm sorry. Of course you do. But what you may not know is that I was nervous. Young, and nervous. I worried about every single thing that I said. You'll know what I mean, once you start work. Early on, one worries about every damn thing. And now – here we are. It's a kind of vindication, I think. For us both.'

'You never seemed nervous,' I said.

'Good.'

'Are you sure, though? That this is it?'

'Yes,' she said, 'I am. You've done it, Lex. You, and me, and the Jamesons. And I know that there were some terrible days, and things that were very hard to hear. Yet here we are. With the rest of your life waiting.'

She had already been drinking that afternoon. There was a mania to her joy which I hadn't seen before. In the autumn, when I started law school, I read that she had been appointed as a guest fellow at Harvard, and I wondered if this had been the day she found out. In that case, it wasn't just that she had served her purpose to me, but that I had served mine to her.

'It's up to you, of course,' she said. 'We can see each other for however long you would like. All I'm saying is that we no longer need to.'

'It seems like the right time,' I said. 'I guess.'

We talked into the darkness, even after the champagne was gone. I told her that Dad was considering retirement: 'But who will I call,' she said, 'when I'm losing all faith in humanity?' I told her that he had cried at graduation, straggling behind Mum as they walked across the lawn after the ceremony, using the spare few seconds to scrub his eyes. 'That,' she said, 'doesn't surprise me at all.'

I had a strange desire to give her a happy ending in every respect, so I told her, too, about the man whom I had met a fortnight earlier, at one of the university balls. It was four o'clock in the morning, and breakfast and the day's papers were served in the gardens. He was standing behind Olivia and me in the queue for bacon sandwiches, and as we approached, it became clear that they were running low. I tried to calculate if there would be enough left for me, but I was too drunk, and too tired. 'This'll be close,' he said.

The server handed me the final sandwich, and offered him a vegan patty.

'I don't suppose you feel like sharing,' he said. He had a long-broken nose and he ate like he was starving. He had opened his collar and lost his dinner jacket, and I could see the press of his shoulders against his shirt.

'Not really,' I said, and took a bite.

'It's terrible hospitality,' he said. 'I travelled from London for this.'

'To deign us with your presence?' I said, and regretted it right away. I understood that there was a difference between being playful and cruel, but I only ever recognized it once the words were said. He chewed a mouthful of his patty, still smiling, and shrugged.

'You don't sound like you're from London,' I said, to make amends.

'It's a recent thing. But be warned. When you leave this place, you have to become serious. I'd advise against it.'

'His name's Jean Paul,' I said, to Dr K. 'But he isn't French. Don't you think that's odd?'

'I think that his parents might be odd,' she said. 'Certainly.'

There were things that I didn't tell her. The following afternoon, after we had slept apart, I took him to the all-day breakfast cafe in town. That was our first in-joke: the bacon sandwich. That night, in my room, he asked if I was usually so bad at sharing. 'I'm sharing my bed,' I said, 'so perhaps you should be more careful.'

'Let me guess. You're an only child.'

I hadn't expected that. 'Yes,' I said, reminding myself that he was older than me, and already a barrister. I would probably never see him again, and the lie would neither need to be maintained nor corrected. He laughed.

'Me, too,' he said. 'And there's no way I would have shared it.'

Dr K took my disclosures as an offer; she felt that she owed me something in return. She leaned into me, close enough to see the pores and the lines beneath her foundation, and to smell a warm champagne burp which popped from her throat. I had never expected to encounter her this dishevelled, and I never did so again. 'Let me tell you a secret,' she said, 'about the night that you escaped. When something like that happens, the police put together a list. It's like a who's who of practitioners, I suppose. The best psychologists that they've worked with. And for something like Moor Woods Road, everybody wants to be on that list. They only needed a handful of us, of course, and I understand that I was the last one to be included. I'd worked with the DI a few times, and that's what he said: "You were the wild card". But by the time they started to call us – midnight, one o'clock – I was the only one to answer the phone. I was working, I suppose – I don't really remember. Anyway. When they called me, I requested – quite firmly – that I be assigned to you.'

'To me? Why?'

'Girl A,' she said. 'The girl who escaped. If anybody was going to make it, it was going to be you.'

There was no service to London for twenty minutes. A village station on a Sunday evening: it was the loneliest place in the world. I waited in the car, not wanting to be alone on the platform. It seemed important to speak to somebody before the train arrived. Evie answered right away, as she always did. 'Lex,' she said. 'You don't sound well.'

'No,' I said. 'Not really.'

'One moment,' she said, and the noises around her dimmed. 'I'm sorry. It's just—'

'Don't be stupid – you don't need to be sorry. Are you OK?'

'I found Gabriel,' I said. 'But he's so ill, Evie. I don't know if he's going to sign the papers.'

'He isn't?'

'I don't know. He's confused.'

'Don't give up on him, Lex. Ethan – Delilah – they always know what they want. And there's something Gabe'll want, too.'

'It isn't just that, though. It was hard to look at him. And then I thought – when I had left him – about when he was younger. He was such a good kid. For the longest time, he never minded about anything.'

'Stop, Lex. It's OK.'

'I don't know if it is. Seeing him – you just remember things. Don't you? Things that you couldn't think about every day.'

'I'm going to come,' Evie said. 'I can come to see you, and we can sort things out. We can go to the house together. I can come any time this month. Whenever your deal's over.'

'You can't,' I said.

'Let me, Lex. It's been too long.'

'Don't, Evie. I'm OK.'

'Stop it,' she said. 'I'll come with you. I'll come home.'

When she had gone, I saw myself in the mirror, smiling. It was the thought of her, back in the country. In the passenger seat. A stay in Hollowfield, she had said. It isn't exactly the road trip we had planned. I watched the train arrive, pause, depart. There was nobody around to board it. Without Gabriel's signature, the exercise would be redundant. The house would be sold, in ruins, or pilfered by the moor which surrounded it. I started the engine and turned the car around.

The Lifehouse was finished the summer before I started secondary school. For two weeks, Father patrolled the high street, handing out leaflets advertising the grand opening and talking to anyone who would listen about the love of God. At night, he walked the residential streets, posting flyers. He had, he said, left piles of them hidden in the pews of other churches in town, hoping that members of the congregation would sense that God was directing them elsewhere. On the eve of the opening, he instructed us to wear our red T-shirts from the holiday to Blackpool. Mine was embarrassingly tight at the chest and Ethan's tore at his shoulders. When we congregated in the kitchen, Father surveyed us with disgust. 'What's wrong with you?' he asked. We were permitted to wear something white and modest, instead.

Jolly travelled from Blackpool. Evie cut chains of paper angels to string in the windows. Mother descended from her bedroom and baked late into the night. It had been a long time since she was pregnant, and Father had prescribed rest, with a doctor's certainty. When she emerged, she looked white and lumpen, like part of the bedding.

Before I went to sleep, I wandered to the kitchen and offered to help her. She was surrounded by sponge cakes, whipping cream, her eyes fixed on the spoon in the bowl. 'Aren't you too clever for this kind of thing?' she said, but she didn't refuse. The kitchen bulbs were bright; still uncovered. I could see the psoriasis at her elbows and throat. As soon as I took the bowl, she folded herself away from me and gripped at her sleeves.

'Is there anything else to do?' I said. 'After this?'

'The other one needs icing.'

'Leave it for Evie. I'd probably destroy it.'

Our reflections hovered in the kitchen window, expressionless and close.

'The new school,' she said. 'What's it like?'

'It's OK. We did a lot of the stuff already, at Jasper Street. Or else Ethan told me it.'

'Are you still at the top?'

I glanced up. She was turned away, picking at baking paper. 'I don't know,' I said. 'Probably.'

'Make sure of it.'

I spread the cream onto the sponge, and Mother manoeuvred a second one on top of it. She took her hands away tentatively, trembling, and covered her eyes. 'Please, God, let this be a success,' she said, and I realized that I had never heard her pray like that before – like God was in the kitchen.

We were at the Lifehouse at eight o'clock the next morning, carrying decorations and baked goods. I had visited the weekend before, to touch up the paint, and I had liked the new wood smell. I could see, tying balloons to the pulpit, that Father had created something simple and strangely beautiful from the husk of the shop. Light fell through the old glass windows and careened down the aisle. There was a neat wooden bar at the back of the room, where Mother had laid out the cakes.

The service was due to start at eleven ('To ease them in,' said Father), but with five minutes to go, nobody had arrived. We had spread ourselves out, tactically, across the first two rows. Ethan turned around every few seconds to check the door; after a time he stood, straightened his shirt, and joined Father outside. I could hear snippets of their conversations with passers-by, some of them gentle and some of them scoffing. Two teenage girls slipped in, giggling, and took a handful of Mother's flapjacks each. They sat on the back row, close to the door. A pensioner joined them, and one of the drunks from the pub across the road. Somehow, this meagre crowd – witnesses to Father's embarrassment – was worse than no crowd at all.

At quarter past eleven, Father stepped up to the makeshift pulpit and cleared his throat. He had never needed a microphone. I heard Ethan slide into the pew beside me, but I didn't look at him; when Father caught our eyes, I knew that it would be important for him to see that he had our absolute attention. 'Welcome to the Lifehouse,' he said.

Late that night, when I couldn't sleep, I heard somebody in the kitchen. I untangled my body from the sheets and walked down the hallway and the stairs, knowing them now, stretching my feet to the quieter floorboards. I hoped that it would be Ethan, that we would be able to discuss the day. Downstairs, I stood in the darkness and watched Father at the kitchen table. He held the liquor in one hand; with the other he gestured, his lips moving but no sound coming out. The final sad sermon of the day. I thought for a long time about joining him. I still think of it now. I have selected the exact verses that might have offered him comfort. Instead, I made my way back to the bedroom. That night, eleven and confused, I didn't yet know what to say.

The palace was orange and pink beneath the evening sky. This time, I didn't park between the lines, or speak with the receptionist, or wait to be summoned. I arrived at Gabriel's room out of breath, with a nurse at my heels.

'There'll be something for addiction,' I said. 'At the community centre. It'll be a condition of the proposal.'

Gabriel was in institution pyjamas, propped in the chair at the window. 'I thought that you would be back,' he said. And to the nurse: 'It's OK. I know her.'

'There could be meetings,' I said. 'Drop-in sessions. Whatever – whatever you think might have helped.'

'I'd like that,' he said. His fingers and thumbs shaped a plaque in the air. 'Funded by Gabriel Gracie,' he said.

'That's right.'

'And will I be able to take part, do you think? I could speak there – if that would help.'

'Maybe. When you're better, and you're out of here, you can do whatever you want.'

'You think so?'

'I know it.'

'Whatever you did,' Gabriel said, 'it worked.'

'I'm sorry?'

'He didn't come by,' Gabriel said. 'After you left. He passed a message to one of the nurses, instead – just to say goodbye. He did love me, Lex. In his own way.'

Perhaps, I thought. In his own way.

Gabriel stood to navigate the little room, touching the furniture as he went, as if we were in the dark. He took the papers from his bedside table and handed them to me, and I saw that they were already signed.

'Out there this afternoon,' he said. 'You reminded me of Delilah.'

'I'm not nearly that fierce, Gabe.'

'What did you say?'

'Nothing exciting. The law, mostly.'

'Delilah uses books in her way,' Gabriel said. 'And I guess you use them in yours.'

5

Noah (Boy D)

LATE IN THE EVENING, waiting for Devlin to call, I opened my favourite bookmark and checked the weekend's results. On Sunday, the Cragforth Under 17s Junior Cricket Team had been all-out for ninety-seven, and defeated. Not such a good week.

I hovered at the tab beside Results, which was How to Find Us.

'Come on,' I said, to myself, and wandered down to the kitchen. With a kind of mundane magic, the lights in the corridor flicked on ahead of me. It was three thirty a.m. I assembled a bowl of cereal and black coffee, and returned to my desk. Devlin hadn't called. The cursor still rested on How to Find Us.

I had only heard of Cragforth once, many years before. I was twenty, and had just secured my place at university. My parents and I had been for dinner, and Mum was upstairs, getting ready for bed. Dad and I sat at either end of the sofa, our legs touching in the middle, reading different sections of the newspaper. He balanced a glass of whisky on his chest.

My reading was a sham. In my head, I drafted and rephrased a question I had contemplated for some time. I had plotted various routes to it, discounting some and awaiting the right weather for others. This, I decided, was the day of the attempt.

'I wonder if the others will go to university,' I said, not looking up from the paper. 'Besides Ethan, I mean.'

'I don't know,' Dad said. 'You'd hope so. But take you – it's not as if it was easy. You had a lot of catching up to do.'

I turned the page. 'That would be true for Delilah, too, I suppose,' I said. 'But the others were younger. Do you think Noah will, Dad?'

'Noah's different. He isn't expected to remember anything at all. And he had an easier time than the rest of you. As things went – in that house – he was lucky.'

'Where is he?' I asked, and Dad stopped reading and stared at me.

'Lex. You know—'

'I'd just like to be able to think of him. That's all.'

A toilet flushed upstairs, and I knew that Mum would soon be on the way down, coming to say goodnight and another congratulations. She was fiercely professional – she protected patients' confidentiality like state secrets – and she wouldn't entertain this line of questioning.

'I don't know much about it,' Dad said, 'other than that he's well. The family who adopted him were in a little town – Cragforth, I think it was.'

I returned to the paper. He was strangely still, and no longer reading.

'What?' I said.

He shook his head.

'Nothing.'

In the weeks that followed, it was clear that Dad deeply regretted this disclosure. The morning after, he arrived in my room in his dressing gown, bearing a teacake. 'This feels like a bribe,' I said, and propped myself up in bed.

'I had trouble sleeping last night,' he said. 'I shouldn't have told you that, Lex. You need to promise me that you won't use that information for anything at all.'

He was unable to say Noah's name. He handed me the plate and sat at the end of my bed.

'If you were anybody else,' he said, 'I would hope that you might just forget it.'

'I won't do anything,' I said. 'Really. I just wanted to know where he'd ended up.'

'No emails or messages?'

To my dad, both the Internet and my intellect were all-powerful. I could be on a video call with Noah that afternoon.

'No.'

He was beginning to smile. 'And no carrier pigeons, either.'

'Nothing, Dad.'

And for a while, that was true. At university, I often searched for Noah and Cragforth online, but with a habitual curiosity, the same way that I checked the weather or legal updates. I had become accustomed to the three results which returned to me on each occasion: a theological essay by Bradley Cragforth of Wisconsin State University, which involved a close analysis of Genesis (and which was, I thought, rather good); details of Cragforth Primary School's reception class syllabus, which included 'listening to and discussion of stories from both the Bible and other religions (e.g. Noah and the Ark)'; and an advertisement for the amateur dramatic performance of *The Grapes of Wrath*, held in Cragforth Park in the summer of 2004, which featured Gary Harrison as Noah Joad.

I considered the options. His family might have moved to another town, or abroad. They might have changed his name.

I was twenty-eight and in New York before a fourth result appeared. It was past midnight, and I was waiting for documents from the Los Angeles office. There were few people left on the corridor. I typed the old combination into the search bar and hit return. At the top of the page was a new link. This was a team listing for the Cragforth Under 15s Junior Cricket team. The Vice-Captain was Noah Kirby.

I leaned back in my office chair and crossed my arms. Noah Kirby, of Cragforth. I clicked through to the results for the season so far. They hadn't been updated for several weeks, but as of mid-July the team had won two games, lost five, and had one rained off. A trying season. If somebody had emerged at my office door and asked me why I was crying, I wouldn't have been able to answer them. I didn't know.

The summer before I started high school, we lived under Father's regime. On the first day of the holidays, when we scrambled down for breakfast, there was a brilliant gold parcel on the kitchen table.

'What's inside it?' Delilah asked. The parcel was tied with a bow. It was the size of a small television, or a whole stack of books.

'Six weeks,' Father said, 'of good behaviour.'

'And then we can open it?'

'That's not much to ask,' Father said. 'Is it?'

It was a slow, dank summer. At the front of the Lifehouse, Father sweated for the empty pews. A congregation of flies weakened at the windows, unable to find their way to the door. The garden at Moor Woods Road was rain-logged, and most of our games involved navigating the swamp. When Father was away, we clambered over the fence and scattered across the moors, combing for sheep bones and slow worms. On the boldest days, we arranged a mission to the river at the bottom of Moor Woods Road, moving single-file and close to the wall, with the nominated lookout – Gabriel, usually – giving us the all-clear at the bends. We washed in the shadow of the mill, in the black tea water close to the banks, and when we returned to the house, the present surveyed us from the kitchen table.

Mother's womb was still empty. That was how Father said it. When I looked at her, I thought of a cavern beneath her clothes, cool and dark. She had become a strange, rare sight: a blink of white nightdress between a parted doorway, or cracked feet, retreating up the stairs to bed. Each evening, we filed into my parents' room and kissed her goodnight, while Father watched us. She touched bones new-risen, like rocks at low tide. 'Small again,' she said. 'Like when you were babies.'

There would be another child, Father said. But we would have to be ready. We would have to be deserving. Week by week, he adjusted the rules of the house, tuning to a pitch which the rest of us couldn't hear. We would wash only our hands, and only to the wrists. The Lifehouse would run three services on Sundays, rather than two. We would demonstrate our self-discipline.

The child would come.

There were lines on my arms where the dirt began, like a tan in reverse. The edge of the pew had printed a bruise at the top of my spine. Our portions had shrunk, and on other days, when he dined with Jolly, Father made nothing at all. When I thought about starting at Five Fields Academy in the autumn, slick with sweat-dirt and the smallest in my year, my stomach ached. The library only had half of the reading list. I hadn't even got a uniform. And I had seen the students in Hollowfield before, on my way home from the primary school. The girls had curated faces, and wore their uniform so you thought of what was underneath it. They moved in tight, glossy packs, like a whole different species.

By September, we were scavengers. We sniffed at the parcel, hoping to catch a food-smell. We poked at the cupboards and scoured for leftovers at the back of the fridge. Father's refusal to throw anything away meant that there was always something there, mouldy or unrecognizable. The question was whether you were hungry enough to try it.

It became a game to us, which we called Mystery Soup. The name came from our first discovery: a murky substance sealed by clingfilm, in a drawer at the bottom of the fridge. Evie dipped in a finger, licked it, and nodded.

'It's actually pretty good,' she said.

'But what is it?' I asked. She shrugged, and fetched herself a spoon.

'Mystery soup,' she said.

Anything could be Mystery Soup: cheese, coated in emerald fur, languishing on the counter; a few scraps of fried chicken, in paper from the takeaway on the high street, which Father abandoned on the kitchen table; a year-old box of cereal, never unpacked from the move. I have an encyclopedic recollection of the meals at Moor Woods Road; they were so precious that I stored them in my memory, to eat again.

A week before school began, with Father in Blackpool, we fanned across the kitchen and searched the cupboards. Gabriel, scouring the drawer where Mother had once kept vegetables, shrieked, and emerged with a handful of pulp, which he dropped onto the kitchen table for inspection.

'That's not Mystery Soup,' Delilah said. 'That's disgusting.'

Gabriel waved his hand in her face, and she ducked away, squealing.

It looked like it might once have been a potato. It was the shape of a fist, with soft black patches, and green tufts sprouting from its skin.

'Bin it,' I said.

'*You* bin it,' said Delilah, and at that moment, with the five of us clustered around the table, Father opened the kitchen door.

'What's this?' he said.

He was impossibly early. We had been left with instructions to collate passages on determination, in our bedrooms. He took a seat at the table and started to unlace his boots.

'Who found it?' he said, and Gabriel, his expression lurching between fear and pride, said: 'It was me.'

'And where did you find it?'

'Nowhere. In the vegetable cupboard.'

'And what were you doing in the vegetable cupboard?'

'We were – we were just – checking.'

Now Father stood to remove his shirt, and sat back down in a white vest, tight at the shoulders and gut. His arms dangled behind the chair, and he studied his tableau, not yet satisfied.

'If you're so hungry,' he said, 'why don't you eat it?'

Spines and jaws stiffened around the table. Gabriel giggled, and saw that none of us were laughing. The giggle cut with a gasp. He looked from one of us to the next, with wide, imploring eyes. I stared at my feet, and to Delilah, who was looking at her own.

'I don't want to,' Gabriel said.

'So – you're *not* hungry.'

'I – I don't know.'

'Unless you want to starve,' Father said, 'you're going to eat it.'

He sat, waiting.

Gabriel reached out a hand and closed his fist around the pulp. The flesh of it squeezed between his fingers. He lifted it from the table and gave it a long look. Then, with his brows set, and the four of us gaping, he raised it to his mouth.

Father stood from his chair, strode around the table, and clapped Gabriel on the back. The Mystery Soup fell from his hand, and onto the kitchen floor.

'You didn't actually think I'd make you eat it,' Father said. 'Did you?'

Instead, he took the golden parcel from the table, and carried it from the room.

The night before the new term, I woke to somebody at the bedroom door. For the first bleary seconds, I thought that it was Father. He was on his haunches, arranging something at the threshold. But when he stepped back, into the hallway lights, I saw that it was Ethan.

I hadn't heard him crying in the night-time since we arrived in Hollowfield. He had shaved his head to the skull, and he was as tall as Father. He no longer seemed to lose his belongings. When he joined Father and Jolly in the kitchen at night, I heard a new, affected guffaw ascend through the floorboards. He had even spoken at the Lifehouse, when only the family was in attendance. He delivered a passionate, sincere sermon on filial duty, and I thought of the boy in Blackpool, five years before, who didn't believe a thing.

I cracked the bedroom door, to see what he had left. It was a high school uniform. The standard-issue jumper and skirt. It was faded, but clean. It would fit.

I stopped at his bedroom door the next morning. 'Thank you,' I said. He was hunched over a pocket mirror, scrutinizing the skin at his neck, and he didn't look at me.

'Where did you get it?' I said.

He did look up, then. He had an expression of curious disdain. I had seen it on so many strangers' faces, but on Ethan, it had a savagery of its own.

'I don't know what you're talking about,' he said.

Five Fields accepted students from Hollowfield and the four villages around it. Three of these were also suffixed with 'field';

the last, Dodd Bridge, had been outvoted on naming day. The school consisted of a vast concrete playground, surveyed by classrooms on three sides and a wooden hall on the fourth. The hall had been opened by a minor royal, and must once have been a source of pride, but now it was blackened by moor rain, and smelt of PE. On my first day in secondary school, I sat there beside Cara – one of two hundred eleven-year-olds promised the best seven years of my life – and concluded that I shouldn't have worried about my hair, or shoes with holes in them. This would be an easy place to disappear.

'Whoa,' Cara said, as soon as the welcome address was over. She took my hands and held them out at my sides. 'You got skinny.'

She looked a little frightened, but mostly impressed.

'And you,' I said, 'you got tanned! How was France?'

We compared timetables. We shared three classes, which I hoped was enough to stick together. In the early autumn, that was the case: each break time and lunch hour, we met in the same spot outside the school hall and ate our sandwiches, huddled against the wooden walls. We didn't have enough to say to entertain the hour allotted to lunch, but Cara brought in books from home: whatever she was reading, and a spare for me.

There were days when I noticed her glancing across the pages to my lunchbox, and the tweak of one eyebrow. Who survived the day on two pieces of bread and a film of jam, or cold soup cooked the evening before? In turn, I examined the contents of her lunch. There were so many different components: a salad or a stuffed sandwich; fruit or vegetables, preserved in their own bright Tupperware box; a cylindrical tub filled with chocolate biscuits. My mouth opened before I could determine whether or not to ask it: 'Would I be able to have one?'

Cara was generous the first time, and less generous each time afterwards. A few weeks into term, as she opened a tub of three Jaffa Cakes – that smell, of dark chocolate shot through with orange – she turned to stare at me, and tucked the container closer to her chest.

'You've got to stop looking at my food,' she said. 'It's freaking me out.'

The week after that, approaching the hall, I saw Cara sitting with another girl, Annie Muller. Cara patted the ground on the spare side of her, and I sat down beside them, although my stomach had already started to drop. Annie was mid-monologue as I arrived, and though she waved, she didn't stop talking to greet me. Her lunch consisted of peanut butter sandwiches; Doritos (Cool Blue); and a banana sealed in a banana-shaped container.

'They basically just don't get it,' she concluded. 'They don't understand it at all.'

'Annie's parents are being weird about getting her ears pierced,' Cara said.

'You don't have yours done, right?' Annie said. She leaned over Cara, chewing furiously. 'So are your parents as crazy as mine?'

I unwrapped my two slices of bread – just margarine, today – and peeled off a crust to eat first. 'I suppose so,' I said.

Annie left us just before the bell, and once she had run for the lockers, I looked to Cara for an explanation. She was rummaging in her bag for the afternoon's textbooks, and it was a slow few seconds before she would meet my eye.

'What?' she said. 'Just because you hate everybody else doesn't mean I have to.'

I felt a dull heat rise out of my collar and across my cheeks, and it made me cruel. 'But I'm in History with Annie,' I said. 'And she's stupid.'

'A bit,' Cara said, 'but at least she invites me to her house.'

The discipline of the summer paid off. By late autumn, Mother was pregnant. Father started touching her again. At dinner, they sat side by side, reciting Psalm 127 and smiling over our conversation. They kept having to drop their cutlery to hold hands. When I looked at my siblings, frailer around the table, it seemed like they'd taken a little flesh from each of us, and made something new.

JP selected a wine bar called Graves, two blocks from my hotel. 'It's a pretty morbid name,' I said, when he suggested it.

'It's an area of Bordeaux, Lex.'

'Like you knew that.'

'Since visiting their website – of course.'

I arrived first. I had spent the previous hour in the bath at the Romilly, with a carafe of red wine, reading Bill's guide to planning applications. There was a wooden tray which slotted over the bathtub, provided for this specific purpose.

An evening off.

Graves was at the bottom of a black metal stairway, beneath the ground. Bankers' lamps set in the centre of each table. I held the menu to the dim green light and ordered cognac and champagne. I was halfway down the glass when JP walked in. First I recognized the walk of him, stooped, tilted forward, and then his trench coat, which he had bought because it made him look like a secret agent.

I had loved JP in all of the ways that it's unwise to love another person. Dido on the pyre. Antony in Alexandria. Bitch in heat. Before I left for university, Mum sat on my bed and tried to explain some matters of the heart, one of her hands stroking the cover over my legs. She seemed confident that I would already know about the sex side of things. Love, she had decided, might be a different matter. I was hot beneath the bedding, and aware that I couldn't kick it away without her thinking that I was embarrassed.

'The key thing,' she said, 'is that you never lose your self-respect.'

On reflection, this was sweet, and useful for a while. I had been too much of an oddity at high school to attract much attention – OK-looking, but *so* fucked in the head – but at university I was interesting enough. I could hold court on literature, or, with credit to Mr Greggs, countries that I'd never been to. I studied Olivia's humour and Christopher's optimism. I studied The Sartorialist. I wore tight, dark clothes, and a smile that I'd practised. Despite the showers and the CK One, I stank of somebody who might need saving, and men liked that best of all.

Sometimes I recall them: the odd pageant of men who tried to save me. They tried to save me by making love, or dinner, or, on one stilted, final date, a Build-a-Bear. Clever men from solid schools, destined for great things (or good things, at the very least). They parade through my head, with their tentative hands and concerned frowns. They ask why I'm reticent about my family. They touch my surgical scars, deliberately, to demonstrate that they're not afraid. They come bearing handwritten letters, or hand-cuffs with fur – with fur – on a special occasion. They lick the wrong parts of my skin and dip their fingers inside me like they're testing my temperature. They try to convert me. Lie still, they say, it will be different with me. This is always inaccurate. Ultimately, they're angry and disappointed. Maybe I'm not that mysterious, after all. Why must you request such strange things; why would you ask that I hurt you; why won't you tell me what *happened* to you? Maybe I'm just a bitch.

And then there was JP, and I prepared my self-respect, and served it to him, delicate, on a plate.

I spent most of the summer after university in London. Dad dropped me at the station on Friday afternoons, and I sat on the train in the same seat – one hour and seventeen minutes – with butterflies battering around my belly. They had claws; they had teeth. The hot, rattling carriage, and then the shade of the plat-form. JP waited behind the barriers at London Bridge, past the initial crowd, and I liked to see him just before he saw me, his eyes sweeping the different faces for mine. Each time we met, it was as if we started again: for twenty minutes we were shy together, one talking over the other, both of us with too much and too little to say. We took the tube to his flat in De Beauvoir, walking from Angel and holding hands, and as he talked about his week and his friends and his ideas for the weekend, the butterflies became drowsy, and slumbered. His flat had long windows facing west, so that the evening light fell in neat stripes across the floorboards, the bookshelves, the bed. He resisted all decoration. There was never anything on the floor.

I tried to remember to urinate on the train, right before it reached London, so that as soon as we were inside he could set me where he wanted to: on the sofa or on the desk, or through and into the bedroom. This sex was always inelegant, half-dressed and hurried, and never lasted long. 'I need to be inside you,' he would say, and I enjoyed the needing, as if it was something he would have to do, whether I liked it or not. As soon as he came, we removed the dregs of our clothes – a stray sock, or my bra pushed above my breasts – and lay naked together on the bed or on the rug. He propped himself up on one elbow and reached for me, his eyes creased in a smile and barely open.

'Tell me,' he said, during one of the first weekends, starting to touch me. 'Tell me what you want.'

I rolled onto my stomach and rested my head on my arms.

'I want you to hurt me,' I said.

'Say that again.'

I did so, obedient. A smile rose across his face, sun-slow. 'How fortunate,' he said.

When I had met JP in my final weeks of university, I had assumed that his family would be comfortable, and as tidy as he was.

There would be a mother and a father, and a house in the home counties. He would be able to ski, and play a musical instrument. He spoke with a soft, placeless accent, and he was endlessly generous; he would insist on paying for extra rounds and dinners and my train fare home. When I refused, I would find the exact sum hidden in my shoes, or fluttering from a book when I unpacked.

After several months, I realized that I had been wrong, although I knew that JP appreciated the assumption. It was, after all, a testament to his life's work. His mother lived in Leeds, and he visited her three times a year, returning sullen and withdrawn. Her house was cluttered with kitsch ornaments and kitchen paraphernalia, and he couldn't stand it. He had been made to watch whatever came onto TV next. He had lost brain matter. But he was simple to appease. I waited for him on the sofa or at his desk, sometimes in the position which he requested and sometimes intending to surprise him, and when he walked into his flat he smiled, dropped his bag definitively upon the floor, and unbuckled his belt. 'There's no place like home,' he said.

When I found JP looking at me – returning to our table from the bar of the local pub, or grinning over his shoulder from his desk – I wondered about his own misapprehensions. I had told him everything about Mum and Dad. He knew the layout of their cottage, the best of Dad's stories, my teenage grudges against them. To somebody else, it might have seemed strange that my memories started at fifteen, but JP's reluctance to discuss his own childhood made my omissions much easier. We had his cases, and Olivia's on-off relationship with his senior colleague, and the impending start of my job, and which books we should take with us to Croatia, in order that we would both be happy to read any one of them, and Christopher's new boyfriend, who was earnest, which we both agreed was one of the worst things you could be. The past was one of the few foreign countries which neither of us wished to visit. There was always so much else to talk about.

My lies ran out when I realized that he would have to meet my parents. It had been over a year, and we planned to leave our separate flats and to move together, to somewhere new. I was pretty sure that Mum and Dad would lie for me, if I asked, but when I pictured them in the garden in Sussex, nudging one another to remember the facade, I didn't want them to have to.

'If you're going to do it,' said Olivia, 'then just do it, before you drive yourself crazy.'

'But doesn't it have to be the right moment?'

'Come on, Lex. There isn't a right moment for something like this.'

Now that the decision had been made, the thought of it loomed over my desk at work, and sat beside me in the taxi on the way home. It stood beside our bed at night, glancing at its watch.

I waited until a summer Bank Holiday. A Friday-night train to the Lake District, with cans of gin and tonic. We reached the bed and breakfast after midnight, and by the morning, the landscape had emerged, bright and textured from black silhouettes, as if it had been finished overnight.

I waited a mile into the first walk, when we were off the road and beginning the ascent. I recalled Dr K's old adage, about the difficult things being easier to say when you don't have to look at somebody, and I waited until a narrow path between bracken, single-file only.

'I think that there's something which I should probably tell you,' I said.

'This sounds like a good start to the weekend.'

'I'm adopted.'

'OK. By your parents in Sussex?'

'Yep.'

'How old were you?'

'Older than you would expect. Fifteen.'

'God, Lex. So – you know who your birth parents are?'

'Yes,' I said, and felt the shift in the comfort between us. Here we were, on the edge of it, together.

I told him only what he would have been able to read in a news report from the time. When I had finished, he was silent for a moment, and in my head I implored him to turn around, so that I could see his face. 'God,' he said. 'Lex, I'm sorry.' And, at ten a.m. and because he could never stand to be serious for very long: 'You should have told me later in the day. When we'll be closer to a drink.'

He turned to me and gathered me up towards him. 'We can speak about this whenever you want to,' he said. 'But I don't mind if you don't.'

We staggered together for a time up the little path, until it became too narrow for two, and he was ahead of me again. That was JP: walking away from me, with his forward-lean and a light pack, towards the skyline. Following my months of indecision, he was able to discard my revelation back there on the path, a fruit skin, or else its core. By the summit, he was talking about lunch.

That night, after sex, we lay on top of the sheet in the inn, as far away from one another as we could be. Just our hands touching. Silence extended in every direction, so that the little human noises of our room – the toilet flush, or music from his phone – seemed loud, and embarrassing. I closed my eyes, and started awake with the sense of something missing. 'Here,' I said, and collected the bed covers from the floor. Beneath them, he turned to me.

'I feel worse,' he said, 'about the things that I do to you. That we do together. After what you told me.'

'Why? It's what I want.'

'Yes. But still.'

'You know – for what it's worth – they're not connected. And even if they were—'

'Yes?'

'Would it matter?'

'I don't know,' he said.

It was too dark to read him. I reached for his face and found hair, then the notch of an ear. He shifted closer.

'When I'm away,' he said, 'and I need something to think about. You know? I think of you very early on. We were in my flat. You looked at me, and – you told me what you wanted. The way that you said it. It was more than I could have hoped for. And I was terrified, of course.'

'Good,' I said.

We were a few seconds from falling asleep.

'There's a lot that I'm ashamed of,' I said. 'But not this.'

I had assumed that JP was being disingenuous; that in time he would be curious, and begin to ask his questions. I was wrong. JP – who was so boundlessly fascinated by matters of morality, or of the law – had little interest in old suffering. His acceptance of my confession, without any disquiet or judgement, lulled me into a sense of absolute security; not just that he loved me, which he had already said, but that it was possible to overcome the past as comprehensively as Dr K had promised. I, too, could be happy.

We lived as I had only secretly hoped that I might live. During the week we worked, arriving home at ten, eleven, midnight, and talking together in bed, in the precious last minutes of that day, and sometimes over into the next one. A lost hour of sleep – the denser fogginess in the morning – seemed like a relatively small price to pay. At the weekend we saw friends, or travelled to Europe late on a Friday evening, landing weary and excited in Porto or Granada or Oslo. I bought postcards for Evie, and wrote them at my desk when I was back. Usually something dull or hideous, chosen to make her laugh. Highways of Norway, or a llama drinking port. Other times, my sentimentality won over. I picked a shot of the Alhambra at dusk, just as they lit the walls. Do you remember, I said, when we saw it in the atlas?

Foolish: to assume that we would live that way for ever. Two years in, JP's mother visited us in London. His history on the doorstep, wearing coral lipstick and mid-heels. He booked dinner for the three of us at a sleek basement bar in Mayfair. There was a sake list, and small plates. I knew as soon as I met JP's mother that it was a terrible choice. At the restaurant, she complained about the comfort of her chair and the complications of the menu and the lighting at the table. 'It's ever so difficult,' she said to the waiter, 'to see what I'd like to eat.' The waiter returned with a small torch which could be clipped to the menu, and JP winced.

When the food arrived, she took fussy little spoonfuls from each dish and moved them around her plate. JP ate in silence, enjoying nothing. 'This is great,' I said, and went for seconds.

'You've got a big appetite,' JP's mother said, and I shrugged.

His mother was staying at a bed and breakfast by Euston, and we hailed a taxi and stopped at the address. JP and I came out of the taxi to say goodbye. It had rained while we were eating. Puddles of light beneath the streetlamps. The building was a dirty cream, and flower baskets drooped on either side of the entrance. 'It's perfectly fine,' JP's mother said, 'although the room's a little warm.'

'Happy birthday,' I said. We watched her totter across the street. At the hotel door, she stepped onto a loose paving stone, and a puddle lapped over her shoe.

We ducked back into the taxi, and JP lay across the back seat, his head in my lap. 'Fucking hell,' he said.

'Come on,' I said. 'She's not that bad.'

'She's terrible,' he said. 'You wouldn't be the first to say it.'

'She's fine,' I said. 'You know, there was a time when ordering from a menu was the most stressful thing that I could think of.'

'But not any more.'

'Well, no. Not any more.'

JP sat up. 'And I love you even more,' he said, 'for that.' He extended one of his hands and bent me towards him. 'You know – one day,' he said, 'together – we're going to have the family we both deserve.'

There it was: the gut punch of it. Harder than anything I'd ever requested. His words spread under my skin and into the tissue, so that later, when he watched me undress, I was surprised that he couldn't see the mark of them. That to him, I was unchanged.

Here is an old legal principle: *Caveat emptor*. Buyer beware. You are selling a property. The walls are solid; the roof is new; the foundations are strong. You know all of this: you built the house yourself.

Each spring, fleshy roots infest your garden. They grow fast. Canes emerge, bloated and purple. Their leaves are like hearts. Through summer, the canes grow at a rate of ten centimetres each day. You attempt to cut the plant at the canes. Within a day, it returns. You attempt to cut the plant at the roots. Within a week, it returns. You seek consultation.

This is Japanese knotweed. By now, its roots will have penetrated the foundations of your house. They will have nestled three metres deep. In time, it will destroy your property. If a single stem is left in the ground, reinfestation will occur. Its removal is prohibitively expensive.

Should you disclose this invasion to your buyer? If they ask you: yes, of course. But how specifically must the buyer ask? If, for example, they enquire about environmental problems, or contaminative materials – what then? Shouldn't the buyer have been more explicit? How should you respond? How will you feel at the thought of them unpacking their lives in your empty rooms, with the plant stirring beneath them?

For a second, JP looked at me as a stranger. Then I half waved, and his face softened.

I had selected my outfit with great care, and following two consultations with Christopher. ('Promise me,' he had said, 'that we will never be above such things.') I wore a golden silk vest (the one item in my suitcase that I remembered JP had liked: I thought of him), a leather skirt with a heavy buckle (did he recall the feeling of the material in his fingers, and the resistance of pulling it up to my waist, when he didn't want to fumble with the belt?), and quilted Chanel pumps (I was richer than I had been when I last saw him, and was, generally, doing well).

'Hello,' he said. 'And sorry I'm late. This client – well. Let me tell you with drinks.'

Our conversation was more civilized than I had expected, although I shouldn't have been surprised. Neither of us enjoyed deep and meaningful disclosures, and we had the benefit of having a lot in common. It was the kind of discussion you have with a former colleague, with genuine questions to ask and enough gossip to be entertaining. He talked about his client, who had a penchant for shredding documents, and meetings in international waters. He asked, politely, about Devlin, whom he had always considered crude, and not quite as clever as she thought she was. One of his old law professors had died. JP returned to university for the funeral, and at the dinner afterwards, when he was asked about his career, somebody said: You know, I always thought you looked more like a bouncer than a barrister.

'I'm sorry,' he said. 'I'm boring you.'

'Talking of boredom,' I said. 'I have a legal question. For you.'

'A legal question?'

'I'm not joking.'

'I'm sure you're not. Can you afford me?'

'I don't know. You're pretty overpriced.'

I reached for my drink, but it was already finished.

'Let's say you were the executor,' I said, 'of a will.'

'Your mother's will? For example.'

'For example. And a house has been left to this person's surviving children. But one of those children – they were adopted when they were tiny. Years and years ago. They were too young to remember a thing. Technically, they're a surviving child. But they don't even know it.'

'Lex,' he said, and shook his head.

'Do you need to tell them?'

'I don't know the answer to that question.'

'Come on,' I said. 'What would you do?'

'You want it to be watertight?' he said. 'Then yes. You do.'

'But.'

'But what?'

'But that isn't what you think I should do.'

He gathered the glasses and stood over me, with his body turned to the bar and his face turned to mine. 'That,' he said, 'is beyond the scope of my retainer.'

I had seen JP in court once, although I had never told him. He had always resisted any suggestion that I might attend one of his hearings. It was a minor case by his standards, and pro bono: he was acting for a young mother whose divorce lawyer had failed to explain her basic rights. The woman was left with nothing, yet still expected to pay the fees. I had little on at work, so I caught a bus from the City to a miserable courtroom in East London. I had brought a notebook in the guise of research, but now that I was here, it seemed to make me more conspicuous. But JP didn't even look at the gallery. He was cutting and concise, polite to the judge and to his learned friend. I awaited his every phrase with an exhilarated terror. I thought that you have to care about somebody very much to have the energy to hope that they don't stumble over a word. I guessed that it was the kind of caring that most people save for their children.

He set down new drinks. We touched glasses. 'Tell me about New York,' he said.

I had been select in my reports to colleagues, and even to Olivia and Christopher. But JP really did want to hear about New York. I told him about my runs in Battery Park, which had to be early: everybody got to work so fucking early in New York. I had my own office overlooking the Statue of Liberty – 'So, you really are a big deal,' said JP – and my favourite places for coffee; ramen; books; tacos; pastrami. The New York bar exams had been easier than I expected. I spent many weekends in Long Island, where Devlin owned a house. On certain summer evenings, a rich bronze light extended from the horizon across the ocean and the sky, and landed on the long metal table in Devlin's kitchen, where we worked. 'It's the champagne light,' Devlin would say, and would pad to her cellar to fetch a bottle. Sometimes, if it had been a long week and the champagne light was tenuous, Devlin determined that it would soon be on its way, and visited the cellar early.

'Do you have many friends out there?'

'Not many,' I said. 'Some people from the office, I guess.'

I thought of the early weekends, when my voice would catch in my throat on a Monday morning, after two days of disuse. I thought of recent weekends. There is a boutique hotel, I thought, in Midtown. I know the smell of the rugs. I know where to kneel, if they want to watch us in the mirror. I meet friends, there.

'Devlin and I drink together,' I said. 'And I have an elderly flatmate called Edna.'

'Edna?'

'She's good company.'

'Oh, Lex.' He grinned, but it fell fast. 'We were going to go there,' he said. 'Weren't we? Just before—'

'The hotel was booked. But we got our deposit back, I guess.'

I remembered us at the table in our flat, laptops up, sharing Lonely Planet. He planned a precise route for our days. Williamsburg; Harlem; Beacon, on the Hudson. Places we had planned to see together, which I had ended up liking alone.

'Perhaps we'll visit you someday,' he said. The sting of the plural. He cleared his throat.

'I have to tell you,' he said. 'Something—'

He loosened his tie further from his neck. I dipped my head, craning for his eyes, but he looked to the bar. The lamps around us had been extinguished as each table departed, and it was very dark.

'I've got some news,' he said, 'that I didn't want to tell you on the phone. But I know that you'll be back in New York any minute, and I suppose it may be – it may be some time before we see one another again.'

Even drunk, I was practised at impassivity. I steadied my gaze and waited.

'Eleanor and I are going to have a baby,' he said. 'I'll be honest with you in that it wasn't necessarily planned – I think that we both might have liked to marry first – but she was excited about it, and we're lucky enough to be in a position where we can manage it, we think. Although I suppose that you don't know, do you, until it arrives—'

I had watched videos of filibusters in the Senate – I liked the sheer bloody-mindedness of the concept – and I wondered if that was what JP was attempting; maybe, with the drinks and his dread, he would be able to make it through until morning.

'So, you see,' he concluded. 'I hope that you understand.'

'Yes,' I said. 'Yes. Of course I do.'

I hauled up my smile.

'It's wonderful news,' I said. 'But I wish that you had told me at the beginning. It might be too late for a toast, now.'

He looked bemused. He looked, I decided, disappointed.

'So,' I said, 'when will the baby come?'

'In two more months.'

'Jesus. You should be at home, preparing. All you'll get here is wine and debate.'

In the middle of the table, he reached for my hands and entwined them with his own. I looked at his wrinkled palms and the mounds of veins and the hair between his knuckles, and I thought of the many, varied times when I had taken one of these hands in mine. On aeroplanes and after dinners, in my college room the day after we met, walking into a restaurant or into a party, and in the taxis which we sometimes shared on our way home. I held his hand when it was too hot to embrace at night, and to guide him to the right place – just there – between my legs. When we were outside in wintertime, he enveloped my fist in his palm to keep it warm. His child would have improbably minute hands, barely big enough to clutch a finger.

'Why are you so sad, JP?' I said. 'Why are you so sad, when you got everything you ever wanted?'

We finished our drinks, and he walked me across the two streets to the Romilly Townhouse. There was nothing left to say, and we both produced our work phones, and began to scroll through the messages we had missed. Devlin had been in touch: our client was comfortable with the commercial terms for the purchase of ChromoClick, and it would be bought within the fortnight. *Full steam ahead!* said Devlin. We had been drinking for some time, and I didn't trust that I could respond with the alacrity her message required.

At the entrance to the hotel, JP opened his arms. 'It was great to see you,' he said, and at the same time I said, 'Congratulations again.'

Like this, with his arms around me and my lips against his jaw and the wine nudging me towards my worst ideas, I said, 'You should know that I still think about us when I masturbate.'

He took my shoulders and held me at arm's length, and I smiled stupidly. He was three-headed, and each head was shaking. Cerberus in disapproval.

'I'll always be heartbroken about what happened to you,' JP said. 'But don't do this, Lex. Don't do it.'

The second time I met JP's mother, it was Christmastime, and the week before he left me.

Christmas had invaded JP's childhood home. His mother had a real Christmas tree, which looked like it belonged in a bigger house; you got a faceful of pine on the way to the kitchen. It was laden with stringy tinsel and glittering baubles. There was a singing, sensor-operated Father Christmas in the kitchen, which startled me each time I walked past. She had purchased a stuffed elf, the kind that parents relocate while their children are asleep. 'It's an Elf on the Shelf,' she said. 'But he's been all over. In the oven. In the washing machine. On the TV.'

I thought of her at bedtime, carrying the elf through the rooms of the house.

'Who knows,' she said, 'where he'll be tonight.'

'Who knows,' JP said. He had bought the *Financial Times* at a service station on the way, and he was working through it, word by word.

'You never could get him to believe in Christmas,' JP's mother said to me. 'And I *did* try. He was five years old – four or five – when he started questioning the logic, you see. "But he can't reach all of the houses in the *world*." I tried some stories, but they didn't convince him. And a year later I was receiving a list of demands for his stocking.'

'You should have been more convincing, then,' JP said.

'Tell me about your Christmases, Lex,' JP's mother said.

That night, in a small, floral guest bed, JP pinned his knees to my shoulders and choked me. For five seconds – ten seconds – more. His mother still pottering in the kitchen below us, preparing tomorrow's food. Relocating her fucking elf. Through the darkness, there was something different in JP's face, something passive and devoid of pleasure, and I signalled for him to stop.

'But you like it.'

'Yes. But not like that.'

'Like what?'

'Like you're angry.'

That was Christmas Eve. On Christmas Day, before JP was awake, I went for a long, cold run through the town, waiting for the moment when the exhaustion of it erased everything else. Most of the houses were dark, but there were lights on in a few bedrooms. Fairy lights tracing the windows and doors.

We opened our presents with mugs of tea, JP's mother in her dressing gown. She gave me a Christmas jumper and a book on meditation. 'It's changed my life,' she said.

'Like colouring books for adults?' JP said. 'Like Zumba?'

They argued over dinner, too. We pulled crackers and wore the thin, obligatory hats. I ate quietly, watching my food and monitoring the contents of the side plates. Condensation thickened across the windows, sealing us in. JP was talking of our family – the family we would have together.

'You see it in the people who've lived in London their whole lives,' he said. 'People whom Lex and I know. It's this – this confidence, I suppose. You grow up surrounded by culture, by sport, by commerce. None of it comes as a surprise. It's the only place we'd want to have children, I think.'

'Right in the centre? Where you live now?'

'Right in the centre.'

'I don't know why you'd do that. It's incon*ceivable*. Just the two of you, without any family around. With the fumes, and all of those people.'

'As opposed to here? In a shithole?'

'JP,' I said.

'I would advise *against* having children,' JP's mother said. 'If this is the kind of thanks that you get.'

'Actually,' I said. 'That's already decided.'

JP stopped drinking. We looked at one another. He stood up so quickly that his chair teetered, and fell to the floor. 'Excuse me,' he said, still watching me. His mother giggled.

'Don't worry about him,' she said. 'He always knew how to throw a strop.'

'Thank you again,' I said. 'It was a great dinner.'

She smiled. 'It's a thing worth learning,' she said. She was playing with the keyring from her cracker, dangling it from a finger. I was sure that she would keep it.

'I should check on him,' I said.

I opened the sliding doors to join him in the garden. A little island of concrete, encircled by wet grass. We stood together on the paving stones, neither of us dressed for the weather. I removed my cracker hat. The sky was a murky white, like day-old snow. In an hour it would be dark. I had the sense of Sunday evening, or the journey back from the airport after a holiday. The feeling of things coming to an end.

'Why would you say that?' he said. 'Where did that come from, Lex?'

'I don't know,' I said. 'She just – you were being cruel to her.'

'She says stupid things. What do you expect?'

'I don't know.'

'You humiliated me. Do you understand that? Here – you're supposed to be on my side.'

'I'm always on your side.'

'But you weren't then, were you? There always has to be – your objectivity. And – speaking as somebody who has to be objective a great deal of the time – it isn't always appreciated. I need you on my team.'

'You sound like a child,' I said. 'Teams?'

'You don't understand,' he said, 'what it was like. Growing up in this house. It was miserable, Lex.'

'Was it?' I said. 'Was it really so fucking bad?'

He flinched. They're just words, JP, I thought, and then, knowing that I could think something like that: Well. I suppose this is it.

'What did you mean,' he said, 'about children? About that being decided?'

'You want the truth?' I said. 'There's something you should know. About our future family.'

That wasn't the end of it, of course. There was the journey back to London on Boxing Day, suspended in traffic with a Christmas playlist, which JP cut midway through. There were the messages exchanged at work, spiteful and sad, while we sat at our desks with still faces. There was the fact that we were still fucking, hating each other a little more every time. There was the last time, when the hating outweighed the pleasure. There was the conversation when JP said – and I quote – 'You should have told me that you were—'

'Go on. Say it.'

'That you were— Fine. Broken.'

For the first time in many years, I considered seeing Dr K. She had celebrated the beginning of it: let her commiserate the end. I had recognized the relief in her expression, that evening in her office garden. That I might have found somebody who would offer normality, ambition, forgetting. She had expected that JP might drag me with him, and I had hoped for the same. But my past wasn't something which could be left behind us on a footpath, or in a cluttered house in a distant city. The facts of it lived inside me, and if he was going to take me with him, he would need to bear them, too.

Instead, Evie came to stay. She took a train from Gatwick and arrived before sunrise. I found her huddled by my door in a thin jacket, her hands tucked underneath it for the warmth of her body. 'Surprise,' she said, although she had called from the airport, to check that I was awake. 'You didn't need to,' I said, and it was true: I was dry-eyed and showered, and dressed for work. 'I know,' she said.

She cooked dinners; she sourced terrible television; she wore my sweaters, until everything smelt of her. After the first time, we didn't talk about JP. 'Listen,' she said, once I had explained it. 'Fuck him.' At the weekend, we dressed beautifully and visited a bar, and danced recklessly on an empty dance floor, ignoring the people watching. We walked home together, across the river in a thin, fine drizzle, both of us stopping to vomit into the Thames. We slept until Saturday afternoon, our limbs entwined. Beneath the pain, I felt better. Devlin's reputation had drifted across the Atlantic, and I had already scheduled a call. I cancelled JP's flight to New York, and upgraded my own. Another escape.

In Soho, I awoke suddenly in the night, as if the recollection of our parting had startled me. It wasn't so bad. I had been telling the truth. For the most part, anyway. And there were far more embarrassing things that I could have said. About loneliness, for example. In the face of his gibbering – all of the fucking melancholy – I had been so composed. It had never been likely to last.

I reached for the light switch and wandered through to the bathroom. I had been too tired to shower when I got in, and now I felt dirty and nauseous. I had thought in the evening that there had been longing in JP's face, but, sober and alone in the night, I concluded that it had probably been pity. I turned the shower as hot as I could stand it and stepped inside. My hair collapsed across my face, and my skin became a hot, porcine pink where the water hit it. I cleaned my body, the folds of it, the old scars, as carefully as if it was somebody else's, and afterwards I held the skin above my womb, trying to imagine it taut with a child. Sometimes I dreamt about it, in vivid, mundane dreams, but when I was awake it was no good. Even the imagining was impossible.

There were two events which marked the end of my time at Five Fields. The first was Father's disappearance. The second was the opening of the computer shop in Hollowfield, although I didn't realize its significance at the time. That came many years later, and only with Dr K's assistance.

Father went missing on my final day at Five Fields. I had just left English, which was one of the few classes I shared with Cara. Homework had been handed back – it was our first essay on *The Bridge to Terabithia* – and she was bad-tempered and cold. I had received an A, and she had been awarded a B+. 'How is it,' she said, 'that I'm the one who has to bring you books to read, and you still find a way to beat me?' I had nothing to say to that. We walked in silence, heading for the final class of the day. Everybody in our year ended Thursday afternoon with mathematics, and there was a crush of students waiting in the maths corridor. Cara was in the set below me, and I was relieved; tonight, Evie would congratulate me on the A, and by break time on Friday, Cara would be appeased by the proximity of the weekend.

At first, the woman in the corridor was a glimpse of white between the blue jumpers. She was walking in our direction, a head taller than the students around her. As we approached her, Cara stopped and seized my arm.

She wore a white gown to the floor with yellowed patches at the neck and armpits, and a rumpled quality which gave the impression that she hadn't changed for many days. Her hair hung flat against her back and then dangled down to the knees. She was anxious in the hallway, turning this way and that, and flinching when a pupil came too close to her. Where she passed, the hubbub softened to a hum. It was the pitch of stage whispers, and feigned horror. She was gaunt other than for her jowls, and the hangs of her belly and breasts.

'Oh my God,' Cara said. 'Is she OK?'

I realized with a slow, hot humiliation that the woman in the corridor was Mother.

'Don't worry,' I said. 'I know her.'

Cara turned to me, incredulous.

'It's my mother,' I said. 'Something must have happened.'

I considered my hard-won invisibility. Its cloak was beginning to slip, and in moments it would be on the floor.

'I should find out,' I said. 'But break time tomorrow?'

Cara was backing away from me against the corridor wall. She took timid little steps in her school shoes, as though I might not notice her departure. Already, I knew, she was thinking about who might be her new best friend.

'I'm sorry, Lex,' she said. 'I'm really sorry.'

Alone, I approached. Mother was trembling. 'Is it Evie?' I asked, and Mother shook her head. I hadn't seen her outside the house for so long that I had forgotten her twitchiness. Without Father at her side, she moved like a cornered sheep, twisting for an escape. She placed a hand on my wrist and I saw her fingernails as the other children would see them. Not resting harmlessly on her duvet when we said goodnight, but overgrown and jaundiced, with shadows of dirt trapped beneath them.

'Can we go somewhere else?' she said. 'The office was incompetent – I didn't know where to find you.'

'Of course.'

She fed her arm through my elbow, and the sea of children parted to let us pass. Cara would do well from this, I thought: she could testify to my secrecy, my strange habits. Her statements would be in high demand. Just before the door to the playground closed, I heard the eruption behind us.

Cara contacted me once, when I was living in London with JP. She had found me on LinkedIn, and hoped that we might connect. She didn't mention Five Fields, and she didn't refer to the events at Moor Woods Road. She was a solicitor too, she said. I hadn't heard of the firm, and I didn't respond to Cara, but not out of any sense of resentment. We had never had very much in common, other than being a little cleverer than our peers; since then I had met many clever people, and knew that it was an insufficient basis on which to build a friendship. If I had been kinder, I might have let her know that I didn't begrudge her that day in the corridor. People have done far worse things to survive being a teenager.

Mother and I stood in the playground in near-darkness. The moorlands were already black against the sky. I could see flickers of lessons through the classroom windows. Across the road, older boys ran on the football pitches, orange beneath the floodlights.

'What happened?' I asked.

'It's Father,' Mother said. 'He hasn't come home.'

He had driven to one of Jolly's sermons that morning, before sunrise. He had kissed Mother through her half-sleep, and touched her stomach, like a charm. He would be home for lunch. I tried not to think about the stretch of Mother's days, now that we were at school, and she had nothing to soothe. She had spent the morning preparing for Father's return, her fingers laced with pastry and meat. She had left the pie to cool and fallen asleep on the sofa, amongst her blankets. She woke in the mid-afternoon with the shock of the empty house.

'Where is he?' she said.

She had passed by the Lifehouse. The windows were dark.

'Let's get the others,' I said. 'Let's get everyone home.'

The school office was decorated for Christmas. Pink tinsel hung around the secretary's desk, and a plastic tree had been unfolded outside the headmaster's door. I asked where I could find Ethan, and the secretary informed me that he had been marked absent that morning, and every other morning that week. 'Aren't you his sister?' she asked.

'I think that there's been a mix-up,' I said. 'He was here this morning. I mean – we walked here. Together.'

'Well, that's not what the register says.'

The secretary had a heater beneath her desk, and she rested her bare feet between its gratings. She stared at me, as if she was waiting for me to leave. Through the doors, I could see Mother, huddled against the wind at the edge of the playground. An uncollected child at home time.

'Thanks, anyway,' I said.

By the time we returned home, Ethan was waiting for us, impatient and confused. 'Shouldn't you be in bed?' he said to Mother. He listened to the story of Father's disappearance with ever-widening eyes, and as soon as Mother was finished, he sat at the kitchen table and commandeered the phone. There was nobody at the church in Blackpool. Jolly's phone rang out. Mother stood over him, trembling, with her fingers at her throat. Delilah called to her from the couch, asking for a hug, and as soon as she was in the other room, Ethan started ringing hospitals.

Without Father, it was a strange, quiet evening. I divided the pie into six precise slices, and we ate in the living room, gathered at Mother's feet. Evie curled in my lap, feline with contentment. We prayed into the night, with full bellies and bowed heads. I could feel the jitters of a smile on my face. I didn't know what to pray for. I had the kind of ideas that I knew landed you in hell. Father's van was upturned on the moors, with a Father-shaped hole in the windscreen. Father was hanging from the bracken. We would eat well for the rest of time.

Amen.

Some time after midnight, headlights swung through the window.

Father came in the door breathless and pained, like the last survivor of some bloody crusade. He called for Mother, and she went to him. They staggered together to the kitchen, and she served him tea and crisps, tenderly, beneath the bright electric lights. While we were waiting for him to talk, I brushed down the empty pie plate and returned it to the cupboard.

'I've been,' Father said, 'with the police.'

They had picked him and Jolly up from Dustin's, mid-breakfast. The food had just arrived. Full English, with extra black pudding. When the officers approached the table, Jolly set down his knife and fork, and sighed. Father narrated this part of the story with the kind of hushed awe which he usually reserved for the Old Testament God. 'At least,' Jolly said, 'let us finish our fucking breakfast.'

The inquisition happened at the station. They were charging Jolly with money laundering and fraud. The fraud related to Jolly's use of religious donations from the residents of Blackpool, and was, of course, a complete fucking fabrication. I thought of his congregation, their faces turned up to catch some of his light. They would have counted out precisely what they could afford, and pressed the notes into his warm, damp hands. The police asked Father how Jolly spent his money; where Jolly kept his records; why Jolly hadn't shared his proceeds, if they were such close friends. Once Father had prayed for them, he knew exactly how to answer. 'No comment,' he said. He no-commented all afternoon.

They released him in the late evening. When they returned his belongings, the officer flicked a few thin coins onto the floor, so that Father had to stoop to collect them.

'Don't spend it all at once,' the officer said.

Father gathered us to him, then. 'There's persecution out there,' he said, 'for people who desire to live the life that we do.' I thought of the laughter in the school corridor, as Mother and I had left it. Father lay a hand on my neck, still cold from the drive home, and I warmed it with my own.

That night, for the first time in many months, Ethan wanted to talk with me. He called to me from his room as I passed to go to bed, so softly that I thought I had only hoped for it. He called again, and this time I knocked on his door and went in. He was lying on his bed in his school trousers with the Bible held above him. As soon as I was inside the room, he threw it at me, too fast for me to catch it. It hit me in the chest, and stung. 'So,' he said, and laughed. 'Thou shalt not steal.'

'We don't know anything yet,' I said, and he laughed again.

'What do you think he spent the money on? I bet it was something really dark. Old Jolly. He was always a complete lunatic, but I wasn't expecting this.'

'Do you think Father had anything to do with it?'

'I doubt it. I don't see Jolly as a man who would have shared his proceeds. But – put it this way – I don't think that this will help with Father's state of mind.'

'What do you mean?' I asked, and because I couldn't resist it: 'Like you're his great confidant.'

'At least I have a seat at the table.'

Ethan stood up. He had always been taller than me – even Delilah was taller than me – but in the last year his body had acquired a new power. There were cuts of muscle in his arms and across his chest. I heard him exercising in the evening, the noise of each odd movement repeated again and again, accompanied by his breath. He was beginning to refine himself. He stopped a foot away from me. I held back my shoulders, as Father had told us that we should, and adjusted my face so that I wouldn't look afraid.

'I think that he's losing it,' Ethan said. He spoke so softly that I stepped closer to him still. 'He already thinks that the world conspires against him. He talks of creating his own kingdom, right here in this house. This thing with the police – it just confirms what he's always suspected.'

Ethan still revelled in the transmission of knowledge. Part of the deal was your gratitude, which he looked for to confirm that he was cleverer than anybody else. I nodded, as though the information was taking some time to process, and asked the only question which seemed to have any worth. 'Then what do we do?' I said.

'You look after yourself, Lex. I won't be able to do it for you.'

I suspected that Ethan had requested my presence with this conclusion in mind. He was resigned to our fate and had no interest in an alliance. As I turned to leave, I recalled the one thing that I knew, and he didn't.

'Why weren't you in school today?'

'I was.'

'You weren't. Mother came to collect us, and I couldn't find you. You haven't been in all week.'

'Maybe there's nothing left to learn.'

'Don't be stupid.'

'Fine, then. I spend my time doing things that are a little more worthwhile. Sometimes I go to the library. You don't get bothered there. And sometimes—'

'Yes?'

'Sometimes I ask people for money.'

'You what?'

He contorted his face into an anxious smile. 'You don't happen to have a spare pound, do you? My mother forgot to pack my sandwiches.' The smile trembled, and cracked into laughter. After a few seconds, when I didn't join him, he wiped his eyes and lay back down on his bed.

'I don't think that school will be much of a concern any more,' he said. 'In the parish of Moor Woods Road.'

I didn't acknowledge it, but Ethan was right about school: I never did go back to Five Fields Academy. The day after Jolly's arrest, I heard Father moving through the house in the early morning. It was still dark outside, and I was comfortable and warm. I wasn't even hungry. I closed my eyes and drew up the covers, and when I next woke it was light. The alarm clock was missing from its place on the floor. 'Did we sleep in?' Evie asked, emerging testudinate from the duvet.

'I don't know.'

Still in bed, I pulled on my school jumper over pyjamas, and braced for the cold. In the kitchen, my parents sat hand in hand, Mother stroking the hair at Father's temple. There was a collection of clocks on the table in front of them, not just our alarms but the clocks from the hallway and the living room, and the pink plastic watch which Delilah had received for her ninth birthday. Mother and Father shifted as I entered the room, and Father smiled at my choice of dress, the way that you smile at a child's faux pas. 'You won't be needing that,' he said.

In place of the kitchen clock, he had hung the cross from the Lifehouse. Suspended embarrassingly above the hobs.

'Why don't you wake the others?' Mother said. 'And we can share the news.'

When we were assembled in the kitchen, Father began to talk. What had happened to Jolly, he said, was an abomination. He had long been suspicious of the authorities' attitudes to religious groups, peaceful though those groups may be. He had seen the influence of those attitudes in our despondency and our self-consciousness; in our sins and – he looked at me – in our cynicism. He had decided that we should commence a freer, more focused way of living, outside the shackles of public education. He would teach us himself.

Only Gabriel rejoiced at the news. 'So we don't have to go to school?' he asked. When Father nodded, he gasped and clutched his fists to his chest.

Father had ideas about how we would structure our days. Time was an unnecessary distraction, and he would monitor it himself. This was a world without the dictation of the school bell, or going-home time. There were books we had studied which we would need to discard, and which he would collect later that day. It would be up to us to discard the ideas which we had acquired from them.

'There are some things that you'll need to forget,' Father said. 'But there's so much for you to learn.'

That morning, Father wrote two letters: one to the headmaster of Five Fields Academy, and the other to the headmistress of the school that Evie, Gabriel and Delilah attended. The letters were polite and perfunctory. Father wished to exercise his right to educate his children at home. He had reviewed the curriculum ('curricula,' Ethan mouthed to me, unable to stop himself), and was confident that he and his wife would be able to deliver them. He would welcome visits from the council.

'Do you know where we are on their to-do list?' Father asked. Mother gazed up at him, wide-eyed, and shook her head.

'Below the bottom,' Father said. 'Last in line.'

He signed, with a flourish.

During lunch, I excused myself to use the toilet. In our room, I surveyed the small pile of books on the floor, which I had checked out of the school library the week before. I had already read them all; things had happened too quickly for me to return them. I thought of the disappointment of the school librarian, who had praised me for never incurring a fine, and who had once told me that there were days when she much preferred books to human beings. I knelt down and examined the spines. There were fantasy novels, and an R. L. Stine, and something by Judy Blume. I couldn't hide them all: they would have to go. I took the book of Greek myths and unwrapped it from my jumper, touching the cover and the golden fore edge. It was, I thought, the nicest thing that I had ever owned. I tucked it beneath my mattress, where Father couldn't find it, and where we could still reach for it at night. In the bathroom, I stared at my reflection for some time. 'Think,' I said. I watched my lips pull back over the word. For the first time, I saw myself assembling a rucksack of belongings, and leaving Moor Woods Road in the middle of the night. I could do what Ethan had done, and ask people for money. I could reach Manchester, or even London. I could find Miss Glade, and beg to live with her. I straightened up. It was a ridiculous idea, and besides, I couldn't leave Evie. I was overreacting. I lifted the skin at the sides of my mouth, and I returned to the kitchen, smiling.

The computer shop opened two doors down from the Lifehouse, just before the church closed. It was called Bit by Bit. 'Fucking imposters,' Father said, when he first saw the signage, hurrying us behind him.

Whenever we passed – to the weekend services, or to a prayer session in the evening – the shop was busy. At the till, there was a young woman with a shaved head and a jungle of tattoos. There was a leaflet in the window advertising free computer lessons for the elderly. We had Information Technology classes at school, which mostly involved the boys trying to breach the school's safeguards to find pornography, but I knew how to send an email and format a document. Father had taught Ethan more than this, but lessons had not been extended to the rest of the family.

I mentioned Bit by Bit to Dr K in passing. We were talking of Hollowfield, and how little of it I remembered, and she held up her palm and frowned. 'Let's talk about this shop,' she said. 'And what it meant to your father.'

'He didn't like it,' I said. 'I think that much is clear.'

'And why do you think that was?'

'His own enterprise hadn't worked out. He was jealous, I suppose.'

'Wasn't this the ultimate reminder of his failures?' Dr K said. 'Which he had just tried – had relocated – to forget?'

'It was just a shop.'

She rose from her chair, as she did when she was animated, and walked to the window. It wasn't the long window of Harley Street. This was in our early days, when we met in a hospital in South London. Her office was on the ground floor, and she had to keep the blinds closed; the doctors liked to smoke just beside it.

'Entertain me, Lex. Slip into his head – oh, I know, it's an unpleasant place to be – and consider the litany of his failures. The coding classes. His employment in IT services. The Lifehouse. The fall of his idol. Failure on top of failure. Men like your Father are odd, delicate things. Easily cracked – just a hairline fracture in the porcelain.' She turned back to me, smiled. 'You don't realize that you've broken them until the shit floods out.'

'Lots of people fail,' I said. 'Every day. All of the time.'

'And everybody's brain is wired that little bit differently.' She shrugged, and returned to her chair. 'I'll never ask you to pity him,' she said. 'Only to understand him.'

We sat as we often did, in deadlock, each of us waiting for the other person to speak.

'I ask you,' she said, 'because I think that it might help you.'

It was a weekday evening, in my first year back at school. I still had to attend a physiotherapist appointment and finish my homework. 'Are we done?' I asked.

She gave it a final try. 'Do you remember when the shop opened,' she said, 'in relation to the Binding Days?' I was already standing, pulling on my coat.

'I need to go,' I said. 'Really. Dad'll be waiting.'

He wasn't. I sat in the hospital reception, watching the strange cast pass through the sliding doors, hidden by the water fountain in case Dr K emerged from her office and found me in the lie. When I thought of Father, all I could see was the collection of photographs published by the papers after the escape. Here was Father at the pulpit (The Preacher of Death); here was Father on Central Pier (They Were Once a Normal Family). His real face – the tics of pleasure and disappointment – eluded me. He would have liked that, I thought. The idea that he couldn't be captured.

Of course, Dr K was right. Bit by Bit had opened a few months before the Binding Days began. The last time I had walked by, in the days when we were still walking, the shop window was broken. The crack had been taped up with cardboard, and a cheerful note: Still open for business.

For a fortnight, my world was compressed to the office and the hotel. Black taxis moved me between them, turning on their lights when I approached. I slept little enough that there was no discernible ending or beginning to the days. The numbers at the bottom of my screens blinked from one date to the next.

I kept the probate documents in the safe in my room, to alleviate the strange fear that I'd return to find them gone. I requested that Bill reschedule our visit to Hollowfield, and he was silent; for a moment, I thought that he would refuse. An article had appeared in a tabloid, under the headline 'Hollowfield's House of Horrors: Where Are They Now?' I imagined the members of the council assembled around it, wondering which of us had been paid for the commission. It was a double-page spread, with the famous garden photograph in the centre. Our forms had been removed, leaving seven black silhouettes and the letters of our pseudonyms. In the margin, the journalist summarized us. Ethan was 'an inspiration'. Sources close to Gabriel reported that he was 'troubled'. Girl A was 'elusive'. Bill sighed. He would give me one more week.

Jake signed the documents on behalf of ChromoClick at eleven forty-seven, thirteen minutes from our client's deadline. It was a subdued gathering. Devlin was in New York. ChromoClick's solicitors dispersed. When I asked the night secretary for a bottle of champagne and two glasses, she sighed, and walked slowly to the firm's kitchen. When she handed me the bottle, she scowled. 'Congratulations,' she said.

Jake stood at the window of our meeting room. When he

turned to me, he was grinning. 'There aren't many moments like this in a lifetime,' he said. 'Are there?'

I knew precisely how much richer he had just become. 'I think you're doing well if you get one,' I said. 'Cheers.'

'Do you get your life back now?'

I laughed. 'This is my life.'

'And you don't get tired?'

'Sure. But I don't mind it. There's always something to think about. Somewhere else to go. I've been bored in the past – really bored, in fact. And – well. This isn't so bad.'

'Your boss seems like a pretty hard taskmaster.'

'She's been in this firm for thirty-five years,' I said. 'I don't think she had much of a choice.'

We looked back to the window. There were a few bodies left in the next office along. There was a certain comfort in that; in the City, somebody was always having a worse night than I was.

'I used to play this game,' I said, 'with my sister. What would you do with a million pounds? Am I allowed to ask you what you have in mind?'

He laughed. 'And the rest,' he said.

'I didn't want to be impolite.'

'I'll build a house,' he said. 'There's a particular kind of house that I've had in mind, since I was a child. Very different from the house where I grew up. Isn't everybody's answer some variation on that?'

'Well, we were children. I wanted a library. She wanted a convertible.'

'She'll have change.' He was quiet for a moment. 'I have no doubt,' he said, 'that you'll get your library.'

We shook hands at the lifts, on his way down. The adrenaline was seeping out of me. I could sense myself becoming smaller and flatter.

'Hey,' he said. 'I just thought – did you ever do it? Your ChromoClick results?'

I laughed. 'No,' I said.

'Let me tell you a secret,' he said. His lift was here, and between the closing doors, he said: 'Me neither.'

I walked past the empty offices to my desk. There was a message waiting for me from Devlin: 'Give me a call when you can,' she said. She had sent an email, too, which said: I left you a voicemail.

'Congratulations,' she said, as soon as she picked up the phone.

'Thanks. This was a good one.'

'You were excellent. Everyone's happy. There'll be a dinner in New York.'

'Just what I wanted to hear.'

'Not for a while. Jake's flying out. Some of the other partners. I hope that you'll be back here by then.'

'I'm nearly there. There's just one last thing to do. And my sister's flying in to help out over the weekend. It'll be easier, once she's here.'

'Good. Take a few days. There's a lot in the pipeline, but nothing this week.'

'I'm happy to talk about it now.'

'Well, I'm not. Go home, Lex.'

I began to order a taxi, then changed my mind. I had spent every hour of daylight in the office for twelve days now, and most of the night-time hours, too. I kicked off my loafers. I would walk.

I passed through the dark lobby and out into the City. The nights had become colder. The wind skimmed across empty pavements and between gaps in the grand, dark buildings. I walked along the walls of the Bank of England, past its pompous columns and the sculptures labouring above its doors. From his horse, Wellington presided over the late traffic. I walked past the old trade halls on Cheapside and through St Paul's churchyard, beneath the glowing grey dome. I recalled the promise which the City had held when I had first arrived in it, as hopeful as I had ever been, discharged by Dr K and falling in love. It was hard to subdue the memory of the feeling, which wasn't so different from the feeling itself. The place still held a few modest hopes. I hoped to complete this deal or that. I hoped to keep Devlin happy. I hoped that I made enough money so that I would never concern myself with paying for breakfast, or a pack of tampons. I passed Millennium Bridge and the cloistered quads around Temple. JP might still be at work, hunched in the dark of a labyrinthine chambers; there had once been an infestation of moths in his office, who had left holes in his gown and wig. At Aldwych I turned north, back towards lands of the living. As he did each evening, the doorman at the Romilly greeted me, and wished me goodnight.

I left London early on Thursday morning. There were still foxes sniffing the rubbish bags in Soho, and the sun wasn't up. I drove straight through to Leicester and ate breakfast on the embankment at a service station, watching the traffic beginning to clot. A message from Bill to confirm my appointment the next day. A lorry driver stopped beside me to finish his coffee; he asked where I was headed. 'I'd get a wriggle on,' he said, 'if I was you.' I had seven hours before I needed to collect Evie from the airport and drive on to Hollowfield, but I intended to make another stop on my way. 'Thanks,' I said, and he waved. I returned to my porridge.

I waited for the traffic to clear, and continued on to Sheffield and into the Peak District. We had been scattered so far apart, when you thought of it: there was no reason to our whereabouts other than people's willingness to take us. It had been one of the reasons that the proposed meetings between us had rarely taken place. The terms of Noah's adoption meant that he would never be able to attend them; Evie was hesitant, and preferred our long phone conversations, or to visit me alone; Ethan had secured his place at university and lost interest in the reality of us: strange children, gathered in a room designed by a committee. The Coulson-Brownes had always brought Gabriel along – I expected that they were watching for some new nugget of horror to feed to the press – and Delilah had come reluctantly, chewing gum and distracted by a new gadget, right up until our final argument. I couldn't recall a meeting after that one. Dr K had advised that it was for the best, and it wasn't like I had missed them.

At Cragforth Cricket Club, I pulled onto the grass and pushed my sunglasses up my nose. As soon as I stood from the car I saw that an old man, all in white, was walking towards me. He held a stick in one hand and a bucket in the other, and for an impossible moment I believed that I had been caught; the whole town had been awaiting my eventual arrival and would guard Noah however they saw fit.

'It's a fifty-pence donation,' said the old man, 'for the car park.'

'Oh. Sure – of course.'

The end of his walking stick had been carved into the shape of a cricket ball. It even had the seams, etched into the wood. 'I like that,' I said, and he chuckled. I produced a ten-pound note – it was an embarrassing amount more than he had requested, but all that I had – and dropped it into the bucket. 'I don't need change,' I said.

'You should save some for yourself. It's two for one at the clubhouse bar, provided you buy before six.'

'Thanks. That sounds good to me.'

He was already looking for the next car, but he waved over his shoulder, and I waved back.

I walked around the pavilion and to the pitch beyond it. The town was encircled by soft green hills, and I could see walkers on the nearest ridge, minute against the sky. There were a few benches in the shade of the buildings, just below the scoreboard, but the spectators were gathered at the edge of the field, in the sunshine. I stood a few metres from the little crowd and surveyed the scoring. JP had been devoted to the game, and I understood it well enough. When he had to work at the weekends, in the summer, the sound of *Test Match Special* filled our flat. The warm lull of it. Father had called cricket a game for faggots.

The Cragforth team was batting. Fifty-two for three. One of the batsmen had only just come in; he was batting timidly, leaving most of the balls. I looked back at the boys waiting in the stands, unsure what I was expecting to see. One of the men in the crowd wandered along the boundary to join me. He was wearing a Cragforth Cricket Club cap.

'Hello,' he said. 'Not a bad start.'

'No.'

'Are you one of the mothers?'

'No. I'm just stopping by.'

'It's a nice way to spend an afternoon.'

'Yes.'

I was already sweating. I adjusted my sunglasses and shook the hair from my face. 'I'm going to grab a drink,' I said.

'Oh, yes. There are some end-of-summer deals, I think.'

'I'm driving. It's a shame.'

The clubhouse was cool and dark. There was a moss green carpet and a whole wall of team photographs. The man from the car park sat at the bar with a new pint in his hand.

'You didn't take much persuading,' he said.

I laughed. 'Just a Diet Coke,' I said. The girl behind the bar nodded.

'It's on the house,' said the old man, and to the girl: 'She blew her savings on the car park.'

'Thanks.'

'Did you travel far?' the girl asked, waiting for the glass to fill.

'From London.'

'No wonder you look so bloody miserable,' said the old man, and I grinned, and carried my drink back out to the sunshine. My friend in the cap still stood alone, and it seemed odd not to rejoin him. The timid batsman was out and conversing sternly with his father. 'You haven't missed much,' my friend said.

'Do you come every week?'

'I try. My son used to play for this team, you see. It was a happy time.'

'Oh.'

He smiled. 'It's a nice community,' he said. 'People look out for each other. You don't get that everywhere.'

'No. I guess not.'

A new batsman was on strike. He played an effortless drive to the boundary. I finished my drink and sucked the ice. This pair were more interesting to watch: they were reckless and aggressive, and they called inaudible instructions to one another across the central strip. I felt warm and lazy. I could spend the afternoon just here, I thought, and order a gin and tonic every few overs.

'Do you follow the game?' my friend asked.

'A little. I had a boyfriend who liked it. That was a while ago, now, though.'

'At least you got something out of it.'

'True.'

A few balls later, the original batsman fumbled his shot, and the ball looped into a fielder's hands. My friend winced, and was the first to break into applause. The batsman shrugged. Alone, he began the long walk back to the pavilion. Pressed cream uniform against the electric green grass. As he went, he removed his helmet.

I pushed up my glasses.

Noah Gracie.

He was a head taller than me. He had our pale hair, whitened from the sun. Alone on the pitch, he seemed very young, but when he neared the clubhouse I understood that he looked no younger than the other boys waiting to bat. It had been the fact that – when we were children – we had looked old. He met two women at the boundary, set up with folding chairs and a cool box in the shade of the building. I was too far away to hear what they said. One of them handed him a banana, and he jogged to join his team.

Noah Kirby.

The boys welcomed him into the thick of them. One handed him water. Another ruffled his hair. The man next to me was still clapping. 'He's had a good season,' he said. I nodded, unable to speak, and joined the applause. I was watching the women at the boundary. One had opened a beer and a paper, but her partner was folding her chair, and gesturing towards the village. By the time she reached the car park, I was following her.

The Lifehouse had a short, inglorious existence. It closed its doors around the same time the new baby was born, so the house on Moor Woods Road suddenly felt a lot fuller. There was the baby, with his cot crammed into the corner of my parents' bedroom, and his cries rebounding from floor to floor. There was Father, muttering between the rooms, with nobody left to preach to but us. There was Mother, appeasing them both; when we heard her hushing and cooing, we were never sure who was in her arms.

The Lifehouse had been populated, for the most part, by my siblings and me. In his efforts to convert the people of Hollowfield, I recognized that Father's charm had faded. His old devotees – restless mothers, and bored girls hoping for an adventure in salvation – no longer glanced up when he passed by. His body was taut and restless, his veins closer to the skin. His sullenness, which had once been seductive, had become frightening: mothers shifted their children politely out of his path. He had a gut, and holes in his clothes. He didn't look like somebody who could save you.

I had hoped the new baby might placate Father. A little reminder of his vitality. The truth is, our new brother was difficult and sickly. He was born a month early, and was jaundiced; at first, he had to stay in hospital, beneath artificial light. For two weeks, Mother was missing, and Father sulked at the kitchen table, criticizing our writing, our attitude, our posture. We ate little, and I was relieved when the child came home. Evie presented Mother with a card, with a drawing of Jesus, still and serene in the manger, and Mother parted the blankets so that we could see the baby's face. He was raw and scrawny, writhing to escape her arms. Evie took back the card.

'Maybe he'll look like this when he's older,' she said.

I noticed that Mother tried to keep the baby from Father. She zipped him into a coat and took him for long walks on the moor, even though she was still stooped from the birth. During our lessons, they sat in the garden, bundled in blankets in the thin winter sunlight, the baby's cries subdued by the kitchen door. One night, collecting glasses of water, I found them there past midnight, a hunched creature with two clouds of breath. It was March, and there was snow on the ground.

Father believed that there was something wrong with the baby. 'The crying,' he said. 'What child cries like this?' He constructed strange theories about the fortnight at the hospital. 'Did you keep an eye on him?' he asked Mother. 'All of the time?' And, when the crying was loudest: 'Are you sure that he's ours?'

First the books had gone, then the luxuries: colourful clothes; shampoo; our old birthday presents. Father sealed the windows with cardboard, so that the authorities wouldn't be able to see in. It wasn't that we were forbidden from going outside – not at first – but that we didn't want to. I had three T-shirts on rotation, which smelt warm and rotten, and tracksuit pants with holes in the crotch. I contemplated meeting Cara and Annie on the high street. I directed whole scenes of my own humiliation: this time they would run from me, shrieking; this time they would feign politeness, and exchange a long, incredulous look, just before I turned away. Only Gabriel accompanied Father to the supermarket, and he returned snuffling or bruised. He had seen things that he wanted, and forgotten that he wasn't supposed to ask for them.

The area beyond the house began to soften, then to blur. I could recall the direction of Moor Woods Road – the slope downwards, which started gently and steepened to the junction – but not the appearance of the houses, and not the details of Hollowfield. I dreamt of walking between the shops on the high street. They came to me in order: the bookshop; Bit by Bit; the charity shops; the Co-operative; the doctor. The shutters where the Lifehouse had been. I purchased paper bags full of food, taking my time, talking to the shopkeepers. Dreams ordinary enough to be true.

We were expected to learn together. Father taught us little that I didn't already know, so instead I observed my siblings. Delilah sighed, perpetually and dramatically; sometimes she swooned face-first into her journal, exhausted. Gabriel held books a few inches from his face and stared at the words in frustration, imploring them to share their secrets. Evie was serious and studious, noting each word that Father imparted.

Once or twice a week, Ethan offered to take me off Father's hands for a few hours. He did so begrudgingly, with feigned exasperation, and only when he had thought of something which he wanted to discuss. He had managed to retain more of his belongings than the rest of us, and in his room, he would settle himself on the bed, with his back against the wall, and open *Mathematics for Economists*, or *The Canterbury Tales*. 'Come here,' he would say, without looking up, and when I was seated next to him, he would begin to talk, in quick, concise sentences, waiting for the dot of my full stop before he started on the next.

I longed for the evening. After the tedium of our lessons, and our exercises, and Father's dinnertime games. Evie and I had been left with three books: an atlas; an illustrated dictionary; and the myths beneath the mattress. When the house was still, Evie tiptoed across the detritus of our bedroom floor and lifted my duvet. First the cold of the room, then the warmth of her body, taking its place. 'What tonight?' I asked. It seemed important to ration the books, so that we didn't become bored of them.

'I don't mind.'

'Come on. Choose.'

'But really. I like them all.'

I could sense her smile in the darkness. I thought that I could hear it. She switched on the bedside light.

Her favourite word was Car, which was accompanied by a photograph of a Mustang on an ocean road. My favourite word was Defenestration. Our favourite country was Greece, of course. We had found the routes of our heroes in the atlas, tracing them with our fingers, planning a journey of our own.

On the first warm day in spring, we sat in a half-moon in the garden, facing Father. That day, he was soft and charismatic. Mother was inside with the baby, and the afternoon was quiet. Father changed the syllabus, and we learnt about discipleship. 'Obey your leaders and submit to them,' Father said, 'for they are keeping watch over your souls.' He closed his eyes and turned his face up to the sun. 'There are no Judases,' he said, 'at my table.' It seemed obvious to me that Judas was the most interesting character in the Bible. I liked his sad attempt to return the silver paid for betrayal. Like that would do any good. Ethan and I had discussed the disparate accounts of his death, which we agreed was evidence enough that you couldn't take the Bible as historical truth. If you were a real person, you only died once.

After our lessons, there was time left for play, and we spun across the garden in a game of tag, Father watching us from the kitchen door. I was It. I darted at Delilah and seized her shins, and we tumbled together into the soil where Mother's vegetables were trying to grow. In the falling sunlight, I looked up from the ground and my siblings scattered away from me, bent-double, half laughing and half gasping, and I understood that if somebody were to come around the house and through the garden gate, they would see our beautiful family, us with our matching hair and our strange, antiquated clothes. There would be nothing to worry about at all.

And then there were other afternoons.

There was the afternoon when Gabriel smashed Father's liquor. There was no longer any need for one of us to fetch the bottle: it stood in the middle of the kitchen table, like a condiment. Father had been drinking at lunch, and the bottle had moved to the edge of the table. It wasn't that Gabriel gestured, or brushed it as he passed by; he set his palms on the table to stand up and placed one on top of the bottle. There was an odd second before we could see liquor or blood, when it seemed like the bottle might have survived, and in the next second, it shattered across the room.

Father was somewhere else in the house. Upstairs, the baby's muffled screaming. We waited, none of us looking at Gabriel. Blood flashed down his wrist. He stood alone at the centre of our circle and started to cry.

'Jesus, Gabe,' Ethan said. 'Stop it.'

Slowly, taking his time, Father came to the kitchen. There was no need to ask what had happened. He ran his finger across the damp tabletop, and sucked it. 'Oh, Gabriel,' he said. 'Ever cumbersome.'

He touched his palm to the side of the little boy's face, cradling it.

'What will we do with you?' he said, and the cradle tightened into a tap, gentle at first, as you would touch somebody whom you needed to wake, and then harder. A slap.

'Do you know how much that costs?' Father said, and his hand changed again: now it was a fist. I moved between Evie and the table, so that she wouldn't have to watch.

'No,' Father said. 'You know nothing of worth.'

'Stop it,' Delilah said, and Father laughed and mimicked her: Stop it, stop it, stop it. One for each impact. Delilah stepped from our circle. I hadn't looked at her – really looked at her – for a while. She was so much thinner than I remembered. There were sinkholes around her eyes and beneath her cheekbones. She gripped Father's hand with cadaver arms.

'Don't you understand?' she was shouting. 'He can't see!'

She clutched Father's fist as if it was a wild animal which she wanted to soothe. Their faces were a few centimetres apart. The kind of proximity where you can taste the other person's mouth.

'He can't see,' she said again.

Gabriel sat back in his chair. Blood had collected in his Cupid's bow. He had stopped crying.

'We can clear it up,' Delilah said.

'All of my children can see,' Father said, and left the room.

And there was the afternoon when Peggy visited. The incident was omitted from her book, which surprised me more than it should have done. She wouldn't have come out of it well. When I finished the book – *Sister's Act: A Tragedy Observed* – under the supervision of Dr K, I flicked back through to make sure, with a kind of nauseous elation. I wouldn't have come out of that afternoon well, either.

It had been a difficult day. The baby had started to cry before dawn. The miserable persistence of it, pervading the rooms of the house. I had heard Ethan groan, then throw something at the wall between us. I clung to sleep for as long as I could, cover drawn up against the first thin light. Evie lay on her back, her lips moving, telling herself a story. Even when the baby stopped, I could hear his cries, living between the walls.

Autumn again, and the kind of weather which never commits to daylight. Father instructed us to write in our journals. I sat at the kitchen table, looking at the empty page. Contemplating what I would write, if it wouldn't be subject to inspection. As it was, my entries were all comically dull. *Today, we spent a long time considering the fact that Jesus never raised the issue of homosexuality. I agree with Father's opinion that this omission cannot be taken as permission to participate in homosexual behaviours.* I glanced at Evie's page. She was drawing a garden, completing the veins of each leaf and shading the shadows underneath them. 'Eden?' I said.

'I don't know. Just somewhere I think about.'

I couldn't draw: I was stuck with this world. *We had a tiring night*, I wrote. *The whole family was awake early. I love having a new sibling, but I hope that he starts to sleep a little more.*

On days like this, I thought of codes and messages. How to capture – quietly – the extent of our boredom? How to record each little assault? At the table, Gabriel hunched his back, to position his eyes a few centimetres from the page. And the pervading ones. How to translate the hollowness of starvation? The feeling that something was feasting on the walls of my stomach, chewing it from the inside out?

Mother is getting stronger every day, I wrote, pathetically.

There were two figures in Evie's garden, walking hand in hand in silhouette. Their heads tilted together, as if they were lost in conversation. 'Are you sure it's not Eden?' I asked.

'Yep.' She pressed her lips against my ear. 'It's us.'

She touched a finger to her lips, smiling. I rolled my eyes, smiling too.

And then the knock at the door.

My pen jerked across the page.

Delilah stood up.

'Who is it?' Evie asked. Beneath the table, I took her hand.

Another knock.

Father came softly into the kitchen. 'We have a visitor,' he said. His hands were pressed together, as if he was just about to begin a sermon.

'Let's all be very, very quiet,' Father said. 'And very calm.'

He placed his hands on my shoulders.

'Lex,' he said. 'Come with me.'

In the hallway, he knelt down in front of me. For a long time, I had avoided looking him in the eye, and now that I did, I saw that he was tired and wild. Clumps of grey hair stuck to his forehead. At the edges, his mouth slumped into his jowls. There was a smell coming from him, not just from his mouth but beneath his skin, as if something had hidden there to die.

'I need you to answer the door, Lex,' he said. 'But it's more than that. This is your chance, you see – to prove your commitment to this family.'

He took my hair in his hand – as long as Mother's, now – and tweaked my head to face him.

'It's Aunt Peggy,' he said. 'You know how she likes to interfere with us. You know how she'd like to see us suffer. All you need to say – all you need to do – is say that your mother and me are out. You say that everybody's well. You don't let her inside. Do you think that you can do that, Lex?'

I looked longingly back to the kitchen.

'Come on, Lex,' Father said. 'It's very important to me. It's very important to us all.'

That's what I think of, when I remember the afternoon. Father's faith in my loyalty. In my obedience.

A tendril of shame, stirring in my gut.

Father stood, and kissed me on the forehead. He watched me walking past the living room and the bottom of the stairs. The warmth of his eyes, nudging me along the hallway. I was already smiling. I opened the door.

Peggy Granger started. She was a few steps from the threshold, looking up to the bedroom windows. She was rounder and older and blonder than I recalled. Beyond her, I could see Tony, parked on Moor Woods Road, watching us from the car.

'Hello,' I said.

Peggy examined my face and neck, my dress and ankles and feet. In the daylight, I was dirtier than I had thought, and I crossed one foot over the other, to hide some of the grub.

'Is that you, Alexandra?'

I laughed. 'Yes,' I said. 'Yes, Aunt Peggy. Of course.'

'How are you?'

'OK,' I said. 'Good.'

Then, thinking: 'How are you?'

'We're very well, thank you. Listen. Are your mum and dad home? We were in the area.'

'Not at present,' I said. 'They're out.'

'And when will they be back?'

'I don't know.'

'That's a shame. I hear I've got another nephew. I'd love to meet him. How's he doing?'

'He cries a lot,' I said, and Peggy nodded, satisfied. Still susceptible to a little schadenfreude.

'He's OK, though,' I said.

'Good. Well. We'll be heading home.'

She lifted an arm to wave, but didn't move. She looked to her shoes, like she couldn't convince them to retreat.

'Listen, Alexandra,' she said. 'I'm a bit worried about you. You don't look very well, if I'm honest. Not very well at all.'

I opened my mouth, then closed it again. Codes. Messages. A few vague ideas, which I was too tired to enact.

'Alexandra?'

Peggy took a step closer to the door. An imploring look on her face, as if she wanted to say it for me.

'Are you all right, Lex?'

A fierce little figure assembled herself beside me, obscuring the view between the doorframe and my shoulder.

'Hello, Aunt Peggy,' Delilah said.

'And this must be Delilah! Look at you. Like a model.'

Delilah curtsied, and did the thing with her face which made Father forgive her trespasses.

'Girls!' Aunt Peggy said. 'What are you like?'

'I'm sorry, Aunt Peggy,' Delilah said. 'But we were playing a game. And Lex is holding everything up.'

'Well, that won't do.'

Peggy laughed. Delilah laughed. And, after a few seconds, I laughed, too.

Delilah pinned her arm around my elbow.

'You ask your parents to give us a ring,' Peggy said.

'We will.'

'Goodbye then, girls.'

'Goodbye.'

I closed the door and turned back into the gloom. Father waited there, still and smiling, then advanced, one arm raised, ready to use it when he reached us. I shut my eyes. When I opened them, his hand was on Delilah's head, cradling her scalp, with his stare settled on me.

'Well done, Delilah,' he said. He looked satisfied, the way he looked at the end of a good, long lunch. 'Well done.'

No Judases at his table.

That was when the Binding Days began.

I followed Noah's mother through the village. There were spindly stone cottages craning to see the road. The bells were ringing at the church, but there was no one around. There was a cafe with a queue of walkers, and dogs lapping at water bowls outside. There was a noticeboard advertising the choir and Kittens For Sale. I passed a sprawl of teenagers at the cenotaph, sucking on ice lollies, their limbs entwined. The hills were speckled with mountain bikers and sheep.

Noah's mother walked fast, with the chair in one arm and the other arm swinging. Her legs were scrawled with varicose veins, but otherwise, I could have been following a child. We crossed a stream, subdued by the summer and busy with ducks, and turned down a new road. Here, the houses were bigger and further apart. She stopped at the third one on the street and propped the chair against the wall.

'Mrs Kirby?' I said, and she turned around, with her face open. The front of her T-shirt said Bondi Lifeguards.

'One of them,' she said. 'My wife isn't home.'

'I think you have a son,' I said, 'called Noah?'

'I just left them,' she said. 'Is everything—'

She looked at me properly, then. She had the door unlocked, but she didn't open it.

'No,' she said.

'I'm not—'

'Please,' she said. Her mouth was clenched in one straight cut, and as she shook her head, the sun-ruined skin at her neck went from taut to slack. 'Please.'

'I just need a minute,' I said.

'Tell me who you are. And tell me what you want.'

'My name's Lex,' I said. 'I'm his sister.'

I shrugged.

'Girl A,' I said.

She slumped against her house. I thought that she didn't know whether to plead or to gut me. I took a step away, back onto their lawn. I had been holding up my hands, but I realized how stupid I must look, and dropped them.

'Early on,' she said, 'I expected this every day. Every time the door went, or the telephone – I'd think: This is it. Then a bit of time goes past, and you start to think it might be all right. The press, the family – they might never look for you. You start to think you've got away with it.'

She closed her eyes.

'Sarah always said that someone would come,' she said. 'But the last few years – I didn't think about it at all.'

'I'm not looking for him,' I said. 'I don't need to see him. It's just – administration.'

'Administration,' she said. She laughed.

'I just need a signature. For our mother's estate.'

'Your mother,' she said.

She opened the door and entered the house. 'You can't be here,' she said, 'when they get back.' In the hallway mirror I saw the two of us together. My face looked sunken and stunned. A whole different species. She stepped onto the side of her trainers to take them off, and I reached for my shoes.

'Don't,' she said.

She walked barefoot through her home. There was one great white room, with the garden behind it. Along the back windows was a wooden table, with two benches, and a scatter of belongings: keys, envelopes, something half knitted. She wrestled with the patio doors, and heat fell into the room. A cat padded after

242

it. I sat slowly, expecting her to tell me to stand. Instead, she handed me a glass of water and sat opposite me. Her eyes twitched across my face. She was looking for her son, I thought. Like there were parts of him I'd already stolen.

'You might have seen,' I said, 'that my mother died.'

I laid the documents across the table, and I explained them to her the way I would explain them to a client. I talked with a performative precision, a notch louder than usual. It was one of the few times I could hear my own voice. Here was a photocopy of the will. Here were our applications. Here was where she should sign.

'Give me a minute,' she said.

She collected reading glasses from between the cushions of the sofa. Above the mantelpiece, there was a dreamcatcher and a photograph of my brother's family. I tried not to look at them. While she was reading, I checked on Evie's flight. She was mid-air, bouncing towards me every time I refreshed the map. The cat hopped onto the table and surveyed me with great disapproval.

'Don't worry,' Noah's mother said. 'She looks at everybody like that.'

She tightened her ponytail.

'How are the rest of you?' she said.

I thought: How long do you have?

'We're doing well,' I said. 'All things considered.'

'And do they know,' she said, 'where to find us?'

She dug a pen out of the fruit bowl and clicked the end of it.

'No. They don't.'

'When we first brought him home,' she said, 'Sarah would have visions. Nightmares, really. Cameras in the cradle. Your mother, driving down from Northwood in the middle of the night. She bought a bespoke alarm system. The ones with lasers, like in the films. A badger would come up the side of the house, and she'd be out there, with a torch and the Stanley knife. It took years, for her to sleep the way she used to.'

She signed, with her face close to the paper.

'I told her she was going mad,' she said. 'We could usually laugh about it, in the daytime.'

She slid the documents across the table. She was looking over my shoulder, out to the hot, bright street. 'Now,' she said, 'I'd like you to leave.'

I nodded. We stood together, in synchrony, and across the table I held out my hand. She took it. An old habit: to shake hands over a deal, at the end of a meeting.

'The community centre,' she said. 'It's a good idea. I like it.'

'Thanks. It was my sister, mostly. She's better than the rest of us.'

She followed me back across the house. I went slower, this time. I took in the bee-print coasters and the dead orchid on the bookcase. I took in the wedding photographs up the stairs, and the light of bedroom windows, falling into the hallway. There was a row of Marvel figurines guarding the fireplace. There was a basket of hats and gloves and sunglasses by the door.

'It's hot out there,' she said. 'I can get you some sun cream. If you want.'

'Don't worry. I'm parked pretty close.'

'I'm sorry,' she said. It was easier to be sorry, I thought, with the documents signed, and me on the front step.

'It's OK,' I said. 'I won't come back here.'

'Is there anything that would help?' she said. 'I mean – is there anything that you would want to know?'

I smiled. You don't need to tell me, I thought. I already know. When I was at university, he was learning to ride a bike. In the winter, he plays video games and runs cross-country. He doesn't think about money or God. He moves easily through the school corridors, and he walks into each classroom knowing exactly who he's going to sit next to. There's a five-tier bookcase in his room. I think of you on Sunday evenings, having dinner together, and some nights – I see it – you stay at that table when the meal's over, talking about the cricket club, or the week ahead. I won't search for him, any more. I already know.

'No,' I said. 'That's OK.'

She started to close the door, but as she did, her head moved to fill the gap, and then the crack. I knew that kind of love. Too ferocious for niceties. She had to make sure that I'd gone.

'Still,' I said. 'Thank you.'

In another long night, the baby's cries came down the hallway, ever louder. Then the door opened, and Mother ducked into the room.

'Girls,' she said. 'Girls. I need your help.'

Her arms were full of blankets, and within them the baby, the little twisting tremors of him. She knelt down in the Territory and unravelled the material from his body, and stepped between us, loosening the bindings.

'Girls,' she said. 'You have to make him stop.'

She looked from me to Evie.

'Please,' she said.

Babies were OK, I thought. There had always been one around. I liked their softness and their strange preoccupations. They would laugh at all of my tired games. I lifted the child and lay him in the hollow between my thighs. 'Hey,' I said. 'Hey.' His eyes veered past me, through the ceiling and the roof. Seeing him here, like this, there was something odd about him. Something missing. I realized then that I hadn't really looked at him before. There had been a time when I had stopped thinking much beyond our room.

I leaned over and touched my nose against his. He smelt of the house, which smelt of worn clothes; stale plates; shit.

'Why won't he stop?' Mother said.

'Here,' Evie said, and peek-a-booed over my shoulder.

'It's been days,' Mother said. 'Your Father—'

She looked to the door.

'You're supposed to be clever,' she said. 'Aren't you? So – fix this.'

I held the baby closer, his head nestled against my shoulder. Crying, still.

'Not that clever,' Mother said.

'I read somewhere,' I said, 'that the more a baby cries, the smarter it is.'

I tickled the soles of my brother's feet. When he writhed, Mother lifted him from my arms and entombed him beneath her blankets. She ignored us now. It was just Mother and the baby. She murmured a prayer, part to God and part to the child, whispering his name. Imploring him to save himself.

For the first two weeks of his life, he had been nameless. The tag on his wrist said Gracie, so the nurses knew which mother to look for when they lifted him from the incubator. When he returned from the hospital, Father declared that he had already survived a fortnight in the lions' den. He wanted to give him a name which belied his half-formed frame. His tissue-thin skin. As if in naming him, he could reform him, and begin again. My parents congregated in the kitchen, and when they emerged, they declared that they would call him Daniel.

6
Evie (Girl C)

AT THE AIRPORT, I swung the car into the pick-up queue and looked for Evie. I had heard my phone vibrating on the passenger seat, and I was pretty sure that it would be her. The end of the summer, and waves of people returning home, wheeling suitcases and trolleys through the sliding doors. She was sitting apart from them, cross-legged against the wall and with one hand on her rucksack, keeping it close. She wore sunglasses and a hanging white dress, the straps fastened to the bodice with big red buttons. She had bundled her hair on top of her head in a precarious blond turban. I waved manically, as you can only really wave to people you love, and she looked up and tilted her sunglasses down to be sure it was me. I waited for the recognition to click. When it did, she jumped to her feet and darted through two lanes of traffic. 'You could have got a convertible,' she said, and kissed me through the open window.

'There was a limited choice. Anyway – the sunshine breaks tomorrow.'

'Well, that sucks.'

The driver behind us leaned on his horn.

'Can't he see,' Evie said, 'that we're busy discussing the weather?' She waved an apology and bundled her rucksack into the boot. The car behind us honked again. 'Jesus,' I said. Evie landed in the seat beside me, just as the driver shouted something from his window.

'Dick,' Evie said, and we pulled away.

'Next stop Hollowfield?' I asked, and she groaned.

'You know, we could go anywhere from here. We could be in Hong Kong, or Paris, or California—'

'All of our old atlas targets.'

'I don't know if I'd trust it,' she said. 'It was so old.' She spoke about the book like a mutual friend, one whom we missed. 'I'm pretty sure we intended to visit both parts of Germany.'

'Have you been?' I asked.

'West or East?'

This was Evie's approach to questions: she dodged around them, as she had danced between the cars in the traffic. Her life in Europe was uneventful, she said, but she maintained a casual mystery about her days. Her friends had first names and no backgrounds; she called from the city or from the apartment or from the beach; she had boyfriends and girlfriends, but never anything serious. Whenever I asked her about returning to England, she became quiet. 'I've spent my whole life,' she said, 'travelling away from our room. I can't stop now.'

Thinking of the house, she flinched. It was one of the reasons that I had resisted her arrival. Hollowfield still held its scrawny grip on her, tighter than it had on the rest of us. Sometimes she called in the middle of the night, late into the New York evening, and narrated a night terror. They always started at the front door of 11 Moor Woods Road, but inside there would be some strange landscape of Father's design: the family in crucifixion, or a biblical plain, with plagues on the horizon.

But in the daylight she was quick and freckled and light on her feet, and with one of her arms around my neck, and her smile radiating from the passenger side, I felt that our time in Hollowfield would be tolerable, at least. We would meet with Bill and representatives from the local council, and we would present our proposal to obtain funding for the community centre.

'Will there be a cheque?' Evie asked. 'One of the huge ones?'

'If I wanted a photo opportunity, I would have brought Ethan.'

'I'm not interested in the photo,' Evie said. 'I just want to know how it works. Do they take it to the bank?'

'Why don't you do less talking and more directing?'

Evie laughed and turned on the radio. 'We'll lose it in the hills,' she said, 'so we might as well enjoy it now.'

'Turn it up, then.'

We arrived in Hollowfield just after seven. There was a moment in the journey – I couldn't identify the exact point – when I began to recognize the landscape. The bends of the road were familiar, and I knew the number of miles to each of the next towns, promised on square blue signs. Already some of the moorland was purple with heather, spreading on the land like a new bruise. Daylight lasted longer here than in London, but the darkness would be dense and difficult for driving, and we were short of time. The moon was on the windshield, fingernail thin. We descended into the valley.

Hollowfield idled in the last stale summer light. The sun sunken behind the moors. The grass in the gardens and church-yard had receded, exposing graves like old teeth. A blank-faced girl rode a horse towards Moor Woods Road, pinching its dumpy belly between her legs. I turned onto the high street. It was difficult to distinguish between what had changed and what I had forgotten. The bookshop was still there, flanked by a book-ie's and a charity shop. The Lifehouse had last been a Chinese restaurant; it was boarded up, and for sale again. There were still a few shrivelled menus taped to the inside of the window.

Evie and I had booked into a twin room at the pub on the corner. I parked beside a tip, in the shadow of the building, and we looked at one another. A waitress sat on a bottle crate, smiling at her phone. My fingers left dark prints on the wheel. Evie took my hand.

Inside, locals guarded the bar. This had been one of Father's recruitment grounds, and I glanced at their faces, looking for members of our congregation. The floors were coated in a tongue-pink carpet, and there were photographs of old demolitions on the wall. The pub, perhaps, or Hollowfield in its early days. All of their occupants humourless and male. The landlady, laden with jewellery and holding her own glass, looked at me strangely when I mentioned our reservation. We were foreigners in this land, as we had been many years before. She led us to our room in silence, letting each door slam behind us on the way up.

'Well,' I said, when we were alone, 'she was friendly.'

'Come on, Lexy. She was fine.' Evie nudged me in the ribs. 'You,' she said, 'with your fancy hotels and your New York expectations. I want to hear all about it, by the way. New York.'

'Let me take a shower. I'll tell you over dinner.'

Like lovers, we talked as we undressed and dressed again. There was nothing of my body that she didn't know. Our room had two single beds, one against each wall, and without speaking we pushed them together.

At some point I dipped into sleep, and Evie woke me a few minutes later. She had rolled across the divide, and pressed her body into mine: nose in hair, arm against ribs, her ankle twisting around my shin.

'I'm cold,' she said.

'It's boiling. Are you OK?'

'Maybe it was the flight.'

'Come here,' I said, and turned to face her. When I wrapped my arms around her, her skin was cool. I tugged the duvet up to our eyes, and she laughed.

'How will the house look?' she whispered.

'Insignificant,' I said.

'I hope so.'

'What we really need here,' I said, 'are the Greek myths. They were much better than the Atlas.'

I liked to exaggerate the importance of Miss Glade's gift to my and Evie's survival. We had, after all, paid a high price for our stories.

'Do you know why I think that we liked them?' Evie said. 'They made us feel better about our own family.'

'You've told us little about this time,' Dr K said. 'When you were fourteen. Fifteen.'

'I don't remember as much of it.'

'That's understandable. Memory's a strange thing.'

This was a month after we first met. I remained in the hospital, but I had started to walk. I had an earnest physiotherapist called Callum, who looked like a Labrador. He celebrated each of my steps with an enthusiasm which I found difficult to take seriously. In each session, I scrutinized his face for mockery, but I never found it.

Dr K and I sat in the hospital courtyard. The square scrub was still frozen at mid-morning, hemmed in by the wards. The sun somewhere unseen above us, bleaching a corner of the sky. I had walked here myself, lurching on the crutches, and now I was tired and quiet.

'The things that you've told me about,' Dr K said. 'The lighting. The absence of any point of reference for the date, or the time. They're old disorientation techniques. It's OK to be confused, Lex. But you'll need to try.'

One of the detectives hovered around us with a notepad open in his hand. 'It's the critical period,' he said. 'Those last two years.'

'We're aware of that,' Dr K said. 'Thank you.'

She stood from our bench and knelt down before me. The hem of her dress touched the soil.

'I know how difficult it'll be,' she said. 'And your memory won't always help you. You see – it protects you from the things that you don't want to think about. It can soften certain scenes, or bury them away for a long, long time. A shield, of sorts. The problem, right now, is that it's protecting your parents, too.'

'I want to try,' I said. Ever eager to please. 'But maybe not today.'

'OK. Not today.'

'Did you bring any books?'

She straightened up, smiling. 'Maybe.'

'*Maybe?*'

But she was thinking of something else. Her hands were encased in black leather gloves, and she twisted and unravelled them, as if she was weaving.

'It's a particular interest of mine,' she said. 'Memory.'

The detective was watching us.

'We'll be able to use it,' she said.

The crawl of somebody else's hair against your skin. It was the first thing I was aware of, before the room unfurled from the darkness.

The ceiling in Moor Woods Road was white, too.

And in the first few moments you might try to stretch, forgetting that you couldn't. And then you could begin the first checks of the day: for new pain, and secretions in the night, and the rise and fall of your sister's ribs, shallower some days than others.

I lifted my arms, waiting for the present to return to me.

The walls were papered with flowers; Father would never have entertained wallpaper like that.

Evie was awake. She lay on her side, watching me. 'Hey,' she said. So much older, now.

She rolled across the division between the beds and rested her head on my chest. It had been a few years since I had shared a bed, and there had been times when it felt like my whole body craved the comfort of it. To sleep, I would twist my limbs together, pretending each belonged to another person. There had been a time – after I first moved to New York – when I had tried to stop this exercise. It wasn't possible. It was the kind of indulgence which I allowed myself: the only person to witness the humiliation of it was me.

Breakfast was included with our stay. 'Typical Lex,' Evie said. We sat in a dim room beyond the bar, facing one another, with a view to the car park. A dim concrete light fell across Evie's face. She tucked her legs beneath her on the chair and traced the crescents of last night's drinks on the table. She wasn't hungry.

'You're sure?' I said, when the food came. There were cold triangles of toast assembled in an elaborate silver structure, and a pool of grease on my plate, which shifted with the tilt of the table. A smile blinked across her face.

'Positive. But thank you.'

'OK. Let me know if you change your mind.'

She was still looking at the table. 'You always worried about me far too much.'

'Somebody had to.'

She looked up. 'Do you remember Emerson?' she said.

I had forgotten, but I remembered then. Emerson was a mouse. This was in the Binding Days. He appeared at odd intervals, scuttling across the Territory or beneath our bedroom door. We named him after the editor of our dictionary, Douglas Emerson, whom I always imagined bespectacled and hunched, in a study full of books. Whenever I've seen a mouse since – flashing past the threshold of my office, in the early hours of the morning

– I've thrown a document in its direction. But we weren't afraid of Emerson. Day after day, we hoped that he'd visit us.

'I still gather the strays,' she said.

A feral cat had appeared outside her apartment. A temporary place, in Valencia. Close to the beach. The cat was old, she thought, and skeletal. She could trace its ribcage, protruding through the fur. One of its back legs was contorted. She cornered it in the communal courtyard and took it to a veterinary surgery.

'It was furious,' she said. 'Even the vet thought so.'

The animal underwent several hours of surgery to correct its leg, and required an overnight stay with the vet. Evie paid over five hundred euros for the treatment. Two weeks after the animal was discharged, it died peacefully, in Evie's bed.

'My friends think that I'm crazy,' she said.

I looked down at my plate, saying nothing.

'Lex?'

I started to laugh.

'That cat,' she said. 'God.'

She reached for my tea and took a swig, laughing too.

But after breakfast she was tired. She spent half an hour in the bathroom, and emerged slumped and clammy, with her hands nursing her stomach.

'This place,' she said, smiling. 'We should never have come.'

'*You* should never have come. But I already told you that.'

'I'm sorry, Lex.'

'Let me do the meeting. You stay here. Rest up.'

'But it's why I came.'

'It'll be boring anyway. I'll be fine.'

I had packed my most serious work suit. Slate jacket and cigarette trousers. From her bed, Evie watched me dress, her smile widening.

'Look at you,' she said. 'Ready to take over the world.'

My documents were stored in a neat leather sleeve which I had taken from work. I checked them, then tucked them beneath my arm.

'I'd say that your parents would be proud,' she said. 'But let's be honest—'

I kissed her on the forehead.

'I'm proud,' she said. 'Does that count?'

'Yes,' I said. 'That's better.'

The ceiling in Moor Woods Road was white, too.

Beneath it, Evie and I spent our months. I had once monitored the dates in my journals, but over time I missed a Tuesday, then a weekend. My last entry didn't help me: my recordings were so banal that the days were impossible to distinguish. Had these events taken place two days ago, or three?

Together, we sank into the sludge of time.

Our lessons were disarrayed. We'd start on Sodom and Gomorrah, with a focus on the sin of homosexuality and its increasing prevalence in the modern world. ('The men of Sodom are at our gates,' Father said, with a conviction that made me glance out of the kitchen window, expecting a mob.) Father had little to say about Lot offering his daughters to the crowds – 'Protecting angelic guests,' he said, 'requires great sacrifice' – and then we were onto the death of Lot's wife, metamorphosed for turning back towards home.

'Why would she turn back?' Father asked.

I thought of Orpheus, turning back on the edge of the Underworld. 'With concern?' I asked.

'With longing,' Father said. Lately, longing for the past was one of the worst sins of all.

It seemed impossible that Cara and Annie still met for lunch beneath the gymnasium. Along the school corridors, behind closed classroom doors, knowledge continued to be imparted. The bell still rang. Beyond Moor Woods Road, I imagined acquaintances discovering sex; driving; exams. Love, even. Their world hurried on, while we were stunted at the kitchen table, children for ever. It was one of the few thoughts which still made me want to cry, and I didn't want to be turned into a pillar of salt, so I tried not to think about it very much.

Exercise was curtailed. There were inherent risks in being outdoors, and besides, we needed to conserve our energy. The fact was, there had been an incident. One afternoon, Delilah had stopped running in the very centre of the garden and turned towards Father, watching us from the kitchen door. Her mouth moved, as if there was something she wanted to say. An empty speech bubble of breath suspended over her head. Her eyes flicked to white, and she fell back onto the ground with a thud. It was just like Delilah, to faint the way people fainted in fiction.

Father lay her on the kitchen table, like a feast. Gabriel took her hand. Mother dipped a soiled kitchen cloth beneath the tap and wiped her face. Somewhere above us, Daniel was crying. Delilah coughed and squirmed. Her eyes were still damp from the cold, and she wrung out a few tears, reaching for Father. 'Daddy,' she said. 'I'm so hungry—'

Impatient, he stepped out of her reach. He opened his mouth to speak – to send us back to the garden – and stopped. Mother looked at him over their daughter, across the table, with an expression that had its own language. Father took Delilah's hand. It seemed entirely possible that Mother's face had moved his bones.

Delilah ate well that night and the next. Over her plate she watched me, fork sliding between her lips. A smile small enough to get away with. At night, she was free to wander between the rooms, and she opened our bedroom door in the late evening.

Light exposed the sullied mattress, and Evie curled away from it, closer to my chest. Delilah remained at the threshold, back-lit, so that I couldn't see the expression on her face.

'What?' I said.

She stood there for a minute, then two.

'Delilah?'

'Goodnight, Lex,' she said, and left us together in the darkness.

Always back to the bedroom. Father had procured a bed for Evie, but there were many nights when she slipped from the bindings and picked her way across the Territory. The slight compression of the mattress, ghost-light. I was usually awake, to welcome her into my arms, but sometimes she arrived when I was asleep, and our bodies collided happily in the night.

Other evenings, Evie and I ventured into the Territory and established a world there. Ithaca, maybe. The interior of a Mustang, heading for California. I found it easy to suspend the events of the day and slip into my self-appointed role. But as the months passed, Evie was more weary, and less convincing. She didn't want to play Penelope; couldn't she be Eurydice, where you got to stay in bed? She couldn't hold a plate at shoulder-height, and would let it fall into her lap; you could never do that with a steering wheel. I tried to compensate. My performances became more maniacal. There was some embarrassment to that, I thought, being five years older. All the same, I knew that we couldn't stay in the room. Not every night. There had to be some world apart from it.

Bill waited for me outside the council office. He had a super-market bag looped around one wrist, and half of a sandwich in his hand. Everything about him was soft: his stomach and his eyes, and the place where his face met his neck. He was smiling, as if he was thinking about something special and specific.

'Hello,' I said, and he blinked.

'Alexandra. I didn't recognize you.'

'It's good to see you,' I said, and meant it.

He held out a hand, and I shook it.

'I know that you don't have to be here,' I said. 'I appreciate it.'

'You don't want to face those cronies on your own.'

'I think that I could handle them.'

'Oh, I think that you could handle anyone.'

The truth was that Bill had done it all. He had recommended a probate lawyer to review the documents signed by my siblings. He had appointed a surveyor, and read their report. He had investigated the council's budget and assessed its current offerings. He had lunched with the councillors themselves, who were old fashioned, sure, but easily charmed. He had procured our Friday-morning appointment, when everybody – he was sure of it – would be in a good mood.

'Are you ready?' Bill asked.

'I've got notes. And the plans.'

The plans were my only contribution. Christopher worked as an architect at a great glass studio in North London, and had agreed to spend an afternoon in Hollowfield, composing a first set of drawings at a discounted rate.

'Could I make a weekend of it?' he asked, when he was booking a train.

'I wouldn't.'

He had hand-delivered a neat wooden tube to the Romilly. When he passed it over, his hands were quivering. He crossed to the window and waited there, watching the street below, while I unravelled the paper across the duvet. There were layers of it, so that the community centre appeared at first from the outside, encased in metal and wood. Beneath that, the external walls were removed and the interior exposed. Figures walked between the rooms and met at tables, in corridors, at the kitchen sink. On the last sheet, the building was a shell, to reveal the garden behind it. I traced the fine pencil lines with a finger, trying to consolidate this with the house I remembered. Even the form of it was incompatible with Moor Woods Road, where each sheet of paper had been dog-eared, and drawn on before.

'There's something uniquely embarrassing,' Christopher said, 'about creating something for a friend—'

'It's perfect,' I said, and started to laugh. 'Is it expensive?'

'Well. It *could* be—'

Inside the office, the receptionist stirred, like somebody waking up.

'They're waiting for you,' she said.

Together, we took the drab corridor. There seemed to be a grandeur to these buildings in London, cared for quietly through the nights, but here there were vacant bulbs and piles of tatty flyers. Events long passed, and poorly attended. The carpet was matted with dirt and gum, and curling away from the walls, as if it had decided that the time had come to leave.

The councillors received us in their chamber, which was just a small, hot room, with heavy curtains and a table too big for its inhabitants. I had prepared myself to recognize them – to be recognized – but they were all old and unfamiliar. I thought of Devlin, always the first into the meeting room, her hand outstretched, her mouth on the brink of a smile. Devlin would devour them whole.

'This is Alexandra,' Bill said.

'Hello,' I said, and shook five hands. There were a dozen spare chairs at the table, but I stayed standing. Let them see me, I thought. Give them a tale to tell at tonight's dinner table. Let them look.

I had expected them to be stern and suspicious, but now that I was here, they seemed mostly sad.

'You may know me better,' I said, 'as Girl A.'

Let me tell you about the community centre.

The building would be constructed from wood and steel, and it would rise from the side of the moor. There would be a long wooden ramp from Moor Woods Road to the glass front. Already you can see the welcome area, with communal tables and a row of computers. For the first year, it smells of lumber. There will be coding classes, hosted by a local IT consultant; she once owned a computer shop in town. An open corridor extends to the back of the building, and on either side of the corridor is a door, each facing the other. Behind one of the doors is a children's library, with bean bags and bookshelves, and stencils of two children on the wall, guiding your way. Behind the other door is a hall, with a small stage and couches to rest from the dancing. On certain afternoons, adults gather in a circle here, talking when they wish. If you pass them both, you will find that the corridor expands into a further room, cut with skylights. Our kitchen was once here, and there is still a counter and a sink and a fridge, for events. The fridge is usually full. You slide back the glass doors at the end of the building, and step onto a veranda. On summer evenings, once the clouds have burnt, you can sit on this terrace and watch the hills eclipse the sun. There will be small events: a choir recital, or a beer festival. There will be music.

I understood the curse that we had cast on the town. Once the mills had spun cotton and money. Canal boats jostled for a mooring. Loud men came from cities you hadn't seen, to survey their investments. Now your town is known for something individual, rather than communal. For something cruel and small. I know how that feels. You can demolish the house, or request us to sell it. But you can't erase the past, or make it right, or misremember it as something better than it was. Take it, and use it. It's still possible for you, like us, to salvage something good.

'It's ambitious,' I said. 'I acknowledge that.'

The councillor in the middle of the row gestured for me to sit down. I understood that the others were watching her. Waiting for her to speak.

'There are worse things than ambition,' she said. 'That's for sure.'

I sat opposite her, and from my folder I took Christopher's drawings and the accounting sheets, and the planning application which I had worked through with one of my colleagues, late into the night.

'Do you have a name?' the councillor asked. 'A name for the place?'

I hadn't; and then, once she asked, I had.

'The Lifehouse,' I said.

There were more and more days when we weren't allowed from our rooms, and so there were events – a noise, late in the evening, or a missed meal – which I have never understood. The lost stories of the house. Performed still in a bedroom in Oxford, in the hospital room in the Chilterns and in rented apartments across Europe, during those multitudinous hours when nobody else in the world seems awake.

For example: one morning, Mother left the house with Daniel, his cries fading down Moor Woods Road. They returned in the middle of the next night, with footsteps on the stairs and the touch of my parents' bedroom door. For a handful of days after that, Daniel was quieter, and Mother didn't look at Father, not even when he gathered her body against his, and kissed her face.

Or: Noah's birth, which happened in my parents' room, without ceremony, so that one day Daniel's cries divided, and he was demoted from the cradle to the sofa, or to the kitchen table, or to the floor.

Or: Ethan's conversations with Father. Father deigned to allow

Ethan his freedom more often than the rest of us, and sometimes I heard them in the garden, talking together; mostly Father talking and Ethan assenting, laughing, the same laugh which he had refined at the dinner table with Jolly, when we still went to school. I prised a few snippets of conversation through the bedroom window, all of them useless:

'—but you must have thought about it—'

'—our own kingdom—'

'—the eldest—'

I spent each of these days willing Ethan to come into our room. He would know if things had gone too far, I thought. He would know exactly what to do. There was one afternoon – it was the time when Father would have been resting – when I heard his footsteps on the stairs. He walked past the room where Delilah and Gabriel were bound; past Mother and Father's doorway; past his bedroom. The footsteps paused. Evie was asleep, a muddle of limbs beneath the sheet. 'Ethan,' I said. My voice was timid; it didn't even reach the door. 'Ethan,' I said, louder, and one of the floorboards shifted in reply. His footsteps retreated.

Then the day of the chains.

It started with Father's form through the morning light, releasing the bindings. The troughs of muscle shifting beneath his shirt. Bread for breakfast, and the usual slew of lessons. It was always the Old Testament, now. ('There are times,' Father said, 'when I think that Christ was a moderate.') In my memories of this day, Gabriel and Delilah sit together at the kitchen table, their heads touching. It's difficult to make out whose hair is whose.

I was thinking about the possibility of lunch as a percentage, based on the data of the last ten days. That was as far back as I could remember, and it made the calculations easy. Starvation was such a boring affliction: the thought of food coated the words of the Bible, until I could no longer read them; it spilt into my games with Evie, so that midway down Route 1 I would suggest a stop for hamburgers and become lost in the thought of mince, onions, bun, swallowing down my saliva, no longer able to speak or imagine. I dreamt of feasts. When Mother served us, I divided my portion into small, delicate mouthfuls, and moved them to each corner of my tongue before I would swallow.

'Alexandra?' Father said.

'Yes?'

'Back to your rooms. Contemplation.'

Not today, then. I adjusted my calculations.

In our room, we sat in my bed, Evie's spine against my ribs. She took the myths from beneath the mattress. I read and she turned the pages, as if we were at a piano. Midway through the siege of Troy, I reached the end of a paragraph and the page didn't turn. I shifted the book from her hands, gently, so that she wouldn't wake up, and turned to the illustration of Thyestes' feast. The smell of baking rose from the kitchen. Maybe just from the pages. I wasn't interested in Thyestes' feud with his brother, or how he came to eat his own sons. I just wanted to look at the pictures of the banquet.

Leaves scuttled across the window. Evening arrived, darkening the corners of the room. I thought that it was September, or maybe October. We should be summoned soon, for dinner or for prayer. I crossed the Territory and eased open the bedroom door. Across the gloom, the hallway was empty. All of the doors were closed.

I returned to my bed.

At some point I was asleep, because the noise woke me. A man crying out, once. I came to midway through it, so that I couldn't understand what he had said. At the end of the hallway, where Gabriel and Delilah slept, there were a few frantic thuds, the house reverberating with them. Then a softer sound, the noise of a more malleable thing.

Evie stirred, and I pulled the covers over our heads.

There was a new noise, now, something human and wet. A kind of gurgling. Over it, the tone of Father's voice, continuous, calm, as if he was coaxing a small child into something which it didn't want to do.

'What's happening?' Evie said, and I started; I had hoped that she was still asleep.

'Nothing,' I said.

'But what time is it? Night-time?'

'It doesn't matter. Go back to sleep.'

I lifted the corner of the duvet, and listened.

That night, Mother didn't visit us, and Father didn't fasten our bindings. Still he spoke, late into the night, in that same low, slow tone. I lay with my hands over Evie's ears. The room became cold, and in time the gurgling stopped.

I talked about that night only once, with Ethan. He visited me at university, and we met at a tea shop in the centre of the town. I hadn't wanted him to see my room, with decorations from the Jamesons and photographs of my friends. He would find something to ridicule. It was March, on the cusp of rain. Tourists were fumbling for anoraks. I saw him before he saw me, walking easily across the cobbles with a newspaper in his hand, amused by something on the back page.

'Is it always this dreary?' he said, when I was close enough to hear him, and I was glad that we embraced, so that I didn't have to think of a clever answer.

We sat in the window, facing out to the street. In that first hour, we were at our best. We talked about my degree and the odd cast of college. We talked about the students in his class, and how so many of them reminded him of one of us. We talked about my visits to London to see Dr K. The grandeur of her office there. 'She did well out of you,' Ethan said, and I shrugged.

'Do you tell people where you're going?' he asked. He laughed, anticipating his own absurdity. '*Who you are*,' he said, cinematic-dramatic.

'Not yet,' I said. 'But I think that I will.'

He raised an eyebrow. 'That's unexpected,' he said. 'From you.'

'Well, I have friends here.'

'Oh, I don't blame you. It's an excellent story. You get to be the one who escaped, after all.'

'I wonder about that, though.'

I was warm and content. It was good to sit here like this, with him, talking as friends. As friends, I wanted to confide in him.

'There was a time,' I said, 'in the last year. In the last few months. I don't remember. Somebody else tried to escape, I think. Gabriel. Maybe even Delilah. I heard this scuffle, on the stairs. Somebody stopped them. After that, there was this terrible noise, like someone being – I don't know – like one of them was injured.'

He had ordered a second scone, and he took a bite.

'Do you remember?' I asked.

His mouth was full. He shook his head.

'The next day,' I said. 'Father brought home the chains.'

He swallowed. 'That,' he said, 'I remember.'

I turned away and watched the rain coming down, sliding across the window and jumbling the view, resting on the pavement and between the cobbles. 'That night,' I said. 'I thought that I heard you. I thought that you might have been the one to stop them.'

'I don't remember this at all, Lex. There were all sorts of kerfuffles in that house. It could have been anything.'

'But it's strange, isn't it?' I said. 'That after those noises – literally, the next day – Father changed his approach?'

'Lex,' he said. In the time that I'd looked away, his face had altered. 'Now that you're here – now that you're a little older – isn't it time to stop making things up?'

The chains were three millimetres thick; one point five metres long; a bright, zinc-plated finish. They were sold as suitable for fixing hanging baskets, or chaining dogs. At Mother's trial, the prosecution referred to this fact on several occasions. An easy headline.

I spent many days contemplating the practicalities of this purchase. Father, in the aisle of a hardware shop – B&Q, perhaps – selecting the right tools for the job. Did he have a shopping trolley, or a basket? Did he make small talk with the teenager at the checkout? Did he ask for a carrier bag?

The handcuffs were purchased separately, online.

The chains were absolute. There were no evening congregations in the Territory, or readings of the Greek myths in the night. There was no Mystery Soup. There was no option to wriggle free and use the toilet, or the pot in our room. The first time I wet myself, I called for Mother for two or three hours, as the distraction became pain, then agony. The promise of relief, just behind it. Noah had whined through the day. I hadn't heard Father's footsteps since the early morning. 'Where are they?' I said, to Evie. My stomach was hot, distended; I didn't want to move. I squeezed my knees to my belly.

'It'll be OK, Lex. Hold on.'

I was starting to cry; I couldn't seem to help that, either.

'It won't be, though.'

The sensation of it came back to me in a taxi in Jakarta, with Devlin, on the way to the airport. One of our first business trips together. It was raining, the roads bulging with water and traffic. A closed rank of cars on each side. We were static for over an hour. 'How long?' Devlin asked, and the driver laughed.

Devlin looked at her watch. 'We're going to miss this flight,' she said.

'No – there must be something—'

'Lex,' she said, and threw up one arm, presenting four walls of vehicles. 'Come on.'

'Can we call the airline?'

'They don't hold planes,' Devlin said. 'Even for me.'

It was the helplessness of it: back to the bedroom at Moor Woods Road and the warmth of urine spreading beneath me. I thought of our plane, reversing from its stand.

'We can pay,' I said, to the driver. I gathered my bag from the seat and combed for my wallet. He laughed again, harder this time.

'Keep your money,' he said. 'It's no good here.'

'Lex,' Evie said.

Some time in the night. I had been asleep, oblivious, and for a moment I couldn't speak. I was too angry with her.

'Lex?'

'What?'

'Daniel doesn't cry any more.'

'What?'

'Not for three days.'

'How do you know?'

'Didn't you notice? The quiet. It's new.'

'He's getting older.'

'But isn't it weird?'

'He's just growing up.'

'He's still tiny, though.'

'What are you trying to say?'

'I don't know.'

'Then go back to sleep.'

'It's strange, though. Isn't it?'

'It's OK, Evie.'

'Promise?'

'Promise.'

The silence lasted so long that I thought she was asleep. Then, after half an hour – longer:

'But why isn't he crying?'

I closed my eyes. I summoned Daniel, small and warm in my parents' bed. Growing older, beginning to sleep through the night.

Evie's eyes, possum-wide in the darkness.

'I don't know,' I said. 'I don't know.'

After the council, the house. We bought coffee and tiffin, and walked in quiet to the car. Sun seeped through the clouds, and the moors glinted bronze where it hit them. Bill had parked outside the pub, and I looked up to the window of my room, hoping for some sign of Evie. The window was closed, and nobody was in it.

'You were wonderful,' Bill said. 'Truly. I didn't have to say a word.'

'Were you expecting to?'

'I didn't mean it like that. Just – you were very impressive. That's all.'

'Thank you.'

An intimidation of men passed, bare-chested, and looked at me curiously. Not Girl A; just a stranger in a suit, on one of the hottest days of the year. I took my sunglasses from my bag. I didn't belong here now, any more than we had done then.

'They shouldn't make us wait more than a few days,' Bill said. 'A week, maybe. Ready to roll?'

When he had pulled out, and he no longer had to look at me, he said: 'Your mother would be very proud of you.'

I didn't respond. His words sat with us in the car, a sour passenger.

The house had made its own strange headlines. When Mother was imprisoned, she asked for it to be sold. Kyley Estates, based in one of the other -field towns, presented the listing: 11 Moor Woods Road was a detached, four-bedroom family home with exceptional views and easy access to Hollowfield's high street. It had a modest garden, ripe for landscaping. It might benefit from some updating. For weeks, there was no reference to the events which had taken place there, and very few enquiries. The slideshow pictured grubby carpets; chipped paint; the moor encroaching the garden. A local journalist eventually exposed the story. *House of Horrors to be sold as family home.* After that, Kyley Estates was inundated with interest. People requested tours at dusk; they brought cameras; they were found trying to detach sections of the wallpaper to take home with them. The listing was removed, and the house started to rot.

We turned onto Moor Woods Road, and Bill dropped gears.

'Did you know the neighbours?'

'No. There were horses, though. In that field. We'd stop and talk to them, on our way home from school. They didn't think much of us.'

'You'd – what? Feed them?'

'Feed them? No.'

I laughed. I could see the house coming silently beyond the car windows.

'No,' I said. 'That wasn't really an option.'

Bill pulled onto the driveway and cut the engine.

'Do you want to get out?' he asked.

The husk of the house against the white sky. Every window

was shattered or absent. A few rags of curtain hanging in the upstairs bedrooms. The roof drooped in on itself, like the face of a person after a stroke.

'Sure.'

It was cooler here. A wind was blowing from the moor, telling of the end of summer. I walked to the side of the house and surveyed the garden. There were waist-high weeds and clusters of rubbish. The grass was tangled with outdated wrappers and strips of material, unidentifiable as clothes. Scorched rings in the earth, where teenagers had lit fires. Bill was at the front door, talking, his voice muddled by the wind. There were a few lank flowers left at the threshold, still shrouded in plastic. I touched them with my shoe. I didn't read the card.

'I guess people still leave flowers,' Bill said. 'That's nice.'

'Is it?'

'I thought so.'

It had happened at the hospital, too. My room was populated with new toys and second-hand clothes. With white bouquets, as if I was dead. Dr K appointed nurses to sort through the accompanying labels, which could be divided into three categories: acceptable, well-meaning but misguided, insane.

'Do you think they know what they're letting themselves in for?' I asked. 'The council?'

'They've got the figures.'

'Yes. I suppose so.'

'Is it like you imagined?' Bill said. He knocked briskly on the front door, once, and I had the desire then to frighten him, to say: Don't you want to see what's inside?

'I didn't,' I said. 'Imagine it, I mean.'

He had imagined it, I thought. He had been imagining it for a while.

I crossed back to the car, and held the handle, waiting for him to unlock it.

'The next time you come here,' Bill said, 'the whole thing'll be gutted.'

'The next time?' I said.

In the car, at the bottom of Moor Woods Road, I pointed to a spot beyond the junction.

'That's where the woman found me,' I said. 'The day we escaped.'

'Just there?'

'Thereabouts. Do you know what the driver said, when she was interviewed? She thought that I was a ghoul. Those were her exact words. She thought that I was already dead.'

I prepared my smile. It was the face which I presented at interviews, or at the check-in desk at the airport. When there was something I wanted.

'Can I ask you something?' I said.

He glanced across at me, then away.

'Why did Mother appoint me,' I said, 'as executor?'

'I don't know the answer to that.'

'Come on, Bill. All of the things that you've done. Helping me. Arranging the meeting. Speaking to the probate lawyer. You must have known her pretty well, to bother doing all of that.'

'It's my job. Isn't it?'

'Is it?'

He sighed, and his cheeks deflated. I liked the advantage of him driving, so that I could scrutinize him as I wished.

'Fine,' Bill said. 'We got on. I wanted to help her. You have no idea how vulnerable she was. The vitriol that woman faced, by virtue of making it out alive. But I don't imagine you want to hear about that. About the size of the cells, or the abuse, or the mothers in the mess hall—'

'Not really,' I said. 'No.'

'It *is* my job, by the way. I always thought that I'd work in human rights. Help people that way. Be a barrister. I wasn't clever enough, I suppose. I went to all of the interviews in London, just after university. No – I wasn't nearly clever enough.'

There was JP, ascending some great stone staircase, with papers clutched in his fist. Precisely clever enough.

'This job,' Bill said, 'I still get to do that. You help people nobody else thinks are worth helping.'

His hands left sweat prints on the steering wheel.

'Anyway,' Bill said. 'If you ask me, I think that she respected you the most.'

'Respect,' I said. 'Really? That is unexpected. I mean, that really is a surprise.'

I made myself laugh, although it wasn't funny. More than anything, I wanted to injure him.

'I think that she tried,' he said. 'I actually think that she tried. She mentioned this scholarship. A scholarship you could have applied for when you were at school. She said that she spent weeks talking to your father about it. Nagging away at him – that's what she called it. She said that she had to be subtle – you always had to be subtle.'

We were past the mill and turning back towards the town.

'She was certainly subtle,' I said. 'I'll give her that.'

'Do you know what she said,' Bill said, 'when I'd ask if I should contact you? When she was dying, I mean. I'd ask if you might visit, if I got in touch. And she just said, oh, no. Lex is much too clever for that.'

A dull red blush advanced to his ears, and he was no longer interested in looking at me. I tried to think of something pleasant to say, to fill the rest of the drive. I thought of him arriving home, hours late, to a plate warming in the oven. He clawed off his shirt and trousers, and calmed himself – sensibly, alone – in a quiet bedroom. *That ungrateful fucking bitch.* He would, I admitted, probably never think something like that.

He didn't get out of the car to say goodbye. I clambered out and stood on the pavement, watching him through the open window. I had sweated through my shirt and suit, and I tucked my hands beneath my arms, afraid of what he might gather from the patches.

'I appreciate your help, Bill,' I said. 'But I can take it from here.'

He didn't look at me. His eyes were fixed on the dull road home.

'Your father,' Bill said. 'Did you ever think about what he did to her?'

'You know,' I said, 'there was always so much else to think about.'

Evie was waiting for me in the room above the pub, tiny amidst the two beds. She was pale and slouched, but still she smiled when I walked through the door.

'Tell me. Tell me everything.'

'How are you feeling?'

'I'll be fine. Come *on*, Lex!'

While I showered, she sat in the corner of the bathroom, the knobs of her spine against the radiator. I narrated the day from the cubicle, gesturing through the stream of water, ducking out to catch the expressions on her face. 'You nailed it,' she said. 'Absolutely.'

When I spoke about Bill: 'How the hell did Mother manage that?'

In response to the house, she was quieter. 'I need to go back there,' she said. 'What did you feel?'

'Nothing.'

She smiled. 'That's such a *Lex* answer. "Nothing".'

'I don't know what else to say. It was just an ordinary house. Are you going to tell me how you're doing, now?'

'Not so good.'

'Allergic to Hollowfield?'

I had been joking, but she considered it. 'I don't know. It started when we arrived. A kind of – fear, I suppose. Like – dread.'

'We can leave now. Stay somewhere in Manchester, or back in London. You should see the hotel—'

'I'm too tired, Lex. Tomorrow.'

'First thing tomorrow.'

I bought a bottle of wine from the bar and we finished it in a chair beneath our window, waiting for the storm. The wind blew down from the moors, already damp from where it had come. Sky the colour of sand. I wrapped a blanket around Evie and set my feet on the window ledge. Down on the high street, people scurried beneath shopfronts and back to their cars. It was good to be here, inside and together, and close to the end of the day.

'I'm worried about you,' I said.

'I'm just tired.'

'You're tiny. You need to eat.'

'Sh. Tell me a story. Like you used to do.'

'It was a dark and stormy night.'

She laughed. 'A good story.'

'A good story? OK. At the beginning of the story, there are seven brothers and sisters. Four boys; three girls.'

'I'm not sure about this story,' she said. She glanced at me, one eyebrow raised. 'I feel like I know how it ends.'

'What about if they live by the seaside? In a great wooden house over the beach.'

'Better.'

'Their parents work hard. Their dad runs a little IT business. Their mum's the editor of the town paper.'

'She survived the journalism cuts?'

'They had an exceptional website. Her husband designed it.'

'Touché.'

'Sometimes the kids like each other and sometimes they don't. They spend their whole childhood on the beach. They read a lot. They're each good enough at something. The eldest one – he's the cleverest—'

'That isn't true.'

'—He's the cleverest. He has ideas about how the world should be. He has all of these convictions—'

'The girls. Tell me about them.'

'Well, one of them's unspeakably beautiful. She takes after her mother. She works in television. She can make anybody tell her anything. She knows what she wants, and precisely how to get it.'

'The other two, though.'

'Oh, they're all over the place. One of them wants to be an artist. The other one doesn't know what she wants to do. She might be an academic. She might be an escort. She might be a lawyer, even. There's plenty of time for them to think about it.'

'They can be anything they want to be.'

'Exactly. Before they decide, they set off from the wooden house, and they travel the world. They have a bucket list from the books they've read. They're away for many months – for years.'

'Living the dream.'

'Then they're close to home. They come to a small, strange town. More like a village.'

'Is it called Hollowfield?' Evie asked. 'By any chance?'

'It's called Hollowfield.'

'OK.'

'It's a day's travel back to their house by the beach, but they're tired. They need to stop. They check into a room. They have a bad feeling about the place, as if they shouldn't be there. As if they're not welcome. Or – perhaps – as if they've been there before.'

'And what then?'

'Nothing. They sit at the window, uneasy. Trying to put their fingers on it. The next day, they pack up and go on their way.'

'Do they know how lucky they are?'

'No. I don't think so.'

'I wish I could tell them.'

'No. Let them be.'

'I'm so tired, Lex.'

'That's OK. We don't have to talk any more.'

When I looked at her, she seemed to have regressed; she looked twelve, or thirteen.

The sound of the storm came first, the edge of the rainfall advancing along the high street. I closed the window and lifted Evie to the bed, and sat vigilant against the headboard, watching the room become dark.

In the night, Mother. She sat hunched at the end of my bed. She held her head in her hands, the fingers swollen apart and encased with old dirt.

Before I spoke, I listened for Evie's breath. The room cold enough to see it. The white of emaciated arms stretched above her head.

'Mum,' I said.

'Oh, Lex.'

'Mum,' I said. 'We need to do something.'

I had started to cry. I prided myself on how little I cried, just like all of my favourite characters. But it was harder than they made out. You couldn't even indulge the thought of tears, and this time, I had left it too late.

'Please,' I said.

'Temporary,' she said. 'Just a temporary thing.'

'Evie's starving,' I said. 'She has this cough—'

'I don't know if there's anything – anything that I—'

'There are things that you could do,' I said. 'There are.'

'What? What could I do?'

'You're out shopping,' I said. 'Maybe tomorrow. Maybe the day after. You can build up to it. You go up to someone – to anyone. Just start talking. You can tell them about Father. You can just – you can explain. You can explain that it got out of hand. How he started to change. You can tell them that you're frightened. You can tell them – about Daniel.'

A sob shredded from my throat. I swallowed it.

'Please,' I said.

She was shaking her head.

'But how could they understand?' she said.

'It just got out of hand. That's all.'

'Yes. It wasn't meant to end up like this, Lex. You understand that. We were trying to protect you. That was all that we wanted. There was no other way—'

'Yes. I understand that. Father had his ideas – his dreams. And when they didn't go right—'

'It was longer ago, Lex. It was so much longer ago than that.'

'You can tell them everything,' I said. 'But soon. It has to be soon.'

She touched my shoulder and then my face, left the chill of her handprint in the space between my chin and jaw.

'Maybe I could,' she said. 'Maybe I could.'

She didn't, of course.

Ethan in our room, unchained, with pink material in his arms.

'You're to wear these,' he said. 'And clean yourselves up.'

He had the key to the cuffs, and when he leant over me, I clutched at his hand. He shook his head. 'If you try anything,' he said, 'he's going to kill us both. Not today, Lex.'

'When, then?'

'I don't know.'

I sat on the bed and stretched out my body. Muscles shifted and grumbled. As soon as Evie was free, she dashed across the Territory and onto my lap, and locked her arms around my neck, like a sloth on a limb.

'It's a temporary thing,' Ethan said. 'I wouldn't get too excited.'

He was wearing old, odd clothes. A double-breasted black suit with dusty shoulders, and a clip-on bow tie. It was the kind of outfit you would find during an exhumation.

'One of you should get in the bathroom,' he said. 'One at a time.'

After locking Evie in the room behind us, he held my elbow along the landing. I assumed that he was supporting me, but when my legs started to work, I felt the pinch of his grip and understood that wasn't the case. At the bathroom, he wedged a brogue against the door, and waited.

'I can't just leave you,' he said. 'You know that.'

I stepped onto the tiles, and peered into the bath. Tepid water, long-run, and grey with the dirt of other bodies. I turned back to him, and before he could look away, I pulled my T-shirt over my head.

'Can't you?' I said.

I sat in the bath with my knees to my chest, and rolled a wizened bar of soap along my limbs. I was whiter than the tub. When my teeth started to chatter, I climbed out, and dried myself with a vile towel left in the sink. Ethan handed me the pink material, his back still turned, and I held up a dress, high at the neck and long to the shins.

'What is this?' I said. 'Ethan. What is it?'

He half turned to me, so that he could whisper. 'He's calling it a ceremony,' he said.

'It's OK. You can turn around.'

'You look ridiculous.'

'Well, you look like you're dead.'

I waited on my bed for Evie, trying to formulate a plan. I could hear her coughing from the bathroom. The panic of the opportunity. I lifted the corner of the cardboard at the window. Beyond it there was only the black-blue of the closing dusk, and rain on the panes.

The door swung back open, to fuchsia.

'Do you like it?' I asked Evie, and she cocked an eyebrow. It was something we had been practising through our listless days: the raised eyebrow.

'No. Me neither.'

In our party dresses, we descended the stairs. Ahead of me, wet hair slapped between Evie's shoulder blades. The living room emitted a soft, warm light, but otherwise, the house was dark.

We were the last to arrive. The room had been rearranged to a makeshift aisle, with the sofas facing one another, and Father at the top of it. He had assembled a strange pulpit: a cassette player and the Bible; a page of handwritten notes and a clutch of heather. Gabriel and Delilah already sat on one sofa, with Noah between them. I knew from looking at them that we were coming to the end of ourselves. The details of bones protruded beneath their clothes, and their eyes were wide and wild. Gabriel's face seemed different, misshapen, as if the bones had shifted. Where's Daniel, I thought, and the words settled into a refrain in my skull: Where-is-Daniel?

'Good evening,' Father said, 'to our little audience.'

He gathered his notes and closed his eyes, and I tried to get underneath his lids. He was delivering an address to the Lifehouse, with hot crowds pressing around him, and children held aloft.

Stragglers spilled onto the high street, so that they had to divert the traffic.

He opened his eyes.

'We are so incredibly alone,' he said. 'That's inevitable. If you're not shunned, you're not living according to God. If you're not questioned, or isolated, or persecuted, you're not living according to God. That's the burden we bear. But, you know, truly – I have never had to bear it by myself.'

He pressed Play. There was the rustle of the cassette turning, and then a sad, beautiful song adjusted the room. It wasn't religious, but an old love song, a vestige of a world outside the house, which was still turning. It had been so long since I had heard music that I gave in to the lull of it, and when he glanced to the door, I saw that Father was crying.

Mother came slowly from the hallway. She wore her wedding dress, which I knew from cheerful yellowed photographs. The dress had yellowed, too, and now her flesh bunched over the top of it. On her way past, chiffon brushed my foot; until then, I hadn't been convinced that she was real. She didn't look at any of us. She kept her eyes on the altar, and she returned to him.

At the top of the aisle, Father enveloped her hands in his.

'We've been married twenty years,' Father said, with fissures in his voice. 'I loved you at the beginning. And I'll love you right to the end.'

He took her unresisting into his arms. He covered her. Her face moved in and out of the lamplight, gold and then grey, and things moved across it, each of them beneath the surface, failing to emerge into an expression.

Again and again, Father played that song. 'Everybody,' he said. 'Everybody up. Everybody together.' Evie and I stood and danced, clicking our fingers and twirling the material of our skirts. She kept having to retreat to the sofa for breaks. Delilah spun between our parents, stroking Mother's rags. I danced as close to the threshold as I could, squinting to see the locks on the front door. Five footsteps. A second, to flip the latch. Two more for the chain.

I swayed closer to the hallway. Four footsteps, now. Father's eyes were closed against Mother's head, and her hair was stuck to his lips. He was rotating away from me, on a slow pivot. I would have my seconds.

I stepped out of the room, into the darkness between the kitchen and the door. Here it was: the body-clench, belly-thump of adrenaline. I looked to the locks.

'Lex,' Mother said. 'Oh, Lex.'

As they turned in the dance, she had come to see me. My parents' bodies came apart, and something sour filled the space between them. Father reached to cut the music. Mother held out her arms, palms up, and waited for my hands to fill them. 'Why don't we stay here,' she said. 'Like this.'

Father was surveying the route of my dance, as if I might have left footsteps on the carpet. His smile was starting to change.

'Actually,' he said, 'I think that it might be bedtime.'

He nodded to Ethan, who started to gather us, first me and then Evie, who was holding the sofa, breathing hard.

'Come on, Eve.'

He guided us from behind, scruffs of skin in his hands. Just before we were through the door, Evie stretched out an arm and wedged herself in the room.

'Where's Daniel?' she said.

'He's sleeping,' Father said. Mother nodded, as if the music was still playing. Not assent, but an old song, on repeat: Yes, yes. He was sleeping.

We slept more and more. The scant light in winter compressing the days. Evie woke herself in the night, coughing, her body bucking against the chains. Go back to sleep. What else to say? Go back to sleep. My mind had started to betray me: saviours came from the blackness, bearing water, blankets, bread. Miss Glade or Aunt Peggy, whispering in strange, gentle languages which I didn't understand.

Sometimes, it was Mother. I thought of how she had loved us best, when we were inside of her, silent and entirely hers, and I allowed her to care for me. Sometimes she brought milk, or scraps of food. She fed us by hand. Other times, she brought a towel and a plastic bowl of water. She knelt by my bed. She talked to herself quietly, as if she, too, was a child. All the time, the towel moved across my body, between the collarbone and the ribs, over the empty pockets of skin at my chest and buttocks, still distended, anticipating flesh, and down between my legs, where there was always a mess, an embarrassment, my body unable to stop its attempts to be human. In these moments, softened by her tenderness, I understood what defeat would feel like. Not to think of escape, or protecting Evie, or the requirement to be clever. The pleasure of that. I would slip into it, like clean sheets.

Dark, flimsy dreams. I woke up cold with old sweat and reached across the bed, waiting for my hand to touch Evie's body. Further; further. The other edge of the mattress. I sat up and fumbled across the covers. A cold, tidy space. She was gone.

'Evie?' I said.

I tore from the bed and across the room and hit the one switch I knew, by the door. The hot little room, empty and exposed. Everywhere the warm, sour smell of the bar. The bathroom was dark, but I opened the door anyway, and the shower curtain after that.

'Evie?'

I started to dress.

Downstairs, the landlady was at the cash register. The overripe smell of yesterday's drinks.

'Excuse me,' I said.

She glanced up, said nothing.

'Has my sister come through here?'

There were little stacks of change spread along the bar. She frowned. I had interrupted her calculations.

'My sister,' I said. 'I arrived with her. She was here at breakfast, today.'

'What?'

She looked at her hands. Her palms were grubby from the notes. It was as if she was trying to grasp something – some final sum – before she could give me her attention.

She shook her head. 'Nobody's come through,' she said.

I checked the breakfast area. I walked to the toilets and opened the three cubicle doors. I returned to our room. The crumpled duvet, and no sign of a note. I thought of the streets to the house. The curve of Moor Woods Road, as it rose towards the moor. I pulled on my shoes.

I stood in the empty road. There was the tap of water dripping from the rooftops, and a rivulet of it somewhere beneath me, in the drains. Dark but for the streetlamps. Two o'clock in the morning, and the whole town asleep. Even the drunks had retreated.

'I need to go back there,' she had said.

The hired car was still in the car park, glinting. She had left on foot. I contemplated her, ill and confused, fixated on the house. I could be there in twenty minutes. Half an hour, maybe. She was unwell. I could catch her before she reached Moor Woods Road.

I set off in the centre of the street, following the white lines. Jolting at the movement of myself in the black windows. At the end of the shops, I followed the road down across the river. I could hear the noise of it before I saw the bridge. There was a straggle of limbs caught between its banks, the water lumpy over boulders and a few stray shopping trolleys.

I passed the mill which marked the edge of the town, and began to climb.

It was still drizzling beneath the trees. On either side of the road were empty fields, extending fast into darkness. Everywhere the damp, fleshy smell of the earth, like long-dormant things coming to life. I scanned each turn of the road for her: a thin figure, bent into the night. I had expected to catch her by now.

Moor Woods Road rose ahead of me. I passed beneath the final streetlamp and paused at the edge of its light.

Everything more frightening at night.

I thought of small, mundane comforts: the phone in my pocket, and drinks with Olivia and Christopher, early the next week, where I would narrate this story over the last spritzes of summer. 'And then,' I would say, while they watched me – mouths agape, providing me with just the right reactions, the way that good friends do – 'I headed for the house.'

With the phone, I lit a ring of road ahead of me.

It wasn't far. When I remembered the day of our escape, I was sure I had been running for ten minutes or more. In fact, it was a few hundred metres to the house. I passed the field where the horses had lived, and cast the feeble light over the fence. It lit a patch of cracked earth, then faltered against the darkness. It was an absurd idea, I thought; the horses would have died years before.

'Evie?' I called, across the field.

I turned back to the road. It had always been so quiet here. Too quiet for anybody to come by accident. The community centre would need extensive advertising. We would need to ensure that there were funds for that.

The house waited, silent, the rooms of it looming behind the long-rotted wood. I stood at the end of the driveway, facing it.

'Evie,' I said, and then, as loud as I could: 'Evie?'

The front door was long boarded-up. I stepped over the flowers and pushed at it, first with my hands and then with my whole weight. Scratches of paint shed in my hands, but the door held.

The kitchen, then.

I waded through the wet grass, following the walls of the house. There was a padlock looped between the back door and its frame, but it was rusted and severed, and came away in my hands. I let it fall onto the grass and swung the door open.

There are things that your body doesn't allow you to forget.

In the late afternoon, Father came to our room. The noise of the key in the lock. He had been outside, and he smelt of the cold. His face was flushed and happy. 'My girls,' he said, and touched each of us on the head.

These days, he spoke less of God. He talked of more modest things. He was contemplating a holiday, he said. We had never been on an aeroplane. That had to be addressed. Did we remember the weekend in Blackpool? How the sea looked in the mornings? I nodded. We could get more T-shirts, Father said. A different design, this time around. We would need seven of them, he said, and in my head, I said: six.

'This family's been through so much,' he said, and when I turned to look at him, standing at our window with his face turned to the scant light, I knew that he believed it.

Across the room, I saw Evie shaking her head, her eyes locked on my bed. Her whole body was contorted in terror.

I traced her stare.

There it was: the corner of the book jutting out from beneath my mattress.

Our book of myths.

Father turned back to us. He eased himself onto my bed, and the weight of his body rolled me towards him. He laced his fingers through my hair. 'Alexandra,' he said. 'Where should we go?'

I closed my eyes.

'I don't know.'

'But you and Ethan know all about *geography*. Don't you?'

'To Europe,' Evie said.

'See. Eve knows where she'd like to go. You had better have a think, Alexandra.'

'Or to America,' Evie said, her eyes wet with fear, trying to keep his eyes upon her, shaking with the bravery of it. 'They have Disney.'

'Yes. You'd like that. Wouldn't you?'

'Yes,' I said.

He sighed, and stood.

'My girls,' he said, again, and leant to kiss me.

I felt his body stop, his lips suspended against my skin.

'What's this?' he said.

He reached for the corner of the book and tugged it. Here the beautiful cover and the golden pages. He opened it in the middle and stared blankly at the story, as if it was something he couldn't understand. His face was beginning to change, veering between shock and triumph. It settled at a kind of madness, as if a revelation had come to him, and I thought of Jolly at the pulpit. But Jolly had only ever pretended to be mad. Father was different.

'All of this family's misfortunes,' Father said. 'And now we know.'

Get it over with, I thought. Quickly. How does it feel? Will you be able to stand it? And stand it defiantly – do you have that in you? You. Always so eager to please.

He wrapped his fist around my neck. Between his arms, I saw Evie struggling against the chains, her whole body taut. Don't look, I wanted to say. You won't be able to unsee it. And Evie was so young. She was so good. It was suddenly very important, that she didn't look – one of the last few important things. I tried to say it with my eyes, but it was impossible. Still she was fighting.

'Do you want to die?' Father said. 'Do you want to die and go to hell?'

He threw me back to the mattress. There was no need to pretend any more, and I started to laugh.

'Where are we now?' I said. 'Come on. Where are we now?'

He walked from the room, his whole body trembling. In the few seconds before he returned, I looked across at Evie. 'Lexy,' she said.

'You'll be all right,' I said. 'You'll be OK, Evie.'

'Oh, Lex.'

'It's OK. But promise you won't look.'

'I'll try.'

'No, Evie.'

'OK. I promise.'

'OK.'

When he came back, he was holding something in his hand. A kind of wooden baton. From the cross, I thought. From the kitchen wall. From the Lifehouse. He bent over me and unlocked my wrists, a last tenderness to that, and I hauled myself up to face him.

'God,' Father said. 'God, I loved you.'

He hit me in the stomach, and something there collapsed, burst, changed state. Then there was the sensation of my body being opened, the dumb vulnerability of it, with its nerves and its holes, and the soft insides.

And that was it. After that, Evie stopped speaking, and I knew that soon – very soon – we would need to escape.

Coldness and damp. The floor was soft and the last scraps of linoleum shifted beneath my feet. I stepped between weeds and new shoots of grass, where the moors had started to reclaim the house. Everywhere was the sound of dripping water. Through the darkness, my torchlight lit tumours of mould growing from the ceiling, reaching for the last ruins of the kitchen, the hobs bloody with rot and the fridge on its side on the floor. Particles of dust fluttered in the air, invisible until the torch beam moved between them.

A rat dashed from the hallway and I danced away from it, too frightened to yelp. I wondered then if Emerson had been a rat, if we had called him a mouse because the thought of a rat was too horrifying to sleep with.

'Evie?' I called. 'Evie? Please?'

I passed by the living room and cast the light up the staircase. It was too dark: the beam hit the first few steps and faltered against the blackness. I knelt to examine the bottom stair. The first layer of wood had decayed, exposing the soft underbelly, yellowed and beginning to rot. I pressed my back to the wall and let it take my weight, body stiffened and one breath for each stair climbed. Floorboards creaked in the rooms above me.

The landing came into view, doorway by doorway.

I stopped at the threshold of Gabriel and Delilah's room. Behind the sound of the water was another noise, the gurgling. The house leaking its old secrets. The first miserable little bedroom, the corners of it dark enough to evade the torchlight. Flaps of paint hung from the walls. The wind moved through the house, and the door shifted, but I caught it before it could shut.

There was a noise behind me, at the other end of the landing. My heart beat in my skull and hands and stomach, and I held the door and turned across the hallway.

'Evie?'

The door to our bedroom was closed.

I crossed the landing, thinking of nothing, sure that any memory might conjure the thing itself out of the night.

I reached out a hand, bright white in the torchlight, and parted the bedroom door.

I knew then that there was something in the room. The beds had been removed as evidence, many years before, leaving white relics on the wall. The Territory was a wasteland. The carpets and the walls had eroded, exposing the flesh of the house, the white plaster and the floorboards bony underfoot. The terrible shape was huddled in the corner, where Evie's bed had been. Something small and still. When the torch beam reached it, it twitched. I wasn't frightened any more. Here she was, waiting for me.

'Evie,' I said.

'Oh, Lex,' she said. 'Do you really think I ever left this room?'

7

All of Us

I LEFT ENGLAND IN the autumn. In early October, I crossed Soho, collar-up, and collected my belongings from the Romilly Townhouse, where they had been packed from my room and stored since my visit to Hollowfield. 'How was your stay?' the receptionist asked, and I opened my mouth, then closed it again. She looked at me, knowingly. There were few secrets to be kept in a hotel. 'It was eventful,' I said.

'And what now?'

'Now,' I said. 'A wedding.'

By the morning, I was propped up on pillows in a hospital bed, surrounded by the chatter of nurses and machines. It wasn't the same hospital we had been taken to after the escape, but in the first strange minutes, I was sure that it was. It had the same sweet, chemical smell, which still made me feel relieved. I watched my hand reach to the ceiling, testing its freedom, and Dr K nodded, watching too.

She had been waiting for me to wake up. She looked pale and old. She wore a beautiful cream dress which hung haplessly from her body and exposed the sinews of her neck. I couldn't reconcile her with the woman who had sat by my hospital bed when I was a child. She was like a world leader at the end of her term. We met eyes and she smiled, without much conviction.

'Lex,' she said.

'Are we still in Hollowfield?'

'Not far from there.'

'Where did they find me?'

'Between the town and the old house. A factory worker had just finished the night shift. Not far from where you were rescued the first time, I suppose. You were disorientated – exhausted.'

'Lucky again, I guess.'

'The hospital called me at five. It would appear that I'm still your emergency contact.'

'Don't read much into it,' I said. 'Other than a lack of viable alternatives.'

I understood that it was still my turn to speak, but not what I was supposed to say.

'I didn't want to worry anyone,' I said. 'I was just there to see the house. You'll have heard about Mother. She made me executor. We have these plans for Moor Woods Road. I was there to sort things out. Being there – I must have been overwhelmed.'

She rested her elbow on her knee and her chin on her fist. I hadn't said what she was hoping to hear.

'My parents,' I said. 'Are they here?'

'Yes,' Dr K said. 'Greg and Alice.'

'I'd like to see them.'

'In a moment,' said Dr K. 'I think that we should speak first. The man who found you – you told him that you were looking for your sister.'

'I did?'

'Yes.' She started to say one thing, then stopped, and said something else. 'I've been trying to reach you since you landed,' she said. 'But I could never get through. I was concerned – as soon as I heard about your mother – that something might happen.'

I turned my head away from her. 'I don't think I was ready,' I said, 'to take your call.'

'That,' she said, 'I understand. We should see that as a positive thing. Don't you think? I believe – I believe you knew what I would have to say.'

A lump clotted in my throat.

'I appreciate how my methods may seem, Lex,' she said. 'Many years later. It was different, at the time. In those first few months following the escape. It helped you. I thought that by the time I told you everything – all of it – you would be in the right state of mind to process it. To recover.'

'You lied to me,' I said. 'Isn't that what you mean?'

'Yes. For a short period of time. And since then, I've spent a long time asking you to accept the truth.'

She drew herself up in the chair and looked through me.

'Tell me,' Dr K said. 'Tell me what happened to Evie, Lex.'

'You used to tell me that the ends had justified the means,' I said. 'Well. Look at us now.'

The tears rolled down my face and into my ears.

'Lex,' she said. 'I need to hear you say it.'

The police reached the house thirteen minutes after I left it. The smell of it made the first responders recoil from the doorway. They found Father slumped by the back door, as if he had tried to run and then thought better of it. Mother was with his corpse, of course, and wailing. They found Daniel like an afterthought, in a plastic bag and bent into a kitchen cupboard; he had been matter for many months by then. Noah was in his crib, matted with his own faeces. Gabriel and Delilah were wide-eyed and skeletal. Ethan waited calmly on his bed, considering exactly how much he would say. Evie was still in our room, and still in chains. She was unconscious. When a policeman lifted her, she felt as light as his own daughter. His own daughter hadn't started school. He went against protocol, and broke the chains himself. He carried her from our room and down the stairs, and out into the road for the arrival of the paramedics. Girl C. Ten years old. She was pronounced dead at the hospital, a day later, having never regained consciousness. For me, that was the worst part of it. The last thing she could have known was that room.

After two nights in hospital, there was little left to do but to go home. Mum and Dad collected me from my room and walked me to the car, and I sat in the back seat, observing their hair over the headrests, like a child.

When I woke up, we were in Sussex, and close to home.

The cottage is at the end of a shady track, off one of the roads out of town. There is a bench next to the front door, with Dad's papers spread across it, each supplement weighed down with garden stones. When it rains, articles break off and dissolve between the slats. Behind the cottage is the garden, stuffed with bees; herbs; trampoline. From the cottage, you can cross a stile to a great field, stretching across to the Downs. A single white windmill turns whimsically against the sky.

It was some time before I understood what had been sacrificed in the relocation. Just before I left home, I found a set of photographs of the old house outside Manchester, which had three floors and an elaborate mosaic path leading to the door. Here, we had two and a half bedrooms, and the land bulged with my parents' projects. Something was always dying because it had been eclipsed by something else. Mum had been a lead nurse in accident and emergency; now she worked in a general practice, dispensing vaccinations and conversation.

'It's not as simple as that,' Dad said, when I questioned him.

'It looks pretty simple to me.'

'Believe it or not, there are some things that you don't understand.'

At the cottage, he extracted himself from the little car and took my suitcase from the boot. 'Let me,' I said, but he shook his head, and lugged it through the door.

'Home again,' Mum said.

The sun teetering on the ridge of the Downs. We passed into the shadow of the house and beneath the hanging baskets, and set about making tea.

The first time that I had come here, Dr K and Detective Jameson were in the front of the car. Me in the back, with Detective Jameson's wife. During the drive, her hand hovered between us, as if she was frightened to touch me. At the service station, she bought me a packet of Quavers, and told me that I could call her Mum – if I wanted.

There was still a For Sale sign outside the cottage, which I didn't like; Dr K had told me, in no uncertain terms, that this place would be my home. 'Perhaps you could take a photograph?' Mum had said, and the three of us, my new parents and me, huddled at the doorway, unsure whether to smile.

'I took a few,' said Dr K.

Once the photograph was done, the three of them ducked into the house. I stood at the threshold, a bedraggled vampire, waiting to be invited in.

I spent September reading and sleeping. The sleep of the dead, happily dreamless. In the morning, sunlight puddled across the duvet and illuminated childhood books; posters; the framed certificate of my degree. I woke up knowing exactly where I was.

On Saturdays, Olivia and Christopher spilled from the train. Edna called, questioning my whereabouts and financial prudence; paying for an unused room, she said, indicates poor monetary policy. Devlin sent flowers and emails. Her messages read like extracts from a particularly direct self-help guide.

> Don't be embarrassed. Think of all of the shit that didn't get done because of embarrassment.
> Fuck those stale swamp nuts. I'm keeping you on the payroll.
> Jake is asking for you, so marrying a millionaire remains a viable option.

I replied asking for details of autumn deals, and she sent those, too.

I refreshed my inbox as many times as I could stand it, hoping for news from Bill. Whenever I did, I thought of him in front of a battered laptop, refreshing his own inbox, waiting for my apology.

I read, ran, masturbated, bathed, ate. That was the problem with coming home: you also had to come home to the self which resided there. When I talked to my parents, we discussed the easier things. There was the weather, of course: the summer was always just about to end. Mum asked about Olivia and Christopher; about Devlin, and the wilder clients in New York; about JP, with disdain. I accompanied her to the supermarket and to the newsagent. I spent some days with her in the surgery, assisting with her filing, the two of us sitting on the floor, back to back, besieged by paper. 'Expect an invoice,' I said.

We didn't talk about Hollowfield. We didn't talk about Ethan's wedding.

I recognized that my parents were older, and that some of that was my fault. The unanswered messages. The phone call from Dr K, in the early, early morning. Weren't those the things that aged people, more than the fact of time? Sometimes I listened to the tone of their voices, in their bedroom in the night, and knew that they were talking about me. The pockets beneath Dad's eyes had descended, like an extra set of jowls, and he had developed the habit of following me from room to room. He would wake from an afternoon nap and rush up the stairs, tapping at my bedroom door, or arrive in the kitchen with inexplicable urgency, to stand sheepish over my breakfast. 'What are you worried about?' I said, and he shook his head, unable to say it.

'I don't know,' he said.

On a warmer afternoon, I took a bucket of water across the garden and cleaned the trampoline. The best spot in the house for reading. I brushed away the leaves and started to scour it, first the mat and then the springs and the legs. It was just sturdy enough to support me when I was still; if I jumped, I'd land on concrete. I gathered a blanket and a cushion, and read until the light in the garden was hazy and soft. Not long before Dad came out to find me. I watched him cross the garden. The slow, careful steps of him. His hands held against his back. When he reached me, he turned back to the house and heaved his body next to mine.

'Dad. What are you doing?'

'Joining you. How's the reading?'

'It's fine.'

'Do you remember the hours that we used to spend on this thing?'

'Of course.'

'I thought that you would kill me.'

'Come on. You liked it.'

'I did. I really did. We were so sure – well.'

I put down my book and turned to look at him.

'Lex,' he said. I waited for him to say something else, but he only lay there, watching the lull of the branches.

'You can stay,' he said, finally. 'You can stay for the rest of the year.'

'Dad—'

'Stay, Lex. Don't go to the wedding. I mean it. You can stay for for ever, if you want.'

'I can't, though. You know that I can't.'

I could have done, though. Above us, the Downs were patched green and gold, stitched with hedgerows and chalk paths. I could see myself in ten years' time, and then twenty, living in the perpetual childhood which I had missed. The posters in my bedroom bleached by decades of sunshine. Still sleeping well, in a bed which had sides to it.

'Unfortunately,' I said, 'I have to live in the real world.'

He was nodding. It had been worth a try.

'I'm a pain,' he said. 'I know that.'

'You're not a pain, Dad.'

'When you first came to us,' he said, 'I'd have this dream about you. You were always so little. We'd run into each other, as if we already knew one another, and we'd talk for a while. Sometimes we were at the supermarket, or you'd be in the garden, on the trampoline. You were tiny. Just six or seven. Long before I could have known you. They started off as nice dreams, really. But then there would always be the moment when you would have to go. It was like I knew all along that it was coming. And somehow – somehow I knew what you would have to go back to.'

He was crying. I turned away, knowing that he wouldn't want me to see it, and he pressed his eyes with his hands.

'I would always wake up then,' he said.

'Dad.'

'God,' he said. 'Sorry.'

'It's OK.'

'And once you're awake,' he said, 'even if you try – once you're awake, you can't get back into it.'

A condition of my freedom was that I would agree to see Dr K. She was in the process of finding me a psychologist in New York, she said, but it would take time. It had to be just the right person. In the meantime, we would meet once a week.

We would talk.

I didn't want to visit her office in London, and I hated the thought of her in the cottage, assessing our dynamics. Greeting Dad as an old, lost friend. We came to a truce with a cafe in town. It had dismal service and artfully distressed furniture, but excellent coffee; on that, we agreed.

She no longer concerned herself with pleasantries. She was usually there first, with her handbag on the table and her trench coat occupying a spare seat. She had always already ordered, a coffee delegating my place. She didn't stand to greet me.

Above our table, a chalkboard said: Live. Laugh. Love.

'How are you?' she said, and I answered the question as she required: simply, sticking to the facts of it. I was fine. I was looking forward to resuming my work. I was preparing to return to New York. Evie had died many years before, shortly after we escaped from the house.

'And why do you think that you've been unable to accept this,' Dr K asked, 'for such a long period of time?'

Some days, I entertained this line of questioning. The body is notoriously efficient at forgetting pain, I said. Is it any great surprise – with a little encouragement – that the mind can do the same thing? Or just: because you gave me the chance. In the destitution of those early hospital days, you offered me a lie, and I staggered inside it and closed the door behind me. By the time you told me the truth, I was already living there. I had unpacked, and changed the locks.

On other days, I couldn't see the worth of conversation. I had told myself stories: that was true. What of it? What of convincing yourself that certain things had happened in a different way? Ethan and Delilah and Gabriel and Noah: they each had their own fiction. Who didn't tell themselves stories, to get up in the morning? There wasn't so much wrong with it. Those days, I considered leaving Dr K at the table. Let me stay in this fiction, I would say. Like this.

The only thing we didn't discuss was the wedding, and the reason we didn't discuss the wedding was because I had told Dr K that I wouldn't be attending it. She had asked about each of my siblings under the guise of academic curiosity, but when I was talking, she had the look of a parent at the school gates, comparing other children with their own. I described Ana, and Ethan's various successes; I softened the scene in the bedroom, and emphasised the protagonists' love story.

'I hear that Ethan's getting married,' she said.

'Yes. In October.'

'A family affair?' She wasn't smiling.

'I think that he wants the spotlight,' I said, 'without sharing it with the rest of us. You know Ethan.'

She nodded. 'Ethan,' she said, holding his name in her mouth, like she was trying to identify a particular ingredient. 'I hope that he gets the life he deserves,' she said.

I consoled myself with legal theory: it was more of an omission than a misrepresentation, and there was little wrong with that. The Devlin in my skull raised an eyebrow. In that case: I hadn't wanted to waste a session on something happy and mundane.

But before Dr K left, she paused at the table, her coat buttoned and tied. 'About the wedding,' she said. She didn't look at me: that made it easier.

'Yes?'

'I'm glad,' she said. 'I'm glad that you're not going.'

At other times, it was as if we were there for her own sanity. She spoke more during these meetings than she had across the years I had known her. In the blunt light of the cafe, she was haggard and illuminated.

'I don't forget the expression on your face,' she said, 'when I first told you the truth. I think about it all of the time. It was during your third month in the hospital. You had been asking about her for days. You'd become wild. This thought of her, installed with a new family. You asked again and again – you know – why can't I join them? Now that you were so much better, I had started to question my approach. There was no ending to it, you see. Or rather – there was only one ending. To tell you.

'So I did. We visited our courtyard, in the hospital. And when I said it, you didn't say a word. You just looked at me, with this – pity, I think. As if you felt sorry for me – that I could say something so stupid. You started off on another topic, something different altogether. The quality of the hospital lunches. Like you hadn't even heard me.

'After that, it was as though we started again every day. You would remember the writer of an obscure poem that I mentioned, in passing, or the name of an animal which you'd never seen. But this – you were always capable of forgetting it.

'We tried time and again. What was there to do? You had a new family, and a new school in September. You were walking again. You were doing so well, Lex. Just as I had hoped. The Jamesons had their child, and I had my vindication. And to tell you the truth, I think that we assumed you would grow out of it.'

'Like a comfort blanket?' I said. 'Or – what? Sucking your thumb?'

'Do you know what Alice used to say? "An imaginary friend – what child doesn't have one of those?"'

The loyalty of that. I tried not to smile, but I could feel it on my face.

'Eventually,' Dr K said, 'I stopped asking about it. Why? Well, I think that now. But it's obvious. Isn't it? Because in every other way, you were my greatest success.'

At first, there had been failures, too. There was, for example, a great deal of concern about my lack of friends.

In the late summer, Mum had accompanied me up a wide driveway lined with trees. We walked from sunlight to shadow, each of us nervous. Her hand bumped against mine. A clock tower waited for us at the end of it, and beneath it a headteacher, with his hand outstretched.

That morning, I sat in an empty classroom and completed three examination papers. Lawnmowers hummed across hidden court-yards, and a bored young man gave me notice when I had half an hour left, and then ten minutes. Afterwards, in a bright wooden study, I spoke with the headteacher, who asked me, in turn, about what I was currently reading (*The Magus*, by John Fowles; my parents knew only that it was about Greece, but not about the sex scenes); the Bible (where to begin?); whether I knew what philosophy meant (yes); and the most interesting place to which I had travelled (Blackpool). A week later, and six years late, I had my school scholarship. For the purposes of the national curriculum, the headteacher said, I would need to join the school two years behind my age group. Academically, I might find that I was a little bored; if that was ever the case, then I shouldn't hesitate to make it known.

As it turned out, I was never bored.

There were seven lessons a day. There was learning to fasten a tie. There was homework. There were swimming lessons, where I floundered a few widths and disrupted the other students' lengths. There was operating Microsoft Word. There was an extensive school library, where you could take out eight books

– '*Eight*,' I said to Mum, on our way home – and where the librarian informed me that she could procure any book which I believed was missing, provided that it wasn't pornographic or *Mein Kampf*.

I was assigned two welcome buddies, girls from my class who accompanied me to lunch and between lessons, ensuring, at all times, that I had somebody to sit with; that the correct text-books were in my bag; that I knew exactly where I was going. After the first week, I no longer required their services, and in time they peeled away and left me to navigate the corridors alone. The other students were pleasant enough, but in the evenings, I missed the slew of text messages that would form tomorrow's gossip. After my first term, I wasn't invited to many parties.

Still, then: friendship eluded me. I studied the students at lunchtime and in our breaks, trying to understand this particular form of magic. They laughed so easily – stupidly, really – about anything. None of them seemed as interesting as Ethan, or as bright as Evie.

'It isn't magic, Lex,' Dr K had said. 'You just have to' – she shrugged – 'put yourself out there.'

I imagined this: sidling up to a table of my peers and setting down my lunch tray beside them. 'Which school were you at before here?' somebody would ask, as they had done already, and I would shift forward in my chair: 'Well—'

I raised an eyebrow, and Dr K started to laugh.

'For what it's worth,' she said, 'I never found it particularly easy myself.'

And I wasn't unhappy. Each evening, at the dinner table, my parents were endlessly interested in my day. At night, I spoke to Evie, at first as if she was there, beside me in my new, clean bed, and later with my phone held to my ear, so that it was easier to believe. Nobody laughed when I responded to a question in class, or read my essay aloud. I was strange and tolerated. 'I'm not lonely,' I said, to Dr K, and that was the truth of it.

And there was the day when I ate Christmas.

My first December with the Jamesons. We had performed all of the traditions of a family. Tentatively wearing our new lives. We had walked to town to collect a tree, which smelt like the cold, and which was much, much too tall for the living room. 'It will never fit,' I said to Mum, waiting outside the garden centre for Dad to pay; this seemed like a waste of expenditure, and it concerned me.

'I wouldn't worry,' Mum said. 'This is an annual event.'

And when she saw that I was still frowning: 'We'll laugh about it later. I promise.'

I had a new range of Christmas paraphernalia: a CD of classic Christmas songs, and an advent calendar, and a jumper with penguins on it. To my scepticism, I had a stocking.

'Santa Claus doesn't exist,' I said.

'Well, yes,' Dad said. 'But presents do.'

We spent Christmas Eve finalizing our preparations. I wrapped presents at a glacial pace, with a stern eye for detail. 'They don't have to be *that* neat, Lex,' Mum said, but I was determined that they would be. Carols pealed from the kitchen. Mum baked in a frenzy, so that every half an hour, the oven alarm signalled a new smell. We were summoned for strange, specific tasks: dressing the gingerbread men, or counting the cheeses.

In the night, the smells stirred all through the house. I lay in bed, glowing with the pleasures of the day, contemplating everything that we had made: the crimped crusts of the mince pies; the snap of each gingerbread man; the vat of custard, speckled with vanilla. My stomach churned, haunted with the ghosts of hunger past.

I lifted my arms over my head. Freedom.

First the stairs, and then the kitchen. The fridge bulged from the darkness, stuffed. Just one thing, I thought. Something small.

I heaved the cheeseboard from the top shelf, and set it on the kitchen counter. I unwrapped the first little paper parcel and tugged away a slab of Comté. My hands were shaking. The taste of it spread across my tongue. Already my fingers were unravelling the next wrapper. Please, I thought: stop. This is a terrible idea. I was eating faster, now, and the hunger demanded something new. In the first cupboard I tried was the Christmas cake, sealed in its special festive tin. That, then. The gingerbread men lay beside it, and I took them too.

For fifteen minutes, I feasted in the dark. A starved Christmas spirit, gorging at the family table. There was food on my chin, and beneath my nails. A dull, helpless horror had set across my limbs, weighing me to the table. By the time my parents reached the threshold, I was contemplating my next, grotesque course: the plump, pink turkey, or the dish of brandy butter in the fridge door.

In the kitchen light, I could see that it didn't look good. The cake was a rubble of fruit. The gingerbread men were massacred. Cheese sweated across the table. The fridge door was still parted, and humming.

I swallowed.

'I'm sorry,' I said. 'I don't—'

'God,' Mum said. 'It was meant to be perfect.'

There was a thing on her face which I hadn't seen for a while. The wrinkle of it in her mouth and between her eyes. Dad saw it, too, and took her arm so hard that she yelped.

'Don't you—' he said, and she turned to him. He said something too quiet for me to hear. He was still holding her arm. When she looked back to me, the ugliness had gone, and she was only incredulous. She was just about to laugh.

'We thought that you would be looking for presents,' she said, and instead of laughing, she turned into Dad's chest, and started to cry.

The days were long, but weeks were passing. When I had last spoken to Ethan, he had been terse, and uninterested in how I was.

'You wouldn't believe,' he said, 'the questions that I've been asked in the last fortnight.'

I was in my bedroom, with a book to hand, and I opened it. 'Such as?' I said.

'About how we would like to be *announced*,' he said. 'About whether we would like champagne brought to us *pre-* or *post*-confetti.'

I found my place. There were a few neat flecks of rain on the window, and below it, Mum was gathering laundry. The lull of a dull Sunday.

'About the placement,' he was saying, 'of fucking cutlery.'

He paused.

'You're still coming,' he said. 'Aren't you?'

'I hope so,' I said.

All of the arrangements had been made. I could see the journey: the train to London and the flight to Athens; the smaller plane after that, and a drive to a pink villa, fifty metres from the sea. Sometime after that, Ethan at the end of an aisle. Pleased to see me.

'It means a great deal to me,' he said, 'that you'll be there.'

'As I said. I hope so.'

I spent the final afternoon in my bedroom, gutting the contents of my childhood and filling a bin bag with the scraps. The letters and gifts had continued to arrive long after the escape, even after we left the hospital. The nurses forwarded them to the cottage, accompanied by a series of wry covering notes. About a metre-high teddy bear: *We're not sure that this is age-appropriate.* About a dismal, hand-painted replica of the photograph from the beach at Blackpool: *We thought that this would give you a laugh.* About a bottle of champagne: *We don't know what they were thinking.*

That first year, there had been a novelty in owning things. My bed was lined with stuffed animals, the kind made for children of five or six. I erected a little shrine of gifts in the corner of my room, which I could peruse every day, inspecting a T-shirt or a football or a book, and setting it back, just where it had been. I arranged my cards along my windowsill, at just the right distance between the glass and the rim. *Dear Girl A . . .*

Even when I realized the absurdity of it – the fact that people at school selected their own belongings, rather than relying on the morbid fascination of strangers – I couldn't bring myself to throw all of the items away. Now, filing through the remains of them, I shrank at the embarrassment of it. They were cracker gifts, unwanted and odd. There were picture books; board games with missing pieces; letters offering me a whole multitude of thoughts and prayers, with little idea of what had been lost. There was one letter which I had been waiting for, and when I came to it, I uncrossed my legs and crawled up to my bed, making myself comfortable. I wanted to savour it.

Dear Lex, the letter said. *I have spent some time trying to put into words what I wish to say to you. You may not remember me. I taught you at Jasper Street Primary School between the ages of nine and ten. At the time, I was deeply troubled by your family's situation. I think that I believed that education and books might be enough to save you – the notion of a young, naive teacher, who didn't realize that she was out of her depth. I have spent many years regretting my failure to act on my concerns, both before and after I learnt what had happened to you and your siblings. I am so very sorry that I didn't do more to help you. It is something that I will think about for the rest of my life. All the best, Lex, and – though books cannot save you from everything – I hope that you are still reading.*

There was Miss Glade, her hand raised at the end of a cheerful corridor. I read the letter again, one more time, and added it to the black bag.

The last supper. In the afternoon, Dad disappeared, and returned with two bottles of the same red wine, held aloft.

'Your favourite,' he said. 'Isn't it?'

I didn't recognize the label, but I nodded, and took the corkscrew from the drawer. 'Thanks,' I said.

'To Lex,' Dad said. 'Always one for a comeback.'

The three of us drank, then took our seats at the table. For the first time during my stay, we were awkward, and I kept drinking, to hide it.

'I didn't do enough vegetables,' Mum said. 'Did I?'

'It's great,' I said.

'How did the clearing go?'

'Another few bags. I'll leave them in the bedroom. There's a lot more space, now – you could use it.'

'The way those parcels came,' Mum said, 'in the beginning. We thought they'd never stop.' She glanced at Dad. 'Dr K wanted us to throw them away. Do you remember that?'

'Yes. I remember.'

'I didn't see the harm in it,' she said. 'Well. Except for the bees.'

It had been the first record in our family's folklore. A large rectangular box arrived at breakfast time; the postman held it straight before him, like an offering, and set it on the doorstep.

Handle with care, it said. Package Bees. 'I've never seen anything like it,' he said, and retreated. The three of us stood at the front door and surveyed the box. Serious as a bomb disposal unit, and still in our dressing gowns. The bees were accompanied by an earnest, handwritten note, wishing me well, which concluded: *We have found beekeeping to be extremely therapeutic.*

'Therapeutic,' Dad said, laughing still.

A local beekeeper had retrieved the package. He was, he said, grateful that we had thought of him.

We ate on, to the chimes of metal on china.

'There's one thing,' Dad said, 'and I have to say it—'

He set his hands on the table, palms up, as if he was about to begin grace. I took one hand, and Mum took the other.

'This wedding,' he said. 'We're worried, Lex.'

A petition, then. I let go of his hand, and kept eating.

'Seeing them isn't good for you,' Mum said. 'Isn't that what Dr K says? We just – we want you to get back to New York. Back to work – safe and happy. You don't owe Ethan anything.'

'It's a family wedding. A holiday.'

Mum looked to Dad, and Dad looked to me.

'What did Dr K say?' he asked.

The old trust between them, forged in hospital corridors and windowless rooms.

'She isn't concerned,' I said.

'In that case—'

My parents looked at empty plates, like they were still waiting for a serving of reassurance.

'If you have to know,' I said, 'I have a date.'

Olivia and I flew out in the middle of the week, and early. At the airport we moved listlessly from WHSmith to Boots, bug-eyed and bored, looking at things which we would never buy.

We tried on sunglasses, none of which concealed how old I looked at this time in the morning.

'Champagne?'

'Sure.'

There was one of those obnoxious white bars, dumped in the centre of the departure lounge. A few long-dead lobsters languished on ice.

'Did you see that JP's baby was born?' I asked.

There had been a picture of JP online, with a white bundle in his arms. Mother and baby were doing well. They had called the child Atticus, and even alone, I had rolled my eyes.

'That's nice,' Olivia said. 'I suppose.'

'I hope that it's a difficult baby,' I said. 'Nothing wrong with him, obviously. Just difficult.'

'Furious,' Olivia said.

'Fucking incandescent, to be honest,' I said, and she snorted into her champagne flute, and reached for my hand.

Olivia had instructed me to start spending more money, so I hired the single convertible from the island airport. It was just like I had expected as a child, with one button to roll back the rooftop. As soon as she saw it, Olivia started laughing, and she laughed all along the road, gripping her sunglasses and handbag and hair.

Pebbled steps led to the pink villa, with its veranda and shutters, and geckoes flashing up the walls. The hill of the island hovered in the distance. The garden was shaded by a fat fig tree, and tapered into a scrub of wildflowers and pine trees; below that was a cove, and the ocean. We left our suitcases on the veranda and scrambled down to the beach, neither of us ready to speak; the quiet was so absolute that you imagined somebody must be listening. A makeshift jetty bobbed in the tide, the wood of it slick and splintered, and in the shade of the cove there was a rudimentary rowing boat, upturned and missing its oars. There was something improbable about the mundane items in isolation, as if they must be magical, or cursed.

Olivia sat down on the pebbles and pulled off her shoes and socks, and then her jeans. 'Come on,' she said. 'It's too good to wait.'

We staggered to the sea, hand in hand, and into the shallows. Feet alabaster beneath the water. Shoals of translucent fish swarmed between us, neat as starlings.

That first night, in a strange bed with the wrong kind of pillows, I received an email from Bill. *They'll fund it*, the email said.

I lay there for a few long minutes, reading the message again. The happy thumping of my heart was too loud for the bedroom. Olivia was already asleep, and I couldn't speak to anybody else I'd have liked to tell. I padded down to the kitchen, poured a glass of wine, and took it out to the veranda. The night was warm and silvered, and I raised my glass, to no one in particular.

Soon, there would be a curtain of scaffolding around 11 Moor Woods Road, and behind it, the house would change.

The rooms are full of people, bearing power tools and flasks. They drain the floors and the garden. They shift the upstairs weight from the old walls and knock them through. They joke about the contents of the garden, but only in the daylight. Christopher visits, wearing cashmere and high vis. Nobody wants the site waste, even for scrap. They plaster in the New Year, then leave the house to dry. They fit windows, lights, sockets, switches. They hang the doors and furnish the rooms. Last of all, they decorate. In the library, a local artist paints a girl and a boy, hand in hand, life-size. They are running, in motion, about to slip from the wall. The boy is seven or eight, and the girl is already a teenager. They are older than they have ever been, and they share a knowing smile.

We lived for three days in extended celebration. Slow and planless, and often drunk. I ran in the morning, when the light was still cool and new. We swam before lunch. Olivia crawled far out, beyond the cove and into the open water, until her body was indistinguishable from the sea and the sunlight. I stopped when the water line cut my throat and hovered there, inelegant, listening to my breath and the lap of the tide. I surveyed the beach and the rocks above it. The whole island dotted with secret coves and olive groves. You could believe the myths, when you were here. You could believe anything. I waded back to the shore and across the pebbles, trailing saltwater.

It was the kind of happiness which you try to preserve for more difficult days. I was blonde again: Ethan will approve, I thought. We drank through the afternoons and cooked extravagant dinners: a fish course, a meat course. Cheese. We sat on the veranda late into the night, talking or reading. Olivia didn't ask about the events of the summer, and I didn't speak of them.

'When we're old,' Olivia said, 'we can buy a taverna.'

'Without any customers, though,' I said.

'God, no.'

'We'll turn people away,' I said, 'even when there isn't a soul in the place.'

'"Have you got a reservation?"'

On the day before the wedding, I woke to voices from the cove. An intrusion; maybe something left over from a dream. I climbed from bed and wandered to the bottom of the garden, coffee in hand. A yacht had moored at the bay, fifty metres out to sea, and the dinghy was already on the beach. A man sprang from the jetty, rolled in the air, and crashed through the water. When he surfaced, he shouted back to a group on the deck, at breakfast. English. I felt bitter disappointment. The magic was broken. The wedding guests had started to arrive.

That night, I kept Olivia on the veranda for as long as I could. Past midnight, and after the music from the yacht had died; into the second bottle and then the third. 'I'm retreating,' she said, close to two, her palms held up in defence. 'And my strong advice is that you should, too.'

She returned one more time, with her toothbrush hanging from her mouth.

'You know,' she said, 'you don't even have to go to this stupid wedding.'

'Goodnight, Olivia.'

'Go to bed, Lex.'

Sleep was unfeasible. I cleared the table. I showered. I opened my bedroom window and lay on top of the covers, surveying the night. I was too drunk to read. The silence of the house extended on every side, out to the ocean and to the road; to Delilah and Ethan, alone in rented rooms; up to the town and to the venues in wait. It seemed that everybody else on the island was asleep. For something to do, I hung my wedding suit from the bedroom door and surveyed the hollow clothes, as if they might entertain me. Double-breasted blazer and wide, slack trousers. Flamingo pink.

Let them look.

When there was nothing left to do, I thought of the three a.m. things. My last meeting with Dr K, when I had told her that I was looking forward to landing in New York. My parents' petition at the kitchen table, and the cross-mattress wrangling which would have led to it. What I had said to Delilah. Not in the Romilly, but the time before it.

It was the last of our miserable family meetings. Each session was held in some form of centre, with bright, obvious objects intended to distract us. There had been a facilitated conversation and a group exercise; now we were in Free Time. Ethan was revising, with a hand held to his forehead, and a pen tucked behind one ear. Gabriel was focused on his PlayStation: a biped rat was fleeing from a boulder, and was crushed on each run, without exception. I was beating Delilah at Scrabble.

'What's your house like?' she said.

'What?'

'Your house. Where you *live*.'

'It's nice,' I said. 'Really nice.' I thought about it. 'I have my own bedroom,' I said.

Delilah snorted. She was surveying her letters, in disgust.

'Everybody has their own bedroom,' she said. 'What about your parents? Are they strict?'

'What do you mean?'

'I mean, I can do what I want. Can you?'

'Sometimes.'

'Sometimes?'

She was watching me, her whole body still. Coiled. I returned to my letters.

'I saw them, when they brought you in,' Delilah said. 'The people who adopted you.'

I looked up.

'They're kind of old,' she said.

I thought of Mum and Dad: how they had accompanied me on the train to London that morning, with homemade sandwiches and two copies of the same newspaper. I was wearing a new dress which Mum and I had selected, at length, for this meeting, and which had started to itch as soon as we left the house.

Delilah wore ripped denim and a hooded sweatshirt.

'I suppose that's what happens,' she said, 'when you're the last one left.'

I took the edge of the Scrabble board and threw it in her direction. The board missed her, and folded on the floor. Letters careened across the room. A few bounced from her face, and landed, anticlimactically, in her lap.

'How did you get to survive?' I said. My voice embarrassingly loud in that little plastic room. 'When—'

Doors were opening; hands were reaching for us. In that moment, Delilah was wounded. She wiped her mouth with her hand, as if checking for blood. As if I had hit her.

'You should have died in there,' I said.

I started calling for Evie, then. It was the shock of her absence in the room. In each family, you have your allies, and mine was lost. After all of my efforts, I was alone and ashamed, with old parents and a cheap dress. I called for her as I had done in the early days in the hospital, like she was waiting just behind the windows. Delilah held to a minder, and Ethan held to his desk. It came to them slowly, in the nights that followed. I called for her like you only call for somebody you're expecting to come.

All up to the church there was a queue of cars. There had been a series of printed signs on the way – *Two miles to the wedding! One mile to the celebrations!* – so that Olivia had turned to me, deadpan, and asked if I was sure we were going the right way. Now we joined the procession, caught between a Bugatti and a dusty cab, crawling towards the square.

From the road to the church was a canopy of flowers, and beneath it a purple carpet across the cobbles. I surveyed the guests, waiting in bright, beautiful huddles, taking photographs of one another. There was nobody I knew; that was to be expected.

'I'll wait up for you,' Olivia said, and I clambered from the car, before I could change my mind.

I had been considering how I would greet Ethan. At the church doors, the light dipped, and he was the first thing I saw in the shade, tuxedo and sincerity, with a queue for his attention. He didn't look nervous. The man he spoke to was nodding; laughing; nodding again. I stepped past them, slid into an empty pew, and arranged a benign smile. At the front of the church, Christ surveyed me with his hands spread, unconvinced. Like: Oh, *please*.

Dr K and I had talked of religion, at times. 'How do you feel about it?' she asked. It was the same question she asked about everything else.

'About what?'

'God,' she said. 'For example.'

I laughed. 'Sceptical,' I said.

'Not angry?'

'What's the point?'

We waited.

'It wasn't exactly his fault,' I said. 'Was it?'

'That might depend whom you ask.'

'No. It wouldn't.'

The doors of the church were closed. Ethan took his place at the end of the aisle, alone. The priest was here.

I set my hands together. It's OK, I thought. My usual prayer: I don't blame you. In the silence before the priest began to speak, I glanced up. Over the bowed heads and hats, Ethan was watching me.

Once the confetti was thrown, we thronged the streets of the town, all the way to the hotel. A tangle of cables and ivy above us. Strangers waving from precarious balconies. The sun flashed between the buildings, and the shadows were starting to lengthen.

I found Delilah in the hotel gardens. The land was staggered: first a terrace, where the tables were set for dinner; then a grassy verge, with a swimming pool and a set of tepees, down to the town walls. Delilah sat at the edge of the earth with a glass of water and a cigarette, in a black dress which exposed the dimples of her spine.

'Wasn't it *beautiful*?' she said.

'I was very moved,' I said, and sat beside her.

'You know,' she said, 'I think they might actually have married for love.'

'As opposed to what?'

'Oh, all sorts of things. Do you think it'll last?'

'For so long as it's useful to Ethan, I suppose. Have you seen the drinks?'

'They're hiding them in the room next to the toilets. Get me one, will you?'

On the way, I passed Peggy and Tony Granger. They were sitting at a table in the shade, with sunscreen and their anonymous sons. Peggy fanned herself with the order of service. I suspected that Ethan had invited them not for their company – they weren't nearly important enough for that – but to display the splendour of his life. As I passed, Peggy glanced at me, and when I smiled, pointedly, she looked away. I collected four glasses of champagne and returned to Delilah.

'Have you seen that Aunt Peggy's here?' I said, and Delilah rolled her eyes.

'Did you read her book?' I asked.

'Oh, Lex. You know that I'm not a reader. But put it this way. It wouldn't be the first book I would try.'

'She did everything that she could to save us.'

Delilah laughed. 'Well,' she said. 'Fuck me.'

'How's Gabriel?'

'He hasn't killed himself yet.'

'That's good.'

'Yes,' she said. 'I suppose it is.'

She rested her drink on the ledge, the alcohol slanting right to the brim, and peered over the wall.

'You must have thought about it,' she said.

'All of the time.'

'You know,' she said, 'I spent so long looking through the Bible for something which forbade it. Something he could hang onto, I suppose. And what is there? Fuck all.'

We drank for a while, in quiet.

'Delilah?'

'Yes?'

'Seeing what you've done for Gabe – I'm sorry about what I said. At the last of our get-togethers. It was a terrible thing to say.'

'It was rather dramatic,' Delilah said, 'I admit. But you never liked me very much, Lex. You don't need to start now.'

I waited, with nothing left to drink.

'It's OK,' she said. 'In fact – looking at it cynically – it's in my interests to believe in forgiveness.'

'I'm sorry?'

She started another glass and another cigarette, all hands and vices.

'You asked me before,' she said, 'about whether we tried to escape. Me and Gabe.'

'I heard you. One night – near to the end—'

'We didn't try to escape, Lex. I can see why you'd like to think it. That we couldn't stand it – the same way you couldn't. But that isn't what happened at all. Gabe and I – we were so bored. I'd come up with these missions, just to entertain us. You know Gabriel. He would always do exactly what you told him to. Just stupid stuff. Get out of the bindings. Who can touch the lowest stair? That kind of thing.

'And that day – I decided that it was my birthday. Uncelebrated, obviously. Undiarized, too. I'd been trying to count from Christmas, so I might have been close. And it was one of those days with the cake smells in the house. You know those days. I'm not a glutton, and I wasn't then – but those could be long days. So I proposed this idea, that perhaps Gabe should get me a present. Not *seriously*, of course. I was expecting him to turn around and tell me where to go.'

'He wouldn't ever have said that to you,' I said.

'There I am, talking about presents, and candles, and how this is the worst birthday ever. And that day – the bindings are loose. He's off the bed, and he's through the door, with that smile – you know it – like he's champion of the world.

'I guess I thought he'd be OK. Father was asleep. Mother was with the babies, in their room. So I lie on the floor, and watch him go down the stairs. Lower than we've ever gone. He looked back at me at the bottom, and he's still smiling, and – I mean this, Lex – I remember thinking: he's got this.

'So then he's in the kitchen, and I'm lying there on the floor, on stake-out, waiting for him. When he comes back out, he's carrying two of the biggest pieces of lemon cake I've ever seen. I mean – *slabs*. And I'm already thinking: Gabe, you're not covering this one up. But it wasn't like there was any going back. I'm just willing him to make it up the stairs, and then – once he's in the room – we can figure it out. We can make a plan. And on the second-to-last step – because he can't see a fucking thing, of course – he tripped. Lemon cake, everywhere. Gabe all over the floor. And whose bedroom door opens?'

She looked back at Ethan, who was surveying Ana with studied devotion, as the photographer had instructed.

'I thought he'd help us,' she said. 'In those first few seconds – I really thought he would.'

'But he didn't?'

'Oh, Lex. You know the answer to that one. It was one of the reasons I agreed to come today. I thought that I might be ready to forgive him.'

Here she stopped, mustering the rest of it. This was the part of the story that she couldn't make funny.

'Gabe never mentioned my birthday,' she said. 'It went on all evening, and he never mentioned it. Father told me to turn around – to protect me, I guess – and I did. But you could still hear it. He was different after that. The fits started. He was the best little boy, and that was the end of him.'

I thought of the noises that I had heard, all the way along the hallway, and how they might have sounded in the small, dark room, with your face to the wall. In the sunshine, Ethan was gathering Ana's family for a photograph. The flower girls vied for his arms; he plucked one of them from the ground, and swept her, squealing, over his head.

'And was he there then?' I asked. 'Into the night?'

'Come on, Lex,' Delilah said, and for a long moment I didn't look at her, knowing that the answer would already be there, on her face. 'Who do you think held him down?'

Ana insisted that we have a family photograph of our own. She summoned us across the reception with eager, unignorable gestures, and Delilah and I exchanged a glance.

'I don't think they're optional,' I said.

We carried our glasses up to the swimming pool, where an archway of flowers divided the terrace from the grass. I slid my sunglasses back over my eyes. We waited for Ana's family to finish up: they had been split into two ranks, with half of them kneeling down at the front. The flower girls sat happily in the dust. 'Now a silly one,' the photographer said, and Ethan flung Ana over his knee and kissed her, while her family cheered.

Then it was our turn. Delilah stood beside Ana, and I stood on the other side, next to Ethan. The weight of his arm on my shoulder felt crushing, like a little world. 'Is this everyone?' the photographer asked, and Ethan nodded: Yes, this is all of us.

At dinner, I was placed between Delilah and one of the bridesmaid's husbands. He wore black tails, and as soon as he found his name card, he took a napkin from the glass at another setting and mopped the sweat from his face.

'So,' he said. 'Who do you girls know?'

'Ana,' Delilah said.

She reached for my knee, and squeezed it.

'We're old friends,' she said. 'I met her at a gallery.'

'*Artistes*, then,' he said, and poured three large glasses of wine. I wondered how often Ethan dined with people like this. Did he suffer them with subtle mockery, or had he actually started to enjoy their company? He and Ana were walking between the tables, hand in hand, each fixated on the other, and our companion leant forward, conspiratorial.

'How much do you know about him?' he said, after the applause. 'Other than the obvious thing.'

'The obvious thing?' I said.

He swallowed. 'You don't know?' he said. 'The child abuse thing.'

He paused, waiting for us to take it in.

'It was big news,' he said. 'Huge. Ages ago. There were these parents keeping their kids like animals. Cages, starvation. It had been going on for years. Somewhere up north, of course. And – I'm not making this up – he was one of the children.'

'That's a little dark,' Delilah said. 'For a wedding.'

'I feel unwell,' I said, 'just thinking about it.'

'What does that *do* to a person?' Delilah said.

'That's exactly my point,' he said. 'How do you trust somebody like that?'

'Can you pass me the bread?' I asked.

'What happened to the rest of them?' Delilah said.

'God knows. A lifetime of therapy. You know, I think a few of them might have died.'

'Just a few,' Delilah said to me, and shrugged.

'What do you do?' I asked.

'I work in money,' he said, as if whatever it was, I wouldn't understand it.

I said: 'I'm a lawyer.'

'A good one?'

I was eating. Delilah leaned across me. 'The best,' she said, and that was the end of it.

The dance floor was assembled at the bottom of the gardens, where Delilah and I had been drinking before dinner. Generations of Ana's family, moving in time. The flower girls darted between them, or else rolled in the grass, snatching at one another's dresses. Somebody had thrown Ethan into the pool, and now he was in the centre of things, hair slick and bow tie unbuttoned, dripping across the dance floor. I was sinking into myself, I knew. Becoming sadder and softer. Something about the dancing.

Delilah collapsed into the chair beside me.

'What's wrong?' she said.

'Nothing.'

'I got the impression you were looking for someone.'

'No. Just watching.'

She closed her eyes. 'Always watching,' she said. 'What about dancing?'

She rested her head on my shoulder.

'That man,' she said, 'at dinner. Who did he remind you of?'

He was at the edge of things, talking to a girl in a dress which looked cheaper than everybody else's. Her head was tilted, as if she was trying to decide whether to be impressed or dismissive.

'Father,' I said.

'That's the thing, you see,' she said. 'The world's full of them.'

She stood up and swayed, and I offered my hand to steady her. She lit a cigarette and lifted her drink, and backed away from me, starting to move and at the same time starting to laugh, reaching back for me. For a while, I watched her dancing, smiling at the absurdity of her – at the way that everybody moved out of her way. At the end of the song, she turned back to me and made a heart with her index fingers and thumbs. Love. That was Delilah: an easy convert to whatever the celebration required.

At two o'clock, I retrieved my blazer and bag. The dance floor was quiet; the last guests sat in huddles in the garden, or drinking from wine bottles on the terrace. I found Ana lying in a tepee, sharing a Magnum with a bridesmaid.

'Where's Ethan?' I said, and she shrugged.

'Come here,' she said, and opened her arms, like a child waiting to be lifted. I held her from above, my face in her hair, and like that, close enough for secrets, she said: 'Today was a good day.'

'It was. It really was.'

'I'm sorry. About the last time—'

'Don't be.'

'Hey,' she said, as if the memory had just bobbed to the surface. 'At dinner – did you and Delilah pretend to be somebody else?'

When she had finished laughing, she kissed me on each cheek.

'Send Ethan to me,' she said, and I nodded. On the cusp of the goodbye, I turned back to her.

'When we're next together,' I said, 'not tonight, of course – we should talk.'

I walked backwards away from her, with my hands already in my pockets.

'We should talk about Gabriel,' I said. 'He's doing better. I think that you'd like him.'

Ethan wasn't in the gardens or in the hotel reception. I asked for a taxi to collect me at the square, and walked back up through the still, dark streets. A few stray guests writhed in a doorway, and a girl stumbled past me, headed for the hotel. The shutters of the town were closed, but between a few of them I saw television lights and the faces of the people watching them. I buttoned my blazer, walking into the wind. In a week, the planes would stop running. The end of the season.

I found Ethan in the square, standing at the church doors. He was looking down the aisle, an amber drink in his hand. I took the few stairs up to meet him. At the threshold, I could see the glint of icons beyond us, waiting in the dark.

'Ana's looking for you,' I said.

'Lex. We've hardly spoken. Have we?'

'People say that's what happens when it's your own wedding.'

'For the most part,' he said, 'I would rather have been talking to you.'

Wind whipped between the doors, and in the church, something fell.

'I'm going to head off. I just wanted to say goodbye.'

He rested his hands on my shoulders. He seemed to be thinking of something to say – something which would be just right – which kept eluding him.

'And congratulations,' I said. 'Again. I'm going back to New York. It'll be a while before we see one another, I think.'

I covered his hands with my own, and lifted them away from me.

'Don't fuck it up,' I said.

Olivia waited for me, as she had promised. She was reading on the veranda in a white plastic chair, with her feet on the table. Moths fuzzed around the light above her hair. There was a rusty glass on the table, and an empty bottle of red. 'I meant to save you some,' she said, 'but you were later than I expected.'

I dragged up a chair and slumped down, and rested my feet on the table, next to hers.

'How was it?' she asked. She reached for my hand, and I allowed her to take it.

'It was OK.'

'Good food? Good wine?'

'Yep.'

'We can talk about it some other time, if you want.'

'Yeah. I'd prefer that.'

She picked her book up from the table, and started to read. After a moment, she set the book back down and looked at me over her glass.

'All of it?' she said.

'OK. All of it.'

In the morning, I woke up cold and muddled, contorted on the mattress which we had brought out to the veranda. Something about wanting to wake up facing the ocean. It had seemed like a good idea at the time.

I could hear an engine. Olivia's suitcase was at the door. She descended the stairs with her arms full of unpacked belongings, ring-eyed and moving gingerly. 'This is un-ideal,' she said, when she saw me. 'We should have stayed another day.'

'Another year, maybe.'

We were whispering, the way you do in the early morning. She crammed the last items into her case, forced the zip, and grinned. 'Bloody hell,' she said. She gathered me into her arms and kissed my hair, and then the suitcase was in her hand, and she was out into the morning.

My flight was in the mid-afternoon, and there was little left to do. I removed my pink suit and walked between the rooms, picking up the lovely objects. An old stone paperweight on a bedside table. A model rowing boat, painted by hand, in the same colours as the one in the cove. We had opened every window, and the noise of the tide lapped through the house. It was the first time that I had been alone in so many weeks.

In the shower, I thought about New York. I thought about the ChromoClick dinner, and how I would dress for it, with Jake across the table. I thought about the new psychologist, and all the work that we still had to do. I knew that Dr K intended to help me, and that she expected me to help myself; the plan was that we would talk again as soon as I landed. I was undischarged. That was how she had put it. We were standing outside our cafe, a few days before I left, and she was searching in her handbag for one of her cards. Even though I had all of her details. Had had them for years.

'What if it takes for ever?' I said.

'Then it does,' she said, and when she straightened up she looked at me with the one thing which had always been there. Fierce now as the very first time. Pride.

I dressed in white and set my suitcase in the car, and walked from the house down through the garden. The limbs of the trees shifted in the breeze, like a person stirring in sleep. The yacht was gone from the cove, and the sea lulled undisturbed beneath the sunshine, translucent by the pebbles and a deep, brilliant blue beyond them. Cicadas sung across the afternoon.

A few final moments. This was where I would come to, I thought, to retreat from the sadness of the city.

I lifted a hand to my eyes.

There was somebody coming up the beach.

She walked determined towards the water. The movements of her tendons and muscles and bones. Her skin warmed from the sun. She was as I had always imagined she would be.

I picked my way through the trees and down to the cove, pine needles sticking to the soles of my feet. I understood that there was no need to rush. She would wait for me. I knew exactly how she would smile. We made it here, she would say. After all of this time.

I stepped into the sunshine and called her name. She was at the edge of the water now, facing the sea, and she turned back to me and raised her arm, beckoning, or waving.

ACKNOWLEDGEMENTS

Thank you to my glorious agent and friend, Juliet Mushens. I can't imagine this wild journey without you. Thanks, too, to the fabulous Liza DeBlock, for all of your practical magic.

I'm grateful to all of the co-agents and editors who have championed this book.

A special thank you to Phoebe Morgan and Laura Tisdel, for your insight, brilliance, and humour. This book wouldn't be what it is without you. Thank you, too, to Julia Wisdom and the marvellous A-team at HarperFiction, and to the whole Viking team in the US, for your extraordinary creativity and support.

I'm hugely grateful to my colleagues, old and new, for so much encouragement and understanding.

Thank you to the many teachers who urged me to keep writing. In particular, I'm grateful to Mr Howson and his English department, who showed me boundless kindness when I needed it the most.

Thank you to my wonderful friends and family. Thanks to Lesley and Kate Gleave, and to the Trinick family. Thanks to Anna Bond, Marina Wood, and Jen Lear, for all of the time spent talking books. Thanks to Will Parker, Anna Pickard, Elizabeth and Paul

Edwards, James Kemp, Tom Pascoe, Sarah Rodin, Naomi Deakin, Sophie and Jim Roberts, and Rachel Edmunds, for sharing the earliest excitement.

Thanks to Gigi Woolstencroft, who believed in this book long before I did.

Thanks, especially, to Paul Smith, Rachel Kerr, Matthew Williamson, and Ruth Steer, for so many years of laughter and love.

Thank you to my parents, Ruth and Richard Dean, who filled the house with stories, and who have always, always been there for me.

Finally, thanks and love to Richard Trinick, my greatest supporter and toughest adversary, who never did stop believing.